To Flip,
Merry Christmas and thanks
for all your help.

Jeff Robenalt
2012

The Bloody Frontier

Saga of a Texas Ranger

Volume 3

by

Jeffery Robenalt

Strategic Book Publishing and Rights Co.

Strategic Book Publishing and Rights Co.
12620 FM 1960, Suite A4-507
Houston, TX 77065
www.sbpra.com

ISBN: 978-1-62212-838-9

Design: Dedicated Book Services (www.netdbs.com)

Dedication

This book is dedicated to my wife Lizabeth and daughter Emily. Thank you for bringing love and happiness into my life.

"Give thanks to the Lord, for He is good, His love endures forever."   1 Chronicles 16:34

Prologue

The first glimpse of the picturesque hacienda from the high ridge overlooking the Colorado River was a welcome sight to the weary travelers. It was late in the afternoon of Christmas Eve 1849, and Texas Rangers Caleb McAdams and Bigfoot Wallace were returning from New Mexico. Four months prior, the Rangers had set out from the Rocking M to avenge the murder of Caleb's mother-in-law, Maria, and the nearly fatal shootings of his wife, Lucinda, and his brother-in-law, Pedro. The pursuit of the Pate brothers had eventually ended in a bloody gunfight in Santa Fe, only the most recent incident in an entangled feud between the McAdams family and the Pates of Tennessee that had stretched back over the years.

In the intervening years since the untimely death of Caleb's family at the hands of the Comanches, he and his father-in-law and business partner, Felix Vaca, had built the Rocking M into one of the finest horse and cattle ranches in Texas. The ranch now employed more than thirty vaqueros, most of them Felix's nephews and cousins from Mexico, and spanned some twenty-five thousand acres along the north bank of the Colorado between Austin and Bastrop. Felix had also been instrumental in the design and construction of the beautiful hacienda that now graced the low ridge above the river.

The hacienda, surrounded by an eight-foot adobe wall with a sturdy oak gate banded in strips of iron, stood at the western end of a huge central square. Rows of small cottages, where the married hands and their families lived, and a long bunkhouse and storage shed formed the north and south sides of the square, and a blacksmith shop, a barn, and a spacious corral enclosed the eastern end. The hacienda and the buildings that formed the central square were constructed of whitewashed adobe brick and roofed in Mexican red tile, making them both pleasing to the eye and essentially fireproof. The overall effect of the arrangement was to create an easily defensible fortress, a fine idea for any ranch located so close to the bloody Texas frontier.

Instead of heading for the corral when they rode into the square, Caleb and Bigfoot reined toward the hacienda's open gate. Ilse and Gretchin were restless after a long, hard day in the saddle, and the horses could be taken care of later, once the girls were settled in. The Rangers, along with the help of an old mountain man named Frost, had rescued the little German girls from a Kiowa war party on the Santa Fe Trail after the savages had brutally murdered the girls' parents.

The Kiowas had destroyed any evidence that might have led to the girls' identity, and Caleb decided to adopt the waifs and bring them home to his wife, Lucinda. She had lost their first child when she was wounded in the ambush initiated by the Pates, and the doctor feared that the miscarriage would prevent her from ever having any children of her own.

The big central square bustled with activity in preparation for the holidays and Bigfoot laughed as he looked over at Caleb. "Damn partner, this place looks more like a Mexican village than a ranch. I ain't never seen so many Mexicans in one place this far north of the border."

Caleb smiled, knowing Bigfoot's remark held no malice. "Most of 'em are family and damn good ranch hands, too. In fact, there ain't a hand on this ranch I wouldn't trust to watch my back in a tight scrape."

The majority of the ranchers in Bastrop County were down on Caleb for hiring so many Mexicans, but he paid little heed to their complaints. The tall Texan would stack his ranch hands up against any of the local Anglo ranch hands. The vaqueros were not only good with cattle, but fantastic horseman as well, and crack shots to a man.

Jesus Vaca, one of Felix's nephews, stood guard on the wall beside the gate. He waved the riders through with a smile. The family had been alerted to Caleb and Bigfoot's approach by the outriders who constantly roamed the confines of the Rocking M, and Lucinda, Felix, and Pedro were standing on the porch waiting to welcome them home. Caleb could not help but notice Lucinda's eyes. They never left the little girls when he dismounted and looped his reins over the hitching rail.

Reaching up, Caleb lifted Ilse out of the saddle and Bigfoot handed little Gretchin down to him. He turned to Lucinda with a big smile. "Merry Christmas, love, meet our new daughters. This is Ilse, and this is her little sister, Gretchin. Their English is better than it was when we left Santa Fe, but they still speak mostly German." The questions in Lucinda's expression were many, but Caleb only added, "It's a long story, but for right now just say hello."

Caleb stood the girls on the porch and Lucinda knelt down, taking each of them by the hand. "Welcome to your new home, *ninas*. I am your mother."

PART I

Chapter 1

The morning sun had climbed its way well into the clear azure of the Texas sky east of San Antonio by the time Caleb rode into the main plaza of the old mission town and dismounted in front of the Pellham Hotel. The wide plaza was lined with low, flat-roofed buildings constructed of adobe and stone, many of them painted in a multitude of brilliant colors. Across from the hotel stood the San Fernando church, an imposing pink structure topped off by a dome and a tall bell tower. The church was surrounded by a low wall that enclosed the Campo Santo cemetery. Soledad Street ran north and south in front of the cemetery.

Caleb was convinced that former Texas Governor George Wood had been instrumental in setting the frontier aflame when he disbanded the Texas Rangers as a cost-cutting measure right after the war with Mexico, and as far as the veteran Ranger was concerned, the only way to contain the flames was to reestablish the organization. That was why he had decided to stop over in San Antonio on the way to his meeting with Bigfoot. He wanted to discuss the issue of the frontier with his longtime Ranger commander, Colonel Jack Hays, and also say goodbye to Hays, who would soon be departing for a new life in California.

As a sixteen year-old youngster, Caleb first met Jack Hays at the Battle of Plum Creek, after Caleb's family was massacred by the Comanches in the Great Raid of 1840. At the conclusion of the battle, Caleb signed on as a member of Hays's Ranger Company, and for the next six years he had ridden with the Texas Rangers during many engagements against both the Comanches and the Mexican soldiers who refused to respect the independence of the Republic of Texas.

During the recent war with Mexico, Caleb fought with Colonel Hays and the Rangers alongside General Zachary Taylor at the battles of Monterey and Buena Vista and with General Winfield Scott on the long road to Mexico City. Caleb looped the reins of the big Appaloosa stallion he called "Nasty" around the hitching rail, removed his old gray sombrero, and entered the lobby of the hotel that served as the unofficial San Antonio headquarters of the Rangers.

From behind the registration desk, the owner of the establishment, Alexander Pellham, greeted Caleb with a big smile. "I haven't seen you around these parts for quite a spell."

"Howdy, Pell," Caleb replied as he strode over to the desk and shook the hotel proprietor's offered hand, "good to see you. Have you seen Colonel Hays?"

Pellham nodded. "He's in the café. He told me to watch for you."

When Caleb shoved his way through the batwing doors and entered the café, he hardly recognized Hays. Instead of his usual buckskins, the former Ranger Colonel was decked out in a fine, dark-blue suit complete with a silk waistcoat and a gold watch chain. Jack Hays was clean-shaven with neatly trimmed hair and piercing blue eyes. He looked every bit the prosperous gentleman surveyor he had become since the end of the war.

Hays stood, and the two men shook hands. "Pull up a chair and make yourself comfortable, Caleb."

Caleb's size had always impressed Jack Hays. The young man stood six-feet four inches tall and carried two hundred and twenty pounds on his lanky frame. Curly, copper-red hair hung down to his shoulders, and his keen, slate-gray eyes seemed to take in everything at once. Caleb was dressed, as usual, in a fringed buckskin hunting shirt and faded-blue army trousers tucked into a pair of tall, moccasin-like boots. A bushy red mustache drooped down over the corners of his mouth, giving his handsome, still youthful features a mature look. His face, burned brown from long hours in the saddle, was marred by a small, fishhook-shaped scar on his right cheek; the gift of a Mexican ricochet at the Battle of Monterey. The holster tied down to Caleb's right thigh held a huge Walker Colt revolver, and a sword-like Bowie knife hung from a beaded sheath on the left side of his gun belt.

"When do you leave for California, sir?" Caleb asked as he pulled out a chair and took a seat.

Hays smiled. "Next week. I'll be guidin' a party led by Major John Caperton of the Army Engineers as far as El Paso and helpin' to survey a route for a planned road along the Rio Grande. I'll make my own way from El Paso to San Francisco and send for my wife later on. She'll come by ship. If you can believe it, a group of local California businessmen have already asked me to run for sheriff of San Francisco County when I get there."

Caleb smiled. "I believe it alright. You'll make a great sheriff." Hays had gained quite a national reputation as a Texas Ranger before and during the war. "By the way, sir, once you get settled, I'd appreciate it if you'd take a look around for Ned and Mike Pate. I'd sure like to know what they're up to."

"I'd be happy to." Hays knew the Pate brothers were involved in a longstanding blood feud with Caleb's family. The feud had originated years ago in Tennessee when Caleb's Uncle

Liam killed old Salem, the patriarch of the Pate clan in a duel. The killings had continued over the years, and then the Pates had brought the bloodshed to Texas by twice attempting to kill Caleb and killing both his younger brother-in-law, Luis, and his mother-in-law, Maria, in separate ambushes.

"What makes you think Ned and Mike are in San Francisco?" Hays asked.

"It's either there or the goldfields," Caleb replied. "That's where Elijah sent 'em before the gunfight in Santa Fe."

Hays nodded. "Either way, I should eventually get wind of 'em. I'll be sure and write if I hear anything."

"Thanks, Colonel, I'd be much obliged. That brings me to the other thing I wanted to talk about. It's been more than two years now since the army took over the duty of protectin' the frontier, and the problems with the Comanches are gettin' worse, not better. Nearly two hundred settlers north and west of Austin were killed or carried off in the last year alone. I organized a volunteer Ranger company and we're doin' our best, but Governor Wood refused to provide any financial help, and the army won't cooperate with us either. At least, now that Pete Bell has replaced Wood, I'm hopin' he'll do somethin' about the situation. I plan to meet with him when I get back home." Hays took a careful sip of the hot coffee just delivered to their table.

"I understand your frustration, Caleb," Hays continued, "but Texas represents a unique situation for the federal government. Most other states went through a territorial stage before they were admitted to the Union. Their Indians were either killed off or removed long before statehood. Then along comes Texas with a readymade Indian problem, and not just any ordinary problem. As you well know, the Comanches are a warrior race who live to raid and make war. It's the only way of life they know. The army has tried to keep 'em away from the settlements by buildin' a string of forts from Fort Worth in the north to Fort Inge in the south, but the forts are too widely scattered to do much good, and worse, the army still has no cavalry. The last bunch of infantry they sent out here were dragoons mounted on mules, as if that would do any good."

"Texans also look at the Comanche problem differently than the federal government," Hays continued. "That's the main reason the army refuses your help. They plan to make treaties with the Comanches and try and set up reservations. The Texans know damn well the answer is complete victory. The Comanches will never understand anything short of that. You're doin' the only thing you can right now with your volunteer company. At least you're a real Ranger, and you know what you're doin'. Since the war, a lot of the volunteer outfits are bein' led by incompetents. That's another reason the army is leery about cooperatin' with you. But don't give it up. The settlers on the frontier are gonna need your help. Keep workin' on the governor, too. I'll write Pete a letter before I leave. It may help some."

The two longtime friends swapped small talk for the next thirty minutes until Caleb rose from his chair and offered his hand. "Thanks for takin' the time to see me, Colonel. I wish you the best of luck with your new life in California, but Texas and the Rangers are gonna miss you somethin' fierce."

Jack Hays rose and took Caleb's big hand in both of his. "Take care, old friend, and give my best to your lovely wife. We've certainly had some wild times, and it's been one hell of a ride. I'll be sure and keep my eyes open for the Pates once I get to San Francisco."

"Now that I think of it, there's one more thing I'd like you to do for me out there, Colonel," Caleb added.

"Sure thing," answered Jack, "what is it?"

"There was an old mountain man who rode the Santa Fe Trail with me and Bigfoot when we chased the Pates. His name is Frost, Nathan Frost to be certain, but he always went by just Frost. His hair and beard are snow-white, but the old cuss is some kind of a man. In fact, we might not have accomplished what we did without him. Anyway, after me and Bigfoot took care of the Pates, I asked him to come back to Texas with us. Bein' an independent soul, he decided to head for the gold fields instead. If you happen to run into him, tell him I said the offer to come to Texas is still open if he ever changes his mind."

Hays nodded. "I'll be sure and do it. You keep after the Governor, too. The problem with the Comanches certainly won't get any better by ignorin' it. The more the government neglects the situation, the worse it's gonna get."

Some miles to the west of Austin, Jack Hay's words were about to be proven prophetic. A settler leaned on his hoe, took off his old slouch hat, and used his dirty bandana to swipe at the sweat burning his eyes. Taking a moment, the man admired the long, straight rows of corn he was weeding, newly ripened tassels gently waving in the light breeze. In spite of many warnings that the frontier west of Austin was too dangerous without the protection of the Texas Rangers, the settler had been determined to move his family far enough west to find a piece of good land he could claim for his own. He found the land too; land rich beyond belief. The dark loam covering the bottomland along the Colorado had produced a crop far better than he had dared to hope for.

The settler had come to Texas with little money, but on the Texas frontier, money to buy land was unimportant in the overall scheme of things. The key to land ownership was to successfully farm the tract you chose and to hold it safe from all other claimants, including the dreaded Comanches. After all, the settler thought, his Scotch-Irish ancestors had fought Indians from the time they began their slow, steady migration westward more than a hundred years ago; first through western Pennsylvania and the Ohio country, and then on into Illinois and beyond the Mississippi. Many of them made their fortunes, and now it was his turn to accomplish the same thing in Texas. He would allow no Indians, including the Comanches, to interfere with his plans. Shoving the sweaty bandana back into his pocket, he took hold of the hoe and resumed his efforts.

Unfortunately, the settler had made a serious mistake in judgment when he ignored the warnings he had received about the Comanches, and he and his family were about to pay the ultimate price for such foolishness. As Texans had learned over the years, the Comanches were not just another Indian tribe to be pacified as the American frontier continued to move west. Along with their blood cousins, the Kiowas, the Lords of the Plains had stormed out of the north more than a hundred and fifty years ago, driving all other tribes, including the staunch Apaches, completely out of central Texas. Even the Spanish and the Mexicans were unsuccessful in their efforts to subdue the fierce warriors. The Texans knew the frontier would never move further west until the Comanches were defeated once and for all.

As the settler continued to hoe his field, he had no idea he was being watched by a small Comanche war party sitting their ponies on a wooded ridge overlooking the small homestead. An impressive warrior, mounted on a large gray stallion with blue hailstones painted across its rump to ward off evil and lightning bolts painted down its legs to give the big horse speed, led the war party. The war chief's black hair, adorned by a single eagle feather signifying bravery in battle, was not cropped on one side in the usual Comanche manner, but flowed to his wide shoulders. He carried a colorful buffalo bull hide shield and was armed with a long red war lance decorated with several scalps. Wide stripes of vermilion and yellow war paint disguised his features, but he would have been recognizable to most Texans by the ancient Spanish armor covering his broad chest. Iron Jacket was fast becoming the scourge of the Texas frontier.

Iron Jacket's gaze momentarily left the settler and moved to the small cabin sitting on a little rise further back from the Colorado. The settler's wife was returning from the river with a heavy bucket of water, and the infant she carried on her hip was howling its displeasure. Two other small children, one looked to be a boy and the other a girl, played on the hard packed earth in front of the cabin.

Since the big war between the Texans and the Mexicans ended, dogged pursuit of the war parties by the hated Texas Rangers had steadily decreased, and their harassment was now almost nonexistent. Bluecoat soldiers had taken the Rangers' place, but either on foot or mounted on slow mules and living in a few widely scattered forts, their efforts at curtailing the Comanches' raids were nearly laughable.

Iron Jacket signaled to his warriors and led them down the ridge at a slow walk. The foolish settler was unarmed and did not notice their approach until one of the ponies whinnied when the warriors reached the edge of the corn field. Yelling out a cry of warning to his wife, the settler took off running toward the cabin. Iron Jacket heeled the gray stallion into a long lope and easily overtook the white man, spearing him through the back with the long war lance and pinning him to the ground. Leaping from the back of his horse, the war chief quickly ran the blade of his knife around the crown of the white man's head and ripped the bloody scalp free, eliciting a dying scream of pain from his victim, before raising his trophy high in the air.

The remainder of the war party continued on to the little cabin where they quickly broke down the door and dragged the screaming woman outside. One of the warriors yanked the crying baby from her arms, grabbed it by the heels, and slammed its head against the broken door jamb. The woman was hysterical, but the Comanches ignored her cries for mercy as they scalped her alive in front of her children before crushing her skull with a savage blow from a war club. After finishing with the woman the warriors looted the cabin and set it on fire, then slaughtered two hogs and a milk cow that were wandering free nearby. The old plow horse was also put down, but the saddle horse, cor-ralled near the cabin, was a prize worth keeping.

The Comanches were soon mounted again, along with the two small children, and Iron Jacket led the victorious war party north-west along the river. The children would make excellent slaves or even additions to their band if they proved tough enough. If not, they could always be dispatched on the trail back to the village. A cruel sneer played across Iron Jacket's features. One less Texan would now scar the land that belonged to the People.

Several hours later, in the thriving, California gold rush tent city of San Francisco, six men were involved in a high stakes game of five card stud. Caleb McAdams would have instantly recognized the big man with stringy blond hair and watery-blue eyes who was in a debate with himself whether he should call the most recent bet or fold his hand.

Ned Pate held two pair, a five in the hole and a five and a pair of threes among his face cards, but after taking note of the fives and threes already dealt, he knew only the five of spades was left in the deck. A long-faced gambler sat across the table from him with three hearts on the table, including the ace, and Ned was sure the man's hole card was either a heart or an ace. He had just raised two thousand dollars and everyone else folded.

Ned was a good gambler. He knew the odds dictated that he should fold his cards along with the others, but something inside told him to call the bet. Maybe the gambler's hole card was not a heart. In that case Ned might win the pot with his two pair. And even if the gambler filled his heart flush, there was still an outside chance Ned would draw the five of spades. Ned hesitated for only a moment then tossed the two thousand into the pot. The dealer dealt Long-Face a ten of hearts for his last card. When Ned's last card hit the table it was the five of spades.

With a big grin, Long-Face raised the pot five thousand dollars. Ned immediately called the five thousand dollar bet and raised the pot five thousand more.

Long-Face chuckled as he shoved the five thousand in. "Ain't no way in hell you're gonna bluff me out of this pot with them two little pair, mister. I call."

Ned turned over the five of clubs. "Can you beat a full house? I thought not." He raked the pot in as the gambler sat staring at his hand in shocked silence. "That's enough for me," Ned said as he rose and stuffed the money in his pockets. "I'll see you men some other time."

Without another word, Ned turned and walked out with more than twenty thousand dollars. However, that money was chicken feed compared to the wealth he and Mike had recently stumbled across. As soon as they arrived at the gold fields, the Pates met a prospector in desperate need of a stake. The man had a claim he had worked for a good while, and he was sure it was ready to pay off. The Pates staked the prospector for half the claim, and when they discovered gold, it was a simple matter to see that the man had a fatal accident. Ned left Mike to work the claim, and he headed directly to the assayer's office in San Francisco. The assay confirmed their claim was worth a fortune. Something told him to draw that card tonight, and that something was surely the broad smile of Lady Luck.

Ned smiled. He did not even have to share the claim with Elijah and his other brothers. Word recently reached California that Caleb McAdams had taken care of that problem. Of course, McAdams was still not off the hook. The man had killed several members of the Pate family, and he would have to pay with his life, maybe even the lives of his miserable family. There was plenty of time to plan revenge, and more than enough money to carry out the plan, no matter what it might cost.

Chapter 2

Bigfoot Wallace's cabin sat on a small rise on the north bank of the Medina River, some fifteen miles southwest of San Antonio. It was late in the afternoon, and the big man was out back chopping wood when Caleb rode up and dismounted.

"You swing that ax like you got a purpose in mind," Caleb said with a big smile.

Bigfoot chuckled as he buried the blade of the ax in an old stump to keep the edge sharp and rust free and offered his hand." Will keepin' my butt warm this winter do?"

Taking his old friend's beefy hand in a firm grip, Caleb shook it vigorously. "Its good to see you again, partner."

At six-feet two inches, Bigfoot Wallace was slightly shorter than Caleb, but the breadth of his massive shoulders and the two hundred and forty pounds of muscled bulk he carried on his frame made him appear larger. Coal-dark eyes set deep under a heavy brow served to enhance the big man's menacing appearance. His hair was long and dark and his beard bushy and full. He wore a well-worn set of buckskins tucked into a pair of scuffed, mule-eared boots large enough to justify his nickname. The boots were adorned with a set of silver Mexican pinwheel spurs. A Walker Colt filled the holster on his right thigh, and a large sheathed Bowie knife hung from a thick leather strap that crossed his chest.

"It's been near two years now since we got back from Santa Fe," Bigfoot replied. "How's Lucinda gettin' along with them little girls?"

"We definitely did the right thing by bringin' the girls home, Bigfoot. They took to their new Ma like ducklings to a spring pond. You'd never know they weren't ours except for the golden hair and those big blue eyes."

Bigfoot grinned. "That's damn good to hear. I sure did take a shine to that little Gretchin. What about Ned and Mike Pate, have you heard anything about them?"

Caleb shook his head. "Not a thing, but I asked Jack to check up on 'em once he gets to California."

"Good," said Bigfoot, "you can't be too careful when it comes to them varmints. Let's go take a seat on the porch. I've been lookin' forward to havin' a talk ever since I sent you that letter."

Now it was Caleb's turn to chuckle. "That wasn't much of a letter, but you did make it plain you were in an all fired hurry to see me. What's this about a stagecoach ride to El Paso? I know we got stage lines now that run all across east Texas and on into Louisiana, but I didn't know a line went that far west."

"Come on," said Bigfoot, "let's get us a cool drink of that cider I got stashed in the well and have a seat on the porch. I'll tell you all about it."

Once they were comfortable, Bigfoot's expression took on a serious look. "As of now, there ain't a stage line to El Paso, but a few weeks ago Henry Skillman got himself a government contract to provide mail service from San Antonio to Santa Fe, by way of El Paso. I made a deal with him that I'd take the first few

stage coaches through as far as El Paso. Skillman's got somebody in El Paso who'll move 'em on to Santa Fe." Bigfoot took
a long drink of cider. "If I can keep the El Paso stages movin'
until he can get a few relay stations set up, I'll get me a small
percentage of the contract. You know as well as I do the first run
is gonna be the toughest. I got a good man to ride shotgun, and
three men who used to be Rangers who agreed to ride as guards
and handle the remuda, but I need a good scout. Will you make
the first run with me?"

Caleb never hesitated. "You're damn right I will. You've
always been there when I needed you. Now it's my turn to give
you a hand."

"Thanks, Caleb," replied Bigfoot as a relaxed smile returned
to his face. "This little venture is damned important to me. I was
sure I could count on your help."

"We gonna follow the same trail we took comin' home from
Santa Fe with the girls?" Caleb asked, wanting to put Bigfoot at
ease once again.

Bigfoot nodded. "Pretty close, but instead of usin' Horse
Head Crossin', we'll follow the east bank of the Pecos and cross
further north at Pope's Camp. We were on horseback comin'
home, but the ground east of the river is more favorable for a
stagecoach."

"From what I remember, I agree with you. The east bank it
is. When are you plannin' on pullin' out? The ranch won't be
a problem with Felix and Pedro to look after things. I'm gonna
need enough time to get back home and explain all this to Lucinda, though."

"Skillman said the first stage won't leave until early November," Bigfoot replied as he sat back in his old rocker and put his
huge feet up on the porch railing. "That gives you more than six
weeks to take care of business."

The friendly conversation continued until late afternoon,
when something on the horizon far to the south of the river

caught Caleb's attention. He narrowed his eyes and focused them on the movement. "Looks like you're gonna have some company, partner. I see a rider comin' up from the south."

Bigfoot squinted down hard, but at first he did not see anything. He continued to carefully scan the horizon, but it was another minute or two until he saw a rider approaching the river over a rise far to the south. Caleb's far sight was legendary among the Texas Rangers, and Bigfoot had observed it many times. "That looks like Creed Taylor. He owns a small spread southwest of here near where the Hondo meets the Frio."

The rider pushed his horse at a steady lope, splashed across the Medina, and rode up the rise to Bigfoot's cabin before reining in. "Afternoon, Wallace," said Taylor. He nodded a greeting to Caleb. "I come to get your help. That son-of-a-bitch Vidal hit my ranch early this mornin'. He killed two of my hands, wounded a couple others, and run off with my whole string of saddle horses, all twenty-six of 'em. Thank the Lord I had the good sense to hobble this animal near my cabin. I tracked him and his bunch for a few miles. It looks like they're headed for Laredo."

Bigfoot rose to his feet. "Caleb, are you up for a little ride? That bastard Vidal has stolen horses all over this part of Texas for the last couple years. It's high time somebody put a stop to his killin' and thievery."

Caleb stood. "Count me in."

"Creed, this here is Caleb McAdams," added Bigfoot. "He's a Ranger, and he's been my partner a long time. I ain't never gonna find a better man to throw in with me, so I think it might be best if you to head on back to your ranch and look to your wounded. Besides, there's sure to be gun play before this fandango's over, and you ain't no gunfighter."

A momentary frown clouded Creed's features until he took a moment to think over what Bigfoot said. "I'm not sure I like bein' left out, Wallace, but you're most likely right. I'll go on back and take care of my boys if that's the way you want it. You two be damn careful, hear?"

Bigfoot shook hands with Creed and looked to Caleb. "Let's get saddled up. We got a little daylight left and a long ride ahead of us."

That night Caleb and Bigfoot camped on the south bank of the Frio River, and just after sunrise Caleb easily picked up the outlaws' trail. "Looks like ten of 'em, and they're headin' straight for Laredo like Taylor said."

Bigfoot looked at the trail heading southwest toward the old border town. "I figured that's what Vidal would do. He won't be able to sell the string in or near Laredo with Creed's brand on 'em and no bill of sale. Once he leaves town and gets the horses across the border, though, it'll be near impossible to pick up his trail. I hear tell the varmint has a ranch somewhere on the other side of the Rio Grande. I bet that's where he's gonna take the stock until he can find a buyer. Maybe we can persuade somebody to tell us where it is."

Caleb chuckled. "Now how are we gonna do that, partner?"

"We'll worry about that once we get to town," Bigfoot replied with a smile, "and we ain't gonna get there by sittin' around here burnin' daylight. Let's ride!"

The Rangers rode into Laredo before sundown the following day. Bigfoot had been anxious to push hard and make the sixty mile trip without stopping to rest the horses, but Caleb convinced him to spare the animals as much as possible. One way or another, the hunt for Creed Taylor's horses would most likely require them to ride much further than Laredo, and Caleb wanted their own horses as fresh as possible for the chase.

"We ain't gonna find out much on this side of the border," said Bigfoot. "I'll bet Vidal crossed over as soon as he got here. Let's head on across ourselves."

They forded the river and spent the next two hours looking for Creed's horses or anyone who might have seen them. Most of Laredo's citizens ignored the Rangers questions and went about their business as if the Texans did not exist, making it clear that Anglos were unwelcome south of the Rio Grande. It was nearly dark before they found what they needed to know from an old man fishing alone along the south bank of the river. The old Mexican was uncooperative and evasive like all the others when they first approached him, but when he realized they wanted information about Vidal he talked freely.

"Vidal is a very evil man, *senor*," the old man said to Caleb who had learned to speak fluent Spanish from his wife and in-laws. "He corrupted my daughter by bringing her to town to be his wife. In the end he betrayed her, and now she works as a *puta* in the cantina that Vidal shares with a partner."

"Vidal's also a horse thief and murderer, old man," added Caleb. "We tracked him to town with a bunch of horses he stole from my partner's friend. We're not sure where he took the horses once he got here."

The old man nodded. "Yesterday I was sitting here on the riverbank fishing, just before sundown, when Vidal and some of his men crossed the river with a bunch of horses. He moved them to a corral just down the street from his cantina, but they are no longer there."

"Caleb frowned. "How do you know this?"

"I passed the corral on my way to the river late this afternoon, *senor*. It now stands empty."

"What did he say, Caleb?" asked Bigfoot, growing impatient just listening. Like most Rangers who rode the border, Bigfoot understood a little Spanish. He knew the old man was talking about Vidal and the stolen horses, but his understanding of the remainder of the conversation was imperfect.

"Late yesterday Vidal crossed the river with the horses," repeated Caleb, "but they ain't in town anymore. I was about to ask the old man if he knew where Vidal took 'em."

The old man had no idea when or where Vidal had taken the horses, or if someone else may have moved them, but he did tell Caleb the name and location of the cantina. "It is on the south side of town, *senor*, *La Senora de la Suerte*."

"The Lucky Lady," repeated Bigfoot. "Is Vidal there right now?"

"I think its best we find out, partner," Caleb said as he swung back up on the saddle. "Will you be able to recognize him?"

"No problem," Bigfoot replied when he was mounted. "I've got a good look at the varmint a few times over the sights of my Colt, but he's a slippery critter."

A short while later, the Rangers dismounted in front of the Lucky Lady and looped their reins around the long hitching rail out front. Several horses were tied to the rail. Loud music and boisterous conversation flowed from the dimly lit cantina's batwing doors and open windows, disturbing the tranquility of the street. Caleb drew the Walker Colt from his saddle holster, carefully checked the loads and primer caps in the cylinder, and shoved the big revolver in his gun belt. Bigfoot followed suit. They could well need the extra firepower of their saddle Colts before this little fandango came to a conclusion.

After checking the cylinder of his other Colt, Caleb slipped the big revolver back in his holster. "I'll do the talkin' when we go through the door. You ready?"

Bigfoot smiled. "I was born ready."

Leading the way, Caleb shoved his way through the swinging doors of the Lucky Lady and stepped inside the cantina, immediately moving to his left. Following closely, Bigfoot entered and stepped to the right. Both men stood quietly, surveying the crowd. As one customer after another took note of the Rangers' entry, the blaring noise filling the crowded cantina slowly sub-sided like the passage of a herd of buffalo as it thundered across the prairie and on out of sight. Few Anglos were welcome in the Lucky Lady, and since the war with the United States ended, even fewer had the courage to enter the establishment uninvited. The last of the noise faded to silence when the musicians low-ered their instruments.

Caleb could hear the sound of his own breathing before he began to speak. "Where is Vidal?" He asked loud enough to be heard throughout the saloon.

The bartender was the first man to speak. "Vidal is not here, *senor*. What do you want with him?"

"We aim to hang him for murder and horse stealin'," Caleb replied with an even, unhurried tone in his voice. "Do you see him anywhere?" he asked Bigfoot out of the corner of his mouth.

Being careful to stay out of Caleb's line of fire, Bigfoot ig-nored the murmurs of protest and stepped forward to take a good look around the saloon. "The varmint ain't here, partner," the big man answered as he stepped back without taking his eyes off the crowd. "What are we gonna do now?"

Before Caleb could reply, four mean-looking hombres stepped away from the bar to face off with the Rangers. All of them were well armed, but Caleb paid special attention to a lanky hombre on the far left who wore a fancy black sombrero with a silver hatband. The man held a muzzle loading scattergun in his big hands.

"We ride for Vidal, *gringo*," said their spokesman with an angry snarl, "and you will find it very difficult to hang him or anyone else here. This is Mexico, not Texas." The four men spread out, and the remainder of the saloon's patrons began a wild scramble for the back door as the bartender ducked down behind the bar. The saloon quickly emptied.

Caleb was glad the noncombatants had removed them-selves from the line of fire because all hell would surely break loose with what he was about to say next. "If you men ride for Vidal, ya'll are no good horse thieves and murderers just like him. Either you tell us where he is or be prepared to meet your maker."

A man's eyes always tell the story as Caleb had learned long ago from both his father and Bigfoot. When he saw the leader's eyes narrow, the tall redhead cleared leather so fast the movement was difficult to follow with the eye. The Walker Colt in his right fist roared its defiance and the first ball took the outlaw with the shotgun squarely in the throat before he could bring the deadly weapon to bear. The 44 caliber ball nearly took the man's head off at the shoulders as it tore through his windpipe and severed his spine.

Bigfoot's first shot was an instant echo of Caleb's, and the Mexican on the far right was knocked off his feet when the well-aimed round plowed into the center of his chest. The Rangers' Colts continued to roar until all four bandits were on the floor.

"Keep your eyes on the doors, Bigfoot," said Caleb. After quickly checking the downed outlaws to ensure they were dead, he holstered his Colt and moved to the bar. Reaching over and down, he grabbed the bartender by the collar of his fancy shirt and hauled him up, yanking him halfway across the bar. "I will ask you just once," Caleb said in Spanish. "Where is Vidal?"

"Please, *senor*, do not harm me," the bartender choked out in fear, "I have no idea where Vidal is."

"That's the wrong answer," Caleb snarled as he took hold of the bartender's wrist and slipped the big Bowie knife from the beaded sheath on his gun belt. Holding the terrified man's wrist down on the bar, Caleb laid the razor-sharp edge of the Bowie's blade at the base of the bartender's little finger, drawing a thin line of blood. "I'm gonna start with this finger and work my way across your hand. I'm willin' to bet you'll remember where Vidal is long before you lose all your fingers. If not, I'll start on the other hand."

"Madre de Dios!" the bartender pleaded. "Please don't cut off my finger! Vidal has a *rancho* on the Rio Grande, *senor*, fifty or sixty miles west of here. I am sure he took the stolen horses there."

Caleb smiled. "That's much better. Now all I want to know is when he left here and with how many men?"

This time the bartender never hesitated as he sobbed, "Vidal pulled out early this afternoon with five men."

Caleb slipped the Bowie back into his sheath. "Your fingers are safe unless you lied to me. If so, I'll be back, and cut off your whole damn hand. Bigfoot, cover me from the door while I gather up the horses. I'm pretty sure everybody cleared out, but there ain't no use takin' any chances."

Bigfoot stepped to the batwing doors and took a good look around the dusty street. "It looks clear to me. Go ahead and make your move."

Caleb dashed out to the hitching rail, untied the horses and swung up on Nasty. "Come on partner, time's a wastin'!"

Bigfoot bolted out the door and ran to his buckskin, leaping onto the saddle. "Let's make tracks!" he shouted as he spurred the big buckskin gelding and galloped south out of town with Caleb right on his heels.

The Rangers rode west for a few miles until they were well clear of town, and then swung north to rejoin the river. A brilliant full moon shed its silvery light across the Rio Grande Valley, making the riding easy. Reining their animals west along the river, Caleb and Bigfoot slowed them to a steady lope.

"This full moon is a break," said Caleb. "We can make good time, and there's no way Vidal could've covered that many miles before dark pushin' all them horses. That is if the bartender wasn't lyin' to me."

Bigfoot chuckled. "There ain't no way in hell that man was lyin'. You scared him near to death. Were you really gonna cut off his fingers?"

Caleb glanced at his good friend with a deadpan look on his face. "The little finger was as good as gone. I can't say how much further I would've taken it, though."

Bigfoot shook his head. "Damned if I don't believe you, partner. You're sure a hell of a lot meaner than you used to be."

Ignoring Bigfoot's remark, Caleb began to make plans for the encounter he expected to have with Vidal and his men. "Vidal wasn't worried about bein' followed or he would've left Laredo early in the mornin', so I doubt they'll have a cold camp. With luck, we should come across their fire before daylight. That should give us the advantage we're gonna need to deal with six of 'em. Keep a sharp eye out."

It was still a good two hours before sunrise, when the Rangers spotted the glow of the outlaws' small fire. The full moon was hanging low in the sky. The camp looked to be set up along a small creek in the middle of a grove of cottonwood trees about a quarter mile south of the Rio Grande. A long ridge stretched across the horizon to the south, and the creek twisted its way down from the high ground before flowing through the cottonwoods and eventually emptying into the river.

Caleb looked the ground over carefully. "Vidal most likely put out a sentry if he decided on havin' a fire. I'd guess he's somewhere in the trees north of the camp. We best circle around to that high ridge and approach from the south. The wind's out of the north, too, so their horses won't pick up our scent."

"Sounds good to me," said Bigfoot, "but let's get a move on. We damn well want to hit 'em before sunup."

They reached the high ridge in less than an hour and slowly worked the horses back toward the Rio Grande until they were no more than a hundred yards from the grove of cottonwoods. Caleb reined Nasty into a small arroyo and dismounted. The darkness was complete, now that the moon had fallen below the horizon, and he did not want to risk a stumble by one of the horses that would alert the camp to their presence.

"Leave the horses here," Caleb whispered as he tethered Nasty's reins to some brush. "Follow about ten feet behind me." Caleb moved off. Halting again when he reached the trees, he waited for Bigfoot to move up beside him. "You and them damn spurs, partner." Caleb's soft, moccasin-like boots enabled him to move silently. He always kidded Bigfoot that anyone who needed to gouge a horse to death with big spurs should go ahead and walk. "Sit down and take 'em off as quiet as you can and wait here for me. I'll take a look at what we're up against and come back to lead you in."

Caleb ghosted off before Bigfoot had an opportunity to protest. Moving silently as a stalking cat, he was soon in position to observe the camp. Five bedrolls surrounded a small fire that had burned down to glowing embers. Circling the camp as close as he dared, he began to make his way toward the river. Now and then freezing as he listened patiently to the night sounds. The slow and cautious movement finally paid off when he heard the sentry move restlessly and cough; the movement silhouetting the man's darker shadow against the lighter skyline. Silently sliding the Bowie from his sheath, Caleb slipped behind the sentry, covered the man's mouth with his hand, and drove the long blade of the knife deep into his kidney. Yanking the blade free before the tortured flesh could lock it in place, he drove it home again, and then a third time. The sentry's body twitched before it went limp, and Caleb carefully lowered it to the ground.

A few minutes later, he touched Bigfoot on the shoulder. The big man nearly jumped out of his skin, barely stifling a scream. "Damn you, Caleb McAdams!" he whispered hoarsely, "I done told you to quit sneakin' up on me like that. One of these damn days my old ticker's gonna give out!"

Caleb smiled, his teeth showing white the darkness. "The sentry's dead. Did you get rid of your spurs?" When Bigfoot grunted, he continued. "The camp's just ahead on this side of the bank. I'll put you in position, then circle a little ways to the east, over by their horses. Open fire when I do, but remember, I'll be off to your right. If anyone runs away from the stream in that direction let 'em go. I'll take care of 'em."

"I ought to shoot you any damn way for scarin' the hell out of me like that," Bigfoot whispered, forcing Caleb to stifle a laugh.

Caleb placed Bigfoot where he had a clear field of fire, then found a spot for himself with a good view of the sleeping outlaws. From his position, he could also cover the horses. The sun had not yet poked its fiery face above the horizon, but the early morning twilight provided enough light to see fairly well. Drawing his Colt, Caleb cocked the hammer and took careful aim at one of the sleeping men, then sighing, he lowered the revolver. It was no use. No matter what advantage they might gain, he could not force himself to shoot a sleeping man.

"Vidal!" he screamed, "Texas Rangers! Give yourself up!"

Of course, neither Vidal nor any of his men were foolish enough to surrender to a rope. A hail of lead flew in all directions, as the outlaws blindly opened fire from their bedrolls. The fire was hot and heavy for a moment, and then the bandits broke for their horses. That was the edge the Rangers needed. Bigfoot dropped two men as they rose from their blankets and a third as he was running for the horses. Caleb knocked a fourth bandit off his feet, but the fifth outlaw managed to throw some lead his way and make it to his horse when the big redhead hit the ground to take cover. Mounting quickly, the bandit sawed the reins of his horse around and spurred the animal into a gallop. Caleb rose to his feet, taking careful aim. The Colt roared and nearly fifty yards away the outlaw threw his arms wide as the heavy caliber ball plowed in between his shoulder blades and exploded out his chest, knocking him out of the saddle.

Bigfoot walked up as Caleb was holstering his Colt and finished off a moaning bandit with a round to the head. "The one you just knocked off his horse was Vidal, Caleb. He nearly escaped because of your foolishness in callin' out to 'em. One day you'll most likely get us both killed tryin' to be so damn fair-minded." Tactfully changing the subject, Bigfoot added, "Let's make sure the rest of 'em are dead and round up the horses. Some of Creed's stock broke and ran durin' all the shootin'."

Within the hour, the stray horses had been rounded up and the bodies of the bandits stacked near the burned out fire like so much cordwood. Caleb wanted to bury them, but Bigfoot insisted he would have no part of such foolishness. Then it was Bigfoot's turn to come up with an idea that Caleb refused to have anything to do with.

"You're plum *loco*, if you think I'll help you do somethin' like that," Caleb said when Bigfoot told him what he had in mind.

Bigfoot could not help but chuckle to himself as he tightly snubbed down Vidal's horse to a tree. He then drug the outlaw's body out of the pile of bandits and slipped the big Bowie knife from the sheath that hung from the leather strap across his broad chest. "There won't be much blood, Caleb. He's pretty much drained from that big hole you put through him."

Getting down on his knees, Bigfoot grabbed Vidal's hair and quickly hacked off his head with the big knife. Caleb turned to keep from gagging and walked away. Placing the head aside, Bigfoot rolled Vidal's body over, pulled up his shirt, and using a piece of rope, tied the wooden cross he had already fashioned so that it would keep the Mexican bandit's body upright in the saddle. Then he picked up the body, placed it in the saddle as if it were mounted, and pulled the shirt back down. The mustang quivered in fear as Bigfoot used the pieces of rope he had cut earlier to tie the boots in the stirrups and then lash them together under the horse's belly. Vidal's headless body now sat up in the saddle as if it were ready to ride away. As a final touch, Bigfoot picked up the head, placed it carefully on the saddle horn, tied it down, and fastened Vidal's sombrero to it.

"Come take a look at this, Caleb," Bigfoot called out. Bigfoot waited until Caleb walked over and then released the mustang. The horse bucked wildly under the dead weight, but it could not rid itself of its gruesome burden. Finally the terrified animal gave up and raced off towards the river. "That should serve as a warnin' to any horse thief who thinks about crossin' the border."

Caleb stood, shaking his head in disbelief. "You beat all, partner. You know that?"

Chapter 3

A week later, Caleb crossed the Colorado on the Bastrop ferry and headed Nasty west at a steady lope, following the trail that ran along the river. Soon he was on Rocking M land, riding past two ranch hands hard at work repairing a long, split-rail fence Felix had put up to keep the cattle out of the irrigated fields along the river. Returning their wave, he marveled at the acres of corn, beans, squash, and melons standing ripe in the fields.

Further on, he waved to some women and children who were busy with the harvest. The women and children normally spent part of their day attending Lucinda's school, but during harvest season everyone was in the fields. Counting Caleb's family and the wives and children of the married ranch hands, there were more than sixty people living on the Rocking M, and it took a lot of food to satisfy so many hungry mouths. In the distance, the ranch compound stood on a low ridge above the river, the whitewashed adobe buildings surrounding the big central square glistening in the sunlight.

Within the protection of its eight foot walls, the lovely hacienda formed a hollow square. The front section of the structure had a great room with a large bedroom on each end. A long front porch and four evenly spaced arched windows graced the facade, one centered on either side of the door and one centered on each of the large bedrooms. Both side sections had three smaller bedrooms, and the rear section, enclosing the hollow square, had a large kitchen, with a storeroom on one end and a workshop for Felix on the other. The smaller bedrooms and kitchen also had arched windows, although not as big as the windows in the front of the hacienda. Heavy oak shutters, with firing ports that could be quickly closed and barred in the event of an attack, protected all the windows.

Like all the buildings on the ranch, the four sections that made up the hacienda were roofed in Mexican red tile, and they enclosed a spacious central courtyard with a covered walkway that ran along its entire perimeter. A picturesque well, encircled by a low adobe wall and covered by a small gabled and tiled roof, stood in the center of the courtyard. The contrast between the gleaming whitewash and the rust-red tile was pleasing to the eye, and the two tall live oaks that grew on either side of the well added both color and majesty to the lovely setting.

Manny Flores, who along with his twin Miguel, was among the few hands on the ranch unrelated to Felix, was waiting with the corral gate open when Caleb rode up and dismounted. "*Buenas Dias, Senor* Caleb, I will take care of your horse."

Caleb handed him the reins. "*Gracias*, Manny, but be careful."

"Do not worry, *senor*, I know this *hombre* very well," Manny replied with a smile as he carefully patted the big Appaloosa on the neck and led him into the corral.

As usual, the central square bustled with activity. Caleb was greeted with smiles and friendly nods all across the compound as he headed for the Hacienda. Lucinda and Felix were standing on the front porch with the girls when he passed through the gate. Caleb knelt down and opened his arms. The girls ran to meet him. Sweeping the little blond, blue-eyed cherubs into his arms, he gave each of them a kiss, and chuckled when they both began to dig into his pockets for the expected candy. It did not take them long to find it, and he put them down to enjoy their treat while he greeted Lucinda.

"Hello, love," he said as he stepped up on the porch and took Lucinda in his arms. Lucinda barely came up to his chin, and she was as beautiful as the day they were married more than seven years ago. She had big dark eyes, a cute pert nose, full red lips, and long black hair that glistened like the shimmer of a raven's wing.

"You will spoil the girls with your treats," Lucinda scolded with a lovely smile as she left his arms, "but I am glad you are home safe again."

Caleb turned and greeted Felix with a handshake. His partner was short in stature and growing a little stouter with the years. He had handsome features, with the same dark, expressive eyes as Lucinda, and a bushy black mustache that drooped down over the corners of his mouth. There was no gray in his hair. Without Felix, the Rocking M would never have been as prosperous. The little vaquero, along with Caleb's brother-in-law, Pedro, took care of most of the work it took to operate such a huge spread, freeing Caleb to organize and lead his volunteer Ranger Company.

"It's damn good to see you again, partner," Caleb said when he released Felix's hand.

"Damn good, damn good," parroted little Gretchin as she danced around Caleb's legs.

"That's not nice," said Ilse, scolding her little sister.

Lucinda shook her head in disapproval. "Now see what you have done, Caleb McAdams. You must learn to watch your language around Gretchin. She picks up on everything."

"Damn, damn," Gretchin repeated as she continued to laugh and dance around.

"Consuela!" Lucinda called. "Please come out here and help me with this imp."

Ilse shook her head at her little sister's antics. At nine, she already considered herself a young lady. Consuela bustled out the door and scooped up Gretchin in her ample arms. Felix had hired her and her husband Bolivar to help Lucinda with the household chores, but the couple had become more like part of the family than hired help. The talkative Connie was short, broad, and heavy-breasted with skin as dark as a Comanche, while the usually stoic Bo was tall and rail-thin with a ghost-like complexion and a protruding Adam's apple that bobbed up and down whenever he managed to sneak a word in over his rotund wife. Connie did most of the household cooking, cleaning, and washing of clothes, while Bo cooked for the unmarried ranch hands, took care of the pigs and chickens, and saw to the butchering and smoking chores. The family would have been lost without them.

"Come little one," Consuela said to Gretchin. "It is nearly time for supper and you must take your bath." With a smile, Lucinda and Ilse followed her into the hacienda.

Just then, Pedro came through the gate riding his favorite chestnut gelding. Dismounting, he looped his reins over the hitching rail. Caleb's brother-in-law had Felix's dark eyes and handsome features, but his pencil-thin mustache was well-trimmed and he was a good three inches taller and broader at the shoulder than his father. His blue cotton work shirt and red bandana were faded, and he wore gray wool trousers with a reinforced leather seat tucked into tall, soft low-heeled boots like Caleb's. His outfit was topped off by a well-weathered black sombrero, and he was armed with two Walker Colts carried in a dual holster rig.

"*Hola*," Pedro said as he stepped up on the porch and offered his hand. "How are you, brother?"

"I had myself quite a time," Caleb replied. Ignoring the offered hand, he grabbed Pedro in a bear hug and lifted him off his
feet. "But that ain't unusual with that big ugly partner of mine."

Pedro freed himself with a laugh. "You are getting to be
worse than him."

"Come, said Felix with a smile, enjoying the close friendship between his son and his son-in-law, "we must wash up.
Supper will be ready soon."

Caleb sat back with a sigh after he finished his second slice
of dried apple pie. Consuela had outdone herself in preparing the
lavish homecoming feast. The large oak table in the great room
had been loaded down with food, and he had eaten until he could
eat no more. "Connie," he said, as Consuela and Bolivar were
clearing away the dishes, "thank you for a wonderful meal."

Consuela beamed. "*Muchas gracias*, *Senor* Caleb, I am glad
you enjoyed it."

Lucinda rose from the table. "Ilse, Gretchin, kiss everyone
goodnight. I will read you a story before bedtime."

Felix smiled as he watched Lucinda give Caleb a kiss and lead
the girls away. "Caleb, you did a fine thing bringing those girls
home. I have never seen Lucinda so happy." Pedro agreed with
his father and Felix added, "Let's all have a seat by the fire."

Caleb loved to sit in front of the big fireplace in the great
room and relax. Felix, a fine carpenter, had handcrafted most
of the furniture for the hacienda, including Lucinda's rocker,
and the four comfortable overstuffed cowhide chairs arrayed in
front of the hearth. There was a slight chill to the air on this mid-
September evening, and the small fire felt good.

"Caleb, we have a problem," Felix began. "Now that the
war is over, we no longer have a steady market for our beef.
We make enough on the sale of our horses to make ends meet,
but we counted nearly seven thousand longhorns on our range

during last spring's roundup. Even with the ten thousand extra acres we purchased, the ranch cannot support many more."

"I think it's high time I wrote Josh Tanner a letter," Caleb replied after considering the problem for a moment. "He's the horse trader me and Bigfoot met in New Orleans when we went after the Pates. He promised to pay top dollar for any horses I could trail there, and he mentioned he'd be interested in some cattle, too. What do you think, Pedro?"

Pedro's eyes flashed with excitement. "Others have made the drive to New Orleans, and I would love to see the city. Would this Mr. Tanner be willing to purchase enough cattle at the right price to make a drive worthwhile?"

"I'm not sure how many head he was talkin' about," Caleb replied, "or the price he's willin' to pay, but I can write that letter and find out. I'll send it with the next stage to Nacogdoches when I go see Governor Bell. If we decide to go through with the drive, we should start right after the spring roundup. That gives us plenty of time to get an answer back from Josh. In the meantime, like you said, Pedro, a few outfits around here have made trail drives to New Orleans. I'll try and find out what kind of problems they might've run into."

Three days later Caleb rode into Austin on Water Street and reined up the hill when he reached Congress Avenue. Both sides of the wide avenue were lined with saloons and shops of all kinds, intermixed with various government buildings. At the top of the hill stood the capital building surrounded by a strong log palisade. Austin was growing larger by the day, but thanks to the Comanches, anyone venturing too far west of town still stood a fair chance of being scalped. Caleb reined west on Pecan Street and headed for the Bullock Hotel. The hotel, owned by Caleb's good friend Richard Bullock, featured the cleanest rooms, the finest service, and the best food in Austin. The only drawback to the establishment was the foul odor emanating from the owner's pigsty on days when the wind blew out of the northeast. Thankfully, that was not often.

Dismounting in front of the hotel, Caleb looped Nasty's reins around the hitching rail and climbed the steps to the wide, covered veranda. No one was behind the registration desk when he entered the lobby, so he shoved his way through the batwing doors that led to the hotel's café. Richard Bullock was standing behind the long bar polishing glasses. The burly proprietor looked more like a blacksmith than an innkeeper with his thick neck, wide chest, and forearms corded with muscle. Bullock kept his reddish-brown hair and beard cropped short, and he wore a long white apron over his faded blue cotton shirt. Behind him hung his most prized possession; a large circular mirror shipped all the way to Austin from New Orleans. Rows of bottles climbed to the ceiling on either side of the mirror.

Bullock glanced up from his work and smiled. "Caleb Mc-Adams, you're a sight for sore eyes. How's that family of yours doin'?"

Caleb returned the smile. "Real well, Mr. Bullock thanks for askin'. Lucinda said to be sure 'n say hello." Richard Bullock was always ready and eager for the latest news, and just as eager to pass it on. "I just got back from a visit with Bigfoot. He sends his best. He's lookin' to take the first stagecoach through to El Paso from San Antonio. I plan on makin' the first run with him next month. By the way, you'll never believe what the crazy fool did this time." Caleb went on to relate the tale of the "headless horseman."

Bullock's laughter brought tears to his eyes. "That varmint is plum crazy, but I'm damn glad to hear he's doin' well. Be sure and pass on my greetin' when you see him. So, what brings you to town today?"

"I have a meetin' with Governor Bell this mornin'. I got enough time to enjoy a cup of your fine coffee first, though."

"Are you still workin' on puttin' that regular Ranger Company together?" Bullock asked as he slid the cup of coffee across the bar along with a spoon and bowl of sugar.

Caleb sighed as he added his usual three heaping spoons of sugar before slowly stirring the coffee. "I've been tryin' like hell for a good while without much success. I'm hopin' now that Pete Bell's governor my luck will improve." Caleb had first met Governor Peter Hansbrough Bell in 1840 at the Battle of Plum Creek.

"I hope so," Bullock replied. "The frontier is aflame, and the army can't seem to do a damn thing about it. Without your volunteers, the Comanches would probably be ridin' down Congress Avenue by now. We need some full-time Rangers in the worst way."

"I hope Bell agrees with you," Caleb said as he finished off his coffee and set the cup back on the bar. "By the way, would you mind mailin' this letter on the next stage to Nacogdoches?" He handed Josh Tanner's letter to Bullock.

"No problem," Bullock replied as he added the letter to the stack of outgoing mail that rested under the bar.

Governor Bell's office was located in the same rundown old clapboard building that had been used to house the Departments of the Army and Navy when Texas was still a Republic. The Governor was sitting behind his small desk when Caleb was shown into the office. It was a damn good thing Bell's desk was small, thought Caleb. The tiny office was hardly big enough for a larger desk. A tall filing cabinet stood against one wall and a large map of Texas adorned another. Behind the governor a small window offered little light, but a flickering oil lamp sitting on the desk helped to alleviate some of the problem. Three straight back chairs stood in front of the desk.

Governor Bell arose from his chair and offered his hand. "Caleb," he said as they shook hands, "it's damn good to see you again. Have a seat." The governor was tall and thin, and he kept his wavy brown hair, beard, and mustache neatly trimmed. His dark eyes and hollow cheeks gave him a somber, austere appearance, though he was usually prone to smile. "Have a seat. I received a letter from Colonel Hays yesterday. I don't believe anyone is a more avid supporter of your cause."

Caleb smiled. "I spoke with the Colonel a few days ago in San Antonio. He said he'd write to you. Texas will miss him, sir."

Bell nodded his agreement. "We surely will, and you don't have to sir me. We've been friends for a good while now. I remember when you first joined Jack's Ranger Company at Plum Creek. You were certainly a wet behind the ears youngster then. We served together with Somervell on the Mier Expedition, too, didn't we? And again at Buena Vista when I was a regular under General Taylor and you were ridin' with Ben McCulloch; but enough reminiscin'. In his letter Jack said Texas needs some full-time Rangers back in the field. Keepin' in mind that the financial commitment must be kept to a minimum, what can I do for you?"

"I've been studyin' the political situation closely ever since Wood disbanded the Rangers, Governor. I understand the opposition you can expect from the eastern part of the state, and that whatever you recommend to the legislature has got to be cost effective. For the last two years my volunteers have done a passable job, but volunteers are slow to react. They can't be called together until there's already been a raid, and it takes time to gather 'em up. Then once they're in the field they can only serve for a limited time. We need at least one company of full-time Rangers who can run patrols on a regular basis, react quickly when the situation calls for it, and stay in the field for as long as they're needed."

"What I'm proposin'," Caleb continued, "is a regular company of twenty-seven men; two twelve man troops, two sergeants, and a lieutenant. I don't want or need any pay to command the company, and when the men ain't in the field, I'll house 'em on my dollar at the Rockin' M. The state needs to provide the pay and rations for the twenty-seven men, and all the powder and ball they'll need. The men will provide their own horses and tack. There's one more thing. I want to order sixty new .44 caliber Colt Dragoon revolvers; the latest version of the Walker Colt. The company won't be large, but with the Colts, it'll be damn well armed. I figured you might need the exact numbers, so I put it all on paper." Caleb handed the list to the Governor.

Governor Bell stood and the two men shook hands once again. "I appreciate your time and effort, Caleb, and I'll do my best to get this approved."

Caleb led Nasty onto the ferry landing at the foot of the hill on Congress Avenue and up the ramp to the deck of the Colorado River ferry. After the brief crossing, he mounted and reined the big Appaloosa west on the trail along the river. He was on his way to see Wanda Cooper who operated a one-room school house on a high bluff overlooking the river near Barton Springs.

Wanda and Caleb first met when they were sixteen, soon after Caleb joined the Rangers. He had instantly fallen in love with the tall, blue-eyed, golden-haired girl. Wanda loved him, too, but she had been driven by a desire for an education, and though Caleb had proposed marriage, she insisted that he wait while she went off to school in New Orleans. Then, while attending school, she became involved in an affair with a rich New Orleans dandy named Andre and ceased to answer Caleb's letters. This painful situation had continued for nearly two years until Lucinda Vaca finished her schooling at the convent in Monterey and moved to Texas to live with her parents. After hearing nothing from Wanda, Caleb fell in love with Lucinda and asked her to marry him. Lucinda accepted his proposal and plans for the wedding were finalized when Wanda returned to Austin unannounced, after learning that Andre was far from the gentleman he had pretended to be. Though Caleb knew he still loved Wanda and she loved him, he also loved Lucinda, and he was not about to break his word to her and her father. The wedding to Lucinda went forward as scheduled, but over the years Caleb and Wanda had remained good friends, enjoying each other's company and their lively political discussions.

Wanda's homestead consisted of two separate log cabins connected by a wide dogtrot. The cabin on the left served as a one-room schoolhouse, and Wanda lived in the cabin on the right. Both cabins were well built and chinked against the cold, and their cedar shake roofs were in good repair. A rock chimney stood at the rear of each structure. Today was Saturday so the schoolhouse was closed. Caleb dismounted and looped Nasty's reins around the hitching rail. Stepping up on the porch, he walked over to Wanda's door and knocked.

The door opened and there she stood, beautiful as ever. "Caleb," she cried, "what a nice surprise! It's so good to see you." Wanda held in check the surge of feeling she always felt when she first saw Caleb. She was certain he still loved her in his own way, and she made no secret of the fact that she would have welcomed his advances, but she also knew he was determined to stay faithful to Lucinda.

"Come in and have a seat in front of the fire," Wanda said with a smile, "and I'll get you a cup of coffee."

Wanda's cabin had two rooms; a combination kitchen and living room and a separate bedroom. Directly across the room from the fireplace was a large glass window with frilly curtains that overlooked the river, an extravagant addition Wanda had insisted upon. The bedroom also had a curtained glass window, although not as large. She poured the coffee and sugared it heavily before handing it to Caleb and joining him on the sofa in front of the fire.

"What brings you to see me today?" Wanda asked.

Caleb turned to her and smiled. "I just wanted to see how you're doin' and share a little conversation. How's everything goin' with the school?"

"So it's my school you're interested in and not my body," Wanda teased. She loved the way she could still make Caleb blush after so long.

"I swear, girl, I never know what you're gonna come up with next." Caleb's smile was replaced by a serious look. "Have you been havin' any trouble with the local ranchers lately or the fine citizens of Austin?"

Now it was Wanda's turn to be serious. "Not really. There's been the usual grumbling about my Mexican and free black students, but nothing has escalated into a threat. Of course, since the Compromise of 1850 was passed by the U. S. Congress, my opinions on slavery and secession have begun to create quite a stir."

Caleb shook his head. "When are you gonna learn to keep your opinions about such things to yourself?"

"Never," Wanda stated firmly. "The Compromise managed to settle our western boundary, giving El Paso to Texas and Santa Fe to New Mexico, not to mention the ten million dollars Texas received to pay off its debts. The remainder was simply a weak attempt by Henry Clay to avert civil war. And Daniel Webster, an abolitionist of all people, helped him pass it! Although at least Webster warned the south there could be no such thing as peaceable secession."

Wanda gazed into the fire as she continued. "Clay wanted to pass the measure as one law, but he failed. It was Stephen Douglas who took the bill apart and passed it separately. Some parts of it are fine, like the admission of California as a free state, and the banning of the slave trade in the District of Columbia. I certainly don't care for the provision that allows all the new territories we acquired from Mexico to decide the issue of slavery on their own, though, and the Fugitive Slave Law is a total abomination. The very idea of returning escaped slaves to the south is sickening."

Caleb shook his head in exasperation. "Well I can certainly see why you've been causin' quite a stir, girl. Talk like that around here would get a man tarred and feathered, or even hung by some of the zealots."

Wanda took his hand. "I know you're concerned about my welfare, Caleb, but how do you really feel about all of this?"

"You know damn well I think slavery is dead wrong, Wanda. The idea of secedin' from the Union makes me sick, too, after all that fightin' and effort it took to become a state. Throwin' it all away seems plum ridiculous. Unless I'm pressed, though, I generally keep my opinions to myself. I wish you'd do that more often is all. I worry about you here livin' by yourself."

Wanda smiled as she snuggled closer. "I know you do, and I love you all the more because of it. I promise I'll watch my tongue, Okay?" Wanda stiffened as Caleb sat up and moved further away from her.

"You know we got to be careful, Wanda," Caleb said in reply to her reaction. "It aint fair to Lucinda if we let things go too far."

The conversation continued for another hour, but the intimacy of the moment had been lost. In fact, Caleb felt relieved, although strangely disappointed, when he was back in the saddle and riding toward the ferry.

Chapter 4

It was mid-afternoon on the first of November when Caleb rode into San Antonio and reined in at the Pellham Hotel livery. Bigfoot was busy in the main corral inspecting the mules that would be used to pull the stage to ensure they were all in sound condition. The hotel would serve as the official departure and arrival point on the San Antonio to El Paso stagecoach route.

Caleb had enjoyed his last few days on the ranch with Lucinda and the girls. The weather turned to a brief Indian summer, and they all went on a two-day picnic to the little stream that ran through the east end of the ranch. Several small waterfalls and a good sized swimming hole surrounded by low shelves of limestone rock made the picturesque stream a special place, and Caleb had a great time teaching the girls how to swim and dive. He swung down from the saddle, tossed Nasty's reins over the top rail of the corral fence, and tied the lead rope of the big dun gelding he called Smokey alongside it.

Deep in concentration, Bigfoot failed to notice his arrival, so Caleb stepped up on the lower rail and called out, "Looks like you picked some mighty fine animals, partner."

"Twenty-two of the finest mules I could lay my hands on," Bigfoot said as he turned to Caleb with a big grin, "three teams that been workin' together for quite a spell and four extra mules for spares. By switchin' the teams two or three times, we should be able to cover near forty miles a day. That should put us in El Paso in three weeks or so."

"Why mules?" asked Caleb. "Horses would be a whole lot faster and a hell of a lot less cantankerous."

"That's a fact," agreed Bigfoot, "but horses need grain and a whole lot more pamperin' than mules. Once the stage line gets some relay stations built between here and El Paso, they can go with horses, but right now we're gonna need the toughness of mules. I see you brought your own spare mount. Ain't that the same dun you picked up on the way to Santa Fe?"

Caleb nodded. "Sure is. Smokey's not as fast as some, but he's sure-footed and damn dependable."

"And he ain't near as mean as that big spotted bastard neither," Bigfoot chuckled. Nasty had nipped Bigfoot a time or two, and he believed Caleb had done folks a favor by naming the Appaloosa stallion something that tended to warn people off. "Let's go on over to Juanita's and have us a beer. We'll be pullin' out at sunup day after tomorrow. You might as well meet the boys who'll be ridin' with us."

Bigfoot led Caleb into the cantina and paused for a moment to let his eyes adjust to the dimly lit interior. Juanita's was a popular drinking establishment, and though it was still early in the day, the lively cantina already had a large, boisterous crowd. A young man Caleb recognized waved to them from the long bar across the room.

"George," Caleb said with a big smile as he quickly crossed to the bar and shook hands, "it's damn good to see you again."

George White had distinguished himself during the war while riding as one of Caleb's scouts. At five-foot ten inches tall and 190 pounds, White had a stocky build with dark, wavy hair and brown eyes. He wore a set of fringed buckskins with tall, soft boots and his old gray Ranger sombrero. A Walker Colt filled the holster on his right hip. Caleb also recognized the faces of the two men standing beside George, although he could not recall their names.

"Caleb, this is Sam Anders and Frank Talbot," said Bigfoot. "They rode with Ad Gillespie's Company in Monterey and with me down on the border while you was in Mexico City." Both men wore wide-brimmed slouch hats, faded cotton shirts, and wool pants tucked into tall-heeled boots with pinwheel spurs. They were armed with Colt Patterson revolvers and looked as if they could take care of themselves in a scrape. "Sam and Frank will be ridin' guard for us," Bigfoot added.

"It's always good to have a few Rangers along," Caleb remarked as he shook hands with Anders and Talbot.

"And this here's Mike Taylor," said Bigfoot. "Mike's one of Creed's boys." He is no more than sixteen, thought Caleb, as he shook hands with the youngster dressed in a floppy hat, buckskins, and tall boots. A large horse-pistol was shoved in his belt. "He's gonna be helpin' George tend the remuda. They'll be busy with sixteen mules and twelve horses. The extra horses will give us enough mounts for the rest of you to trade out when me and Pappy are switchin' the mules."

Bigfoot turned to an older man standing at the bar. "Speakin' of the devil, Caleb, meet Pappy Hodges. He'll be ridin' shotgun, and spellin' me at the reins. Pappy, this is Caleb McAdams. Like I told you, we've been ridin' together for quite a spell."

Pappy had gray hair, a scraggly, tobacco-stained beard, and emerald green eyes that sparkled out of his wrinkled, sunbrowned features. The old timer was dressed in a set of greasy buckskins tucked into tall beaded moccasins, and he wore an old straw sombrero. In spite of his years Pappy had a firm handshake.

"Glad to meet you, Pappy," said Caleb."

Pappy's smile showed a few missing teeth. "Pleasure is mine, son. Bigfoot told me a lot about you. Some of it must be true." Caleb smiled.

"You boys got the rest of the day to get your gear together," said Bigfoot after the laughter had quieted. "Don't party too hard. We meet tomorrow, bright and early, at the hotel livery to shoe the mules and horses. There ain't gonna be no smithy where we're headin'. You can take turns pickin' out your extra mounts while we're at it, too. Then we'll load the stagecoach with the mail and the supplies for the trail. As of now, we only got three passengers, so there should be plenty of room in the coach."

"Passengers," echoed Caleb, "you never mentioned passengers."

"Just found out yesterday," Bigfoot replied. "Two of 'em are wives of army officers and the other is a Captain. They're all headin' to Fort Bliss."

Caleb frowned. "The women may well cause us some problems before it's all over."

Bigfoot chuckled. "You don't know the half of it, partner. One of 'em is pregnant. Come on Caleb," Bigfoot added before Caleb had a chance to close his open mouth and comment further, "I got to see Pell about postin' a stage schedule in the hotel lobby. I'll see the rest of you in the mornin'."

Everyone was gathered at the livery by the time the blood-orange morning sun broke free of the horizon and began its daily climb into the kind of clear blur sky that portended a fine fall day. They started with the horses, leading the animals two at a time to the blacksmith shop just down the street. Caleb decided to have Nasty and Smokey shod along with the others. Like

Bigfoot said, why take a chance? Everything went smoothly until it was time to lead the mules to the smithy. Unlike the horses, most of them were stubborn and belligerent creatures, kicking out with their hind legs and biting anything they could reach. It was not until early afternoon before all the mules were shod, and, if not for the knowledge of Pappy Hodges, it would have taken even longer.

Next, Bigfoot had the men drag the stagecoach out of the livery barn. The coach was a brand new Concord, and it was absolutely beautiful. The undercarriage was painted a bright yellow and the body of the vehicle was a brilliant scarlet. On both doors, in ornate gold letters, was painted "Skillman Stagecoach Lines, San Antonio, El Paso, and Santa Fe." Caleb opened one of the doors, and they all took a look inside. There was room for nine passengers, and the spacious interior was plush. All the widows had fancy curtains that could be let down to limit the dust and block out the sun, and the seats were deeply upholstered in a lush purple.

"This damn thing looks like a carriage fit for a king, Bigfoot," said Caleb, echoing the thoughts of the others.

Bigfoot beamed. "Didn't I tell you she was beautiful—and practical too? Take a look underneath at them wide strips of leather that support the body? They're called thorough braces; layers of leather cured as hard as iron. They help spare the passengers by lettin' the coach swing back and forth like a cradle to take up the shocks of the trail."

"Them thorough braces help the mules, too," added Pappy. "If the coach gets stuck in the mud or a bad place in the trail and the mules are strugglin', the rockin' motion helps the coach free itself. I don't understand exactly how it works, but it sure as hell does."

"We best get the supplies loaded," said Bigfoot. "They're stacked in the barn. I plan on usin' the four extra mules and two of the horses as pack animals, so we need to load up six pack frames. We only got three passengers, though, so we can load the frames light and put some of the supplies in the coach. Let's get the coach loaded first."

Under Bigfoot's watchful supervision, the men managed to get a good deal of the supplies loaded in the coach, including a small barrel of flour, where it would stay dry and still leave plenty of room for the three passengers. As Bigfoot said, that allowed the pack frames to be considerably lighter. Two large water barrels were also tied down to the boot of the coach. The barrels would remain empty unless there was a long stretch between watering holes. It was growing dark by the time Bigfoot called a halt, and the exhausted men sought out their bedrolls early.

Everyone was awake well before daylight, and the first order of business was to hitch up the mule team that would lead out for the day. Caleb climbed out of his bedroll and saddled Nasty well before everyone else, so he helped Bigfoot and Pappy hitch up the mules while the others saddled their horses. Once the mounts were saddled, George and Mike gathered the remuda in preparation for the departure, and Sam and Frank brought the pack animals back to the barn to begin loading the pack frames.

Bigfoot selected a team of six gray mules to begin the journey and pointed out a team for Caleb to lead. Pappy led the way from the corral to the barn with the team he had selected. After Pappy's mules were harnessed, Caleb walked his team up to the tongue to be hitched, but they balked and refused to move into place.

"That's the lead team partner," explained Bigfoot. "They don't want any part of that tongue. They're used to bein' up front 'cause they got the experience and confidence to lead. Take a good look at Pappy's team. See how much heavier and muscled they are. They're called wheelers. The one on the left is a near wheeler, and the one on the right is called an off wheeler. They need to have strength and pullin' power. My team pulls from the middle, and they're called swing mules. They need to have good control and balance. Every mule has its own job. That's why I was glad when I found three experienced teams." Bigfoot went back to helping Pappy hitch up the mules to the double trees that were connected to the hitch assembly.

Before they were finished Mike Taylor rode up and reined in. "Bigfoot, George said the remuda is ready to move."

"Tell him to head 'em on out of town," Bigfoot ordered. "We'll be along shortly."

"Hold up a second, Mike," said Caleb. "I got somethin' for you. For y'all too," he called over to Sam and Frank who were busy with the pack frames. "Come on over here."

Caleb walked over to Nasty and untied the flap on one of his saddlebags. He reached in, pulled out a Walker Colt, and handed it to Mike. "This might come in handy before our little ride is over. It's loaded, so treat it that way. Here's the extra cylinder that goes with it. I'll show you how to load it later." He also handed a Colt and an extra cylinder to Sam and Frank. "Pappy," he called, "I got one for you too. I'll give it to you when we finish hitchin' the mules." Mike, Sam, and Frank thanked Caleb with big smiles before heading back to their chores.

"Where did you come by the extra Colts, Caleb?" asked Bigfoot.

"I bought one for every hand on the Rockin' M, and we ended up with a few extras. I wasn't sure how the men you hired would be armed, so I brought four of 'em with me."

Bigfoot nodded. "That was a damn fine idea. We're just about done with the hitchin'. Why don't you check the pack animals? Then you can get an early start on the trail before we take the stage over to the hotel."

Though it was not long after sunup, a big crowd had gathered in front of the Pellham Hotel when Bigfoot and Pappy pulled up with the stagecoach. The first stagecoach run between San Antonio and El Paso was a historic moment for the citizens of the old mission town and many people did not want to miss it. Pell walked out of the hotel with the passengers. He was followed by two hotel employees carrying their luggage. Bigfoot handed the reins to Pappy and jumped down from his perch to take part in the ceremonies and see that the luggage was loaded properly. Sam and Frank remained mounted.

The mayor was in attendance for the departure ceremony along with the members of the city council and Mr. Skillman and his family. Of course, the mayor began the festivities with a few choice words that stretched into a much longer speech than anyone had anticipated. The mayor, Mr. Skillman, and Pell then wished Bigfoot good luck, and the hotel employees loaded the luggage.

Once everything was loaded to Bigfoot's satisfaction, he held the door to the coach open and assisted the first of the women passengers to climb up into the stagecoach. She was young and pretty, with her blond hair pinned up and covered by a brown bonnet that matched her long dress, and she was obviously very pregnant. In fact, so pregnant that Bigfoot wondered just how far along the young lady was in her term. The journey to El Paso would be difficult enough, but the possibility of having to deal with a birth on the trail was unnerving at best. The second woman passenger was dressed in black with a broad-brimmed hat and a veil that covered her face. She was matronly in appearance. The army Captain helped her mount the steps into the coach, entered behind her, and shut the door.

Bigfoot climbed up to his seat on the stage and took the reins from Pappy. Reaching down, Pappy picked up the muzzle-loading shotgun leaning against the foot board and cradled it in his arms. The crowd roared as Bigfoot expertly cracked the whip over the heads of the lead team, and the first stagecoach run between San Antonio and El Paso had officially began.

Chapter 5

When Bigfoot reined the mules up on the bank of the Guadalupe River northwest of San Antonio late in the afternoon of the second day on the trail, Caleb was there to meet the stagecoach. "There's a good ford no more than half a mile west of here," Caleb said. "The bottom's gravel and the water ain't deep enough to come up to the hubs. We best get on down there and cross before we set up camp."

Bigfoot nodded. "Sounds like a damn good idea to me. You know the rivers in the hill country. A good rain could bring the Guadalupe out of its banks in no time."

Caleb reined Smokey around, and with the crack of his whip, Bigfoot whistled up the team and followed him to the ford. Smokey was first into the river and the water was not deep enough to reach the big, jug-headed dun's belly when he splashed across. Reining the lead mules into the river, Bigfoot followed Smokey with no trouble, and pulled the stage up under a tall, spreading live oak on high ground overlooking the river.

Caleb splashed Smokey back across to find George and Mike and lead them to the ford. They might need some help getting the remuda watered and bedded down for the night.

Bigfoot turned to Pappy. "You best fetch some water for the coffee before they get here with the remuda. Them animals are gonna muddy the river up pretty good."

Bigfoot and Pappy climbed down from their perch just as the stagecoach door swung open. Picking up the small water cask, Pappy headed down to the river. The army Captain was the first to exit the stage, and he helped the women get down. The older woman walked up to Bigfoot. She no longer wore the dark veil that had covered her face, and she was quite attractive.

"Excuse me, sir, but might I have a word with you?" she asked.

Bigfoot smiled. "Course you can, ma'am. What can I do for you?"

She returned his smile. "First off, you can dispense with the ma'am, and I'll do away with the sir. Last night we barely had time to roll up in our blankets when we finally halted, but it appears we have a little more time this evening to get acquainted. My name is Main, Gloria Main, and my husband is Colonel John Main, the commander of Fort Bliss. We're going to be seeing a lot of each other before this journey is over, Mr. Wallace. I think it would be best if you called me either Gloria or Mrs. Main, whatever suits you."

Bigfoot was a bit flustered by the lady's presence. "I'm sorry about pushin' so hard, ma'am, excuse me, I mean Mrs. Main. I'm doin' my best to see that we average as close to forty miles a day as we can. By the way, you can call me Bigfoot."

"Forty miles a day is far from an unreasonable rate of travel by stagecoach, Bigfoot. In fact, Mrs. Sutton and I appreciate you going easy on us. Some of the stagecoaches that brought us to San Antonio traveled much further in a day than that. Of course, I also realize they had relay stations at their disposal. "Anyway, what I really wanted to talk to you about was the food."

Bigfoot was puzzled. "What about the food?"

Mrs. Main frowned. "I really don't know how to put this without offending your cook, but the food last night and this morning certainly left something to be desired."

Bigfoot stifled a laugh. "I have to agree with you. Pappy hates to cook, and he don't take much pride in it neither."

Now it was Gloria's turn to smile. "Well, I happen to like cooking, and I would love to take over the chore if you don't mind?"

"That would suit me just fine," Bigfoot replied. "Did you hear that, Pappy?" He called down to the river bank. "Your cookin' days is over."

"Good," said Gloria, "show me where you stow the cooking gear and I'll get started. By the way, this young lady is Anne Sutton, and this is Captain Jeffrey Lyton."

Bigfoot nodded to the young lady and shook hands with Captain Lyton. "I best help Pappy get these mules unhitched. The remuda should be along any time."

It was a pleasure to sit around the fire and savor a good cup of coffee after enjoying the delicious supper Mrs. Main had put together, especially the biscuits. After preparing the biscuit dough, she filled both of the big Dutch ovens with biscuits, covered them with the heavy iron lids, and buried them in the coals of the fire until the biscuits were baked to a golden brown. There was already another batch baking that she would hand out at breakfast.

Caleb took a careful sip of his hot coffee. "Mrs. Main, supper was right pleasin'."

"Thank you kindly for the compliment, Caleb," Gloria replied as she rose from the fire. "Gentlemen, if you'll excuse me I will join Mrs. Sutton and get some sleep. Pappy, don't forget to check the biscuits." Pappy nodded, and the others said goodnight.

Caleb looked across the fire at George. "Did you hobble the mules?"

"Yes sir," George replied, "and we put up a rope corral around the horses where there's some good graze like you suggested."

"Are you expecting trouble?" Captain Lyton asked.

Lyton seemed a decent sort, thought Caleb, not a typical army officer who was sure he knew all the answers. "I'm not sure, Captain. The Comanches should've finished up the fall hunt by now and moved into their winter villages. This Indian summer weather has got me puzzled, though. Here we are into the first week of November and today was a lot more like summer than winter. By all rights we should be bundled up by now in the evenin', but I didn't even cover myself with a blanket last night."

"Have you seen any sign?" Bigfoot asked.

Caleb sighed. "No, not a thing, I just got a feelin' things ain't quite right. I'll get a real early start tomorrow and have another look toward the Llano."

George glanced at Bigfoot. He had ridden with Caleb long enough to grow worried when the redhead had one of his gut feelings. The man had an uncanny ability to sense whenever danger was near.

Caleb's words made Bigfoot uneasy, too. "We're right on schedule, Caleb, maybe even a little bit ahead of schedule. I figure no more than seventy or eighty miles to the junction of the North and South Llano from here. Do you plan on ridin' all the way there before you join up with us again?"

"Right now I ain't sure," Caleb replied. "I'm gonna circle a lot and cover my back trail, so I shouldn't be more than five miles or so ahead of the stagecoach most of the time. I might not make it back to camp tomorrow night, though. If not, make damn sure the mules are hobbled and the horses are line tied. Keep a sentry posted, too, at least until I get back."

It was well after midnight when Caleb rode out of the camp on the Guadalupe. The nearly full moon was low on the horizon, but still bright enough to cast long, faint shadows that lent a ghostly appearance to the wooded terrain along the river. On the Texas frontier a full moon was often referred to as a Comanche Moon because the fierce warriors loved to use its silvery light to raid the settlements. Was the full moon the cause of his uneasiness, Caleb wondered? He kept up a steady pace, wanting to put some distance between himself and the camp before sunup. By the time he could see well enough to search for sign, he had covered nearly ten miles.

Reining Nasty away from the river, the big Ranger headed for the high ridges that formed the north slope of the Guadalupe Valley, not high enough to be silhouetted against the skyline, but well away from the danger represented by the river. If there was a war party in the area, the Comanches would most likely follow the trail along the river. He continued to ride the high ground until he neared the headwaters of the Guadalupe, then headed northwest toward the junction of the North and South Llano Rivers.

Several hours later, after much circling and doubling back on his trail, Caleb set up a cold camp on a small stream he guessed was no more than twenty miles from the Llano. If Bigfoot kept up the pace, Caleb was around five miles ahead of the stagecoach. That was right where he wanted to be. He would sleep for a few hours, and then double back again to the camp Bigfoot set up. If any Comanches were stalking the stagecoach, they would be drawn to the fire from the camp like a moth to a flame, and they would have no idea they were also being stalked.

Far below the high ridge that ran to the northeast of the stagecoach camp, Caleb saw the flicker of Bigfoot's fire set down along a small stream. He had circled to the north and west of the camp. If there were Comanches in the area, they must have approached from the northeast or he would have crossed their tracks long before dark. Dismounting, he tied Nasty to a low bush, where the big Appaloosa could reach some graze, and started down the long ridge on foot. If his fears were real, this would have to be a near silent stalk.

The full moon was high enough in the sky to produce plenty of light and, though he moved carefully, it took less than an hour to work his way to within two hundred yards of the camp. A stifled whinny off to his left led him to what he was searching for. Seven Comanche ponies stood in the middle of a small clearing bathed in silvery moonlight. The ponies were not painted for war, and neither was the lone warrior who stood guard. Making sure to stay downwind, Caleb ghosted past the horses and moved closer to the camp. For the next few minutes, he continued stalking silently down the ridge until a slight movement silhouetted against the light of the fire caught his attention. There they were; six warriors crouched in the undergrowth within a stone's throw of the camp. Caleb could make out a few forms sleeping in their blankets near the fire, but the camp was far from unprotected.

In the bright moonlight he saw Frank walking guard around the stagecoach, and off to his left George was in among the horses and mules. The horses were line tied to a long rope stretched between two trees and the grazing mules had plainly been hobbled. The defensive preparations must have set the Comanches thinking because rather than launching an attack; they slowly began to move back up the ridge toward their horses. Caleb followed the warriors until they were again mounted and stood watching as they rode quietly off to the northeast. Quickly climbing back up the ridge to where he had left Nasty, he swung up on the saddle and followed the small party at a distance for a few miles. Once he was sure they were leaving, he doubled back to the stagecoach camp. By the time he rode in and dismounted the full moon was below the horizon and morning twilight had brightened the sky.

Bigfoot was standing by the fire with a cup of hot coffee in his hand. "Here you go, partner," he said as he handed the cup to Caleb.

Caleb took a sip and grimaced at the bitter taste of the coffee. He would sugar it heavily in a minute, but first down to business. Taking his time, he proceeded to tell Bigfoot about his ride and how closely the camp had been observed. "They weren't painted up like a war party," Caleb related when he reached the end of his tale. "I'm guessin' they were out huntin' and came up on the camp by accident."

Bigfoot stood thinking for a moment before he spoke. "I don't figure leavin' quiet like they did is a good sign. War party or not, if they weren't plannin' on comin' back, they would've tried for the horses or at least a scalp. I'd be willin' to bet a good sum the bastards are planin' to round up a few friends and make a try at us later."

"My thoughts exactly," Caleb agreed. "When and where they hit us is gonna depend on how far their winter village is from here. We're only two days from the junction of the North and South Llano. I can't believe they can get back to their village, put a war party together, and get to the junction before we can. And you know damn well they're gonna make big medicine before they ride out. I'd guess they'll try and hit us somewhere between the junction of the rivers and the headwaters of the North Llano."

Bigfoot nodded. "You're most likely right. They won't attack on the open prairie between there and the Pecos. We could see 'em comin' from a long way off. What you got in mind?"

"You know as well as I do, when you're dealin' with Comanches, it's best to try somethin' they'd never expect," answered

Caleb. "They'll be comin' from the northeast. I'm bettin' they'll try to get ahead of us to set up an ambush. If I keep well to the north and follow 'em until they pick their spot, maybe we can ambush them first."

Bigfoot smiled. "I like your thinkin'. It's a hell of a lot better than sittin' around waitin' to get scalped."

The Comanche hunting party rode into their winter village late that same afternoon, and Running Bull, the leader of the party, went in search of Iron Jacket. He found the war chief sitting in front of his buffalo hide lodge eating a venison stew one of his wives had prepared. Although he was still a young man, Iron Jacket's lodge was painted with many scenes of his exploits. Iron Jacket motioned for Running Bull to sit down and help himself to some of the stew, and the famished warrior finished a large helping of the savory concoction before finally speaking.

"Late yesterday, just before the sun dropped from the sky, the hunting party I led came across a painted wagon some miles to the southwest of here. The painted wagon was driven by two white eyes and guarded by two others on horseback. It was pulled by six mules. We followed the wagon until they made camp along a small stream. They were soon joined by two other men driving a small herd of mules and horses. There were many mules and more horses than the fingers on both hands. There was also a blue-coated soldier and two white women riding in the painted wagon. We meant to attack the camp during the night, but it was too well guarded, and we were only seven."

Iron Jacket was pleased. "You did well in returning to the village, Running Bull. I will call a council of the elders and organize a war party to deal with this painted wagon you speak of."

Word of the proposed war party spread quickly across the winter village and soon a council of elders and war chiefs gathered around a fire in the lodge of Buffalo Hump, leader of the

Great Comanche Raid of 1840, and the camp's most senior war chief. As in all meetings where decisions of great import were made, the ceremonial pipe was passed with smoke blown in all four cardinal directions, first to the east, and finally to father sky and to mother earth; thus ensuring the spirits were involved in the final outcome.

Being the most senior war chief, Buffalo Hump rose to speak when the pipe was set aside. The old war chief was tall for one of the people and heavily muscled, with a prominent hump on his upper back that gave him his name. He wore only a loin cloth and beaded moccasins. A string of colored beads encircled his thick neck. His coarse black hair hung down long and straight, not cropped on one side like many of the other Comanche warriors. Dark features shrouded his serious facial expression.

"Iron Jacket has called this council, and it is for him to explain his reasons." With no more to say at the moment, Buffalo Hump sat down.

Iron Jacket rose to his feet and looked around at the warriors who encircled the fire. These men were the leaders of the Penateka in both politics and war. They were the ones he must convince. Of course, every warrior of the people had the right to go his own way, but Iron Jacket knew he would never get the numbers he was seeking for his war party unless the men who made up this council approved of his plan. Above all, he must take his time and not appear too rash and anxious. Although Iron Jacket had counted much coup for a warrior of his age, many of the older warriors in the council considered him too young and headstrong, especially Singing Grass. The two had remained bitter rivals ever since Singing Grass's good friend, Yellow Wolf, was killed a few years ago in the big fight with the Rangers at Walker Creek. Iron Jacket's friend, Many Tears, was also a member of the council, but, unfortunately, he was considered too young by many of the elders to have much wisdom.

Finally Iron Jacket spoke. "Running Bull returned to the village this afternoon with news of a painted wagon moving west across our lands. This wagon is guarded by six Texans, and a blue coat and two women ride inside. Running Bull wanted to attack the camp, but surprise was impossible because it was too well guarded. He had only six warriors, so he wisely decided to return here and organize a large war party. Six mules pull the painted wagon and many horses and mules trail behind it. When we kill the Texans these horses and mules will be ours along with their weapons and their women. I wish to gather a large war party of many warriors; enough to overwhelm the whites and totally destroy them. To do this I need both the encouragement and the wisdom of this council." Having clearly stated his position, Iron Jacket took his seat once again pleased with his efforts. Now the discussion would begin in earnest.

Of course Singing Grass was next to rise, the doubt he hoped to spread clear in the skeptical tone of his voice. "These mules that Iron Jacket speaks of are only good for eating in the starving times, and we have already killed enough buffalo during this year's fall hunt to easily last the entire winter. Only the white eyes' horses are important, and Iron Jacket has not mentioned their number." Singing Grass sat down.

Leave it to Singing Grass to find the weak link in his argument, thought Iron Jacket as he once again came to his feet. He could not afford to hesitate about the small number of horses, but he must present the number with a strong counter argument. "The Texans have twenty-two mules and sixteen horses, and while this is not a large number, neither is it small. But the number of horses to be taken is unimportant. The white eyes are crossing Penateka land without permission. Are we to sit back and do nothing about this outrage? We must wipe them out to set an example for other Texans who think they can freely enter our territory."

The discussion continued for nearly an hour with arguments and counterarguments on both sides equally balanced until Buffalo Hump arose once again. He had remained ominously silent throughout the long discussion. "There is much to be said for and against attacking the whites," Buffalo Hump began. "I have considered the possibilities carefully."

Buffalo Hump wished his longtime friends, Old Owl and Santa Anna, were still among the living and sitting in this council alongside him, but the white man's fever had claimed them nearly three years ago. Much wisdom had been lost with their passing, but one thing was certain in Buffalo Hump's mind. Though Iron Jacket was a great warrior, he had yet to acquire the wisdom necessary to be a true leader of the Penateka. Therefore, no matter the merit of his plan, he must be taken down a notch in the eyes of the council.

"We have found a fine camp for the winter away from the harsh wind," Buffalo Hump continued, "and the fall hunt, as Singing Grass said, was one of the best in memory. Why then should we risk hearing the lamentations of our women for the few or the many warriors who would surely be lost in such an attack? It would be one thing if the whites were planning to scar Penateka land with their iron blades and stay here permanently, but they are only passing through. I say let them pass and stay content in our winter village. I have spoken."

Of course, with Buffalo Hump's opposition, the consensus went against Iron Jacket and his plan to attack the painted wagon. The young war chief immediately rose to his feet and did his best to keep the childish anger out of his voice as he made his position perfectly clear. "As always I respect the opinion of Buffalo Hump and of this council. But as a warrior of the people, I must also take the path where my spirits guide me. Tomorrow as the sun rises I will ride west to attack the painted wagon. All Penataka warriors who feel as I do are welcome to join me in this ride."

Chapter 6

Caleb was five miles north of the confluence of the North and South Llano Rivers when he finally located the war party. Eighteen warriors slowly trotted past his well-hidden position and continued west; that made twenty-two counting the four scouts he had spotted earlier. The odds could have been a lot worse, he thought. In fact, he had expected to encounter as many as a hundred warriors, depending on the size of the village. It was late afternoon and the stagecoach would soon arrive at the river junction where Bigfoot intended to set up camp for the night, but Caleb did not want the Comanche scouts dogging the stagecoach to spot him, so he decided to wait until dark before entering the camp.

With plenty of time, he circled in a big arc to the east and then south to avoid the scouts and it was an hour after sundown before he neared the campsite. Following his usual practice, Bigfoot had forded the Llano just north of the confluence before setting up camp, so Caleb was forced to swim both the South and the North Llano to approach the site without being seen. The weather was a little chillier than it had been lately, and the night breeze made him shiver in his wet clothes. Dismounting, he tied Smokey off to some brush near the river where there was plenty of graze and began a stealthy approach to the camp.

George White was walking guard in the middle of the horses and hobbled mules when Caleb slipped up to him. "Evenin', George," he whispered.

White stifled a yell of fright. "Damn it, Caleb, you scared the daylights out of me. Bigfoot said to watch for you sneakin' up, but I never heard a damn thing."

Caleb chuckled. "You ain't supposed to hear me. Just be glad damn I'm not a Comanche. Go tell Bigfoot to meet me over by the stagecoach. We got some Comanche scouts keepin' a close eye on the camp, and I don't want 'em to spot me by the fire. I'll watch the remuda until you get back."

When Caleb walked up to the stagecoach, Bigfoot was waiting for him with a cup of hot coffee. "It's just like we figured, partner," he said as he took a welcome sip of the coffee. "The war party crossed the Llano five miles north of here and headed west. Countin' the four scouts watchin' the camp, there're twenty-two of 'em. My guess is they'll be waitin' for us tomorrow somewhere along the North Llano."

Bigfoot nodded. "Twenty-two ain't bad. I was sure there'd be a hell of a lot more. What you got in mind?"

Caleb had been considering a possible plan all day. "We're gonna hit them first, just like we talked about. I want you ridin' with me. Let Pappy drive the stage, and Captain Lyton can ride shotgun. We'll need both Mike and young Taylor to control the remuda. You know damn well the Comanches are gonna go for the horses and mules first. We'll take Sam and Frank along with us. Pappy should move the stagecoach out at sunup and keep as close to the North Llano as he can. Tell George to keep the remuda bunched, but not to follow the stage to close. The rest of us will hit the Comanches when they begin their ambush. That's about it. Can you think of anything else?"

Bigfoot went over the plan in his mind and asked a few questions before he was satisfied, but he liked what he had heard, especially the part where he would ride with Caleb. "It sounds like old times to me, partner. Should I brief the others now?"

"Now's as good a time as any," Caleb replied. "I'm gonna see if I can find out where the war party plans to hit us, but I should be back well before dawn. Make sure Sam and Frank are ready to ride, and that everyone understands what we expect of 'em."

Bigfoot nodded. "Take care of yourself, hear?"

Caleb switched his saddle to Nasty and walked the big Appaloosa west along the river for nearly a mile before mounting and riding slowly north. After a few minutes he picked up the pace to a steady trot, rode a few more miles north, then swung west once again. The further west he rode, the more he angled back toward the river. Slowing his pace, he carefully probed the moonlit night for his quarry. Within the hour, he was rewarded with the faint glow of a small fire in the distance near the river. The Comanches must feel confident we don't expect a thing to light a fire, even a small one, he thought. That is exactly how he wanted them to feel.

As he neared the fire, Caleb dismounted, loosely tied his reins to a tree, and moved forward on foot, taking care to make a downwind approach to the Comanche camp. The camp was situated on a low ridge that offered a good view of the North Llano. Moonlight shimmered off a small stream that wound its way down around the base of the ridge and widened as it flowed into the river. Pappy would have to bring the stage almost all the way to the base of the ridge before he could ford the stream. It was an ideal location to spring an ambush. Satisfied with the knowledge he had gained, Caleb made his way silently back to Nasty and untied the reins, walking the horse a good distance from the Comanche camp before swinging up on the saddle. Now was not the time to be careless. When Caleb arrived in the area of Bigfoot's camp, he made a wide sweep in search of the Comanche scouts, but as he suspected, they had pulled back to make sure their presence did not give away the element of surprise. Though it was still a good two hours before sunrise, everyone in the camp was up and making preparations to pull out when he rode in and dismounted.

"I found the spot where the Comanches are gonna spring their ambush," Caleb said as he walked up to Bigfoot. "We'll ride as soon as you're ready. The scouts have cleared out, so don't worry about them seein' us. Get everyone together while I grab a cup of coffee, and we'll go over the plan."

When the group had gathered near the fire, Caleb knelt down and swept a spot clear on the ground with his hand. Using a stick, he drew the confluence of the two rivers. "Here's our camp," he said as he poked the stick in the ground just north of the confluence. "This line running west is the North Llano. About five miles or so west of here, there's a small stream that winds around a low ridge before it flows into the river." Caleb drew the stream and the ridge on his map. "Pappy, the stream gets wider, and I suppose deeper, as it nears the river, so you'll have to move upstream close to the base of the ridge before you can ford. That's where I think they'll hit the stage. When they do, you best keep movin'." Caleb looked up at Pappy and he nodded. "Captain Lyton, you'll have the shotgun as well as Pappy's Colt, so give the bastards all you got." Caleb glanced up at Gloria who was listening intently. "Sorry about the language, Mrs. Main."

Gloria shook her head. "It was nothing that a soldier's wife has not heard before, young man. However, I'd like to add that I'm a rather good shot. If you give me two or three loaded rifles,

I'll sit on the side of the stage facing the ridge and assist the Captain."

Caleb smiled. "I'll see to it, Mrs. Main. Now Sam, Frank, this is where you come in. When the Comanches spring the ambush on the stage you're gonna hit 'em from the rear, and I mean hit 'em hard. Ride right into 'em and cause as much of a ruckus as you can. I'm bettin' they'll fold their cards quick and skedaddle. Ride on through 'em and join up with the stagecoach. Understand?" Both Rangers voiced their understanding.

"George, Mike," Caleb continued, "the Comanches are gonna come after the remuda with everything they got. That's why I want the mules and horses between you and the river. Me and Bigfoot will hit the war party from the rear as soon as they attack. We're gonna take out as many warriors as we can, then join up with you, and hit 'em again before they have a chance to get reorganized. I'm hopin' that'll drive 'em off for good, but if not, we let the remuda go and ride for the stage. Does anybody have anything to add?" Caleb's question was answered by silence. "Fine, Bigfoot, Sam, Frank, let's get mounted. Pappy, move the stage out at dawn. Good luck to all of you."

Well before the sun rose above the eastern horizon, Caleb and Bigfoot took cover in a ravine less than a hundred yards behind the east end of the ridge from where the Comanches would launch their attack on the remuda. Earlier, Caleb had posted Sam and Frank behind the west end of the ridge where the Comanches would attempt to ambush the stagecoach. From his belly-down position at the lip of the ravine, Caleb counted fifteen warriors milling around noisily on their painted ponies. If that was the case, only seven were posted at the other end of the ridge ready to ambush the stagecoach. With the help of the shooters on the stage, Sam and Frank should be able to handle them, Caleb thought, so he would not have to worry about the coach or its passengers. He was making double sure of his count when the warrior who was obviously the group's leader rode to their front and began to harangue them for making too much noise. With a start, Caleb realized he recognized the war chief.

The big warrior still wore his raven-black hair long and flowing, not cropped off on one side in the usual Comanche manner, and as before, it was decorated by a single fluttering eagle feather. His face, as in the past, was painted in broad horizontal stripes of vermillion and yellow, and he still rode the same magnificent gray stallion with white lightning bolts painted down its legs and blue hailstones daubed across its rump. A few more scalps decorated the long red war lance, and the warrior's broad chest was now covered by an old Spanish breast plate. So the Comanche known as Iron Jacket was the same youngster Caleb had saved from death several years earlier during a Ranger attack on an Upper Colorado winter village. He had regretted his intervention ever since. Hopefully, he would get a chance to rectify that problem today.

Bigfoot was laying belly-down next to Caleb. "This bunch is gonna go for the remuda," he whispered to Bigfoot. "They most likely won't attack until the warriors at the other end of the ridge spring the ambush on the stage. We'll slip back down and mount up when we see the stage comin' and be ready to charge when the shootin' starts. Ride through 'em when they attack, and take out as many as you can. We'll keep the pressure on until we can join up with George and Mike."

When the stagecoach came into view a few minutes later, Sam and Frank were already mounted and ready to hit the Comanches from the rear the moment the savages launched their ambush. The stage came on quickly, and as the lead team neared the stream, Pappy reined them away from the river in the direction of the ridge to look for a place to ford. He soon found a likely spot, but the stage was forced to slow to a crawl as it entered the water and began to plow its way across. Choosing that moment to attack, the Comanches charged down off the ridge, screaming their war cries.

The Rangers galloped after them, but Mrs. Main was the first to draw blood. She fired a shot while the stage was still crossing the stream. The .50 caliber ball from Caleb's Hawken long rifle flew straight and true, and one of the lead warrior's arms flew wide when the ball slammed into his chest, catapulting him off the back of his pony.

Pappy cracked his whip sharply above the lead mules' ears, and the stage jerked up and out of the stream, nearly unseating Captain Lyton. Once out of the stream, the coach quickly gained speed. In spite of being bounced around in the seat, Lyton began to blaze away with Pappy's Colt as the warriors drew closer to the stage. One of his shots found the target, smacking into the shoulder of a luckless warrior and rolling him off his pony into the tall grass. Mrs. Main fired again, this time with Bigfoot's Kentucky rifle, but the jostling of the stagecoach caused her to miss. Fortunately, Sam and Frank had closed in on the pursuing Comanches by then, and when they opened fire two more warriors tumbled off their ponies. The remaining three Comanches broke off their attack when they realized the Rangers were behind them. Circling back, they picked up their wounded friends before disappearing over the ridge.

Distant gunfire echoed from the other end of the ridge as Pappy reined in the well-lathered mules to a slow walk, and the Rangers rode up to the stagecoach. "We'll be okay!" Pappy shouted down to Sam. "Get on over there and see if them others need a hand!" The young Rangers reined around and rode off at a gallop.

Led by Iron Jacket, the Comanches waiting on the east end of the ridge launched their attack on the remuda when they heard the warriors on the west end begin their ambush of the stagecoach. Caleb and Bigfoot had already scrambled back to their horses when they saw the stage approaching in the distance, and Caleb led them along the ravine until they were close enough to be right on the war party's heels when the warriors galloped down the ridge in their screaming charge.

George heard the rattle of gunfire from the attack on the stagecoach, and then saw the Comanches led by Iron Jacket streaming down off the ridge and heading straight for the remuda. "Get 'em runnin'!" he yelled to Mike as he drew his Colt and fired a round in the direction of the oncoming Comanches.

Mike quickly followed suit, and the remuda lit out as one. Following Caleb's instructions, the Rangers reined up and turned to face the surprised war party who expected to see them fleeing in fear. The warriors screamed their war cries, intending to ride right over the foolish Texans, but Caleb and Bigfoot chose that moment to open fire from close behind the startled war party.

Caleb singled out Iron Jacket for his first shot, and he had the middle of the galloping warrior's back dead in his sights as he slowly squeezed the trigger. However, fate once again intervened to allow the war chief to live for yet another day. Just as the hammer of Caleb's Colt struck the percussion cap, an unlucky warrior swerved in front of the muzzle, and the .44 caliber message of death was delivered to the wrong victim. Iron Jacket did not see the ball strike the warrior, but he heard the shot. The force of the impact in the middle of the warrior's back flung him forward and under the hooves of the war chief's galloping gray stallion, nearly causing the big horse to stumble. A quick glance to the rear told Iron Jacket that he was once again facing the hated red-haired Ranger.

No longer able to enjoy the luxury of carefully picking his target, Caleb joined in with Bigfoot, blasting away with his Colt at the warriors riding nearest him. Just ahead rode a young warrior no older than Caleb was when he first joined the Rangers, but young or not, two scalps dangled from his red war lance.

Caleb leveled the sights of his long-barreled Colt and put a ball into the back of the young Comanche's head, splattering brain matter and blood as the body rolled off the painted pony and bounced along the tall prairie grass.

A warrior turned, looking back over his shoulder to launch an arrow from his short bow, but Bigfoot blew him off the back of his pony before he could loose the deadly shaft. Caleb shot the horse out from under another Comanche who had dropped off to the side of his pony. Three more Comanches were quickly unhorsed. Unable to endure such devastating losses, Iron Jacket signaled for the galloping warriors to circle away from the pursuit of the remuda and head back toward the ridge.

George and Mike then joined the fray, charging into the circling Comanches' flank. Their accurate gunfire knocked two more warriors off their painted ponies before the savages rode out of range. Caleb took one more long-range shot at Iron Jacket. Bravely ignoring the near miss, the war chief leaned far off his gray stallion to pull Many Tears up behind him as he rode away. Though Red Hair had shot Many Tear's painted pony out from under him during the brief fight, except for a few bruises, Iron Jacket's good friend was unharmed. Two more wounded warriors were rescued by their friends during the Comanches' hasty withdrawal. Bigfoot and Caleb joined up with George and Mike, and Sam and Frank soon reined in their lathered mounts to a sliding stop alongside them.

Caleb greeted everyone with a smile. "It looks like we took care of business today, boys. Let's round up the remuda and get back to the stagecoach."

The attack on the painted wagon was a disaster, and Iron Jacket was not looking forward to his reception when the war party returned to the village. A sullen silence had settled over the warriors after the fight, and he expected no less from everyone else once the news of the debacle spread across the village. Naturally they would blame him, or at least his poor medicine for this terrible defeat, but even with the unexpected appearance of Red Hair, things may well have turned out differently if all the warriors in the village had joined the war party as he had requested.

That would no longer matter now, Iron Jacket thought. He had been the one to insist on attacking the painted wagon, though many of the elders, including Buffalo Hump, had warned him this was no time to ride off to war, no time to listen to the wailing of the women and children from lodges that would no longer have a hunter to bring meat. Now there would be nine such lodges, and maybe more, if any of the three wounded warriors died before the war party reached the village. The people did not number as the stars in the sky like the Texans, and nine warriors was a fearful price for the Penateka to pay.

The winter will be long and terrible, thought Iron Jacket. Though I will be blamed for everything that has gone wrong on this day, only one man is truly responsible. Iron Jacket had been shocked to the soles of his beaded moccasins when he turned on the back of his gray stallion during the attack and saw the tall redheaded Ranger and his bear-like companion appear, as if out of nowhere, to bring down death and destruction on the war party. What kind of medicine did the Rangers possess to do such a thing? Medicine or not, Iron Jacket vowed, someday I will take revenge on Red Hair.

Chapter 7

Early in the afternoon of the seventh day on the trail, the stagecoach reached a natural spring a few miles past the headwaters of the North Llano River. The spring marked the beginning of a wide and arid plain that stretched all the way to the Pecos River. Except for the immediate area surrounding the spring, the vegetation was sparse, consisting of mostly scrub brush and prickly pear cactus.

Bigfoot handed over the reins to Pappy and jumped down from his seat on the stagecoach, stretching his cramped legs by bending over and touching his toes. "This is as far as we go today, Pappy," he yelled up to the old-timer. "Take the stage over to the shade of those big rocks near the spring and help the Captain with the ladies. Frank, you and Sam help Pappy unhitch the mules, but don't let 'em muddy up the spring. They can cool down a spell, and we'll water 'em with the rest of the stock when George and Mike get here."

The nearby spring was the last good source of water until they reached the Pecos, and it bubbled up crystal clear out of the rocks, creating a good-sized pool before running off to the south in a small stream that dried up to nothing in less than a mile. There was good graze for the animals all along both banks of the shallow stream. The young Rangers began unhitching the mules, and Pappy climbed down from his seat and opened the door of the coach. Captain Lyton, his eyes squinting from the bright sunshine, was the first to emerge from the stage. After Pappy helped Mrs. Main down, they both helped Mrs. Sutton.

"How are ya doin', Ma'am?" Pappy asked Mrs. Sutton. The young lady looked peaked and nearly worn out.

Mrs. Sutton gave Pappy a wane smile. "Thank you for asking. I feel a little better now that my feet are on the ground again."

"She's doing just fine, Pappy," added Mrs. Main as she smiled and took Mrs. Sutton by the hand. "We army women are a tough breed. Come my dear, I'll help you take a seat in the shade on those rocks over there by the pool. Then I'll get supper started."

George and Mike rode in with the remuda a few minutes later, and Bigfoot directed them to the far reaches of the stream, well away from the clear running spring and pool. Sam and Frank had the team unhitched, and Pappy helped the Rangers take the mules over to where the remuda was cooling down before George allowed the animals near the water.

Once the horses and mules were watered, George decided not to hobble them so they could take advantage of the good graze along the entire length of the stream. It might be their last decent feed for a few days. Sam and Frank could help keep watch during the night.

Supper was over and the setting sun was painting a breath-taking panorama of color across the wide expanse of the western sky by the time Caleb rode into the camp. Frank was standing guard on the tall rocks near the pool, and he had spotted Caleb well out on the plain. Bigfoot was waiting when Caleb reined in and swung down from the saddle, beating the trail dust off his clothes with his old gray sombrero.

Bigfoot chuckled. "Looks like it was a might dry and dusty where you was ridin', partner. How'd it go?"

Caleb ignored Bigfoot's attempt at humor and used his yellow bandana to wipe the sweat and trail dust that had smeared his face. "It's eighty or ninety miles to the Pecos and the only water between here and there is in the Buckhorn Draw about half way. Problem is, it ain't too good and there ain't much of it. We're gonna have to pick up the pace some for the next two days or suffer a night in a dry camp."

"I'm for stretchin' the distance," replied Bigfoot. "The mules are well rested and they should do okay. You might want to talk with Mrs. Main before we decide though. Pappy said he don't think Mrs. Sutton is doin' too well."

Gloria Main was standing at the fire stirring a pot of beans left over from supper when Caleb walked up. "I was just getting ready to call you over here. There are still a few biscuits remaining from supper, and I reheated the leftover beans. You must be starving after all that riding." She leaned over and dished up a big plate of beans and bacon, adding two biscuits. "Here, sit down and eat this."

Caleb gratefully took the tin plate and sat down on a big rock near the fire. "Much obliged, Mrs. Main. I'm mighty hungry and this looks delicious. I was just talkin' to Bigfoot about the need to pick up the pace some for the next two days. It's either that or sufferin' a long night in a dry camp, but he's worried about Mrs. Sutton."

"Anne is quite near her term, Caleb, so close that it's uncertain whether she'll have the baby before we reach El Paso," Gloria saw Caleb's eyes widen and was forced to stifle a chuckle. "Don't worry. Women have been giving birth on the trail ever since this country was born, and in spite of the worry Bigfoot and Pappy expressed, Anne's doing fine."

Caleb was not completely convinced by Gloria's assurances. "Are you experienced in such matters, ma'am?"

"Unfortunately, I don't have any children of my own," Gloria replied, her features taking on a wistful expression, "but as an officer's wife, I have assisted in many births. Everything will be fine, you'll see. And please call me Gloria. Ma'am and Mrs. Main make me feel like an old woman."

"Sorry, ma'am," Caleb chuckled, "I mean Gloria. Just let us know if there's anything we can do to help out."

"Now that you mention it," Gloria added with a smile, "there is one thing. You mentioned that the trail is going to get drier. Even though it's rather chilly now that the sun is going down, I would absolutely kill for an opportunity to bathe. I'm sure Anne feels the same way. This spring fed pool would be an ideal place to wash up if you could arrange it"

Caleb returned Gloria's smile. "No problem. Me and the boys will move over to the other side of the rocks. There'll have to be a guard on this side, but I'll use Mike. It's gettin' dark, and he's still too young to risk stealin' a look anyway." They shared a good laugh.

Well before noon on the tenth day of the journey, Bigfoot reined up the stagecoach on the east bank of the Pecos River. They had been forced to dig for water at Buckhorn Draw, but at least they found enough to fill their barrels and water the animals two at a time. However, the last forty-five miles had been bone dry and the animals were anxious with thirst. Caleb knew

Bigfoot would have no problem keeping the team away from the river until they cooled down, but he took special precautions with the remuda, keeping them far behind the stagecoach until the smell of the water on the wind finally brought them to a run.

The muddy Pecos was narrow and deep, with virtually no timber along its banks. In many places, mudflats and pockets of treacherous quicksand waited to trap livestock too thirsty to be wary of the danger. The river was running a little lower than usual and the banks were steep in many places, so Caleb helped George and Mike steer the stampeding mules and horses to a downstream location he had scouted earlier where the banks inclined gently to the water and there was no quicksand to worry about. The water was brackish, as expected, but wet and welcome nonetheless.

After resting the animals for the remainder of the day, Bigfoot had the camp up and on the trail before sunrise, the stagecoach rolling northwest following the course of the Pecos. He kept the stage well away from the river, so the occasional dry wash running in from the east would be easier to cross. The first night on the Pecos, they camped at Horse Head crossing, joining up with several immigrant wagons. Instead of following the stagecoach north to Pope's crossing, the immigrants planned to ford the river in the morning and take the lower trail to El Paso and California by way of Comanche Springs and the Rio Grande.

Horse Head Crossing, eerily marked by stacks of horse skulls, scattered livestock bones, and the graves of Indian massacre victims, was the most famous—and certainly the most infamous—of the Pecos River fords. It served as a crossing, not only for the southern route to California, but also for the Comanche War Trail, which ran from the upper Texas Panhandle southward through the Big Bend country into northern Mexico. The river's alkaline waters poisoned ponies stolen by Comanche raiding parties from Mexican haciendas far south of the Rio

Grande, after the animals had been driven mercilessly northward across sixty miles of open desert.

Five days and another one hundred and fifty miles later, Bigfoot reined up the stagecoach at Pope's Camp, just below the new border between Texas and New Mexico. From there, the upper trail followed an ancient Indian pathway that paralleled the Texas and New Mexico border westward, passing below the southern end of the Guadalupe Mountains and on to El Paso. There were several wagons encamped at the site, some individual horseman, and even a few men on foot. Almost all of them headed for the California gold fields.

Bigfoot's attention was drawn to the newly-constructed ferry that was presently transporting a wagon across the Pecos. "Would you look at that, Caleb? I believe civilization has done reached the Pecos. Ferryin' this damn stagecoach would sure beat hell out of tryin' to swim it. Why don't you take a ride over there and see what the man charges while I get the boys busy settin' up camp for the night?"

When Caleb got back from speaking with the ferryman, Bigfoot had the camp set up and Gloria Main was busy cooking supper. "What kind of money are we talkin' about?" asked Bigfoot as he hungrily watched Gloria fill one of the big iron Dutch ovens with freshly made biscuits.

"Seven dollars for the stage," Caleb replied as he dismounted, "a dollar for each animal, and two dollars for each man or woman."

"The man's a damn outlaw in disguise," Bigfoot complained. "We should hang the bastard!" Gloria chuckled at Bigfoot's angry outburst, and he turned to her, touching the wide brim of his old gray sombrero in apology. "Sorry about that, ma'am." Turning back to Caleb he asked, "What do you think?"

Caleb smiled about Bigfoot's deference to Gloria. "Outlaw or not, he's got us over a barrel. I say we pay for the stage and the passengers. I'd feel a lot better about the ladies floatin' across the river than fordin' it. That'd only be seventeen dollars;

seven for the stage and ten for you and Pappy and the passengers. The rest of us will swim the horses and mules across. I can't see payin' a dime for them or the rest of us either, even if the water is cold."

"Cold water be damned that bastard ain't gettin' two dollars from me," Bigfoot groused. This time Gloria laughed out loud. Turning to her, Bigfoot contritely touched the brim of his sombrero. "Please accept my apology again, ma'am." Turning back to Caleb, he added, "Anyway, I'm gonna swim the damn river with you and the animals."

Bright and early the next morning everyone except George and Mike helped the ferrymen haul the stagecoach onto the ferry and tie it down securely. Captain Lyton helped the ladies enter the coach, and Pappy took his seat up front.

"It looks like we're ready to go," said Caleb. "The rest of you load your weapons, powder, and spare clothes in the boot. There ain't no sense gettin' everything soaked if we don't have to. Make sure you stow George and Mike's gear away, too."

Once the weapons and equipment were loaded, Caleb and the others went ashore and the two ferrymen began the hand-over-hand pull on the long rope that would slowly haul the ferry to the other side of the Pecos. Mounting up, the Rangers headed downriver to join up with George and Mike who had bunched the remuda where Caleb had already determined the banks were not too steep and there was no quicksand to worry about.

"Bigfoot, take the upstream side," said Caleb. "I'll cover downstream. Keep 'em bunched." Bigfoot nodded and reined his buckskin into position. Caleb looked to the others. "Once me 'n Bigfoot get 'em started, make damn sure the rest follow. I don't want any turnarounds."

Caleb reined Nasty to the downstream side and the other men fanned out behind the remuda. When everyone was in position Caleb signaled to Bigfoot and cracked the nearest mule in the rump with his doubled lariat. Bigfoot followed suit. Braying and whinnying in protest, the reluctant animals plunged into the river and began to swim strongly for the other side. Within minutes they were all climbing the far bank. Once the horses and mules were finished rolling themselves dry, Bigfoot and Caleb sorted out a team of mules and headed them to the ferry landing where they helped offload the stagecoach. George and Mike led the remainder of the remuda to some good graze along a small stream.

The ferrymen were grateful for Caleb and Bigfoot's help, and when the stage was again on dry ground one of them turned to Bigfoot as he and Pappy were hitching up the team. "I never thought I'd see the likes of this rig way out here so soon. She sure is pretty. Will the stage run regular from now on?"

"At first just as regular as I'm able to move it back and forth twixt El Paso and San Antone," Bigfoot replied. "But soon there'll be another stage or two makin' the run, and eventually we plan to put up way stations every forty miles or so."

Bigfoot climbed up on the seat beside Pappy and took the reins. "We'll be seein' you boys on the return trip."

He cracked the long whip smartly above the ears of the lead team. The stagecoach began to roll down the trail, throwing up a cloud of dust from its spinning wheels. Frank and Sam followed at a distance, flanking well out to each side of the coach. Behind them came George and Mike with the remuda. Caleb had ridden ahead as soon as the stagecoach was offloaded.

The first night west of the Pecos, Bigfoot set up camp at the headwaters of Delaware Creek. Late in the afternoon of the next day, the stagecoach pulled into the pass that skirted the southern end of the Guadalupe Mountains. Guadalupe Peak, the highest mountain in Texas at well over eight thousand feet, loomed to the north of the pass. Two wagons were pulled up on the side of the trail. A few settlers and their children milled around a nearby campsite, but the only horse grazing nearby was Nasty.

Caleb was standing near the fire talking to a small group of settlers when Bigfoot reined in the lead team. "Hey partner, what's goin' on?" He hollered as he handed the reins to Pappy and climbed down off the seat.

"These folks have had some hard luck," Caleb replied when Bigfoot walked up to the fire. "A bunch of Apaches run off all their livestock early this mornin'."

"That's bad luck alright," Bigfoot agreed, "but you folks were damn lucky you didn't lose your hair along with the horses. I guess them Apaches were a lot more interested in horseflesh than scalps."

Caleb pulled off his sombrero and wiped the sweat off his face with his yellow bandana. "That's exactly what I told 'em. It could've been worse."

"I agree with you, gentlemen," said Gloria as she walked up to the fire. Mrs. Main had climbed down from the stage when she realized the settlers' predicament, and Captain Lyton followed her over. "The Apaches could certainly have killed them all, but these people are still in quite a fix without any horses. How do you propose to help them?"

"What do you mean, ma'am?" asked Bigfoot. "The Apaches are long gone. They won't be comin' back to bother these folks none."

"I'm sure you're right," Gloria agreed, "but these people are stranded." George and Mike picked that moment to drive the remuda into the pass and lead them to water and graze along a nearby a stream that flowed in from the mountains to the north. Gloria looked to them as she added, "Why don't we let the settlers have some of our mules?"

The settlers looked hopeful until Bigfoot shook his head. "I can't do that, Mrs. Main. The mules belong to the stage line."

Caleb sighed as he yanked his old gray sombrero firmly back down over his red curls. He had been considering what to do ever since he found the settlers stranded in the pass. Gloria was right. There was no way they could leave them here, but Bigfoot could not give away the stage line's mules either. As far as Caleb was concerned, that left only one answer. "We'll have to get the horses back for 'em, partner?"

Bigfoot was not so sure. "What about the time it'll take?"

Caleb had been mulling over an idea that might work. "First off, I know we don't have the time to look for days. But what if we let the settlers use some of our mules to get their wagons as far as Hueco Tanks?"

Hueco Tanks was a huge limestone rock formation about two days west of the pass. Rainwater gathered in large natural rock cisterns all over the Tanks and provided a year-round source of drinking water. The site had long been a gathering point for various tribes, and the rocks were covered with ancient Indian art.

"In the meantime," Caleb continued, "you, me, George, and Mike can take some extra horses and do our best to catch up with the Apaches. We'll give it four days, no more; then meet up at the Tanks one way or the other. That's only two days from El Paso. We can send the settlers some help from there a lot easier than here if we don't get their horses back."

Bigfoot ran Caleb's plan over in his mind. Apaches on the run were damn hard to catch. They usually ran their horses to death, and then ate them when they dropped. If each man took two extra mounts, though, they might have a chance. "Okay, let's give it a try." He looked over to the settlers. "I ain't makin' no promises, folks, but we'll do our best." Turning back, he added, "Caleb, Mike stays here. I know he won't like it, but I told his Pa I'd bring him home."

"What about me?" Captain Lyton asked. "I've fought my share of Indians."

Caleb met eyes with Bigfoot, and when the big man nod-ded said, "Fine, Captain, you're in if you've a mind. Pick out three mounts from the remuda and borrow some trail clothes from George. You won't need that fancy uniform where we're headed. One more thing, I know you're an officer, but out there you'll take orders from me, *comprende?*"

Chapter 8

After leaving the mountain pass, the trail of the Apaches skirted two large salt lakes, then headed southwest across a wide, desolate salt flat that eventually lead to the Rio Grande. The war party had a ten hour head start, but Caleb kept the determined riders in the saddle for most of the long night, covering as much distance as possible in a steady, ground-eating lope, and changing mounts on a regular basis. By the time the morning sun had worked its way above the peaks of the Sierra Diablos Mountains off to the east, Caleb was sure they were closing in on their quarry.

The trail was easy to follow, but a good tracker could learn a lot more from a trail than which direction to take. Signaling for a halt, Caleb reined in and dismounted to examine the unshod tracks. "By the look of these tracks, they ain't pushin' real hard," he said, thinking out loud, "and they ain't sent a rider to check their back trail either. Guess I can't blame the bastards though.

After stealin' all the settlers' horses they can't expect to be followed. I make it to be fifteen of 'em, Bigfoot," Caleb added as he mounted.

Bigfoot took a sip of water and recapped his canteen. "Fifteen ain't too bad, as long as we hit 'em by surprise."

"I ain't lookin' for a showdown if we can help it," said Caleb. "I'd just as soon find their camp and steal the horses back without a fight."

"That's even better, if we can pull it off," agreed Bigfoot. "But we're burnin' daylight settin' here jawin'. Let's ride."

Later that morning Caleb spotted the cold camp where the Apaches had holed up for a brief rest during the night. "They didn't stay here for more than two or three hours, but it was long enough for us to gain a few miles. We should be closin' in on 'em by the time we reach the Rio Grande."

In spite of the thirst that was beginning to tire the horses after more than fifty miles with little water, Caleb picked up the pace and held it there throughout the long day. By late afternoon, however, the thirsty animals began to sense the presence of water on the wind and quickened the pace on their own. When the four riders splashed their weary mounts across the shallow Rio Grande, the sun was setting behind the western mountains, sending its last fading rays into a band of wispy clouds floating high above the rugged peaks and coloring them in vivid shades of red and orange.

They let the horses cool down for a few minutes before leading them to the water. Not far from where the horses stood drinking, a small creek added its meager flow to the Rio Grande. In the dying light, Caleb discovered where the unshod tracks of the war party left the river and followed the winding watercourse south.

Dropping to one knee, he took a closer look and picked up some horse droppings. "They can't be far ahead, Bigfoot. There's still water in these tracks and this horse apple's fresh. I'm bettin' they set up camp along the creek not far south of here."

Captain Lyton looked uncomfortable. He did not like crossing the Rio Grande in the first place, and it was high time he spoke up. The war had ended only a few years ago, and the Mexicans were touchy about the border; especially after losing nearly half their former territory to the United States. His superior officers would not be pleased if he were to become involved in an international incident. "We shouldn't be on this side of the river, gentlemen," he said, "let alone ride further south. The Mexican authorities wouldn't look kindly on our intrusion."

Bigfoot chuckled. "When it comes to chasin' Indians and bandits, the border don't mean much to us Rangers."

"That's okay, Captain," Caleb added before Lyton had a chance to become offended over Bigfoot making light of his concerns, "I understand your position, bein' in the army and all. But like Bigfoot said, we're Rangers. We go about our business, border or not. You can still play a part on the Texas side of the border, though, if you've a mind. Once we find the camp, me and Bigfoot are gonna stampede the stolen horses toward the river, but that won't leave the Apaches afoot. Most times Apaches on a war party keep their own mount close by, either by sleepin' with the rein in their hand or staked out right beside 'em."

"There'll only be two of us and a bunch of them," Caleb continued, "so they'll be comin' after us hard. I want you to wait on the north bank with George and the extra horses. We'll join 'em in with the ones we steal back as we ride past you." George was about to complain over being left behind when Caleb added, "I know you don't like it, George, but I want you here to add your fire power to the Captain's. Open fire when the Apaches hit the river. They'll most likely be right behind us. Keep on firin' until you empty your Colts then light out. *Comprende?*"

"We'll be ready," Captain Lyton said with a smile, glad to be of some help. "But what if the Apaches didn't camp on the creek?"

Caleb and Bigfoot mounted. Sensing the upcoming action, Nasty sidestepped nervously, refusing to settle down at first. "In that case, Captain," said Caleb as he reined the rambunctious stallion in, "we did a hell of a lot of ridin' for nothin'. We ain't goin' any further south."

With a steady wind blowing out of the southeast, Caleb and Bigfoot rode well to the west of the small creek to keep downwind of the suspected campsite. They had not ridden much more than two or three miles when Nasty caught the scent of the stolen horses and softly whinnied a warning.

Caleb swung down from the saddle and handed his reins up to Bigfoot. "We best not ride too close to the camp until I get a good look at the layout." There would be a near half moon tonight, Caleb thought, but it had not yet climbed above the horizon and the darkness would cover his approach. "Wait here. The creek ain't far, so it shouldn't take long."

As he slowly closed in on the creek Caleb halted, carefully probing the darkness ahead with his senses. Though his eyes had completely adjusted to the darkness, he could discern only differing degrees of shadows, but his ears and nose told him much more. The babble of shallow water over rocks whispered that he was close to the creek, and the soft snoring of sleeping warriors and the shadowed silhouettes of their horses revealed the location of the camp. Off to his right he heard the stamping of an occasional hoof and the munching of grass. He moved slowly in that direction, making sure to lift the soles of his soft boots and place them back down carefully with each cautious step. He could smell the stolen horses now, and he was thankful for the stiff breeze that blew steadily in his face.

A muffled cough warned Caleb that a sentry stood no more than ten feet off to his left front. As he focused his eyes in that direction, a deeper shadow moved within the other shadows. Caleb froze as the Apache silently swept across his vision and continued to circle the horses. The horses stirred with the sentry's movement, continuing to graze peacefully, and it was apparent the stolen animals had not been hobbled. Waiting until he was sure the warrior was on the far side of the horses, he slowly slipped away. By the time Caleb made it back to Bigfoot, the moon had climbed above the horizon and was ready to begin its nightly journey across the western sky. There was no time to waste.

"The camp's there all right," Caleb said as he swung back up on the saddle. "We'll slide to the south a bit and move in as close as we dare, then stampede the stolen horses straight through the camp. That should cause enough confusion for us to break clear." Caleb slipped the Colt from his saddle holster and checked the loads, then checked his holstered Colt. There would probably be no need to fight their way free with the horses, but it always paid to be ready.

"You lead the way, partner," replied Bigfoot as he finished checking his weapons.

Caleb nudged Nasty with his heels and let the big stallion pick his way slowly through the chaparral and prickly pear that grew thick in the arid waste away from the creek. Bigfoot followed close behind. By now, the half moon had climbed high enough in the sky to provide minimal light, as the Rangers circled to the south and silently approached the stolen remuda.

When he could make out the backs of the stolen horses peacefully grazing along the creek, Caleb drew his saddle Colt, cocked the hammer, and looked over at Bigfoot. "You ready, partner?"

Bigfoot smiled as he followed suit. "Let's give the varmints hell."

With a whoop and a holler the big man raked his buckskin's sides with the rowels of his Mexican spurs. The gelding was off and running like a scalded dog, with Nasty no more than a half a length behind. Both Rangers charged into the startled remuda, firing their revolvers in the air and yelling at the top of their voices. The stolen horses instantly bolted north as one, stampeding straight through the middle of the Apache camp.

The warrior standing guard over the settler's horses drew back his bow, an arrow already notched, but Bigfoot blew him off his feet as he released, and the feathered shaft flew harmlessly skyward. Adding as much confusion as they could, the Rangers fired left and right, emptying their saddle Colts and continuing to whoop and holler as they galloped through the camp. Visibility was poor, and the dust so thick it was difficult for either man to see if they actually hit anything, but the confusion they created served to delay the pursuit long enough to give them a brief lead for the few minutes it took to reach the river.

Hitting the Rio Grande at full gallop, Caleb and Bigfoot drove the remuda straight into the river and splashed them across, turning the extra mounts in with the settlers' horses as they emerged from the shallow water and fled north. The Apaches, howling their war cries like a pack of starved wolves on the hunt, were not far behind.

George White and Captain Lyton calmly bided their time, concealed in a willow thicket on the north bank, until the unsuspecting warriors reached the middle of the river. When they opened fire, the roar of their Colts echoed along the river bottom like the rolling thunder of an approaching storm. Several Apaches were unhorsed in the deadly barrage of hot lead, and two more warriors were toppled from the backs of their ponies. The remainder of the war party reined around hard and beat a hasty retreat back across the Rio Grande.

"That should keep 'em south of the river for a good while," said George as they reined around and lit out in pursuit of Caleb and Bigfoot.

The four weary riders drove the horses into the camp at Hueco Tanks late the following morning after a long, nearly non-stop ride. Mike was mounted and ready to meet them when they reined up and dismounted. "I'll look after the horses," the young man said in greeting. "Y'all look like you could use a cup of hot coffee. By the way, we've had a little excitement of our own while you was gone. Accordin' to Mrs. Main, Mrs. Sutton is fixin' to have her baby."

The settlers greeted the Rangers and Captain Lyton with grateful thanks for the return of their horses, while the trail-worn riders poured themselves a welcome cup of steaming hot coffee. With the first taste of the wickedly strong brew, however, they all knew it had not been prepared by Gloria Main.

"Pappy," said Bigfoot, "this here coffee is your doin', ain't it? There must be enough damn grounds floatin' around in it to choke a shoat."

Everyone standing around the fire laughed, but before Pappy had an opportunity to say anything in his defense; Gloria Main stepped down from the low limestone shelf where she and one of the settlers' wives were busy tending to Mrs. Sutton near a pool of clear water. The self-proclaimed mid-wife immediately became the center of attention.

Of course, Bigfoot stepped forward and asked the question foremost on everyone's mind. "How's Mrs. Sutton doin', Ma'am?"

With more important things on her mind, Mrs. Main temporarily ignored Bigfoot's use of ma'am. "Right now she's doing fine. I think her baby is about ready. Bigfoot, would you please pick up that kettle of water heating on the fire and follow me?"

Bigfoot grabbed a rag lying near the fire and hoisted the big kettle of hot water, following Gloria back to where Mrs. Sutton was being tended. After setting the kettle down beside the women, he made a hasty retreat back to the fire.

Gloria shook her head and chuckled as she looked over at the settler's wife who was helping her. "Isn't that just like a man?

He would gladly face ten Comanches in a showdown to save our lives, but he runs in fear from childbirth."

Not ten minutes later the men at the fire heard a loud squall, followed by some lusty crying. Exchanging glances of wonder, they all hoped everything had gone well. However, their questions were soon answered when Gloria walked up and handed the baby to Caleb.

"You have children," she said. "You should be able to take care of this baby for a few minutes while we get his mother cleaned up. He's a very healthy little boy. Anne named him Jason after her husband's father. Bring the other kettle of water and come with me, Bigfoot," Gloria added before Caleb had a chance to protest that he had never held a baby.

"How about that," Bigfoot said with a huge smile. "Our first stagecoach to El Paso and our first baby, too."

Close to high noon on the third day after little Jason's birth, Bigfoot reined the stagecoach into the large horseshoe formed by the buildings of Fort Bliss and pulled up at the flagpole in front of the long, adobe headquarters building. Caleb stayed outside the grounds of the fort with Mike and George, helping to keep the remuda bunched. A sentry stepped up to the coach and asked Bigfoot his business.

Bigfoot handed the reins to Pappy and jumped down from his seat. "You got a Colonel Main on this post soldier?"

"Yes sir," the private replied. "Colonel Main is the Commanding Officer of Fort Bliss."

Bigfoot smiled. "Well get him on out here. I got a passenger in the stage who'd like to see him."

The soldier shook his head. "I'm sorry sir, but I can't do that. The Colonel is a very busy man."

The stagecoach door opened and Captain Lyton stepped down. "It's all right, soldier. Do as the man said."

The soldier saluted. "Yes sir!"

Captain Lyton returned the soldier's salute, and then saluted smartly when Colonel Main emerged from the front door of the headquarters building a short while later. The Colonel briefly touched the brim of his hat in return. He was as surprised by the appearance of the fancy red stagecoach as he was by Captain Lyton.

"I didn't expect to see you until spring," the Colonel said as he shook Captain Lyton's hand. "When did the stagecoach start to run?"

"Hello, John," said Gloria as she stepped down from the stagecoach and smiled at the look of shock on her husband's face. "My, but it's grand to see you again."

Colonel Main was struck speechless by the sight of his lovely wife, and it took all the decorum he could muster not to take her in his arms and sweep her off her feet. Instead he took both of her hands and looked deeply into her eyes. "It's grand to see you again too, my dear."

"You'll have to forgive me, John," Gloria said, her eyes sparkling with mischief, "and these men too. I insisted on surprising you, and they agreed to assist me."

Colonel Main smiled. "Well, you certainly did that, my dear."

"By the way, John," Gloria added, "the lovely young lady standing in the door of the coach is Anne Sutton. The baby's name is Jason, and he's the brand new son of one of your young officers. Captain Lyton, would you please help Anne and the baby?"

"Why don't you all come in out of the chill?" suggested Colonel Main, after Captain Lyton helped Anne and the baby from the stage. "There's a nice fire going in my office. The weather has finally begun to cool off in the last few days, and a warm fire will feel good."

"That's right neighborly, Colonel," Bigfoot replied, "but this is the very first San Antonio to El Paso stagecoach, and I got mail to deliver before the next driver takes the coach on to Santa Fe. Mrs. Main, it's been a real pleasure to know you, and I wish you the best of luck. You too, Captain."

Bigfoot climbed back up to his seat and took the reins from Pappy. With a whistle and snap of the whip, the Stagecoach was rolling on its last few miles to El Paso.

The sun was slipping behind the mountains west of El Paso, turning the line of fluffy clouds that floated along the horizon to a cottony pink, when Bigfoot reined the stagecoach up in front of the Fuller Hotel. It was the twenty-eighth day of November, and the journey had taken only twenty-five days. Another crew would take the stage on to Santa Fe, while Bigfoot made the trip back to San Antonio on horseback to pick up the second coach. From then on the coaches would cross paths somewhere along the route, as one traveled east and the other traveled west. Caleb and George were returning to San Antonio with Bigfoot. George would act as Bigfoot's scout on the second run to El Paso. Pappy was going on to Santa Fe with the stagecoach, and Sam and Frank were going to try their luck in the California gold fields.

After two days of welcome rest, Caleb, Bigfoot, and George set out for San Antonio on the same route they had followed west. With spare mounts and only a pack horse to worry about, the three Rangers made much better time on the return trip, and they rode into San Antonio on the twenty-first of December. Caleb rested Nasty and Smokey the next day, and early on the morning of the following day, he led them out of the corral at Pellham's Livery. Smokey had to carry the pack containing the Christmas presents Caleb purchased for the family, so he saddled Nasty for the ride home.

Bigfoot closed the corral gate and offered his hand. "Thanks again for makin' the first trip with me, partner."

Caleb smiled as he took Bigfoot's huge paw in his hand with a firm grip. "That's what friends are for. You've always shaded me when there was a need, and I'll be here any time you call. Keep in mind what I said about my Ranger Company though. I got a feelin' Pete will get the authority from the legislature this time, and if he does I'd sure like to have you ridin' with me." Caleb planned to have a meeting with Governor Bell right after the holidays.

"After I see what it takes to get this stage line on its feet and runnin' regularly, we'll have a sit down and talk about it. If you're still plannin' to make that trail drive to New Orleans this spring, be sure and give Josh Tanner my best."

Caleb nodded. "There ain't much choice' about the drive. The Rockin' M is flat runnin' out of range." Caleb swung up on the fancy Mexican saddle that was a long-ago gift from his father. "So long, Bigfoot, you take care now."

PART II

Chapter 9

Felix's nephew, Jesus was waiting at the gate to the corral when Caleb rode into the central square and dismounted. "I will take care of the horses, *Senor* Caleb. Word of your arrival has reached the hacienda, and the family is waiting for you."

"Thanks, Jesus," Caleb replied as he handed over Nasty's reins. "It sure is good to be home. I'll keep Smokey with me for now."

Caleb was greeted with wide smiles and nodding heads over and over again as he strode across the central square toward the hacienda's gate with Smokey at lead. It was Christmas Eve, and the ranch was bustling with activity in preparation for the holidays. Felix, Pedro, and the children were waiting on the hacienda's front porch, but Lucinda was all smiles standing just inside the gate. One of the hands waved to Caleb from the fire step above the arched gate. Caleb returned the greeting, but it was difficult to take his eyes off Lucinda as she hurried to him and practically jumped into his open arms like a little girl. Caleb dropped the lead rope and caught her, whirling her around off her feet before sitting her back down and kissing her long and deep. The family applauded the loving greeting from the porch.

Lucinda stepped away when they finally came up for air, smoothing at her dress, her face flushed and her dark, flashing eyes shining. "My, but you are a romantic one today my husband. I am so happy you made it home for Christmas."

Caleb took a moment to admire his wife's beauty. "I said I'd do my best, and things went pretty well. Bigfoot sends his greetin's."

A look of concern crossed Lucinda's lovely face. "You should have brought him home with you for the holidays. He must be lonesome."

Caleb chuckled. "Not Bigfoot, love. I'd guess he's already left with the next stage by now. He's not one for wastin' time, once he makes up his mind." Caleb picked up the lead rope and took Lucinda's hand. "Let's go greet the family and get inside by the fire." The girls had broken free from Felix's temporary detention and were running toward him with open arms.

Later that evening, everyone sat around the large oak table in the great room while Connie and Bo finished clearing the dishes. The meal had been a feast as far as Caleb was concerned, but according to Lucinda it was nothing more than a good supper compared to the awesome spread planned for Christmas day.

When Connie and Bo returned to their chairs, Felix asked everyone to stand, held up his glass of wine, and proposed a toast. "To the family," he toasted, "to the name of McAdams, to the name of Vaca, and to the name of Martinez, who will soon be joining our family."

"Martinez?" Caleb asked after everyone had taken their seats.

Felix's face lit up with a big smile. "Pedro visited my family in Mexico while you were in El Paso, Caleb. I have been working through my brother for a good while now to secure a proper bride for him. My brother wrote to us just after you left and said he had found a wonderful girl from a good family. Of course, in the American way, my son would have nothing to do with the arrangement until he met the girl in person and approved."

Pedro stepped into the conversation. "I spent nearly three weeks with her family. Her name is Veronica and she is charming, witty, and beautiful beyond belief. How my father managed to find someone so perfect is beyond me." Everyone at the table laughed. "Veronica and her mother will be coming here in June to spend the summer and work with Lucinda to plan for a wedding in August."

Caleb took Lucinda by the hand. "All I can wish is that you and Veronica will be as happy as me and Lucinda."

"When they get here I will move my things to the smaller bedroom next to Pedro's," said Felix. "Then Veronica and Pedro can have the big bedroom after they are married."

Lucinda rose from the table. "It's getting late. Connie, will you please help me get the girls ready for bed?" Ilse and Gretchin had been sitting as quietly as two little field mice listening to the grownup talk and they immediately began to protest. "Girls, stop your fussing! It is past your bed time, and I am sure the men want to discuss the affairs of the ranch."

Bo rose from the table. "*Senor* Felix, would you like me to serve coffee?"

"*Muy Bueno*, Bo, *gracias*," Felix replied. "And please bring the letter from *Senor* Tanner. It is on the desk in my room. The letter arrived here two weeks ago, Caleb. Pedro and I have been waiting anxiously to hear what Tanner has to say."

When Bo brought the coffee and handed Caleb the letter, they all sat down in the comfortable chairs arrayed in front of the fireplace. Felix lit his pipe, sucking gently until he tasted the sweet smoke. There was a definite chill to the air and the fire warmed them as the flickering flames sent long shadows dancing across the whitewashed walls and up into the heavy vigas that supported the ceiling of the great room. Caleb took a sip of his coffee, then opened the letter and began to read. After a few moments, he looked up at Felix.

"What did Josh say?" Felix asked.

Caleb smiled. "He says he's excited about the drive, and that he'll buy up to thirty-five hundred longhorns at twenty-five dollars a head."

Pedro made a quick mental calculation. "*Madre de Dios*, Caleb, that's nearly ninety thousand dollars!"

"Can we put a herd that size together, Felix?" Caleb wondered. "I'm talkin' mostly steers, two years or older. We don't want to be messin' with a lot of calves on the trail." Before Felix could reply Caleb added, "Josh also said he wants a hundred horses. He won't quote a price on the horses until he gets a chance to look 'em over, though. Do we have a hundred horses to sell?"

"The longhorns will be no problem," Felix replied in answer to Caleb's first question, "but I sold seventy-five horses last month to a dealer down from Nacogdoches. Without harming our breeding stock, we can drive no more than seventy-five to New Orleans."

Caleb nodded. "I'm sure Josh will be satisfied with that. I'll get a letter off to him right away and tell him to look for us in Baton Rouge in early June. We can send a message downriver by steamboat as soon as we get the herd there. What have you found out about drivin' cattle to Louisiana?"

"There have been several drives in the last few years," said Felix.

"I ran into Tom Rabb two weeks ago at Mueller's General Store," added Pedro.

Thomas Rabb was an old friend of Caleb's father. Several years prior, Caleb had ridden with him during Colonel Moore's expedition to attack a Comanche winter village on the Upper Colorado. He owned a big spread down near La Grange.

"Tom made a successful drive last year," Pedro continued. "He said there are ferries over the Brazos and the Neches near Beaumont, but we will have to ford the Trinity and the Sabine. From here, we drive the stock west to the La Bahia Road, and then follow the Opelousas Trail all the way to Baton Rouge. It's about four hundred miles. There are a few cattle stands along the trail that offer stock pens, beds, and warm food, too."

Caleb finished his coffee. "It appears to me you two have the drive pretty well figured out, but what about your fiancé, Pedro? We might not get back from New Orleans before she arrives."

"I will write and tell her," said Pedro. "Veronica will understand the importance of the drive. She'll be busy planning the wedding with her mother and Lucinda anyway, and we should be back before the end of June."

Caleb stood. "That sounds damn good to me. I best be gettin' a reply to Josh written and in the mail *pronto*. But right now I have a wife wonderin' where I am."

Winter at he Rocking M was long and restful. Much of it was spent preparing for the spring roundup and cattle drive. There were saddles and other tack to mend, hobbles and quirts to make, ropes to mend and straighten, horses to break, shoe, and trim, cutting horses to train, a wagon to modify, so Bo could use it to haul supplies for the roundup and on the drive, and numerous other tasks that needed to be accomplished.

In many ways a well executed roundup resembled a military campaign, so Felix, Caleb, and Pedro put together a carefully worked out plan to follow. The range on the Rocking M was generally divided east and west by a stream that meandered out of the high ground to the north of the ranch and eventually flowed into the Colorado. Felix was in charge of the overall roundup, and every hand, except those guarding the hacienda, would participate. Pedro and his men were responsible for the eastern half of the ranch, and the others would work with Caleb on the western half.

The cowhands would work their entire area one section at a time, flushing out all the cattle in a particular section and gathering them for sorting, counting, and branding in a central location near where Bo set up the supply wagon and campsite. Once the longhorns were sorted and branded, the Rocking M cattle, except for the steers required for the cattle drive to New Orleans, would be driven back to the section of the ranch where they had been gathered. Any cattle belonging to nearby ranches would be returned to their home range. The steers making the drive would be gathered in the northeast corner of the ranch. The cowhands would then move on to the next section until the whole ranch and the surrounding area had been covered. A remuda would be maintained near the supply wagon where the men would sleep each night. Every cowhand would have his own string of horses in the remuda, so he could change mounts during the day, as required.

Just before sunrise on the first of April, the cowhands participating in the roundup gathered in the central square in front of the bunkhouse. Caleb and the hands working with him headed for the range in the southwest section of the ranch, and Pedro and his men headed for the southeast section. The previous evening, two wranglers had helped Felix lead Bo's supply wagon and the remuda to a central location along the stream that was selected as the roundup's campsite, and Bo started a whole steer slowly cooking on a spit over an open fire. By the time the sun cleared the horizon, the roundup was in full swing.

As soon as they were in place, Pedro and Caleb sent their cowhands out in different directions forming a web across their assigned section of the ranch. There was little chance of cattle escaping the roundup, because when they ran from the path of one cowhand, they drifted into the path of the next man until, eventually, the longhorns were formed up into many small herds.

In the flat expanses of the huge ranch the cattle were easy to find and bunch together, but in the broken country, the cowhands had to search behind every hill, and poke into every mesquite thicket, gulley, and ravine they happened to come across. The cantankerous longhorns did not cooperate willingly. The cowhands were forced to skid their horses down steep-sided banks and washouts and jump them from ledge to ledge as they worked to spook the reluctant longhorns from their hiding places and send them trotting across the prairie toward the central roundup ground.

Standing on the seat of the chow wagon, Felix saw clouds of dust appear far out on the range as the cowhands drove small bunches of cattle before them. The smaller bunches of running longhorns soon began to merge until they had formed one large herd. As the cattle thundered toward the campsite, the hands circled them up, whistling, yelling, and waving their hats, as they moved their horses in close to keep the defiant longhorns from breaking out of the herd. By noon, there was a good-sized herd milling around on both the east and west sides of the campsite, and once the cattle settled down and started to graze, the hands took turns eating their midday meal.

"It feels as if we did a good day's work already," Caleb said when he joined Felix and Pedro at the chow wagon. "I'm nearly starved."

As usual, Bo outdid himself preparing the food. By noon the steer he had started cooking the previous evening was barbecued to perfection, and Bo served it up with stacks of piping hot corn tortillas and tin plates of fiery brown beans. The meal was topped off with the cook's special dried apple cobbler. After the delicious meal, each man scraped his tin plate clean and threw it into the wooden washtub beside the wagon, then went over to the rope corral where the wranglers held the remuda and caught a fresh horse for the afternoon's work.

Today, Caleb had decided to work with the cowhands who would be separating the cows and their calves from the rest of the herd, so he roped Smokey and saddled him up. The big jug-headed dun had especially nimble footwork, and Caleb had trained him all winter to be a cutting horse. Cutting out the cows and calves took a lot of practice, because it required close cooperation between rider and horse.

Riding slowly up to the milling longhorns, Caleb quietly reined Smokey into the herd, doing his best not to upset the cattle. He turned the big dun toward the cow he singled out and nudged her gently away from the rest of the herd, her calf following closely. Once Smokey understood which longhorn Caleb was after, he refused to take his eyes off the animal, and when she tried to escape he stayed close behind her, dodging, twisting, and constantly nipping at her rump until she and her calf were finally outside the herd. From then on, the intelligent dun stayed between the cow and the herd, refusing to let her run back in. Smokey also kept the mother out of the way when Jesus Vaca rode up to rope the calf.

Swinging his lariat over his head, Jesus sent it flying towards his target, dropping the loop neatly over the calf's head. He jerked the rope tight around the animal's neck and pulled the stiff-legged, resisting calf over to the branding fire, bawling all the way. Acting as flankers, Manny and Miguel Flores were waiting in the dust and heat by the fire. They rushed over, grabbed the calf by its flanks, and knocked its legs out from under it, quickly flipping the animal up and out so that it landed on its side. Manny held the calf's head down, and Miguel grabbed its hind legs, yanking them back and stretching the skin tight. Juan Vaca ran up with the red-hot branding iron, and the little calf bawled in panic and pain when the iron was pressed home.

As soon as the calf was released, it scrambled to its feet, shook its head, and ran off looking for its mother. By that time another calf was being dragged up to the fire.

The process continued throughout the long day. An experienced crew, like the men who worked for the Rocking M, could brand sixty calves an hour. It took a little longer and a lot more work to deal with the cantankerous steers that had never been branded or with brands that required freshening. These animals, along with the steers that were already properly branded were kept in a separate herd in preparation for the upcoming trail drive.

The air was filled with dust and acrid white smoke from burning hair and flesh, and the cowhands had to shout to be heard over the commotion of calves bawling for their mothers and cows bellowing for their calves. Quiet did not settle over the scene again until it grew too dark to continue the work.

By the end of the week the roundup was finished and a herd of more than thirty-six hundred longhorn steers was fattening up in the northeast corner of the ranch in preparation for the trail drive. Caleb left the final preparations in Felix and Pedro's capable hands and rode into Austin for his long-awaited appointment with Governor Bell. The Governor only kept him waiting a few minutes before he was shown into the office.

"Caleb," said Bell as he stood and offered his hand, "good to see you. Sorry to keep you waitin', but the legislature is gettin' ready for their summer session and, with them meetin' only every other year, there is much to accomplish. I did speak with Senator Jenkins and a few other legislators about the new Ranger Company. They're lookin' favorably on the proposition. In fact, Senator Jenkins is willin' to sponsor the bill in the Senate, but the main opposition may come from the House." Andrew Jenkins was Caleb's state Senator, and his local Representative from the Bastrop area was the Levi Coleman.

Caleb chuckled. "After the talk I had with Jenkins in March, or should I say to Jenkins, I'm not surprised by his support. What've you heard from Representative Coleman?"

"The Honorable Levi Coleman has remained silent on the issue in spite of my entreaties for help," replied Bell. "His interests seem to lie with the cotton growers in the east for the moment. Do you think you could have a talk with him, too? A little arm twistin' never hurt on any legislation that may be this close."

Caleb thought of the substantial campaign contribution he had made to Coleman's last election bid. "I think with a little gentle persuasion Representative Coleman may well become an avid supporter of the bill. We're gettin' ready to drive a herd to New Orleans in the next week or two, but I promise to pay Mr. Coleman a visit before we head out."

"I appreciate all the help you can give me," said Bell. "The people who think the army alone can deal with the Comanche problem are sadly mistaken. We need the Rangers back in the field soon, before the Comanches push the frontier all the way back to the outskirts of Austin."

"So what are you planning to do?" asked Wanda after she handed Caleb a cup of coffee and sat down beside him on the small sofa.

It was early in the afternoon on Saturday and Caleb surprised her with his visit to her cabin, arriving just before a spring thunderstorm broke in all its fury over the valley of the lower Colorado. They were listening to the rain pound against the big window in the main room of Wanda's cabin between flashes of lightning and claps of thunder, discussing Caleb's earlier meeting with Governor Bell and the legislative authority Bell needed to establish the Ranger Company.

"I stopped by Levi Coleman's Austin law office before I came over here," Caleb replied. "He didn't sound too cooperative until I mentioned another campaign contribution." Caleb took a sip of the hot coffee that was sweetened to perfection. "It's a downright shame, but nothin' seems to get a politician's attention like money. Trouble is I'm not sure if I can rely on his cooperation. Somebody else may offer him more than I did."

Wanda shook her head in disgust. "Politicians like Coleman make me sick. I'll have John speak to our representative. Ashley Garner is a bit of a prig, but at least he's an honest prig. I'm sure he'll do whatever he can. Many of his constituents live on the frontier."

Caleb smiled. "From what I hear he owns a lot of land out west. It would probably sell a hell of a lot faster if he didn't have Comanches for neighbors."

"Touché," Wanda said with a smile as she tapped her coffee cup gently against Caleb's in recognition of the point he had made. "We all have our axes to grind, don't we?" Caleb had come far since the day he first walked into her brother's general store as a green youngster. He may not be an educated and refined gentleman like the dandies she met in New Orleans, but he was an honest, thoughtful man, well-read, and intelligent far beyond his formal education. "How long will you be in town?"

"I'm not sure," Caleb replied as another flash of lightning was quickly followed by a rolling clap of thunder. The rain continued to pelt against the large window. "I only came to town to drop off a letter at Bullock's for Josh Tanner and meet with the governor. I planned on heading back to the ranch this afternoon, but I never expected this storm."

Wanda stood up, placed her coffee cup on the table, and walked over to the window. "I better close the shutters. It doesn't look like its ready to let up very soon."

The pleasant conversation continued into the late afternoon, with little or no break in the violent weather. Wanda prepared a wonderful supper, and the two of them ate in comfortable silence. After helping clear the table, Caleb went to the window and opened the shutters. The thunder and lightning had finally ceased, but the rain continued to pour down. He was glad he had the sense to pile his saddle and gear in the dogtrot and put Nasty under cover in the small corral at the rear of the schoolhouse when the rain first began.

"I best get my slicker out of my bedroll and hit the trail if I expect to get to Bullocks before dark," Caleb said, talking to himself more than Wanda.

"You're welcome to stay here," Wanda said. "You'll be soaked to the bone if you ride back to the hotel tonight. I can make up a pallet for you on the floor in front of the fireplace. A small fire will feel good in this damp chill."

Caleb closed the shutters and turned with a smile, "That's right neighborly of you, Wanda. To be honest, I wasn't much looking forward to going out in this mess."

Wanda went to bed early, and Caleb finally fell asleep after tossing and turning for a good while, finding it hard to relax knowing she was so near. A flash of lightning and a roll of thunder brought him awake again sometime during the night, and he lay on his side staring into the dying flames of the small fire. He heard soft footsteps behind him. The blanket lifted and Caleb felt the warmth of her body through her night dress as she snuggled against his back.

"I'm terrified of storms," Wanda whispered as he rolled over. "Please don't make me go."

Unable to resist any longer, Caleb gently kissed her forehead as he encircled her with his strong arms and drew her close. Outside the storm continued to rage.

Chapter 10

By the last week of April, everything was in readiness for the trail drive. It was decided that Caleb would act as the scout for the drive, riding ahead each day with the supply wagon and selecting locations for the nightly campsite. He would spend the rest of the day riding in a wide arc, looking for possible trouble from outlaws, renegades, or nature. Meanwhile, Pedro would ride herd on the hands to see that they kept the cattle closed up and on the move.

In spite of Consuelo's wailings, Bo would serve as the trail cook and drive the wagon that carried the outfit's food and equipment and the cowhands' bedrolls. He would also have responsibility for setting up camp every night, preparing the meals, and serving as the doctor for the men and the animals, tending to cuts and bruises and dealing with any broken bones and fevers. The cowhands would take their orders from Caleb and Pedro, but the cook was the key to a contented trail drive. That is precisely why Caleb wanted Bo for the job.

Caleb had refused to deprive Felix of the help required to run the ranch or defend it if necessary, so only five of the regular ranch hands would accompany the trail drive. Jesus and Juan Vaca, two of Felix's nephews would ride point, the twins Manny and Miguel Flores, along with two new men, Tulie Perez and Angel Herrera would act as swing riders and flankers, and two young brothers Pedro had recently hired, Luis and Mike Sanchez, would ride drag.

Normally, youngsters would accompany a trail drive to ride as wranglers, but in addition to a remuda of forty extra horses for the cowhands, the drive would also trail seventy of the finest horses the Rocking M had for sale. Therefore, Ernesto Vaca, Felix's cousin and the ranch's finest horseman, would act as head wrangler, assisted by his eldest son, Jose.

The family rose well before sunup on the day of departure, and Bo helped Connie prepare breakfast for what would be the last time in several weeks. Everyone was sitting around the table in the great room, the girls trying to stifle their yawns, when Connie swept into the room with a heavy tray balanced on one hand high above her head. She set the tray on a serving stand then transferred a large platter of scrambled eggs and a platter of fried potatoes from the tray to the table. Bo followed her into the room and placed a large platter of fried ham and sausage on the table along with a pan of piping hot biscuits.

As they took their seats Caleb could tell Connie was still unhappy with his decision to take Bo on the trail drive, but he would not change his mind. The job was too important for everyone's morale, and Caleb would never find a better cook than Bo. Connie would simply have to get over it. He smiled at Lucinda and squeezed her thigh under the table, remembering their last night together with a sly wink that made her blush. He wanted to chuckle when she kept her head down and concentrated on her food so no one would notice.

"Ilse, Gretchin," Caleb said after he had washed a big bite of biscuit down with a drink of coffee, "I expect y'all to be very good for your mother while I'm gone. If you are, I promise to give you a nice present when I get home."

"Will you give us a pony of our own?" Ilse pleaded.

"Yes," little Gretchin added. "I want a pony!"

Caleb chuckled, but he could not help but notice Lucinda's smile turn into a frown. One of the few things they ever argued about was a pony for the girls. Caleb thought Lucinda was being overprotective in denying the girls their own pony. His father taught him to ride when he was much younger than the girls, and on a full grown horse, not a pony.

"We'll wait and see if you've been very good. Then I'll have to talk it over with your mother," Caleb replied. At least that seemed to satisfy Lucinda, if not the girls.

"How long do you expect the drive to take?" Felix asked.

Caleb thought for a moment. "It's right at four hundred miles to Baton Rouge. With luck, we should average around fifteen miles a day. That's twenty-seven days. Allowing a few days for mishaps, let's say thirty days to get there, and a couple days to take care of the sale; especially dickerin' over the price of the horses. The return trip shouldn't take more than two weeks, so I figure there and back at right around six or seven weeks."

"Veronica and her mother should arrive before I get back," said Pedro. "Please take good care of them, Lucinda, and make them feel welcome."

"Certainly we will take good care of them," said Felix, "and do our best to make them feel like part of the family."

Once the meal was over, the goodbyes were swift. Caleb and Pedro were soon riding toward the northeast corner of the ranch alongside Bo and his supply wagon. It had taken two days to gather the trail drive and get a final count of thirty-six hundred and twenty-one steers. The cowhands who would be taking part in the trail drive had spent the night on the range keeping the longhorns bunched and ready to move out. Ernesto and Jose readied the remuda and the horses that would be sold when the drive reached Baton Rouge.

Caleb looked over at Pedro. "I'm gonna find Chako and Juaquin, and check up on the new Lipans. Go ahead and get the herd movin' as soon as you can. I'll catch up."

Caleb reined away and trotted off in search of the Lipans. Knowing they would be somewhere on the north range, he spotted them just after sunrise. There were five Lipans roaming the ranch now that Chako had returned from his village with the three new men Caleb requested. They looked like a small war party as they galloped up to meet him. Caleb made it a habit to constantly remind the nearby ranchers that the Lipans not only worked for him, but also provided security for the entire surrounding area. Chances were good they would spot any prowling Comanche war party long before the savages could do serious harm.

The new men appeared to be seasoned warriors, and as Caleb looked them over closely, they also examined him. To the Lipans, the famed Red Hair was indeed an impressive warrior, and responsible for killing many of their hated enemies. Lipan warriors would normally have nothing to do with working on a cattle ranch, considering many of the chores to be the work of women. However, riding for a war chief like Red Hair was an honor. The Lipans would bravely ride into the blazing muzzles of a hundred rifles to protect him and his family.

Caleb raised his hand in greeting and spoke in Spanish. "The new men you chose look like fine warriors, Chako. How are they called?"

Chako was pleased with Red Hair's praise. "This warrior is called Cuero. This is Nanda, and this is Santana. They are all proven warriors and swear allegiance to Red Hair." All three warriors were dressed in the Lipan way; long-tailed hunting shirts, breech clouts, and calf-high, beaded moccasins, their long black hair tied back with colorful headbands.

"Make sure they become familiar with the ranch," said Caleb, "and see that *Senor* Felix introduces them to all the ranch hands. *Senor* Felix will also provide each of them with a good rifle and a Colt revolver. When I return from the cattle drive, I'm gonna form my own Ranger Company, and you and Juaquin will ride as my scouts. Until then, look to *Senor* Felix for your orders and provide him with any information you feel is important. *Comprende?*"

Chako nodded. "It will be as Red Hair says."

The herd was ready to move at first light, and Pedro rode to the front. "Move 'em out!" he shouted loud enough to be heard by all the cowhands.

Bo led out with the supply wagon, closely followed by Ernesto and Jose with the remuda. Every cowhand, including Caleb and Pedro, had three extra horses in the remuda, and there were also seventy prime head designated for sale, making a total of one hundred and six animals. Old Dog, a big brindled steer Pedro purchased from Tom Rabb to lead the drive, moved to the front of the herd. The veteran steer had previously trailed to New Orleans with Rabb. Juan and Jesus, as the left and right point men, came next, and Manny and Miguel rode on the flanks. Tulie and Angel would ride drag along with Luis and Mike Sanchez until the herd became trail wise.

Old Dog was the only animal in the entire herd with any trail sense. The rest of the longhorns were familiar with nothing except the range from which they were being driven, and to which every last one of them was bound and determined to return. Bunch quitters fled from all points along the edges of the herd and in every possible direction. Only the fact that they were hemmed in by their own numbers kept the others from likewise fleeing to the winds.

Pedro was helping the drag riders at the back of the herd when Caleb rode up. They all wore bandanas to cover their noses and mouths, but the effort did little good. The clouds of roiling dust were so thick they could be cut with a knife, and it was difficult for the riders to see anything except the steer directly to their front. A crazed animal bolted from the herd and attempted to gore Pedro's gelding with the razor-sharp tip of a horn, but a vicious overhand swing of his doubled lariat landed square on the beast's tender muzzle. The steer ran bawling back into the rear of the herd.

"Havin' a damn good time I see," yelled Caleb over the surrounding chaos as he pulled up his bandana. Pedro gave him a nasty look, but Caleb was soon as filthy as the rest of the drag riders. He could feel the grit in his teeth, and the sweat pouring down his face and body burned his eyes and stained the back of his buckskin shirt.

The struggle continued through the early afternoon, and the trail hands barely had time to rope a new horse from the remuda to give their exhausted mounts a break, let alone halt the drive for a noon meal as Caleb had originally planned. In fact, the bunch of ornery longhorns was still more of an unruly mob than a herd, and most of them were crazed with thirst due to their own frantic and totally unnecessary exertions. With their tongues hanging out and bellowing for a drink, all it took was a whiff of water on the wind out of the east and the herd was suddenly gone in a wild, headlong stampede that swept up the remuda along with them.

"There's no way in hell we're gonna stop 'em," said Caleb, "but at least the bastards are runnin' in the right direction. "We might as well mosey along and rest the horses. The cattle will stop at the next water anyway, and it ain't too far from here."

Three miles later the exhausted cowhands reached a small stream. The herd and the remuda were intermingled and spread out along the stream's banks for two or three miles.

Caleb sighed in frustration. "Bo, set up camp right here. I know we got a few more hours of daylight, but we'll be wastin' our time if we use it for anything other than bunchin' 'em up again. Everybody rope a fresh horse and let's get it done."

It was almost sundown by the time they had rounded up the scattered longhorns and moved them to the lush graze along the east bank of the creek. Ernesto and Jose separated the remuda from the herd and moved the horses closer to the wagon for the night. Supper was a quick plate of bacon and reheated beans with corn tortillas. Pedro, Juan, Manny, Miguel, Luis, and Ernesto drew first watch. The remainder of the crew, irritable and exhausted from the long miserable day on the trail, fell into their bedrolls with little laughter or conversation and were instantly asleep. Nothing disturbed the peace and silence of the night except the questioning hoot of an owl or the occasional yip of a lonely coyote.

The wonderful aromas of hot coffee and fresh baked biscuits brought the cowhands awake and out their bedrolls long before sunup, and most of the men who were standing the second watch drifted into camp to join them. After a quick breakfast of biscuits and reheated beans they loaded their bedrolls in the wagon, roped their first mounts of the day, and moved into position around the herd. Bo got the wagon rolling, and Ernesto and Jose whistled up the remuda right behind him.

The blood-red sun was beginning to climb above the eastern horizon when Old Dog moved out at Pedro's urging, and the other steers began to reluctantly follow. If anything, the second day was worse than the first, and before the herd reached the campsite Bo and Caleb had set up along the east bank of a winding stream, every horse and cowhand in the outfit was worn to a frazzle.

Early in the afternoon of the seventh day on the trail, Pedro saw Caleb off in the distance returning to the herd. The longhorns were finally becoming a little trail wise, having plodded along without incident for nearly two days and actually reaching their goal of fifteen miles a day. However, it would still take a good while to make up for the first few miserable days of only six or seven miles.

Caleb reined in a few minutes later. "We finally made it to the Brazos, brother. Bo is setting camp up on this side of the river near the ferry right now. You should reach there with the herd before the end of the day."

"It's about time," Pedro complained as he led Caleb off to the side of the trail so that Old Dog and the herd would continue on while they talked. "We should have been there two or three days ago. What does it look like?"

"The ferry looks to be fairly new and in good shape. It has sturdy-looking side rails, and rails at both ends that swing open like big gates to load or offload the stock. The ferryman said the charge was three cents a head, horses or cattle."

"Let's see," said Pedro. "We have thirty-six hundred and twenty-one cattle, and one hundred eighteen horses, counting the ones we're riding; a little more than a hundred dollars."

Caleb smiled. "One hundred twelve dollars and seventeen cents to be exact, but the ferryman said he'd forget the seventeen cents."

Pedro chucked. "The man is generous to a fault?"

"It sure as hell beats swimmin' the cantankerous critters across," Caleb added with a chuckle. "The river's high. We'd have problems with 'em for sure."

"No doubt about that," Pedro agreed. "How big is the ferry?"

"It's fair-sized. The man said he could move around two hundred longhorns on each trip, so we best figure on spendin' the day at the ferry. We'll take the wagon across on the first trip. That's an extra five dollars by the way. Bo can set up camp early and cook somethin' special. The food and a little rest should lighten the men's mood some after wrestlin' with these critters all week. Soon as I switch horses, I'm headin' back to help Bo set up. Have the men move the herd north of the ferry to water 'em. The bank on that side is a gentle slope for quite a ways. I'll have Ernesto take the remuda on ahead and get 'em watered before the herd gets there."

The cattle were thirsty by the time they reached the river, and Pedro moved most of the hands to the front and sides of the herd to slow the longhorns down and spread them out as they headed for the water. Of course there were the usual uncooperative beasts, but a few whacks across the muzzle with a doubled lariat straightened them out quickly enough, and the entire herd was soon spread out along the river watering peacefully. Ernesto and Jose moved the remuda to some good graze south of the ferry after they were watered.

Bo outdid himself on the meal, and after stuffing themselves, the cowhands sat around the fire relaxing with the usual jokes and tall tales about bandits, Indians, and wild women. Laughter was a pleasant sound for a change, and Caleb and Pedro were pleased that the mood of the men had lightened as they expected it would.

After the cattle were watered, the hands moved them away from the river to some good graze, and the first watch began circling the herd, the soothing notes of a cowhand singing a gentle Spanish lullaby drifting in and out with the wind. Soft hues of pink and purple faded to a deep indigo as the setting sun slowly sank below the rim of the western horizon. Caleb wondered how long the peace and tranquility could last.

The sun was up and the clear azure of the sky promised a fine day when the cowhands began to cut the first bunch of longhorns out of the herd and head them toward the ferry. The wagon and the remuda were loaded and offloaded with little difficulty. After harnessing the team, Bo led the mules across the loading ramp and onto the broad deck. Ernesto and Jose, with help from Juan and Jesus, then drove the remuda onto the ferry behind the wagon, and the near side gate swung closed. When the ferry butted up against the landing, the far side gate swung open, and after Bo walked the team and wagon clear, Ernesto and Jose drove the horses off and bunched them up on some good graze south of the ferry. Juan and Jesus waited on the far side to receive the first bunch of longhorns when they were offloaded.

Two long, sturdy fences formed a wide-mouthed funnel that narrowed down to the width of the loading ramp as it led to the ferry landing. The fences, constructed to make the job of loading longhorns easier, were not needed to load the wagon or horses, but the unruly longhorns were another matter altogether. Even with the funnel, the stubborn beasts still had to be driven forward once they entered, and that was much easier said than done. The cattle plodded along placidly at first, but as the gap between the two fences gradually narrowed, and the longhorns drew closer to the loading ramp, they began to grow wild-eyed and nervous, some of them stopping or attempting to turn back. These actions did not sit well with the animals behind them that were now being forced to move forward by a line of cowhands delivering a series of heavy blows to their backsides with doubled lariats.

Without the fences, absolute chaos would have ensued. Some of the now crazed animals tried to climb their way out of the narrowed chute, but the fence held. Against their considerable will, the longhorns were gradually forced down the chute, across the loading ramp, and onto the deck of the ferry. The wide gate was quickly closed behind the last animal, and the ferrymen who stood safely out of reach on narrow walkways that ran down both sides of the ferry began to pull hand-over-hand on the long ropes. When the ferry reached the other side of the river, the far-side gate swung open and the longhorns, placid once again after the calming ride across the river, trotted off. Juan and Jesus were there to pick them up. The ferry moved steadily back and forth for most of the day before the entire herd finished crossing.

Chapter 11

Caleb was scouting in a wide arc south of the day's intended route for the trail drive when he spotted the tracks of several riders. The drive had not met many riders since pulling out of the Rocking M, and as far as Caleb was concerned, any trail he came across was worth a closer look, especially one that appeared to be heading in the general direction of the previous night's campsite.

Swinging down from the saddle, Caleb untied his yellow bandana, took off his sombrero, and mopped the sweat from his forehead. The day was unusually hot for early May, and the noon-high sun caused shimmering heat waves to rise off the surrounding hillsides. After jamming his sombrero firmly back down on his unruly red curls, he retied his bandana and sank down on one knee to take a closer look at the tracks. There were clearly five riders, but three of the horses were unshod. It was unusual in this part of the country to see Indians freely roaming the countryside, and almost never in the company of whites. Best to follow this trail and see what else I can turn up, he thought.

Caleb followed the tracks northwest to a place where the riders pulled up and dismounted to picket their horses. It was just below a little rise. A careful examination of the site only heightened his original fears. Three sets of tracks were clearly made by moccasins, but the other two were boot prints. Following the tracks as they climbed the rise, Caleb found several places where the heels of the boot prints had gone deep. Behind the deep heel prints were the imprints of big pinwheel spurs, the kind favored by most Mexicans. The men had crouched to the ground before they reached the crest of the rise and crawled to the top on their stomachs. From the top of the rise, Caleb had a perfect view of the previous night's campsite.

Only one logical conclusion could be drawn from the evidence. Scouts for a gang of Mexican bandits and renegades must have spotted the herd. The fact that the riders had lain concealed at the top of the rise while they observed the camp, rather than ride in to seek the hospitality of the drive for a meal, or at least some coffee, only served to further convince Caleb he was right. Of course, he had to admit it was possible his conclusions were wrong, but that was unlikely. Quickly striding back down the rise, he shoved his boot in the stirrup and swung his leg over his saddle.

After seating himself comfortably, Caleb leaned forward and patted Nasty's neck. "It looks to me like we got some trouble brewin', boy. We best follow these tracks and find out exactly what we're dealin' with." Reining Nasty around, he banged the big Appaloosa in the ribs with his heels and set out at a steady, ground-eating lope.

As evening approached, Caleb slowed Nasty to a walk. The last thing he needed was to come up on a bunch of outlaws, if that was indeed what they were, by accident. The tracks continued to run to the southeast, so he thought it would be best to leave them and move further east before the sun went down. Then, if the men he was tracking did turn out to be outlaws and they decided to hit the herd tonight, he would be between them and the new campsite. Besides, with no moon he would not be able to follow the tracks after dark anyway. He would just keep riding south until he saw their fire or came upon them as they were on their way to attack the herd.

Without a moon, visibility was severely limited once the sun went down. Caleb allowed Nasty to slowly pick his own way through the inky blackness of the night, until he was able to spot the fire he had been looking for while he was still a good distance from the camp. There had been no attempt to limit the fire's size or conceal it in any way, so whoever it was, they certainly were not worried about someone seeing it. Of course, the cattle drive camp was much too far away to worry about. Caleb guessed the campsite was a good ten miles south of the trail drive camp. It would be necessary to get a closer look to determine if the people in the camp were a threat to the drive, and if so, how much of a threat.

The wind was holding steady out of the southwest, so Caleb swung a little further to the east. From there the wind was blowing directly in his face. Nasty was already acting up, so the scent of the camp's horses must have been heavy on the wind. Moving cautiously, Caleb approached the camp on horseback until he narrowed the distance, but was still further out than he thought any sentry would be posted. Satisfied he had come as close as he dared on horseback, he dismounted, tied Nasty's rein to a small tree, and began a stealthy approach on foot.

Caleb did not encounter a sentry until he located the outfit's horses grazing along the bank of a little stream to the east of the camp. After a careful recon he located four guards posted around the horses. Two of them looked to be Tonkawas, but the thing that shocked him was the size of the remuda. Though there was no way to get an exact count, there were at least forty horses and quite likely more.

Aided by the darkness, Caleb slowly worked his way close enough to the fire to hear what was being said without being seen. A quick headcount told him there were around fifty men in the camp, nearly half of them Tonkawa renegades. The language was definitely Spanish, and there was a loud argument in progress, the gist of which was whether to move out immediately and attack the trail camp in the middle of the night, or wait until sunup and attack as soon as they located the herd. The men around the fire were a mean, scruffy-looking bunch, and the man who appeared to be their leader was determined the outfit would not move until sunrise.

"Do not be foolish!" the head bandit argued. "We will stumble around blindly in the dark to find the camp now. And even then we will probably end up shooting each other. Besides, our Tonkawa friends will only fight in the dark if the mood strikes them. They usually don't like it." Grumbling from the Tonkawas, who could speak Spanish, seemed to be on the side of the leader of the gang, and after a few minutes there was a general agreement to wait until sunup to move out.

With no time to waste, Caleb made his way back to Nasty as quickly as possible. After mounting, he walked the big Appaloosa until he was absolutely certain he could not be heard, and then, risking serious injury in the dark to an animal he loved, kicked the horse into a gallop. He would alternate between a gallop and a long lope for the remainder of the ride.

It was well before midnight when a breathless Caleb galloped into the trail drive camp and leapt from the saddle. All the cowhands heard the galloping horse approaching the camp, and realizing that it meant danger, everyone who was not standing guard with the herd had gathered at the fire.

"Where have you been?" asked Pedro in a voice heavy with worry. He had been sure something was wrong, and Caleb's wild approach confirmed it.

"We got big trouble, Pedro," Caleb replied as his breathing evened out. "Scouts for a large gang of Mexican bandits and Tonkawa renegades spotted the herd last night. I followed the tracks and got close to their camp about ten miles southwest of here. They plan on hittin' us early tomorrow mornin'." Caleb's words caused a stir among the men.

Pedro was surprised by Caleb's reaction. As a Ranger the big redhead had dealt with many an outlaw, and Pedro never saw him this worried. "We have some good guns in this outfit. If the outlaws hit this camp they may well be biting off more than they can chew."

Caleb shook his head. "You don't understand little brother. There's near fifty of 'em!"

"Fifty!" parroted Pedro, shocked by the number.

"The varmints must make their livin' rustlin' trail drives," said Caleb. "Most outfits don't have any more cowhands than we do. With fifty gunmen they can make off with a lot of cattle and horses, even if we do manage to fight 'em off."

"There is no other choice but to fight," said Pedro. "We certainly can't outrun them."

The cowhands shouted their agreement. No one was willing to give up the stock without a fight, no matter how many outlaws were involved.

Caleb hesitated for only a moment, remembering the horses he and Bigfoot had stolen back from the Apaches during the stagecoach trip to El Paso. "There may be a way we don't have to fight or run. What if we run their horses off tonight? Even a thousand bandits won't be much of a threat if we leave 'em all afoot."

Pedro's frown was instantly replaced by a big grin. "I like it." The rest of the men enthusiastically endorsed the idea. "I'm sure you thought this through already," added Pedro, "so how do we pull it off?"

"The horses are grazin' on the east side of the camp along a little stream," Caleb began. "We have to make sure and take them all, but none of 'em were hobbled or roped off, that I could see. I didn't see any animals picketed in the camp either." Caleb paused for a moment to gather his thoughts. "There were four guards on the horses, but none on the camp. I'd love to hit 'em from the south and drive their horses north, but the wind is still blowin' out of the southwest. There's no way we can get close enough to stampede the herd without their horses givin' us away."

Caleb knelt down and picked up a stick. Then using his hand, he smoothed out the dirt in front of him and drew a quick map of the outlaw camp. "This is the stream where the horses are grazin'." He pointed to the wavy line he had drawn east of the camp. "The camp is here, and the herd is on this side of the creek between the stream and the camp. Pedro, you, Tulie, Angel, and Mike will stampede the herd. We'll rein up a safe distance from the camp, and I'll put the four of you in place just before sunup. Manny, Miguel, and Luis will hit the camp with me and keep 'em busy. Give us ten minutes to get ready, and then you and your men walk your horses toward the herd until you're spotted. When that happens, don't hesitate. Charge in and stampede the horses south for a mile or two before you swing 'em to the east and then north to our camp. The rest of us will ride straight through the outlaw camp, shoot the hell out of anything we see, and then meet up with you on the way back. Juan and Jesus are with the herd now so they stay here. Ernesto and Jose keep a watch on the remuda. What do y'all think?"

"I don't know about the rest of the men," replied Pedro, "but I think the bandits and renegades are in for a very rude awakening come sunup."

Pedro and his three men were already in place when Caleb joined Manny, Miguel, and Luis. He had scouted the area thoroughly before placing the others, and there were still no guards posted on the camp. It was the time of morning when there was enough light to see, but the sun had not yet peeked over the horizon.

"The camp is not far ahead of us, over a little rise," Caleb said, his voice barely above a whisper. "Spread out some and move slowly forward when I do. We should get to the top of the rise before Pedro starts the stampede. Charge straight through the camp when you hear the shootin'; don't stop or slow down, and shoot any damn thing that moves." The men nodded their understanding and began to spread out. When they were ready, Caleb nudged Smokey and they all started moving slowly up the rise toward the camp.

After the ten minutes he and Caleb had agreed on passed, Pedro drew his Colt. The cowhands, spread out to either side of him, followed suit. At the wave of Pedro's sombrero, they began moving toward the horses at a walk, doing their best to stay on line. Suddenly, the guard on the north side of the herd caught a glimpse of Pedro and shouted an alarm as he raised a rifle to his shoulder. Pedro fired first, and the .44 caliber ball from his Colt slammed into the outlaw's shoulder, spinning him to the ground. All hell broke loose as the four cowhands began screaming and firing their Colts in the air, charging into the surprised herd. The outlaw's horses were off and running as one.

Caught up in the excitement of the stampede, Tulie Perez failed to notice the Tonkawa renegade posted on the near side of the horses until the warrior launched an arrow that fanned the air as it whispered close past his shoulder. Dropping off to the side of his saddle, Tulie fired before the Tonkawa was able to notch another arrow. The warrior's arms went wide as the well-aimed ball plowed into his chest. Dropping his bow, the renegade toppled over on his back.

In the swirling dust and confusion of the stampede, the Mexican bandit posted on the far side of the remuda fired at Angel Herrera and missed, before scrambling for cover behind a fallen tree. Angel kept riding, but fired twice over his shoulder at the outlaw to make sure the man kept his head down.

The stampeding horses cleared the camp, heading south at a dead run with the cowhands right behind them, firing their Colts in the air to urge the terrified animals on. Unfortunately, the Tonkawa sentry posted on the south side of the herd had plenty of time to take cover behind some rocks and get ready for the cowhands to ride past. When young Mike Sanchez approached his position, the renegade stood up and launched an arrow that thudded into Mike's saddle, barely missing the cowhand's thigh. Mike threw some hot lead in the Tonkawa's direction, but the warrior stood his ground and notched another arrow. It seemed as if Mike was home free, until the Tonkawa launched the second arrow. Flying straight and true, the shaft buried deep between Mike's shoulder blades. The young cowhand slumped over in the saddle, but Pedro got to him before he fell and kept him mounted until they were well clear of the camp.

With the roar of the first gunshot from the direction of the stream, Caleb's men drew their Colts. Urging their mounts to a gallop, they charged down from the rise straight into the middle of the outlaw camp, firing at any target that presented itself. Chaos reigned, as sleep-dazed outlaws stumbled from their bedrolls only to be knocked off their feet by a hail of hot lead. Smokey jumped the fire, and Caleb fired right and left, blazing away at men who were too busy scrambling for their lives to return fire. He dropped an outlaw with nearly every shot. Galloping through the camp side-by-side, Manny and Miguel covered each other, shooting at targets too close to miss. A feathered shaft whipped past Luis Sanchez's face with a snake-like hiss, but the cowhand turned in the saddle and killed the Tonkawa renegade before the warrior could reach for another arrow.

The four cowhands were through the camp and galloping south before they received any meaningful return fire from the surprised outlaws and renegades. Only Manny Flores flinched as a lucky rifle shot grazed his shoulder, nearly unseating him as they rode out of range. After reining in for a minute to quickly patch up Manny's the flesh wound, Caleb and his men were in a lighter mood as they galloped north, eventually catching up with Pedro and his cowhands who were driving the stolen outlaw horses north at a lope. Pedro saw Caleb and the others approaching and he slowed the stolen horses to a walk.

When Caleb's cowhands reined in their mounts and began to mingle with the others, Luis Sanchez noticed the body of his younger brother lying belly-down over his saddle. The arrow fired by the renegade Tonkawa penetrated the youngster's lung, and he had only lived a few, painful minutes after the incident. Young Sanchez's death put a damper on any celebration that might have occurred, and the stolen herd was driven back to the trail drive campsite in virtual silence.

The Rocking M hands buried Mike Sanchez before sunrise the following morning, all the cowhands standing around the grave with their hats off. Everyone had taken a hand in helping Luis dig his brother's grave. Bo carved a marker from a board he pulled from his wagon, and began the service with a prayer from his Bible.

After Bo finished, Caleb stepped up to say a few words. "Mike was a fine young man who the Lord took to his own," Caleb began. "He'll be missed by his family and his friends, and most of all by his brother, Luis." The men pretended not to notice Luis's tears. "The Good Book says the Lord gives and the Lord takes away, and a man never knows when the Lord will call him yonder. This was Mike's turn, and we'll all have our own turn sooner than later if we ain't careful; ashes to ashes, dust to dust. Amen. Let's get these cattle on the trail and get this sadness behind us."

Everyone mounted, and Bo whistled up the team. The wagon led the way out followed by Ernesto and Jose with the enlarged remuda. There were now forty seven additional horses, some of them prime horseflesh. Pedro got Old Dog moving and the cowhands hooted and waved their hats, cracking a few steers across the rump to get them in motion. The herd was growing trail-wise by now and they straggled along in fairly good order. Instead of riding ahead with Bo, as usual, Caleb circled south to check up on the outlaws.

Pedro was riding beside the wagon talking to Bo when Caleb caught up with them a few hours later. "We won't be havin' any more trouble from that bunch," he said as he reined alongside Pedro. "They're still sittin' around camp arguin' about what the hell to do next."

"Stealing their horses was a damn good idea, Caleb," said Pedro. "I know we lost a man, but it could have been worse, if we had waited for them to attack us."

"I know what you're sayin', brother", Caleb replied, "but that don't ease the fact that we lost a man. We should reach the Trinity tomorrow evenin' and Beaumont a few days after that. Maybe a night in town for the boys will lighten their mood a little."

Chapter 12

That night the drive set up camp on the east bank of a little stream, some fifteen miles from the Trinity River. The cattle were strung out along the water to the north of the camp, and Ernesto and Jose moved the remuda to the south. Bo prepared an early supper, and the cowhands sat around the fire playing cards and jawing until it was time for the first watch. Everything seemed quiet and peaceful.

Too peaceful, thought Caleb, as he watched the blood-red sun slowly sink behind a bank of dirty gray clouds on the western horizon that grew thicker and more ominous as darkness set in. Soon after dark, the wind began to pick up and swing straight out of the west. So far, there had been virtually no bad weather on the drive, but Caleb was sure things were about to change.

Longhorns were a nervous and scary lot, and bad, dark nights were stampede time. Almost any noise or disturbance—a pot falling from a hook in a supply wagon, an accidental discharge of a weapon, or a flash of lightning—could panic a herd and send it into wild flight. All you would hear and feel was the rumbling of hoofs and the trembling of the earth.

Caleb knew it was best not to be caught unprepared. "Pedro, I don't like the look of this weather. We best get everybody in the saddle and bunch the herd and the remuda. I got a feelin' this night is gonna be a long, hard one. If we bunch 'em all tight, we might have a chance to hold 'em."

Within minutes, everyone was in the saddle gathering the herd and the remuda. The wind picked up, and the cowboys tied down their hats with piggin' string, slipped on their gummed slickers, and loosed their lariats, expecting the worst. The wind continued to strengthen, virtually howling to gale force, as it tore at their clothes and hats like clutching fingers and moaned, banshee-like, through the trees and brush along the river. Surprisingly, it was Old Dog who faced the wind and began to bawl mournfully, others joining in until it sounded like an eerie symphony of fear.

"They are getting ready to run, Caleb," Pedro screamed over the rising wind. "Anything could set them off."

"At least if they run, they'll be headin' east away from the storm," Caleb yelled back. "We got half the riders to the north and the other half to the south. Maybe we'll be able to turn 'em."

At least up to now there had been no rain, but when it finally did come, the rain struck with such cold fury that the men were nearly swept off their saddles. The only thing for them to do was turn their backs to the raging wind and torrential rain, like the longhorns were doing, and ride it out. There had been no lightning and thunder, and the cowhands fervently hoped it would remain that way.

Suddenly, a flash of blue lightning dashed their hopes, as it ripped across the shallow sky and struck a tall live oak near the stream. The lightning bolt lit up the pitch dark night as bright as day, splitting the tree down the middle, and setting it afire. The spooked longhorns did not wait for the earth-shaking blast of thunder that quickly followed before they lit out at a dead run, the remuda intermingled with them and running just as hard.

Caleb, Pedro and the others on the north side of the herd raced along in the dark trying to reach the head of the rampaging longhorns. If the fastest riders could manage to overtake the leaders of the stampede, they might be able to turn them from their headlong course. The cowhands could then force the longhorns to start moving in a wide circle that would eventually wind in upon itself like a coiled spring until the cattle began to bunch up and mill about. Only then would the stampede come to an end.

However, much danger lurked in the darkness for the cowhands and their horses. The land was pockmarked with badger and prairie-dog holes, and crisscrossed by cuts and gullies that could trip a galloping horse and send its rider sprawling. If a rider fell from his horse anywhere near the path of a stampeding herd there would not be enough of him left to bury. Both Caleb and Pedro eventually made it to the front of the herd, but nothing they did, not even firing their Colts near the ears of the leaders could turn the stubborn longhorns.

Finally Caleb signaled for Pedro and the other hands to pull up. The rain was beginning to let up now as was the lightning and thunder, but an occasional flash showed the herd continuing to stampede out of sight. "There ain't no way to turn the bastards when they get that frenzied, Pedro. We'll just end up gettin' somebody killed. Let's go on back and break camp. We'll get the wagon packed up and head for the Trinity. I'm bettin' they'll be scattered all along the river by the time we get there."

The sun was well up when the trail hands and supply wagon reached the Trinity, and small groups of longhorns and horses were scattered north and south along the bank of the river as far as a man could see. The cowhands got busy rounding up the herd, and Ernesto and Jose went after the horses. Once both groups were gathered they would need to get an accurate head-count to determine if the job was done properly.

There would be at least one longhorn lost, because they found a steer on the trail in terrible pain with a broken leg. Bo put the animal out of its misery, and several hands helped him string it up to butcher. Fresh barbecued beef would be a rare treat for the cowhands. Though they were surrounded by a sea of beef, the meat for each meal was usually bacon, or, once in a while, one of the smoked hams Bo brought along. There were not enough men to eat a whole cow before the meat went bad, so butchering beef under normal circumstances was considered wasteful.

It took the cowhands the remainder of the day and most of the next day to round up all the scattered animals, but when the head count was complete they were only short ten longhorns, including the one that had been butchered, and nine horses, all but one of them stolen from the outlaws. During the roundup Caleb had circled far back to the southwest to ensure the outlaws were no longer a threat, but the gang had dispersed after losing their horses.

There was not enough daylight left to move the herd, so it was decided to spend another night at the campsite on the Trinity. The delay would have most likely been necessary without the stampede, because the rain had raised the level of the river considerably, and it did not look inviting to ford. They all hoped it would soon be down to a reasonable level.

Early the next morning Caleb stood looking at the river when Pedro walked up and handed him a cup of hot coffee. The current was still running stronger than usual, and the water level remained at a height where the cattle would be forced to swim, but at least the river had narrowed to no more than fifty or sixty feet wide. Occasionally a driftwood snag would bob above the surface and disappear again as it swept past the ford.

"What do you think?" asked Caleb as he took a sip of the heavily sweetened black coffee and smacked his lips in pleasure. "Thanks for the coffee."

"*De nada*," replied Pedro. He continued to examine the river as he added, "I'd like to see the river low enough for the herd to wade, but that could take a week. Besides, by the look of the sky we may get more rain."

Caleb nodded. "That's exactly what I was thinkin'." He knew a river crossing could be a perilous thing when the water was deep enough to force the animals to swim. Years ago on a winter expedition with Colonel Moore a friend of his, Garret Harrell, drowned fording the flooded Concho River. Caleb sighed. "There ain't no guarantees in this line of work. We might as well give it a try."

After giving the problem some thought, they decided Caleb and the hands who were weak swimmers would ford the river first. That way, Caleb could concentrate on getting them across without the responsibility of tending the cattle. After helping ford the wagon, the poor swimmers would be in position to reassemble the longhorns on the far bank when they emerged from the river, keeping them bunched until the entire herd crossed. Pedro would get the herd started into the river, once the wagon was across, and supervise crossing the cattle.

Caleb assembled the men. "It's best to go ahead and ford the river now in case we get more rain. Are there any of you who can can't swim a lick?" Tulie Perez and Juan Vaca raised their hands. "What about poor swimmers?" Now it was Luis Sanchez who reluctantly raised his hand. "Good," Caleb added without comment, "you three will ford the river with me before the herd swims it. After you've helped me ford the wagon, your job will be to bunch the animals and keep 'em together and out of the way once they clear the river. Ernesto and Jose will ford the remuda before the herd, so give 'em a hand with the horses first. Anybody got a question?" The non-swimmers did not look too happy, but they remained silent. "Good, let's get it done."

Everybody helped Bo round up a few good-sized driftwood logs. These were securely roped to the sides of the wagon. The wagon bed was waterproof enough for the short time it would be in the river, but the logs would give it extra buoyancy. Tulie, Juan, and Luis were sitting their horses, watching with dread, as Caleb took the long rope tied to the wagon tongue and led Nasty down to the low bank. With little coaxing, the big Appaloosa plunged straight into the river and set out resolutely for the other side, swimming strongly. The current was not as bad as Caleb thought it would be, and he remained in the saddle as Nasty regained his footing and climbed up out of the river, shaking the excess water from his hide.

With everyone watching them, the three poor swimmers did not hesitate, spurring their horses into the river and staying with them as the animals swam along the rope to the opposite bank and climbed up out of the water. Pedro tied another long rope to the rear of the wagon, and after Caleb and the others dismounted and got a good hold on the rope tied to the wagon tongue, he and his men rolled the wagon into the river with Bo still sitting on the seat. The wagon bobbed up and down like a boat as it was quickly towed across the river. Pedro and his men kept the slack out of their rope so the wagon would not drift downstream. The men cheered when the wagon rolled up out of the river with Bo still sitting high and dry on the seat.

The remuda came next with Jose on the upstream side of the horses and Ernesto on the downstream side. Whistling, yelling, and using their lariats to encourage the slackers, they drove the lead horses into the river, and soon the whole remuda stood on the other side of the river as the horses rolled and shook themselves dry. After a few minutes the hands drove the horses downstream to some good graze to keep them out of the way of the herd.

"Okay!" Caleb yelled across the river to Pedro. "You can start the herd." Now would come the most difficult part of the crossing.

Jesus and Angel were riding at the point when Old Dog calmly led the longhorns down the low bank and into the swift-running river. Of course there were the usual bunch quitters who attempted to turn back at the last second, but the cowhands were waiting to turn them back to the river with a whack to their muzzles and one to their flanks, if necessary, to encourage them. Meanwhile Manny and Miguel kept up the pressure on the rear of the herd, whacking any reluctant longhorn in the behind to keep the contrary beasts moving toward the river.

Caleb sat Nasty on the far bank, watching carefully for any sign of trouble and refusing to believe how well the crossing was proceeding. Old Dog got his footing under him and scrambled up the bank with a bunch of bawling longhorns right on his tail. Juan, Tulie, and Luis were waiting to quickly move the longhorns to good graze upstream. Out in the middle of the river other longhorns were swimming strongly, only their horns and noses visible above the choppy surface of the river as they plowed their way across. Things went smoothly for a while, and they were down to the final two or three hundred cattle when disaster struck. An old uprooted tree swept into the swimming herd like an avalanche, dragging some of the unsuspecting longhorns under and causing instant pandemonium.

Chaos now ruled the herd as cattle began to thrash wildly about, pushing each other under in the confusion, and turning downstream or back to the bank where they had entered the river. Longhorns swimming back to the bank met other longhorns swimming forward and the panic increased. Throwing caution to the wind, Pedro leapt his big chestnut gelding into the river to try and turn the bunch quitters, but, by then, cattle were crawling on top of each other and bawling out their fear. Caleb watched in horror as the tip of a horn caught Pedro in the side and swept him off the saddle. He was thrashing in the water, trying to make it back to his horse, when another panicked long-horn drove him under the surface.

Caleb momentarily lost sight of his brother-in-law, but then saw him bob to the surface downstream from the herd before going under again. Yanking Nasty's rein, Caleb kicked the stal-lion to a gallop and raced downstream until he was well ahead of the place where he last saw Pedro. From there he and the big Appaloosa plunged into the river. Caleb gave the horse his lead, and the big stallion swam powerfully to mid-stream. As if by a miracle, Pedro bobbed to the surface again, within reach, and Caleb grabbed him by the collar. Without need of a rein, the intelligent stallion tuned for the bank, and, swimming strongly, soon had both men back to shore.

Caleb loosed his boots from the stirrups and slipped off the saddle before Nasty climbed out of the water, and, grabbing the unconscious Pedro under the arms, dragged him up the bank. Af-ter flopping Pedro on his stomach, Caleb began to slap him hard on the back with the palm of his hand. On the third slap Pedro coughed, and on the next one he threw up what seemed to be half the river. Caleb relaxed as Pedro's breathing returned to normal. A few minutes later, Pedro had the strength to roll over on his own.

"Thanks, Caleb," he croaked as he looked up at the sky. "I thought it was over when that longhorn took me under." So did the other cowhands who were now standing around mumbling to each other, amazed that Pedro was still alive.

"Y'all give me a hand," said Caleb. "Let's get him moved to the wagon where he'll be comfortable. Bo can take a look at his side."

By the time they moved Pedro to the wagon in the shade of a spreading live oak tree and covered him with a blanket, Manny and Miguel had driven the turnarounds back into the water, and the last of the longhorns were climbing the bank onto dry ground. Bo checked Pedro's wound where the longhorn gored him in the side, and after a putting in a few careful stitches, he said Pedro would only need to ride in the wagon for a day or two.

Three different ferries crossed the Neches River at or near Beaumont. The William Ashworth ferry crossed south of town at the little village of Santa Ana, the Tevis Ferry crossed in Beaumont itself, and the Pine Bluff ferry crossed five miles north of town. Swamps and bayous covered much of the land near the Ashwoth ferry, making it unsuitable to ford cattle, and herds of longhorns were not welcome in Beaumont. The only logical choice for the drive was to use the ferry at Pine Bluff. Pine Bluff had high ground on both sides of the river and no nearby swamps.

The trail drive arrived in the area of Pine Bluff early in the afternoon of the seventeenth day out of the Rocking M and set up camp for the night. The layout at the Pine Bluff ferry was very similar to the ferry across the Brazos, except five hundred cattle could be crossed on each trip. The price was the same, three cents an animal and five dollars for the wagon. Of course, even a higher price would have been acceptable after the near disaster at the Trinity.

Bo got the men fed early, and some of them asked Caleb if they could have an advance on their pay so they could go into Beaumont for a little sport. "I can't see much harm in givin' y'all an advance, long as you watch yourselves and don't drink too much. I want you back here early, though. Who will stay and guard the herd?"

"Jose and I will stay with the remuda, *Jeffe*," Ernesto replied. "The town does not interest me." Caleb smiled at the downcast look on Jose's face.

"Jesus and I will also stay, *Jeffe*," said Juan. "Our wives would not like it much if we went to town."

"That means the rest of you can go," said Caleb. Manny, Miguel, Tulie, Angel, and Luis were all smiles. "Pedro, I'm gonna ride along with 'em, and see if I can get them Indian ponies we stole shod before dark. How's your side? Are you feelin' well enough to ride with me?"

Pedro smiled at Caleb's concern. "Si, the stiffness is nearly gone, and the stitches are healing well. Let's ride."

It did not take long to cover the five miles to Beaumont. When they got to the blacksmith shop with the horses, Caleb had a final word with the cowhands. "Y'all be careful and don't cause any trouble. I only saw two saloons when we rode through town, so me and Pedro will look you up once we make arrangements to have the horses shod." With a whoop and a holler the young men charged off down the street.

Agreeing on a price to have the horses shod did not take long, and the smithy said he could get to them right away. While the blacksmith and his helper worked, Caleb and Pedro got into a conversation with another customer about the ford across the Sabine River just north of Madison, and the trail further east into Louisiana. They talked for a good while before the friendly stranger had to head for his ranch. By then the horses were shod.

Caleb paid the blacksmith. "We best go check up on the boys, Pedro."

The words were no sooner out of Caleb's mouth, when Tulie Perez galloped up, reining tight to a sliding stop and throwing up a cloud of dust. "You best come, *Jeffe*!" Tulie shouted the fear in his eyes apparent. "Angel is in trouble!" Without another word he jerked the rein on his little black and white piebald mare and spurred her back up the street.

Leaving the ponies in the care of the blacksmith, Caleb and Pedro quickly mounted and lit out after Tulie. They followed him to the other end of the street at a gallop before reining in hard at a drinking establishment called the Wagon Wheel. Leaping from their saddles, Caleb and Pedro did not bother to use the hitching rail before charging up the front steps and plowing through the batwing doors right behind the little cowhand. The sight that greeted their eyes when they entered the crowded saloon instantly infuriated them.

Angel was on the floor and a big ruddy-faced man wearing a black vest kicked him in the side and again in the face. "That'll teach you some manners you little Mex bastard!" The crowd yelled their approval as the big man drew back his boot to deliver another kick.

"Kick that man again, mister, and you're as good as dead!" Caleb's loud growl cut the kick short and silenced the raucous crowd.

Two men standing by the bar, who were holding their guns on the remainder of the Rocking M cowhands, spun around to bring their weapons to bear on Caleb. Pedro cleared leather so fast the movement was a blur. His Colt roared as he fanned the hammer twice, and both men were left standing holding bloody arms as their weapons clattered to the floor.

"I will kill the next man who goes for his gun!" snarled Pedro as he waved the barrel of his smoking Colt toward the crowd.

"Manny, Miguel," Caleb said, his voice the whisper of death, "y'all get on down to the blacksmith shop and pick up the horses. Luis, you and Tulie get Angel back to camp so Bo can take a look at him. Do it now!" he snapped when they hesitated. "Don't worry about me and Pedro. We don't need any help to take care of these sidewinders. Now move!"

The cowhands moved quickly, picking up the barely conscious Angel and carrying him through the saloon's swinging doors. Caleb stood listening as the hands got Angel mounted and rode out of town. As the hoof-beats faded in the distance, the ruddy-faced man's gun hand moved toward his holster, and he instantly found himself starring down the .44 caliber muzzle of Caleb's Walker Colt, hammer cocked and ready to fire.

"You don't hear so good, do you mister?" Caleb asked with a wicked smile. "I should blow your stinkin' head off for what you did to my cowhand."

"The little bastard was a filthy Mex just like that swine sidin' you now," the big man sneered as his held up his fists. "Why don't you holster that hog leg and face me with these?"

Caleb's wicked smile was replaced by a grin as he holstered his Colt. "Come on ahead if you got the nerve."

The man charged Caleb with an angry roar, but the roar was cut short when Caleb landed a vicious straight left jab to the middle of the ruddy face that snapped the man's head back, splattering his nose and bloodying his face. Not giving his adversary an opportunity to recover, Caleb stepped in and landed a wicked roundhouse right to his jaw and another straight left to the mouth that sent teeth flying. Another solid right to the stomach bent the man double, and a final right uppercut delivered from down around the knees dropped him like a lung-shot buffalo. He lay on the barroom floor in his own blood, curled up and moaning softly.

Caleb turned to the crowd, his bloodied fists still balled in anger. "Which one of you skunks is next?" No one in the crowd said a word. "The next time y'all decide to single out a man 'cause you don't like his name or the color of his skin, make damn sure he don't ride for the Rockin' M. Pedro, I think it's time we got on back to camp."

Pedro kept the crowd covered as he and Caleb backed their way out the swinging doors, and he did not holster his Colt until they were mounted. Reining around, they galloped out of town, riding a mile or two before slowing to a walk. No one followed them.

Chapter 13

Ferrying the cattle and the remuda across the Neches went off without a hitch, other than the occasional longhorn that needed a whack across the muzzle or across the behind to encourage their good behavior. Angel made the crossing in the bed of the wagon while recovering from his severe beating, but Bo said he would be back in the saddle again in a few days. The second night out of Beaumont the drive stopped for the night at Bellew's ferry on the west bank of the Sabine River a few miles north of Orange, the easternmost settlement in Texas.

Richard Bellew also operated a cattle stand at the site that offered stock pens, hot meals, and decent accommodations. Driving the cattle and horses into the stock pens for the night allowed every cowhand to get a full night's sleep, a rarity on the trail, and the accommodations were primitive but clean, consisting of a long low bunkhouse lined down both sides with rope beds. Each bed had a mattress stuffed with corn shucks and two clean blankets. Though the mattresses were a bit rough, it was a pleasure to spend a night sleeping off the ground.

Caleb and Bo ferried the wagon and the remuda across the Sabine at first light, and, following Richard Bellew's advice, set out northeast to set up the camp for the night, rather than due east. Bellew said the land to the northeast was low enough to cause some problems, but due east was mostly bayous and swamps, as it neared the Calcasieu River, nothing but deathtraps for the unwary longhorns. By late morning, all the cattle had been ferried to the east bank of the Sabine, and Pedro moved the herd out on the trail of the wagon and horses.

The drive covered nearly forty miles the next two days, traveling through countryside that was a cattleman's dream, and Caleb and Pedro wondered why Richard Bellew had been so concerned. Groves of white pine dotted the landscape, tall and majestic. The trees were widely spaced and, in between, thick lush grass grew in abundance. Grazing heavily, the longhorns and horses regained much of the weight they had lost on the trail.

However, as the trail drive closed in on the Calcasieu, conditions began to gradually worsen, and Richard Bellew's words of warning took on much more significance. Countless streams and creeks flowed toward the Calcasieu, creating bogs and small swamps that trapped the longhorns, holding them fast like glue, until three or four cowhands managed to get a rope around their horns and pull them free. A few were stuck so deep that a hundred ropes could not have freed them, and the only recourse was to shoot the poor beasts. Pedro and Caleb helped Manny and Miguel wrestle a longhorn out of a deep bog. The surly beast rewarded their efforts by trying to gore Manny's horse, before bawling its misery as it ran off to rejoin the herd.

Pedro shook his head as he coiled up his lariat and hung it back on his saddle. "I can't imagine how bad it would have been if we had trailed the cattle further south like we were planning."

"I know what you mean," agreed Caleb. "We would've lost most of the damn herd in this muck. At least the horses have faired well. Ernesto and Jose have kept 'em bunched pretty good."

The herd barely plodded along for ten miles that day, and men and cattle alike were totally exhausted when the cowhands drove the bawling longhorns into the stock pens at the Le Bleu cattle stand located on the Calcasieu River. Ernesto and Jose had arrived earlier with the remuda, and the horses were already corralled. The Le Bleu cattle stand was sited on the only high ground along the Calcasieu for miles, and Caleb was sure it would become a virtual island surrounded by a shallow lake during periods of heavy rainfall. He was glad to see the stand included a good-sized ferry to move the cattle and horses across the river. After what the cowhands had already endured, the last thing they needed was to ford another river. The food was not bad, the beds were dry, and everyone was entertained by old Arsene Le Bleu's stories of his days as a pirate with Jean Lafitte.

Caleb and Pedro sat their horses on a low bluff, watching as the cowhands finished driving the cattle and horses into the stock pens along the Vermilion River. The trail had been much better between the Calcasieu and the town of Opelousas, and the drive covered the sixty miles in three days. They were now only three or four days out of Baton Rouge and the end of the trail.

Caleb took off his old gray sombrero and mopped at the sweat, running down his face and neck, with his yellow bandana. "This heat is somethin' fierce, ain't it brother?"

"It's this hot back home, too," Pedro replied, "but the moisture in the air makes the heat feel much worse."

Manny Flores rode up and reined in. "*Senor* Bo told me to come and see you, *Jeffe*."

"Manny, when we get across the river in the mornin', I want you to carry a message to Josh Tanner. Take it to the docks in

West Baton Rouge, and give it to one of the riverboat captains headed toward New Orleans. I'll see that you have a little money to give him for his trouble. The captain will get the message to Josh. That way he'll be waitin' for us when we get to Baton Rouge."

"*Si, Jeffe*," Manny replied, "I will see that the message is delivered."

"*Gracias*," said Caleb, "you can go have a beer with the boys now. Tell everybody I said to stay out of trouble."

"*Si, Jeffe*." Smiling, Manny reined around and galloped back down the bluff.

With a whoop and a holler the Rocking M cowhands drove the bawling longhorns and the whinnying horses into the stock pens located near the levee on the west bank of the Mississippi. They had finally reached the end of the trail drive a full four hundred miles and twenty-nine days after leaving the ranch. The first twenty miles of the drive from Opelousas to West Baton Rouge had been a terrible ordeal. Swamps, marshes, and deep bogs covered most of the land between the Vermilion and the Atchafalaya Rivers, and dozens of unwary longhorns managed to wander off the trail and stumble into them. Eleven head were unaccounted for. Even a few of the horses had to be roped and dragged out of the muck, and the twenty mile stretch took nearly three exhausting days to cover.

Thankfully, the land steadily dried out the closer the trail drive got to Baton Rouge, and the last thirty miles of travel had been relatively trouble free. Baton Rouge was located on the Istrouma Bluff, the first high bluff upriver from the Mississippi delta, and was protected from most of the flooding that plagued the area. The city had been the capital of Louisiana since 1849, and the new capital building looked like a medieval castle sitting on a high bluff across the river. Josh Tanner was nowhere in sight, and after asking around, Caleb learned the next steamboat from New Orleans would not arrive until early the following morning. Exhausted like everyone else, he decided to go to bed early and be there to meet the boat when it docked.

Caleb was standing on the levee with Pedro, watching as the rising sun turned the surface of the muddy Mississippi to a buttery-yellow, when the steamboat, whistle screaming its arrival, rounded a bend in the river and churned its way toward the West Baton Rouge docks. Maneuvering with the precision and skill that only came with years of experience, the captain guided the big stern wheeler alongside the dock and expertly brought the craft to a standstill by reversing power on the wheel. The deckhands tossed the heavy hawsers into the waiting hands of the stevedores, and once the boat was securely moored to the dock, the gangplank was lowered. Caleb saw Josh smile and wave as he started down the gangplank with two other men, and he and Pedro hurried down the bank of the levee and across the dock to meet them.

The old horse trader had not changed much in the last three and a half years, thought Caleb, as he shook Josh's hand. Tanner was stout in build with gray hair and side whiskers. He wore a white suit and highly shined boots, and his outfit was topped off with a wide-brimmed straw hat. When his jacket opened Caleb saw that his trousers were still held up by a pair of fancy red braces. The two men standing behind him were obviously dressed for work in slouch hats, cotton shirts, canvas pants, and scuffed, high-heeled boots with spurs.

"It's damn good to see you again, Caleb," Josh said, "and good to do business with a man of his word. You said you'd be back, and here you are. I'm glad the circumstances are better this time. By the way, what happened between you and the Pates?"

Caleb smiled. "We can talk on that later, if you don't mind. Right now I'd like you to meet my brother-in-law, Pedro Vaca, and then take a look at the livestock. Pedro, this is Josh Tanner."

"Glad to meet you, Pedro," said Josh as he shook hands. "And these men," he added as he turned, "are my two top hands, Ned Potter and Seth Vincent. Now Caleb, what have you got to show me?"

"As of yesterday, when we ran 'em into the stock pens, the count was 3,597 longhorns, all steers, and 146 horses; stallions, mares, and geldings mixed. Outlaws and rustlers donated thirty-nine of 'em, but that's another story."

"One that I'm very much looking forward to hearin'," said Josh. "Seth, you go with Pedro and have a look at the cattle, but don't worry about a head count. We'll use Caleb's number. Caleb, Ned and I will have a look at the horses with you."

"Come on, Seth," said Pedro, "I'm sure you know where the stock pens are."

"The corrals are over that way too," said Josh to Caleb. "Shall we join them?"

Without the bother of a headcount the sale of the longhorns went quickly, and at twenty-five dollars a head the total came to $89,925.00 As Caleb put it when Pedro gave him the number, "Quite a tidy little profit."

The horses were an entirely different story, with Josh demanding the lowest price possible and Caleb digging in his heels whenever he thought the old horse trader was trying to take advantage of him, in a friendly, give and take manner. After haggling for most of the day, only four hoses remained to be priced. Caleb had intentionally held back a big Appaloosa stallion sired by Nasty and three mares. They were all magnificent animals, but the huge stallion was nearly an exact duplicate of his sire. He had a broad, deep chest and long, sturdy legs, and he was gray in the face and down to his withers with mottled brown spots growing in number and size until they merged at his brown rump. Like Nasty, his red eyes clearly spoke of intelligence.

"I can see why you held these four out until now," Josh complained with a good-natured smile on his face. "You obviously remember my outrageous offer for the sire, and you plan to use it to take advantage of me."

Caleb laughed out loud. The total agreed price for all the other horses was $18,500.00, and thanks to the horse trading he had already made more profit for the ranch than he thought possible. "I stuck it to you as much as I could on the other horses," Caleb said when he settled down, "but I know how much you loved Nasty. I'll sell you all four for a thousand dollars. What do you say?"

"Sold," Josh said without a moment's hesitation. The old horse trader knew when he was being offered a gift. "And they won't be up for resale. I'm going to keep them on my ranch for breedin'."

The remainder of the day and the evening were spent relaxing with good conversation and enjoying a special meal prepared by Bo to celebrate the end of the drive. In the morning they would sell the wagon, load their own horses, tack, and Old Dog onto a steamboat, and churn down the Mississippi to New Orleans with Josh. After a few days to relax and see the sights, they would board a coastal schooner and sail to Galveston.

Caleb and Pedro decided to take $25,000.00 in gold back to the ranch. They would leave nearly $85,000.00 in the Bank of New Orleans. There were no banks as such in Texas because of laws making it difficult to incorporate. Most banking in the Lone Star State was done privately, if at all, by freighting or mercantile firms like Cooper's Emporium. Everyone had a good time in the city, with Josh as their host, and within a week they boarded a ship with a promise to Josh that there would be another drive in the next year or two.

Thankfully, the waters of the Gulf were calm and peaceful for the brief sea voyage, and the schooner sailed into Galveston harbor on the morning of the sixth day out of New Orleans. The sun rising at their backs cast shadows of the ship's tall masts across the warehouses along the wharf as the sailors used a long boom, and block and tackle, to hoist the horses and Old Dog off the ship with a wide belly sling. Nasty nearly had a fit during the painless process, attempting to bite or kick at anything he could reach, including Caleb, but Smokey was docile like most of the other horses. Only Caleb brought two horses back on the ship. He was not about to sell Smokey or leave the big, jug-headed dun in New Orleans, and they could use him as a packhorse on the ride back to the ranch.

The married men did some shopping for their wives in the stores along the Strand in Galveston before they took the ferry across West Bay. After walking the horses off the ferry, they purchased the supplies they would need for the trip, loaded them on Smokey, and rode out for home. Heading northwest from Galveston, they forded the Brazos and followed the east bank of the Colorado River through Columbus, La Grange, and Bastrop. The long ride was uneventful, and on the afternoon of the seventh day out of Galveston, they rode into the central square of the Rocking M.

The returning riders were spotted a few miles east along the river trail, and thanks to the swift outriders, word of their arrival had quickly spread across the ranch. Juan, Jesus, Ernesto, and Jose dismounted at the corral, handed their horses to a few friends who were waiting to greet them, and headed over to the cottages where their families had assembled. When Caleb, Pedro, and Bo rode through the hacienda gate, the whole family was waiting on the porch to greet them. Pedro's lovely fiancée, Veronica, was also standing there along with her mother, and Pedro was the first to leap from his saddle as he hurried to greet her.

With her mother standing beside her, he could not very well sweep Veronica up in his arms the way he wanted to, so he settled for respectfully taking her hands in his. "I was hoping you would be here when we got back," Pedro said as he gazed into her beautiful eyes. "How was your trip?"

Veronica gave him her most beautiful smile, also wishing that her mother was far away at the moment. "The stagecoach ride from Laredo to Austin seemed to take forever, but since we arrived at the ranch, Lucinda and your father have taken very good care of us. *Es no verdad, mi Madre?*" Veronica wanted to make sure that, in his excitement Pedro did not forget to greet her mother.

"*Si*, it is true," her mother replied with a smile as Pedro took her hand in greeting. "We have been made to feel very welcome, and our stay has been pleasant."

Meanwhile, Caleb dismounted and took Lucinda in his arms, lifting her for a long kiss, with a little girl hanging on each of his legs, before he sat her back down. "My, but it's grand to see you again, love." He noticed a mischievous smile in Lucinda's eyes, but he would get to the bottom of that later. Bending down, he picked up Ilse in one arm and Gretchin in the other. "What have you little imps been up to?"

"We have been very good, Papa," Ilse said.

"Yes, very good," added Gretchin. "Can we have our pony now?"

Caleb laughed as he glanced at Lucinda. "Like I said before I left, we'll have to talk that over with your mother." Caleb put the girls down and shook hands with Felix. "We lost young Mike Sanchez to some bandits, but everything else went well. I'd like to hire Luis, Tulie, and Angel, and Jose, too. They all did a good job, but we can talk about that and the drive after supper."

"Don't talk for too long after supper," said Lucinda. "I have something important I wish to discuss with you."

Caleb noticed Lucinda smiling slyly at Felix, and once again he wondered what was going on. Before he had a chance to ask, Consuela came rushing out of the hacienda and nearly knocked Bo over as she hugged him fiercely.

Bo had a big smile on his face. "Maybe I should go away more often." Consuela flushed red with the blush of a young girl, and everyone had a good laugh at her expense.

"I told Josh we'd most likely be makin' another drive in a year or two," Caleb said as he took a sip of his coffee.

It was too warm for a fire, so instead of sitting in front of the hearth, Felix and Pedro had joined Caleb at the large oak table in the great room to discuss the trail drive and future plans for the ranch. The flames of two tall candles, sitting on the table in pewter candlesticks, flickered when a light breeze wafted through the room from the open windows. Everyone else had gone to bed, and the hacienda was quiet.

"Bill Meacham died while you were gone," said Felix, "and with no children his wife is planning to sell the ranch along with the cattle." The Meacham's owned the adjacent ranch to the west of the Rocking M. "I am not sure of the exact acreage, but there must be more than a mile of frontage on the Colorado, including some good bottom land for farming. With the extra cattle we would acquire, we could definitely make a drive to New Orleans again next year."

Pedro was enthusiastic. "We should buy all the adjoining land we can get our hands on. Especially with the money we just made on this drive."

"I agree," said Caleb. "I'd rather have our money tied up in land than settin' in a bank. Banks can always go under."

"We need a good amount of ready cash to keep an operation like this going," Felix added. "But that is no longer a problem, and with more land, we can always make more money. I think we should ride over and see Mrs. Meacham tomorrow."

Caleb nodded. "I have to see Governor Bell about the authorization for my Ranger Company, but I can put that off for a day or two. By the way, as part of the deal I struck, if the

Company is approved, the Rangers will be housed here on the ranch. I thought about usin' the bunkhouse, but with the new hands, there won't be enough room. "I'm gonna need a separate barracks."

"How many men are you talking about?" asked Felix.

"Twenty-seven," Caleb replied, "countin' the sergeants and the lieutenant. I was thinkin' about locatin' the barracks east of the compound on the far side of the barn. The barn and corral have always been a weak link in the ranch's defenses, but with the Rangers' barracks there, it'll become a strongpoint." Caleb yawned again. "I'll know more after I talk with the governor, but right now I'm dead on my feet. I'm goin' to bed. Lucinda's probably been waitin' up for me."

Sleep was the last thing on Lucinda's mind when Caleb finally came into the bedroom. He quickly undressed, blew out the candle on the dresser, and slipped under the linen sheet and light blanket they used as a cover in the summer.

Lucinda snuggled up to him. "I missed you."

Caleb tuned to face her. "I missed you, too, love, somethin' fierce. What'd you want to talk about?"

Lucinda smiled. "Dr. Laughton was here just before you got back."

A frown of concern creased Caleb's brow. "Why was Laughton here? Have you been sick?"

Lucinda smiled. "Yes, love, but only in the mornings."

"Why only in the mornin'?" Caleb was puzzled for a moment before he sat bolt upright. "My God, Lucinda, are you gonna have a baby?"

"Yes, my love. Dr. Laughton never said it was impossible for me to get pregnant again after my miscarriage, only very unlikely." Lucinda had miscarried four years prior during an attack on the ranch by the Pate brothers.

"Well, I'll be," said Caleb as he took Lucinda in his arms and they laughed together.

Chapter 14

A week had passed since Caleb's return to the ranch when he entered Governor Bell's office. The governor was hunched over his small desk, reading from a stack of documents. Now and then, he dipped one of the new metal-tipped pens in the inkwell and furiously scratched a series of notes in the margins of the papers he was reading or crossed out lines or entire paragraphs. The metal pen was rapidly replacing the use of feathered quills. He kept at it for a minute or two before finally looking up to call for his secretary.

"Caleb, for heaven's sake, I didn't know you were standin' there. James should've told me. Please sit down." Caleb pulled up one of the chairs in front of the desk. "James!" Bell called out to his secretary. "Come in here and get this legislation." When the secretary walked in, the governor handed him the papers he had been working on. "Incorporate the changes I made and get it back to the Speaker of the House as soon as you can." Bell put down his pen and wiped the sweat from his brow with a white handkerchief. "At times like this it's hard to believe I actually campaigned to get this job. I must've been crazy."

Caleb chuckled. "I can come back later on if you'd like, Governor."

"No, no, please stay! I have the authorization here on my desk somewhere." Bell shuffled through the papers stacked on his desk while he continued to talk. "Jenkins ushered the authorization through the Senate last week, and you must have put a bug in Coleman's ear because he sponsored it in the House. From what I hear, he called in a few favors to boot. I appreciate your help, and so will the settlers on the frontier. Here it is!" Bell handed him the authorization. "I believe you'll find it covers everything we discussed."

Caleb took a minute to look the authorization over carefully. Everything was there in plain and straight forward language, including the authority to order sixty new Colt revolvers. He handed it back to Bell for signing. "Thank you, Governor, and if you run for office again you'll have my support."

Bell quickly scratched his signature on the document. "It's people willing to volunteer their service like you who deserve the thanks, Caleb. By the way, the legislation also allows me to form two more companies if I deem your unit to be successful. There is no doubt in my mind that it will be." Governor Bell stood and offered his hand. "Good luck!"

Cooper's Emporium was Caleb's next destination. Slipping the toe of his boot in the stirrup, he swung his long leg over the fancy Mexican saddle with the silver and turquoise inlays and saucer-like saddle horn. The Emporium was located a little ways up the hill on the west side of Congress Avenue just past Pecan Street. John Cooper, Wanda's brother, was standing behind the counter when Caleb walked into the store. John was a big, clean-shaven man with short-cropped blond hair and blue eyes. He wore a long-sleeved blue cotton shirt and a knee-length, white apron.

As always, John greeted him with a smile. "Mornin', Caleb. What can I do for you on this fine day?"

"I'm about to make you a very happy man, John" Caleb replied. He chuckled when John looked puzzled, then held up the authorization. "I just got authority from the legislature to form my own Ranger Company. I'm gonna need a few things to get started. How do ninety new Colt Dragoons revolvers sound for a starter?"

John was shocked. "My God, Caleb, are you plannin' on startin' an army?"

Caleb chuckled again. "No, but at two apiece, I need near sixty of 'em for my Rangers, and thirty more to replace the Walkers my ranch hands are usin' right now. Course, I expect a damn good deal for such a big order, to say nothin' of all the powder and lead I'm gonna need. I'd like to work out some kind of trade in for the three dozen or so Walkers I already have, too. Would that be possible? They're all in good shape."

"Certainly," John said, his mind racing over the size of the order Caleb was contemplating, "revolvers are always in demand. Given enough time, I'm sure I could resell them for, let's say, a five percent commission."

Caleb nodded. "Done, five percent of whatever you take in is yours."

"Come on over here. I got somethin' to show you before we finalize the order." John reached into a glass showcase and pulled out a new revolver. It looked like a smaller version of the Dragoon. "Take a look at this." He handed the revolver to Caleb. "It's a .36 caliber Colt Navy model 1851. It still has a lot of hittin' power, and you don't have to be a giant to handle it. It weighs a little more than two pounds, and the barrel is only seven and a half inches long. What do you think?"

Caleb hefted the Navy Colt. It felt well-balanced and solid in his hand. There was a picture of a naval battle engraved on the cylinder. "I'd like to give these Navy Colts a try, John. All my ranch hands are average size men. I think they might like the size of the Navy's. There wouldn't be as much weight to tote around when they're doin' their chores either. I'll stick with the Dragoons for my Rangers, though— big men or small, we all used Walkers in Mexico. I like the firepower they provide. Let me take a look at one of the new Dragoons, too."

Like the Walker Colt, the big .44 caliber Dragoon was a natural fit in Caleb's hand, but the new revolver weighed six ounces less than the Walker, and the barrel on this model was a full inch shorter making the weapon easier to handle. The cylinder was also a little shorter, holding fifty grains of gunpowder rather than sixty for safety purposes, and the loading lever was vastly improved. Unlike the Walker, it would never drop down accidentally when the revolver was fired.

"I can give you thirty Dragoons and thirty Navy Colts right now," said John. "That'll take care of most of my stock, but I always say sell 'em when you can. Take a pair of the Dragoons and a pair of the Navy Colts back to the ranch now if you like. I'll go ahead and order three dozen more Dragoons and the gunpowder and lead for your Rangers. Do you need any extra powder and lead for the ranch?"

Caleb nodded. "Now that you mention it, throw in a few extra kegs of powder and twenty pounds of lead. I'll need twenty-seven rain slickers and the same number of good quality wool blankets, too, and twenty-seven gray sombreros."

John nodded as he wrote down the order. "I'll have to order that many gray sombreros, but the rest will be packed and ready for pickup tomorrow, along with the Colts and the gunpowder and lead. You can either pick up the order yourself, or send someone in when you get back to the ranch."

"I don't have a wagon with me, so I'll have someone from the ranch pick it up. It might take a day or so, though."

"That's no problem," John replied.

When Caleb finished at the store, he rode back down to the foot of Congress Avenue and boarded the ferry to cross the Colorado. Once Nasty was settled, he stood and watched the muddy waters of the Colorado roll slowly past as his thoughts drifted to Wanda and the last time he was with her just before the cattle drive. What happened then could not be erased, but he was determined it would never be repeated. If that meant severing all relations between them, even the close friendship he treasured so much, so be it. No matter what the outcome, it was time he faced her and settled the issue. He owed her that much.

When the ferry reached the landing, Caleb walked Nasty off the planked deck and swung up on the saddle. Reining the big stallion toward the trail along the river, he nudged Nasty into a slow walk. He was in no particular hurry to face his medicine. Less than a half hour later, Wanda's cabin and schoolhouse came into view on the high bluff above the river. School was out for the summer, and as Caleb approached the cabin he saw Wanda sitting in the shade of the dogtrot reading a book, slowly rocking in the old oak rocker that had once belonged to the aunt who raised her. She lowered the book and waved a greeting as he rode up and dismounted.

Tying his reins to the hitching rail, Caleb stepped up on the porch. "Hello, Wanda, it's good to see you again."

As she rose from her rocker, Wanda smiled; a hint of nervous tension on her face. She too had thought much about what had happened between them. After considering all the possibilities, she was prepared to continue the relationship in the manner

Caleb thought best. Married or not, she still loved him without question, but above all she did not want to lose the close friendship and respect she felt for this man and deeply hoped that he still felt for her.

"Caleb, I was just thinking about you. Please come in. I'll make some coffee."

As Wanda busied herself in the kitchen preparing the coffee, Caleb sat at the small table and examined her closely. Tall and blond with bright blue eyes, she was the opposite of his Lucinda, but every bit as stunning. What man would fail to be tempted by her beauty? The coffee was soon ready, and after handing him a cup, Wanda took a seat across from him. Caleb hesitated for a moment as he stirred in his usual portion of sugar. Before tasting it, he put his spoon down and reached for her hand, taking it in both of his big, trail-roughened paws.

Looking her in the eyes, he began, "Wanda, we need to talk about what happened. I think you know how much I care about you, and how much I treasure the special friendship we share, but we can't let things go so far again. It's just not fair to Lucinda.

Wanda swallowed the lump in her throat and put her other hand over his. "I understand how you feel, Caleb. I will never regret nor forget the brief moment we shared together, though. As for it happening again, there will be little chance of that. I'm leaving on the stagecoach for New Orleans in the morning."

Wanda's words brought Caleb up short. "New Orleans! Why in the world are you goin' to New Orleans?"

"I have a job teaching there for a year or two," she replied, "but I plan on eventually returning to Austin."

Wanda wondered what Caleb's reaction would be if she told him the real reason for her departure, but the responsibility was hers. She should have been much more careful, and she did not want to burden him with her problems. Anyway, the explanation for her absence would be quite obvious when she returned, and they could deal with the situation then.

Caleb shrugged his shoulders in helplessness. "I know this sounds selfish after what I just said, but I wish you weren't goin'. At least you're plannin' on comin' back."

Caleb knew he had no hold on Wanda, even if she did not choose to come back. Perhaps that is what frightened him the most about her leaving. Putting his confused feelings aside for the moment, he reluctantly turned the conversation to his meeting with Governor Bell.

"I'm glad you received authority to recruit your Rangers," Wanda said. "The settlers on the frontier certainly need the protection. Hardly a week has gone by without news of some atrocity committed by the Comanches. Don't you think you'll have trouble with the army, though?" Wanda knew that animosity had been rampant between the U. S. Army and the Texas Rangers ever since the end of the Mexican American War.

The dominant political view in Texas, as in most of the South, was that the Union was composed of sovereign states. The federal government was seen primarily as a convenient tool to do those tasks too difficult or expensive for the states to handle, like building harbors and roads, establishing postal and diplomatic services, and frontier defense. In fact, defense of the frontier against Mexican bandits and Comanches had been paramount in the decision to accept annexation in the first place, though from the beginning, the federal government had handled the problems poorly. Neither the War Department nor the army understood the Comanches. No other state had come into the Union with more than half its territory unsettled and still occupied by thousands of hostile Indians. Some two hundred Texans were either killed or carried off into captivity in 1849 alone. The army kept only a few thousand soldiers in the state to counter the depredations, and most of them were infantry, who provided practically no defense against the wide-ranging horse-warriors.

Now Governor Bell, over the stringent objections of local army commanders, was once more ordering the Texas Rangers into the field. The problems between the U. S. Army and the Rangers were sure to continue because they operated under conflicting orders. The army was trying to police the frontier by keeping the peace and signing treaties. The Rangers were just as determined to punish the Comanches and push them back.

Staring into the fire, Caleb finally replied, "There'll be problems alright. Governor Bell said a few legislators are talkin' about workin' with the federal government to set up reservations in Texas. That might work for some tribes, but most Comanche bands won't live on a reservation unless we're strong enough to force 'em to. We'll just have to wait and see. Enough of this dreary talk, though, did you hear that Pedro's gettin' married in August?"

Wanda smiled. "No I didn't. Who's the lucky girl?"

"Felix knows her father in Mexico, and he sent Pedro down there to meet her. It didn't take Pedro but a week to fall in love and ask her to marry him. Her name is Veronica Martinez, and she came up from Mexico with her mother to help Lucinda plan the weddin'. They're stayin' out at the ranch. Speakin' of Lucinda, you'll never guess what happened. In spite of what Doc Laughton said about her miscarriage, she's pregnant again, and we couldn't be happier."

Caleb saw a look of utter despair cross Wanda's features before she burst into a fountain of tears and fled to the bedroom. He found her lying face down across the bed sobbing her heart out. He did not know what to think.

"I'm sorry if I upset you," Caleb said, "It's just that we're so happy Doc Laughton was wrong."

Wanda turned over to face him, doing her best to knuckle the tears from her eyes. "That's not what upset me, Caleb," she sobbed. "I'm pregnant, too!"

There, in spite of the promise she had made to herself not to tell him, Wanda felt so low and despondent when she heard about how happy Lucinda was that she could not help herself.

Caleb was shocked speechless for a moment, then he did the one thing she needed the most. He took her in his arms and held her close, whispering that everything would be okay, and that he would love their child as much as any other.

"I'm so sorry," Wanda sniffled. "I thought I was careful, but it happened anyway."

Caleb gently brushed a strand of long blond hair away from her face. "This child is as much my responsibility as yours, Wanda. It takes two people to make a baby. You don't have to run off to New Orleans either. We'll face this together if you want." Then he broke into a big smile. "Besides, any child we make together has to turn out special, no matter what the circumstances."

Wanda's smile finally returned, the strength of her resolve returning with it. "I still think its best that I go off to New Orleans for a year or two. I can always say I was married and my husband died somehow. Not everyone will believe it, but at least as a widow I'll be able to keep my head up. Will you write to me once in a while?"

Caleb smiled. "I'll write as often as I can, and you can write to me in care of Richard Bullock. He's a busybody, but he'll keep his mouth shut for me. Keep me informed how you're feelin' and what you're doin', and write often. I left a good amount of money in the Bank of New Orleans. I'll write you a draft at the hotel tomorrow mornin' so you can draw on it for your expenses. Take whatever you and the baby need. I won't abide any argument."

Wanda knew the road ahead would be long and difficult, but now she no longer felt alone and abandoned to her fate. No matter how things turned out, Caleb would stand by her, and she could draw strength from that.

Caleb helped the driver and the man riding shotgun load Wanda's baggage in the boot of the stagecoach. "Take care of yourself, and write often." He gave her a big hug. "My thoughts and prayers will be with you as always."

"Goodbye, love," she mouthed before he helped her climb up into the coach.

Caleb stood in the street until the driver reined the stage-coach north on Congress Avenue, then turned and walked up the front steps of the hotel, joining Bullock on the hotel's wide veranda. "Mr. Bullock, I got a big favor to ask, and you need to keep quiet about it. I need your word on that."

"Certainly, Caleb, you have my word. What is it?"

"Wanda's gonna be in New Orleans teachin' school for a year or two. She'll be sendin' me a letter from time to time, and she'll mail 'em to the hotel in care of you. Just hold on to 'em for me. Okay?"

Bullock smiled. "I'll be glad to do it, and don't worry. I know how to keep my mouth shut when it's necessary. How about a cup of coffee? I got a fresh pot ready and plenty of sugar to go with it."

Caleb was sitting at the bar sipping his coffee and talking to Bullock when Ephraim Daggett walked into the café. Ignoring the offered hand, Caleb jumped off the stool, grabbed Eph up in a patented Bigfoot bear hug, and then sat him back down. "Damn but its good to see you again Eph. How the hell are you?"

Caleb rode with Eph during the Mexican American War, in the Ranger regiment commanded by Jack Hays. The regiment fought Mexican guerillas to keep General Scott's supply lines open to Mexico City. Eph commanded one of the companies in the regiment, and Caleb commanded the scouts. The tall, lanky Daggett was clean-shaven and tow-headed with sky-blue, expressive eyes. Dependable to a fault and courageous as a lion, he was mild-mannered and soft spoken, unless something or someone riled him up.

"I'm doin' pretty good now," Eph replied. "Lost my wife and child to the fever about a year ago though, and I been driftin' ever since."

Caleb shook his head. "I'm sorry to hear that, Eph. Why don't you pull up a stool and have a cup of Mr. Bullock's fine coffee? Mr. Bullock, I'd like you to meet a damn good friend of mine, Ephraim Daggett. We were in the war together."

"Glad to meet you," said Bullock as the two men shook hands. Bullock slid a cup of coffee across the bar.

"Same here, Mr. Bullock," said Eph as he took a seat. "Caleb, I hear you're puttin' together a Ranger Company." Eph took a sip of his coffee. "I need a job real bad, and I don't mind ridin' as a private if I have to. Can you use me?"

"Sorry, Eph, I don't need any privates right now." Eph looked downcast until Caleb smiled. "I could use a lieutenant to be my second in command though. That is, if you think you can handle it."

Eph chuckled. "You beat all, Caleb McAdams, and thanks. I'll do a damn good job for you. What have you got organized so far?"

"Well," Caleb said, "I ordered two new Colt Dragoons for every man in the company, and I hired my second in command. Now all we got to do is put the company together." Eph laughed. "Seriously, we'll be based at the Rockin' M. My partner, Felix Vaca, is buildin' the barracks right now. We need to recruit men, though. That's where you come in, Eph. Mr. Bullock, Eph will need a room for the next two or three weeks."

Bullock nodded and Caleb continued. "Start puttin' out the word, Eph. You can recruit here a lot better than I can at the ranch. We'll need twenty-four privates and two sergeants—two platoons of thirteen men each. The pay is sixty dollars a month for privates, seventy-five for sergeants, and a hundred a month for you. I'm hopin' George White will ride as one of the sergeants, but you have to find everyone else. There's another slot for a lieutenant in the company, but I'm savin' that for my good friend, Bigfoot Wallace, in case he decides to join us. Get experienced men if you can, but good men all the same. I'll be sendin' a man in from the ranch to pick up thirty of the new

Dragoons and thirty new Navy Colts from Cooper's Emporium. He'll need to pick up some powder and lead too. We might as well go by the store now. I'll introduce you to John, so he'll know you're authorized to sign for the company. That's a whole mouthful. You got any questions?"

Eph smiled. "Let's go on over to Cooper's. I'm ready to get busy."

Pedro hefted the new Navy Colt in his hand, feeling how well balanced it was. Unlike the Walker, which in spite of his average size he used very well after a few years of practice, the Navy Colt felt as if it was designed and manufactured to fit his hand. He remembered Caleb saying the same thing about the Walker Colt, but now Pedro knew exactly what Caleb meant. The Colt Patterson had fit his hand better than the Walker, but it was an inferior weapon. Not so with the Navy Colt. Not only did the size and weight balance the weapon perfectly for a man of average size, but the Navy also incorporated all the improvements of the new Colt Dragoon.

Pedro and Caleb were standing a good distance from the corral on the far side of the main compound. They set up some boards and old boxes with blackened bulls-eyes against the ridge for targets so they could test fire the new weapons, and then paced off twenty-five yards. Pedro took aim at the first target and fired three quick shots with the Navy Colt. All three rounds were center cut in a tight group, nearly touching each other.

Pedro grinned. "This weapon is very accurate. I wonder how much hitting power the .36 caliber ball has." He fired three more rounds dead center.

"There's got to be a little difference," Caleb speculated. "I don't think you'd have any problem stoppin' a man at this distance, though. The .36 caliber ball is a bit smaller, but it's no patty cake. How does it feel?"

"Like it was made for my hand," Pedro replied.

"Now you know how the Walker felt to me when I first picked it up," said Caleb. "I hope this Dragoon is the same."

"I can't wait to get a set of holsters made." said Pedro. "The speed of my draw will surely improve, and maybe even my accuracy because of the weight and balance of the weapon."

Caleb hefted the Dragoon. "This Dragoon has pretty much the same feel as my Walker, but the six ounces of weight Sam Colt got rid of and the inch he took off the barrel make it a little easier to handle. Let's see how well it fires."

Taking deliberate aim at his target, Caleb fired three quick rounds. A silver dollar could have covered the three holes in the center of the blackened bulls-eye. He holstered the Dragoon, and picking out the next target, made a lightning quick draw, firing three more rounds. The second group was nearly as tight as the first. Caleb smiled as he looked over at Pedro. "I guess I answered that question. Let's move back some."

Caleb paced off fifteen more yards, and after switching cylinders both men fired six additional rounds at forty yards, taking careful aim for each shot. This time there was a noticeable difference in the size of the groups. Caleb's group with the Dragoon was nearly the same. Pedro's group was spread out a little more, but still plenty tight enough to hit a man. From sixty yards there was no comparison. Caleb's group was still less than six inches, but Pedro's group was scattered across the twelve inch bulls-eye, with one round outside it. Next, they switched weapons and repeated the test from the same distances. The results were very similar.

"What do you think?" asked Caleb.

"I am going to switch to the Navy Colt," Pedro replied. "The revolver fits my hand much better and the weight and balance are perfect. My two-gun rig won't be as heavy either. I seldom fire at anything further than fifty yards anyway. I think we should issue them to our ranch hands if they like them, too. They can work horses and longhorns much easier without worrying about the weight of that big hog leg."

Caleb laughed. "I was sure the Navy Colt would suit you when John showed it to me. I agree most of the hands are gonna like it a lot better, too. Like you said, they have to carry 'em while they're workin'. I'll stick to the Dragoon for my Rangers, though. Their job is to fight Comanches and bandits, and for that kind of work, I like the hittin' power and range of the Dragoon. By the way, Pedro, you know damn well I'll make a place for you in the company if you want it."

"I know you would, and I have thought much about it. My father is getting older, though, and he needs my full-time help to run the ranch. Besides, Veronica is not as forgiving as Lucinda. She would skin me alive for even considering such a thing right before we get married."

"Come on," Caleb said, laughing at Pedro's response, "let's go see how Felix is comin' along on the barracks."

Felix had already staked out the perimeter of the new barracks, and the rooms he planned for each end of the building. Now he was busy tying cord from stake to stake as a guide for the adobe walls that would soon be going up.

Caleb took a look at the size of the staked area when he and Pedro walked up. "You certainly didn't scrimp on space, Felix. How big will the barracks be when it's finished?"

Coming to his feet, Felix stretched his back before he answered. "The center section of the barracks will be twenty feet by fifty feet, enough room for twelve rope bunks down each side and a big table in the center for the men to eat and work. There will also be two ten by ten rooms at the south end of the barracks for the sergeants and two ten by ten rooms at the north end for the officers. In front of the officer's rooms will be a ten by twenty foot orderly room."

"At first I worried about how to heat the rooms," Felix continued. "That many fireplaces would be expensive and take a long time to build. Then I found this ad in the San Antonio newspaper." Felix unfolded a picture and handed it to Caleb. "It is called a pot-belly stove. A heavy cast iron stove with its own stove pipe that goes out the side of the building. You build a fire in the stove, the fire heats up the iron, and the heat from the iron keeps the room warm. I will space two of them out in the center section of the barracks and put one in the orderly room. There will be four windows down each side and two on each end, all heavily shuttered with firing ports. I have not decided on the flooring, but it will not be dirt. What do you think?"

"I think you're gonna make this place so damn comfortable I won't be able to get the men out of here," Caleb replied with a smile. "How soon will it be finished?"

"It won't take long," said Felix. "There is quite a bit of adobe brick and red tile left over from our other building projects, and I already hired two men to fire the rest of the tile I need. We don't need that many people working in the fields right now either, so I will put them to work on the bricks. The building should be finished in two or three weeks, sooner if I hire extra skilled help to lay the bricks."

Caleb nodded. "Hire as many as you need." I want it done *muy pronto*, and I don't want you doin' the work. You got enough to do runnin' the ranch."

"Don't worry about that. Pedro practically runs the ranch now, and this is the kind of work I love. Also a rider from the Meacham ranch came by while you two were busy shooting up the hillside." Pedro and Caleb chuckled. "Mrs. Meacham has accepted our offer. The Rocking M now has five miles of river frontage and extends north from the river for approximately twelve miles; nearly forty thousand acres or sixty square miles. We can use the Meacham cabin for a line shack and keep four hands there on a rotating basis. The papers will be signed in Austin tomorrow at noon. I also want to get some of the hands working on an irrigation system for the new land along the river.

The farm land there is better than we have now and more plenti-ful. With Austin growing the way it is, we should be able to sell the surplus crops for a good profit."

"It all sounds good to me, Felix," said Caleb. "Let's get it done."

Chapter 15

Three weeks later, Lieutenant Ephraim Daggett rode into the Rocking M at the head of twenty-six brand new Texas Rangers. New at least to Caleb's company, but many of them were veterans with previous Ranger experience. Caleb was standing in front of the barracks alongside Chako and Juaquin when Eph halted the Company, ordering them to dismount. Before speaking, Caleb took a moment to look the men over.

The company was a mixture of Anglos and *Tejanos*, exactly what Caleb wanted, and in typical Ranger fashion, they were mostly long-haired, bearded, and dressed in all manner of clothing. Some wore cotton shirts, either store bought or homespun, and some wore buckskin hunting shirts. Most had leather chaps to protect their legs from thorns and brush. Trousers ranged from heavy-duty canvas to wool with reinforced seats or buckskins. Most of the men wore mule-ear boots with high heels and big Mexican spurs, but a few had soft boots like Caleb's, or even moccasins. Headgear ran the gamut from old slouch hats and sombreros, to fancy, wide-brimmed, flattop hats and well-weathered, Mexican War campaign caps. As a general rule they were armed to the teeth, with every type of weapon imaginable. Texas Rangers to a man, thought Caleb with a smile.

Of course, as Caleb stood looking the men over, they took the opportunity to size him up as well. A few of them, like Eph and George White, had ridden with him before, and many, especially the former Rangers knew the tall, wide-shouldered redhead by reputation as an eagle-eyed, hard riding, straight shooting hombre who could hold his own in any situation. The stocky, well-muscled Indians standing beside Caleb were obviously Lipan Apaches. They wore only breech clouts and calf-high, beaded moccasins. One wore a wide yellow bandana for a headband and the other a red bandana. Both Lipans had a one-gun rig with a Colt and a Bowie knife like Caleb's buckled around their waist.

Caleb cleared his throat. "Welcome to the Rockin' M. Some of you know me already. For those of you who don't, my name is Caleb McAdams. You can call me Captain." It was an old joke, but the easy laughter that followed served to lift the tension of the moment. "We got a tough job to do, men. Y'all know damn well how big the Texas frontier is, and we'll be the only regular Rangers in the field. That means you'll be livin' in the saddle most of the time. The company will be organized in two platoons, so we can cover a wider area and get a little rest between patrols. Don't plan on spendin' too much time in this nice new barracks, though. I can guarantee you'll have good and plentiful food here at the ranch, but when we're in the field the meals may be few and far between. If you look around, you'll see the company is made up of Anglos and *Tejanos.* You will get along or you'll be gone, it's that simple. As you know, the enlistment is for two years. If you take the oath, you'll follow the orders of the officers and sergeants without question or there will be consequences."

"I know every one of you has a good long rifle, but each man will be issued two brand new Colt Dragoon revolvers and two extra cylinders, along with a holster rig like mine." This news caused a stir among the men and Caleb paused for a moment. "I suggest you get a saddle holster made up for the other Colt, but that's up to you. You can have a two holster rig made up or shove it in your gun belt if you like; just so you keep it handy. Sergeants, I'll need to know how many of your men are left-handed. Each man will also get to choose an extra horse from the ranch's stock, and we got some fine horses here. That's about it except for the new gray sombrero and the blanket and rain slicker you'll find on your bunk. The sombrero is our uniform from now on, so you will wear it. Eph, I want to see you and the sergeants in the orderly room. When Lieutenant Daggett dismisses you, go on in, pick out a bunk, and stow your gear. The sergeants will give you a yell when we're ready."

"Oh, one more thing, the Lipan to my right with the yellow headband is Chako, and the one to my left with the red headband is Juaquin. They'll be the company's scouts. They speak good Spanish and passable English, but they understand both real well. If they have somethin' to say, you best listen to 'em. It might just save your life. Eph, take over." Caleb turned and walked into the barracks. Chako and Juaquin followed him through the door and on into the orderly room.

A few minutes later Eph walked in with George White and a man Caleb had seen somewhere before, but could not place. "Caleb, you know Sergeant White," Eph said.

Caleb smiled. "Good to see you, George. I'm glad you got tired of chasin' that stagecoach around. How's Bigfoot doin'?"

"He said to tell you to quit stealin' his employees, and that he's doin' real fine. If he gets a hankerin' to Ranger again, he'll look you up."

Shaking his head, Caleb said, "That sounds just like the varmint alright." He was still trying to place the other sergeant. The man was of medium height and build with short black hair, graying at the temples. His face and hands were burned brown and wrinkled from the trail like an old piece of leather, and he looked as if he'd been born in the saddle. "Don't I know you, Sergeant?"

The man smiled. "I had the pleasure of servin' with the Captain at Monterey durin' the war."

"Jessup," Caleb remembered, "Terrell Jessup. You were Ad Gillespie's first sergeant, right?"

"That's right, Captain," said Jessup, "and there was no man finer man than old Ad. I'll never forget climbin' that damn cliff the day he got killed. He sure as hell thought the world of you, sir."

Caleb nodded. "He was one of the finest men I ever rode with." Caleb had cried like a baby when Ad died in his arms. "You were with us at Walker Creek when Ad took out that Comanche war chief with the long head shot, too, weren't you?"

Jessup smiled. "Yes sir, Captain, it was well over three hundred yards. It took the life right out of that war party, too."

Caleb shook Jessup's hand. "It sure as hell did, Sergeant! I'm damn glad to have you as part of the outfit. Well Eph, if Sergeant Jessup is any indication of the caliber of men you signed up, I think we'll fair pretty well."

Eph smiled. "A few of 'em are pretty young and green, but only the best ride with McAdams' Rangers."

"McAdams' Rangers, I like the sound of that," said Caleb. "Y'all have a seat."

A small pot belly stove sat in the middle of the orderly room with a table and five chairs on one side of the stove, and two small desks with chairs on the other side. The four Rangers sat down at the table, and Chako and Juaquin stood off to the side leaning against the wall, their arms folded across their chests.

"This barracks is a nice setup," said Eph.

"Felix did a good job," Caleb agreed. "The doors over there lead to the officer's quarters. Take your pick, Eph. There are two rooms for sergeants at the other end of the barracks. George, you know I love you, but Terrell's been around a little longer, so he gets his choice." They all had a good laugh. "We'll issue a new Dragoon and a holster rig to each man today, if we don't have too many lefties, and get started on how to take care of the weapons. I set up a range against the ridge not too far from here. Within the next day or so we start target practice. There's plenty of powder and ball, so every Ranger will be damn handy with his Colt before we go out on our first patrol. Terrell, you and George each choose a corporal for your platoon. They'll get five dollars extra a month."

"That's a damn good idea, Captain," said Sergeant Jessup. "The men need to know who's in charge out there if we get in trouble."

"Both platoons go out on the first patrol," said Caleb. "George, First Platoon is yours. Jessup, you got Second Platoon. We'll divide the men before we issue the weapons. After a week or two, First Platoon will return to the ranch for a week and then go back out and relieve Second Platoon. That should establish a regular rotation of two weeks in the field and two weeks back here. Of course, there'll be times like late spring or early fall when we're all out there until we're exhausted, but we can't do that too often. Just keepin' a platoon on the frontier should discourage the kind of raidin' that's been goin' on for the last couple of years. It's time the Comanches learned there'll be consequences for their deviltry. Y'all get your gear stowed away and get your uniforms on." Caleb touched the wide brim of his new gray sombrero and chuckled. "Let me know when you're ready to get started."

Between getting the Rangers ready for their first patrol and the preparations for Pedro's wedding, the pace of the next two weeks on the Rocking M was hectic. In the middle of everything else, Caleb had to make a trip to Austin to pick up the remainder of the new Colts and the powder and ball. Pedro was right about the ranch hands favoring the Navy Colt. With the exception of the Lipans, to a man they all selected it over the Dragoon. The Walkers were collected and crated, and Caleb dropped them off at Cooper's when he picked up the extra powder and ball.

When Caleb was in Austin he stopped off at the Bullock Hotel, and in addition to the first letter from Wanda, there was also a letter from Jack Hays. Wanda had arrived safely in New Orleans, after a long and exhausting stagecoach ride. She was glad she had not waited until she was further along in her pregnancy to make the trip. She was living at her Cousin Amelia's house and had secured a position as governess and teacher for a wealthy planter's children. Even though it was unnecessary for her to work, she found the job stimulating, and thought it would make the time until the baby was due pass much faster. Besides, the planter had a wonderful private library, and she could spend much of her time continuing her own education. She told Caleb not to worry, and that she would write again soon. She also reminded him to write to her. He wrote a short return letter and mailed it that same day, saying he would write again as soon as Pedro's wedding was over.

The letter from Jack Hays was also interesting. As Caleb expected, Hays had been elected sheriff of San Francisco County. He had run as an independent candidate against the Democratic nominee, "Colonel" J. J. Bryant, a gambler who lavishly spent fifty thousand dollars on barroom food and drink during the campaign. On Election Day Bryant staged an impressive parade in the main plaza, but as soon as the parade was over Hays rode in on a black stallion and put on a daring display of horsemanship. After that the citizens of San Francisco rushed to the polls to vote for the famed Texas Ranger.

As sheriff, Jack came to know many of the prominent citizens well. One of them, Luis Peralta, was the recipient of a huge Spanish land grant. Peralta offered to sell Hays a beautiful, oak-covered tract of land across the bay from San Francisco for ten thousand dollars, and Jack wanted to know if Caleb was interested in purchasing a quarter of it. He was sure that sooner or later the land would be worth a small fortune, and he wanted Caleb in on the deal.

The next part of the letter focused Caleb's attention. Hays had easily located Ned and Mike Pate. They were now two of the wealthiest men in the Bay area, having laid claim to a rich gold mine under some curious circumstances. They lived in a mansion on a hill overlooking the bay in the wealthiest section of San Francisco. You might know swine like that would fall into it, Caleb thought. Maybe now that they were rich, the Pates would forget about him and go their own way. He quickly dismissed that idea. Rich or poor, they would remain a threat to him and his family until they were dead.

Hays had also run into Frost, the old white-haired mountain man who had assisted Caleb and Bigfoot in their pursuit of Ned and Mike Pate's brothers on the Santa Fe Trail. The old man had also discovered gold, and although apparently not as rich as the Pates, he was doing quite well. Caleb wrote a return letter to Hays and mailed it along with a letter of credit from Cooper's Emporium for twenty-five hundred dollars. In the letter he sent his best regards to Frost, thanked Jack for the investment opportunity, and asked him to continue monitoring the Pate's activities.

Pedro and Caleb were sitting their horses on the high ridge that overlooked the hacienda. The late afternoon was bright and clear, and the central square was swarming with people, everyone busy with last minute preparations for the upcoming wedding. Veronica's father and the remainder of her family had arrived the day prior, and finding beds for everyone had put Lucinda in a whirl. Most of the guests would not start arriving until early tomorrow afternoon. The wedding was scheduled for five o'clock, and it would be followed by a huge fandango with plenty of food and drink, a fair-sized group of local musicians, and dancing late into the night. All the ranchers in the area were invited, as were the local politicians like Senator Jenkins and Representative Coleman. Richard Bullock would attend, and Bigfoot, Pell Pellham, and Ben and Henry McCulloch were coming up from San Antonio. Even Governor Bell and United States Senator Sam Houston, on one of his rare trips back to Austin, would attend.

"How did things go in Austin?" Pedro asked.

"Real fine," Caleb replied. "I got a letter from Jack Hays. He was elected sheriff of San Francisco."

Pedro smiled. "That does not surprise me. He will be a fine sheriff."

"No doubt about it," Caleb agreed. "He also found Ned and Mike Pate out there. If you can believe this, they found gold and they're now two of the richest men in San Francisco."

At the mention of the Pates, a scowl of hatred wiped the smile from Pedro's face. "Do you expect trouble?"

Caleb sighed. "The money might keep 'em busy for awhile, but as long as they're alive, we can never let our guard down. Jack said he'd keep an eye on 'em, though."

"If you don't mind," said Pedro, "I would just as soon change the subject. When will the company make its first patrol?"

"We'll be headin' out bright and early Monday mornin'," Caleb replied. "Are you sorry you're not ridin' with us?"

"In a way," Pedro stated honestly, "but I thought it over carefully. I guess I'm more my father's son than I realized. I'll never be a skilled craftsman like him, but I love running the ranch, and he's letting me take more responsibility every day. The feeling of excitement isn't there, but the feeling of accomplishment certainly is. Do you understand what I mean?"

"Sure I do. Lucinda once asked me why I don't feel that way, and I couldn't explain it to her. I love the ranch. Its part of me, but the feelin' I get when I Ranger is in my blood. I'm just happy you're here to take over from Felix, so I can still have both." Caleb looked closely at Pedro. "I remember you askin' me on the day before my weddin' if I was gettin' cold feet. What about you?"

Pedro shook his head. "No, I'm ready, but I am glad you will be standing beside me on that platform." Just as he had done for Caleb and Lucinda's wedding, Felix built a platform beside the well in the courtyard of the hacienda, so that all the guests would have a good view of the ceremony. "Our families have been joined for a long time, haven't they, Caleb?"

"For quite a spell alright," Caleb agreed. "I was only sixteen when I first met Felix, and I was just thinkin' the other day that I'll soon be thirty." The sun hanging low on the western horizon cast its dying rays up into a bank of towering clouds, creating spectacular pillars of fire that climbed high into the sky. "We best be gettin' back to the hacienda before dark. Lucinda and Veronica got a big family supper planned, and if we're late there're liable to skin us alive."

Laughing, Caleb and Pedro coaxed their mounts into a trot and headed back down the ridge toward corral at the east end of the central square.

The wedding was a grand success. Caleb thought Pedro was going to pass out when he saw the lovely Veronica begin the walk with her father down the long aisle created by the rows of guests. Veronica was a stunning bride, and Caleb hoped she and Pedro would be as happy as he and Lucinda were. As best man, Caleb had the privilege of making a toast to the newly married couple after they cut the beautiful cake that Consuela had baked for them.

"To Veronica and Pedro," Caleb toasted as he raised his wine glass high, "may their marriage be one of beauty, friendship, and most of all love." Caleb and the guests drank, and they all cheered the young couple's happiness.

Pedro and Veronica received many wonderful wedding gifts, but Caleb waited until everyone else had presented theirs before he stepped up to the long table. Reaching into the pocket of the new suit jacket Lucinda had insisted he wear, he pulled out a folded paper.

"Pedro, I've always been proud that Felix is my partner in the Rockin' M, but from this day forward, you are also officially my partner. Here is a deed for twenty-five percent of the ranch in your name to go with the twenty-five percent your father owns." From now on we split right down the middle. Caleb handed Pedro the deed and Veronica proudly looked upon her husband, a new partner in such a huge and prosperous rancho.

The party lasted until near dawn, and Caleb spent much of the evening talking politics with Governor Bell, Senator Houston, and Felix Vaca. For privacy they made their way to the orderly room in the Ranger barracks. The Rangers were all at the party having a good time dancing and tipping a jug every now and then, although they all knew better than to get drunk and cause a disturbance. Caleb had threatened them with ouster from the company, if their conduct became too rowdy.

Governor Bell took a sip of his wine. "Your hacienda is magnificent, Caleb. I've never understood why most Texans refuse to use adobe for building their homes. Instead we insist on chopping down trees and building log cabins that are stifling in the summer and freezing in the winter. Even this barracks is an impressive structure, and also evidence of your commitment to the defense of the frontier?"

Caleb raised his glass to Felix. "My partner here designed and built the hacienda and all the other buildings that make up the central square, includin' this barracks. Without him, I'd most likely be livin' dirt poor in a little cabin down by the river. Felix is the one who said to use adobe and he was right. Most people around here think anything Mexican can't be good, even if the *Tejanos* were livin' here and adaptin' to Texas long before us Anglos came along."

"It is shameful the way many of the Anglos feel about the *Tejanos*," Governor Bell agreed. "It's a carry over from the war, though, and I'm afraid it won't go away any time soon. Have you received any grief from the ranchers around here about the number of *Tejanos* you and Felix employ?"

"Many of the men who work on the ranch are family, as well as employees, Governor," said Caleb. "They're related to me by marriage. Even the ones who ain't related are loyal to a man. To answer your question, I've heard grumbling and complaints before, but the Rockin' M belongs to me and Felix, and now to Pedro, and we'll keep on runnin' it the way it pleases us, grumblin' be damned!"

"Here, here," agreed Sam Houston as he raised his glass of whiskey in a salute before draining it and pouring himself another, "I only wish the people in Texas had the same live and let live attitude toward the Indians. The United States government has been trying to get Texas to establish reservations here ever since the war. I met with Governor Bell about it only yesterday."

"What Indians are you talkin' about?" asked Caleb. "There ain't no way in hell you're gonna put the Comanches on a reservation unless you trounce 'em good first."

"That's exactly what I told him," said Governor Bell.

"You may be right," said Houston. "The United States has never been forced to deal with Indians quite like the Comanches. What's left of the Tonkawas and Wichitas, though, and a few others are bein' squeezed between the expandin' frontier and the Comancheria. They desperately need a place of their own where they can live in peace."

"There's room for compromise on that point," said Bell. "In fact, the legislature has been discussing the establishment of just such a reservation."

"I wouldn't necessarily be against that either," said Caleb, "but who would operate it, the army?"

"The United States government would appoint a civilian Indian agent to manage the reservation," Houston replied. "Certainly the army would be used to protect the Indians and keep the peace, though."

"That's another thing I wanted to talk to you about, Senator," added Caleb. "Ever since the war, the army has been charged with protectin' the frontier, and they've done a poor job at best. When is somebody in Washington gonna understand that infantry can never hope to deal with horse warriors like the Comanches? The army has set up a few widely scattered frontier forts, but the Comanche war parties ride right past 'em to attack the settlers. And when I did manage to get out there with my volunteers, the army did nothin' but get in our way."

Houston sighed. "The question of the army using cavalry is one of cost, and right now, in spite of my efforts, the United States Congress is unwilling to spend more money on frontier defense. However, no matter what the situation, there's bound to be an ongoing conflict between the army and the Rangers. They have two different missions. The army is there to keep the peace, and the Rangers want to punish the Comanches and drive them back from the frontier."

"You're damn right we do!" Caleb agreed. "There ain't no peace to keep with the Comanches, Senator, and the sooner the army realizes that the better. My company leaves on our first patrol Monday mornin', and I aim to shoot the livin' hell out of every damn Comanche I see raidin' the settlements—army or no army—unless Governor Bell tells me different."

The Governor nodded his approval. "I'm sorry, Senator Houston, but until the situation we face changes or the army does its job, that's exactly what I expect my Rangers to do."

PART III

Chapter 16

McAdams' Rangers rode out of the Rocking M on their first patrol well before sunup the following Monday morning. When they reached the foot of Congress Avenue, Lieutenant Daggett led the Lipan scout Juaquin, and the remainder of First Platoon, up the hill, around the capital, and north out of town toward the San Gabriel River. From the San Gabriel, First Platoon would continue north until they reached the Lampasas River, and then follow the Lampasas northwest until they reached its headwaters somewhere near Indian Gap. The Comanches often used the gap that ran between the Lampasas and the Colorado Rivers to penetrate the rugged hill country northwest of Austin and raid the settlements. If First Platoon did not encounter any trouble by the time they reached Indian Gap, they would swing southwest until they reached the Colorado River, and then follow it back to Austin.

Caleb led the Lipan scout Chako and the remainder of Second Platoon to the Colorado River ferry. Two trips were required to cross the entire platoon, but when they were all safely across, Caleb ordered them to mount and led the platoon west toward the falls on the Pedernales River. The Rangers rode in a long, single file column with Sergeant Jessup in the rear, and Chako riding far ahead. The plan was to spend the night at the falls, and then follow the river west to the German settlement of Fredericksburg. The new army post of Fort Martin Scott was only a mile to the southeast of the settlement, near the headwaters of the Pedernales, and Caleb planned to stop there first and see if the army had had any recent problems with the Comanches.

Evening was approaching when Caleb spotted Chako riding back to meet the column from the narrow trail that led down to the falls. The heat of the late August day was still oppressive, and from the high ridge above the river, shimmering heat waves rose off the surrounding hillsides. The panoramic view of the river valley that stretched out far to the west in cool shades of green and blue was a sharp contrast to the summer-browned hills.

Signaling for a halt, Caleb called Sergeant Jessup forward. "Did you see any sign?" Caleb asked Chako in English when the Lipan reined in. Jessup and most of the other Anglos in the platoon could only speak a little Spanish, so Caleb wanted Chako to improve his English.

"No sign for many days at falling water," Chako replied.

Caleb nodded. "That sounds good. Chako, I want you to ford the river and ride north and west for a few miles to make sure the area is clear. We'll cross behind you and set up camp a mile above the falls." Waiting until Chako had disappeared over the ridge heading for the river, Caleb turned to Jessup. "It's not wise to camp too close to the falls, Sergeant. The water can cover up the night sounds that might warn us of trouble. Take your place at the end of the column and let's move out."

A few minutes later the Rangers reached the point where the trail dropped over the ridge and twisted its way down to the river. Caleb sat back in the saddle, letting Nasty slowly pick his way back and forth down a series of narrow switchbacks. When the Rangers reached the river, the water below the falls was summer-time low, and it muttered and gurgled to them as it splashed its way over and around descending shelves of limestone rock worn smooth by countless rainy seasons. The hooves of the Rangers' horses hardly got wet as they forded the shallow river and climbed the far bank.

Within the hour, the Rangers reached a campsite Caleb found suitable. "Sergeant Jessup, get two sentries posted on the ridge above the river. Let the men have a small fire to cook their bacon and beans, but make damn sure they use dry driftwood. I want the fire out before the sun goes down."

"Do we keep two guards on each shift all night, Captain?" asked Jessup.

"That's right; one with the horses and one on the far side of the camp. I want the horses hobbled in some good graze, too. I'll be damned if we're left afoot on our first patrol."

"I'll see it gets done, sir," said Sergeant Jessup before calling the men together to pass on Caleb's orders.

After a peaceful night, the Rangers were back in the saddle before sunup. Toward late afternoon, they rode into Fort Martin Scott. The buildings that made up the fort were laid out in the shape of a letter U with the headquarters at the base. The headquarters building was constructed of local limestone in the German manner. The left leg of the U was formed by a long stone barracks yet to be roofed, a stable, a good sized corral with a few horses and several dozen army mules, and a log building in the beginning stage of construction. The right leg of the U was formed by a low log building that served as the fort's officer quarters, another log building under construction, and four long rows of tents. Fort Martin Scott was manned by Company C of the Fifth U. S. Infantry and Company H of the Second U. S. Dragoons.

Caleb halted the Rangers at the flag pole in front of the headquarters building and ordered them to dismount. Reaching into his saddle bag, he took out a waterproof pouch. "Sergeant Jessup, come with me. Don't expect a warm welcome. Just grin and bear it no matter what the army has to say." Relations between volunteer Ranger outfits and the army were poor at best, but Caleb was hoping his authorization from the legislature would ease some of the strain. "Corporal Perez, take care of our horses and keep the men here until we get back."

Two guards from the Fifth Infantry were posted in front of the entrance to the headquarters building. They allowed Caleb and Jessup to enter when Caleb informed them they were Texas Rangers who wanted to speak with the commanding officer. The main door led to an orderly room with two desks. The company clerk sat behind one desk working on a stack of paperwork, and behind the other sat a grizzled-looking sergeant.

The sergeant came to his feet when Caleb and Jessup approached his desk. "Can I help you," he said in a friendly voice.

Caleb reached into the pouch and pulled out his authorization from the legislature, handing it to the sergeant. "My name is Captain McAdams, Sergeant, and this is Sergeant Jessup. As you can see from the authorization I just handed you, we're Texas Rangers from Austin. We'd like to speak with your commanding officer."

The Sergeant glanced at the authorization. "Wait here," he said in a tone of voice that was considerably different than the one he had used to greet them. "I'll be right back." Knocking on a door to his rear, he entered without being recognized and returned a moment later. "Go on in, Major Burns will see you."

Caleb led the way through the door, he and Jessup stopping in front of a desk that was much larger than the desks in the orderly room. Four straight back chairs were arrayed in front of

the desk, but the major did not offer them a seat. He had graying hair with bushy side whiskers, and a balding spot on the top
of his head. Ignoring them, he continued to read from a document before signing it and setting it aside. Finally he looked up.
"What can I do for you gentlemen?" The way he said "gentlemen" made it sound like a dirty word.

"Major, my name is Captain McAdams and this is Sergeant
Jessup. We're Texas Rangers." The major made a rude come on
motion with his hand, as if to say get on with it and quit wasting
my valuable time. Despite the hopes he had for better relations,
Caleb could see that being polite would get him nowhere. "Since
my company is authorized by the Texas legislature, we'll be in
the field on a regular basis from now on. I thought it would be
best to touch base with the army, so we might be able to work
together."

The Major cleared his throat. "I can assure you the army
is not interested in cooperating with irregulars like the Texas
Rangers, especially in this area of operations. Are you aware
that the German settlers in Fredericksburg have signed a peace
treaty with the Comanche Nation? The last thing they need is for
your Rangers to foul things up. I have a platoon of Dragoons on
patrol northwest of here right now. Please don't interfere with
their efforts."

Caleb jumped into the conversation before the major could
continue. "As usual, Major, I don't suppose the efforts of your
"mule-riders" will come to much. Unfortunately, I can see this
visit was a pure waste of time, but for your information, all the
settlers in this area ain't protected by that treaty you just mentioned. They've been burned out, scalped, and murdered ever
since the war ended, and the army hasn't done a damn thing
about it. The Comanches have driven the frontier back a hundred
miles while you blue coats sat on your thumbs and did nothin'.
Well, my Rangers are in the field now, Major, and they're here
to stay, whether you like it or not. And we'll, by God, do the job

we've been ordered to do, treaty or no treaty." Caleb turned and stormed out before the flustered Major could respond; Jessup, doing his best to stifle a laugh, quickly followed.

When the Rangers were mounted and heading for the settlement of Fredericksburg, Sergeant Jessup looked over at Caleb and grinned. "Well, sir, you handled that well; especially the way you kept from gettin' angry."

Scowling at first, Caleb finely relented and chuckled at himself. "I hope our meetin' with the settlers in Fredericksburg goes a little better. Let's pick up the pace and make sure we get there before sundown."

The well-organized German settlement of Fredericksburg, located on the upper reaches of the Pedernales River a mile northwest of Fort Martin Scott, was an impressive sight. Most of the town's buildings were constructed of local limestone, not primitive log structures like other Texas settlements. Caleb halted the patrol in front of the general store owned by the town's founder, John Meusebach, formerly Baron Otfried von Meusebach, before he had renounced his royal title on the ship from Germany to Texas. Dismounting, Caleb and Jessup tied their reins to the hitching rail, walked up the stone steps to the porch, and entered the store.

Meusebach was standing behind the counter and greeted them with a smile. "Welcome to my store, gentlemen, what can I do for you?"

The town founder was a tall, stately man in his middle forties with dark eyes set under bushy eyebrows and a high forehead. His hair, mustache, and beard were well-trimmed. Meusebach was instrumental in the signing of a peace treaty between the German settlers and the Comanches that continued to be honored by both sides. Jack Hays once told Caleb the former Baron accomplished the feat by presenting the German settlers to the

Comanches as a people separate from their sworn enemies, the Texans and Mexicans. Caleb thought that was a pretty clever idea.

"Evenin' Mr. Meusebach," said Caleb as he removed his sombrero. "I'm Captain McAdams and this is Sergeant Jessup. We're part of a company of Texas Rangers recently authorized by the legislature to patrol the frontier." A frown replaced the smile on Meusebach's face, but he did not interrupt. "Since we were out this way I wanted to stop by and tell you we'll be runnin' regular patrols around here from now on. We'll do our best not to interfere with your treaty, but not all the settlers around here come under its protection. If a war party attacks any of them, it's our duty to take action. Otherwise, we'll leave the Comanches be, as long as they're dealin' with y'all in a friendly manner."

The smile came back to Meusebach's face. "That's a much more reasonable approach than the Rangers have followed in the past, Captain McAdams. Under the terms of our treaty, we have had five years of peaceful relations with the Comanches. If your Rangers were to attack them when they came in peace to deal solely with us, the peace would be shattered. As long as you agree not to do that, your Rangers will be welcome here."

Caleb stuck out his hand and shook on the agreement. "It was nice to meet you, Mr. Meusenbach. We'll be campin' north of town for the night and headin' to the Llano River and Fort Mason in the mornin'. Let me know if the Rangers can ever do anything for you or Fredericksburg."

Late the following morning, the Rangers rode up to the west face of Enchanted Rock. Caleb called a halt and the men dismounted to rest and water their horses at a steam that meandered not far from the Rock's base. Comanche sign was everywhere, although none of it appeared to be recent. Rising to a staggering height of five hundred feet and covering some six hundred acres, the solid dome of granite that made up Enchanted Rock was much more than an ordinary hill. Said to be the site of human sacrifice in the ancient past, some tribes like the Comanches used the Rock as a rallying point or a site for important ceremonies, and other tribes feared to set foot on it. However, all Indians held the site in awe and reverence.

Once the horses were watered, Caleb was ready to give the order to mount up, when Chako splashed across the small, spring-fed stream and reined in. "Comanches camp to the east last night."

"How many," asked Caleb as Sergeant Jessup joined him?

Chako held up nine fingers. "Comanches have many hoses and two captures. One is woman and one is small child. They ride there with sun." He pointed north.

Caleb turned to Jessup. "If the Comanches pulled out at dawn, they got at least a six hour head start on us. There's another German settlement about twenty miles north of here on the Llano River called Castell. They may be headed there to trade some horses. If so, I don't think they'll push too hard."

"I agree," said Jessup. "That patrol of dragoons sure as hell ain't anywhere around here, so the bastards got no reason to think they're bein' followed."

"We best move then, instead of sittin' around here burnin' daylight," Caleb replied. "Chako, get as close to the Comanches as you can without them spottin' you. If they hole up anywhere get back to us quick as you can. We'll push hard, but I refuse to kill the horses. I got a feelin' we'll need 'em soon enough."

The chase was on, and with the fate of the captives at stake, Caleb felt the tension in the patrol mount as the Rangers rode north at a steady lope. Every so often they would slow the horses to a walk, and then a trot, before once again breaking back into a steady, ground-eating lope. The Rangers covered nearly twenty miles and were nearing the little settlement of Castell when they splashed across a shallow stream and met up with Chako.

Caleb called for a halt and reined up in front of the Lipan scout. Dismounting, he called for the men to follow suit. "Sergeant Jessup, we'll rest the horses here for a few minutes. Make sure they're watered once they cool down."

"You heard the man," said Jessup. "Walk the animals around for a few minutes and then water 'em. Corporal Perez, get somebody to take care of the Captain's horse and mine." He joined Caleb and Chako.

"Are the Comanches close, Chako?" asked Caleb.

"No close now," replied the Lipan. "Some warriors guard captures." He held up two fingers. "Others cross river to white village with horses. They trade horses, come take captures."

"Them bastards didn't want the Germans to know they been raidin' and takin' prisoners," added Jessup.

Caleb nodded in agreement. "How long ago did the Comanches pull out?"

"Leave not long. Go to spring there." Chako pointed northeast. "Not far. Maybe camp there tonight."

Caleb thought for a moment. "He means Valley Springs, Sergeant; a spring-fed waterhole about twelve miles from here." Chako nodded his head in agreement. "Sergeant Jessup, we're gonna ride into Castell after we give the horses a few minutes to rest and make damn sure none of them Comanches stayed in town. Chako, once you find the Comanche camp head back this way. When we're done in town we'll be ridin' to meet up with you."

"I find camp," said Chako. "Be back damn quick!"

The little settlement of Castell and the surrounding area was originally part of the old Fisher-Miller land grant and was settled mostly by Germans. Castell was named for Count Carl Frederick Castell, and the site for the settlement, on the north bank of the Llano, had been selected by John Meusebach. The one street, lined with log and limestone buildings that made up the settlement, was quiet, and the late-afternoon shadows were beginning to lengthen, when the Rangers splashed across the shallow ford on the Llano River and rode into town.

Caleb halted the platoon, drew his Colt, and fired two quick shots in the air. As expected, the gunfire drew an instant crowd of angry Castell citizens, shouting among themselves and wondering what was going on.

"My name's Captain McAdams and we're Texas Rangers!" Caleb shouted, quieting the angry buzz of the town folk. "Seven Comanches rode into town a while back to trade some horses. Are any of 'em still here?"

"What makes you think we'd tell you if they were," yelled out a self-appointed spokesman. "The Comanches are our friends." Many of the others gathered round agreed with the man's sentiments.

"What if I was to tell you your friends have been raidin' Texas settlements south of here to get them horses," replied Caleb, "most likely scalpin' and murderin' too."

"How would you know that?" asked the spokesman.

"That's the way they usually operate," Caleb answered, "but in this case, we tracked 'em straight here. While seven of 'em were busy horse tradin' with you, two more were waitin' out in the brush holdin' their prisoners; some poor woman and her child. I'm not sure we can get the prisoners back, but we're damn well gonna try. We need your help."

Knowing how she would have felt had it been her or her own child, one of the women in the crowd stepped forward. "They were here alright, Captain, but they left more than an hour ago, all of them."

Caleb took off his sombrero to the lady. "Many thanks, ma'am, and I know the woman and child them Comanches are holdin' would bless you too." Raising his voice once again, Caleb spoke to the entire crowd. "I know y'all have a treaty with the Comanches, and me and my Rangers intend to respect it if they come here in peace. But takin' captives ain't peaceable, and we aim to do what's necessary to get 'em back." Jamming the sombrero back down over his curly red hair, he reined Nasty around and shouted, "Let's ride!" The Rangers followed him out of town at a lope.

The deep ebony of the darkness, brought on by the lack of a moon, was thick enough to cut with a knife, and the Rangers were forced to slow their pursuit to a patient walk. It was only an hour before dawn when they finally met up with Chako. Not knowing how far the Comanches were, or even if the scout had found them, Caleb called everyone in close, so they could hear what was said. He spoke quietly. "Did you find the camp, Chako?"

"Chako find," said the Lipan. "Comanches camp at spring like you say. Not far, maybe two miles."

"Is the camp guarded?" asked Caleb.

"Comanches sleep with horses," Chako replied. "No guard camp. No see captures."

The darkness was so complete Caleb had difficulty making out the faces of the men sitting their horses next to him. "Sergeant Jessup?"

"Right here, Captain," Jessup replied not far off from Caleb's left.

"Move the men in closer if you can." Once everyone had crowded in tight, Caleb began. "We're gonna have to be damn careful not to roust the Comanches by stumblin' around in the dark. The wind's out of the north, so Chako will lead us from here single file until we're as close as we can get to the south side of the Comanche camp. Keep it closed up or you'll get lost in the dark. I'll ride right behind Chako and Sergeant Jessup will bring up the rear. When Chako halts and turns his horse to face the camp, I'll halt and turn my horse, too. When I do, the man next to me will follow suit, and then the next man, all the way down the line, until Sergeant Jessup halts and turns his mount. When Sergeant Jessup is ready, he'll draw his Colt, and then the next man will draw his, and then the next man, until it gets all the way back up to me. As soon as I see there's enough light, I'll start forward at a walk. We all advance together on line until I open fire. Then we charge straight through the camp. Be sure and watch for the captives. Does anybody have any questions?" Caleb repeated the plan to Chako in Spanish to make sure he understood his role. "Okay Rangers, let's move out."

Taking his time, Chako allowed his little paint to pick its way through the moonless night, until he was sure the column of Rangers was in the exact position Red Hair wanted them. Only the soft jingle of harness and the muted squeak of saddle leather disturbed the deathly silence of the early morning. Halting, Chako turned his horse to face the Comanche camp that still remained invisible in the inky darkness. Caleb halted Nasty and gently reined him in the same direction. Each Ranger down the line followed suit, until Sergeant Jessup halted and turned his horse to face the camp. Jessup then drew his Colt and each Ranger back up the line followed suit, until Caleb and Chako drew theirs.

All was in readiness. Within a few silent minutes, the deep shadows began to fade and objects slowly took shape in the morning twilight that arrives well before the sun. The shadowy outlines of the trees and bushes that grew in abundance near the spring came first, then the faint outline of a horse as it raised its head from grazing and looked the Rangers' way. As the sky lightened even more, Caleb was momentarily grateful for the brisk north wind, until one of the Rangers' horses nickered at the strong Comanche scent. He immediately started Nasty forward and the line moved forward with him in fits and starts like a flag gently fluttering in a light breeze.

Thirty yards in front of Caleb, a Comanche rose from his sleeping robe. Without any hesitation, the big Ranger leveled the long barrel of his Colt Dragoon and fired. The ball plowed into the warrior's shoulder, spinning him off his feet. All hell broke loose with the first shot, as Caleb dug his heels into Nasty's ribs.

Joining Caleb in the assault, Chako and the Rangers charged the Comanche camp with Colts blazing. Caleb quickly finished off the warrior he had wounded and looked for his next target. Off to his left, Jessup nearly rode a running warrior down, before he put a ball between the Comanche's shoulder blades at close range, slamming him to his face. A Comanche notched an arrow and drew it back in his short bow as Chako charged. Screaming his war cry, the Lipan fired twice, the first shot splintering the bow and the second knocking the warrior off his feet. Chako was instantly off his horse knife in hand, taking his victim's scalp and holding the bloody trophy high.

Six members of the war party were gunned down without mercy in the initial fusillade, but three warriors managed to gain the backs of their ponies in the middle of an avalanche of hot lead. One of the warriors grabbed the panicked woman captive by her long hair as she ran for the safety of the Rangers and slit her throat. The cruel act cost the Comanche his life as he was hit by several shots that flung his body off the back of the pony and danced it around like a puppet, the heavy caliber balls striking him again and again. Everyone emptied their Colts at the two remaining warriors as they fled the camp, but the range was too great and the Comanches rode away unharmed.

A few Rangers wanted to follow the warriors who escaped, but Caleb would have none of it. "Let 'em go!" he yelled. "They got fresh horses and we don't. We'd be wastin' our time. They'll spread the word that the Rangers are back in the field. Make sure the warriors we hit are dead and search the camp for the captives." Caleb had not seen the woman's death.

Sergeant Jessup reined in beside Caleb. "The woman's dead, Captain. I saw a Comanche slit her throat before a bunch of us shot him."

"Over here, sir!" They heard one of the Rangers yell out.

When Caleb and Jessup rode over to see what the Ranger wanted, he was down on his knees with tears in his eyes. The body of a little girl was in his arms. By the look of it, she had been brutally beaten to death long before the attack. Yet another atrocity committed in this seemingly endless war, thought Caleb.

"Bury the woman with the child," ordered Caleb. "She was most likely the little girl's mother." A shot rang out, and then another, Rangers finishing off wounded Comanches. Caleb shook his head at the absurdity of it all. "Gather up any firearms you find and burn the rest of the weapons. Let the Comanche bodies lay where they fell. The vultures and coyotes will soon take care of 'em."

The following week Caleb was sitting in the orderly room with Sergeant Jessup working on his report to the governor, when he heard some horses ride up to the barracks and rein in. A quick glace out the window told him that the First Platoon had returned from their patrol.

"Sergeant White, see about chow," said Lieutenant Daggett, "but make sure the men take care of the horses and clean their weapons and equipment before they eat." A few minutes later, Eph walked into the orderly room.

"How'd it go, Eph?" Caleb asked.

Eph removed his sombrero and tossed it onto a peg in the wall. "Not bad," he replied as he untied his red bandana and mopped the sweat off his face and neck. Taking a dipper full of water from the oak bucket that sat on the table, he quickly gulped it down and refilled the dipper. "We ran into a small bunch up near Indian Gap; seven of 'em. They weren't painted up yet, but I expect they were on their way to do a little mischief." He took another drink from the dipper. "We killed one of 'em and wounded two others. It was lucky for the Comanches that we bumped into each other by accident. If we'd seen 'em comin', we would've killed every damn one of 'em."

"Put it all down on paper, so I can add it to my report for the governor," said Caleb. He then gave Eph a brief rundown of Second Platoon's action at Valley Spring and the unsuccessful meeting with the army at Fort Martin Scott. "I'll be takin' Second Platoon out again day after tomorrow. We'll ride up the Brazos. Dependin' on how things go, I'm plannin' on stoppin' off at Fort Belknap and Fort Phantom Hill. It's about seventy-five miles southwest of Belknap on the Clear Fork of the Brazos. Maybe their Commanding Officers will be friendlier. Next time you go out stop off at Fort Mason, Fort McKavitt, and Fort Chadbourne." Caleb smiled. "We wouldn't want the army to complain to the governor that the Rangers are refusin' to cooperate, would we?"

Chapter 17

Fall stretched into winter, and even though the Rangers
continued to conduct regular patrols, the Comanches had gone
to ground for the cold months as usual and things were quiet.
Relations with the army had not improved, but Caleb was still
hopeful that Lieutenant Colonel Abercrombie the Commanding
Officer at Fort Phantom Hill, and Captain Stephenson, commanding at Fort Belknap would eventually be willing to cooperate with the Rangers on a limited basis. Selling whiskey and
weapons to the Indians was a problem the army had to deal with,
and the mobility of the Rangers might help them put a stop to
some Comancheros operating west of the Caprock on the upper
reaches of the Brazos.

Felix, Pedro, and Caleb were sitting at the table in the great
room one evening in early March of 1853, planning the next
cattle drive to New Orleans, scheduled to depart in late spring.
Since Caleb would be busy commanding the Rangers, Pedro
would act as the trail boss.

"How many head you plannin' on drivin' this time, Pedro?" Caleb asked.

"Counting the cattle we added when we bought the Meacham place, I should be able to put three to four thousand together. I wrote Josh Tanner, and he stands by the price of twenty-five dollars a head. With that much at stake, I want to drive as many as we can."

"I agree," said Felix. "We must strike while the iron is hot and not miss out on such an opportunity. Should bad times come the ranch would be in a position to operate for several years on the cash we make from this drive alone."

"You're right about that, Felix," said Caleb. "With this silly secessionist talk I keep hearin', the New Orleans market might not always be there. In fact, I think we should make a trail drive every year for as long as we can, even if we have to buy some of the cattle on this end to make it worthwhile. There'd still be a handsome profit, if we paid no more 'n ten dollars a head. We might even be able to get some of the cattle on consignment."

Pedro smiled. "That is a good idea, Caleb." Pedro picked up one of the new metal pens, dipped it in the ink bottle, and did some quick calculations. If we paid ten dollars a head here for four thousand cattle and sold them for twenty-five dollars a head in New Orleans, the profit would be sixty thousand dollars.

Felix focused on Caleb's statement about secession. "Do you really think the south will try to secede from the Union, Caleb?"

Caleb nodded. "You're damn right I do! I'm still hopin' Texas won't go along with the states' rights people from the Deep South—so does Sam Houston by the way—but I ain't about to bet on it and neither is he. Even though I think the issue was settled years ago by President Jackson durin' the Nullification Crisis in South Carolina, we got a bunch of fanatics down here in Texas who still believe a state has the right to overrule any federal law they don't like."

Felix shook his head sadly. "What will happen if Texas does secede?"

I don't know, Felix," Caleb replied honestly. "There's always a possibility the North will let us go, but I don't think so. Like "Old Hickory" threatened, I think they'd rather fight to keep the Union together."

"Then we better begin to plan for such an occurrence," said Felix. "Pedro, bring home fifty thousand dollars in gold this time and have Josh Tanner deposit the remainder of the profit, and forty thousand of the money we made on the first drive, in three good Cincinnati banks. From now on, we deposit money in both the South and the North just in case."

"That's a damn good idea," Caleb agreed.

"How's Lucinda doin', Connie?" Caleb asked when the housekeeper scurried out of the bedroom with the stale sheets she had just replaced on Lucinda's bed.

Lucinda was due any time now, and Consuela and the other women on the ranch were bustling around in a flurry of constant activity. For one of the few times in his life Caleb felt absolutely helpless.

"I think it would be best if you fetched Doctor Laughton right away, Caleb," Connie said after a moment's hesitation. "I have delivered many babies, but Lucinda has already had one miscarriage. I am worried about her. The baby could come at any time."

That was all it took to put Caleb in motion. "Keep a close eye on her, Connie! It won't take me long." He was out the front door at a dead run and almost bowled Felix over. "Sorry, Felix," he yelled over his shoulder as he jumped down from the porch and continued to run for the corral. "I have to fetch Doc Laughton."

Caleb had Nasty saddled and on the river trail at a dead gallop in less than ten minutes, and he covered the distance to Bastrop in record time. Sliding the big Appaloosa to a crow-hopping stop in front of the cabin that served as Doctor Laughton's office, he leaped from the saddle and pounded on the door. "Doc, it's Caleb McAdams! Connie says Lucinda's havin' the baby and there might be a problem!"

Doctor Laughton opened the door. It was mid-morning and he was with a patient. "I'll be with you in a minute, Caleb. Get my buggy from the barn and harness the big roan gelding."

It took only a few minutes for Caleb to wrestle the big gelding into the harness and hitch him to the buggy. He had the rig out front waiting when Doctor Laughton walked out the door with his bag a few minutes later. "Let's go Doc," Caleb said his patience wearing thin, "time's a wastin'!"

"We'll make it just fine, young man," Laughton replied as Caleb helped him up into the buggy.

With practiced ease, Laughton wheeled the gelding around and snapped the whip next to his ear. The buggy's wheels threw up swirls of dust as it gained speed and pulled out onto the river trail, Laughton handling the reins expertly. In what was good time, in spite of Caleb's anxiety, the doctor was racing the buggy into the central square of the Rocking M and through the hacienda's gate, reining up in front of the porch along with Caleb. Felix and Pedro were standing on the porch to greet them, and Pedro helped the doctor out of the buggy.

"Go right in Doctor," said Felix. "The baby has not yet arrived and Consuela will be very glad to see you."

Caleb started to follow Laughton, but the doctor turned and faced him. "You stay out here, Caleb. We'll all be very busy in there, and you'll just get in the way." The doctor turned again and hurried through the door.

Time passed slowly and Caleb endlessly paced the length of the porch, not even stopping to eat. If not for the presence of Felix and Pedro, he would have grown frantic. "How'd you deal with this sort of thing when Maria had children, Felix? Not knowin' what's goin' on is about to drive me crazy."

"Everything will be fine, Caleb," Felix said in a soothing tone of voice. "These things take time. You must be patient."

Actually Maria's births had been quick and easy, and Felix was nearly frantic with worry himself, although he knew he had to hide it from Caleb. The young couple had waited so long for a child of their own. It would be terrible if the experience ended in tragic circumstances. A crowd made up of ranch people and many of Caleb's Rangers, sensing the drama of the situation, began to gather in a quiet vigil outside the hacienda's gate. Felix and Pedro helped Caleb entertain Ilse and Gretchin to make sure they did not feel left out by the birth, and it served to keep them all occupied. Another hour slowly dragged by and the sky was beginning to darken along with Caleb's spirits when they finally heard the cry of a baby. Caleb faced the door in expectation, wanting to hurry to Lucinda's side.

A few minutes later Doc Laughton walked out on the porch, wiping the blood from his hands and arms on a clean rag. "Lucinda and the baby are fine. It was an ordeal for her and she's weak from loss of blood, but with rest, she'll be herself again in no time. Go on in, Caleb. You have a fine son."

"I have a son!" Caleb yelled to the crowd at the gate as he shook hands with Felix and Pedro and whirled the girls around in his arms. "You have a new brother, ladies!"

The girls laughed at their father's happiness, and the crowd at the gate began to cheer loudly. Caleb practically floated across the great room and into their bedroom. Connie and Veronica were there, and Connie had just placed a little bundle wrapped in a blanket in the crook of Lucinda's arm.

Caleb stepped up to the bed and went down on one knee, taking Lucinda's free hand in his and pressing it to his lips. "My prayers were answered. You're safe and well, and Doc Laughton said the baby's gonna be fine."

Lucinda smiled, the exhaustion she felt apparent on her face. "Look at our handsome son, Caleb." She uncovered the baby's face. "Come girls," she said to Ilse and Gretchin who were standing wide-eyed in the doorway, "and see your little brother." The baby had reddish brown hair that he got from both parents, curls from his father, and big brown eyes from his mother. "He is handsome like his father. We shall name him Hammond after his grandfather."

Caleb filled the bedroom with his smile.

As usual, Governor Bell was busy reading when his secretary showed Caleb into the office. "Please file this, Nathan," Bell said to his secretary as he handed him the paperwork he was reading before reaching out for Caleb's hand. "It's good to see you again, Caleb. Have a seat. Would you like a cup of coffee? This meetin' may be longer than usual."

"Yes, thank you Governor, I would," Caleb replied, wondering about Bell's remark, "with plenty of sugar."

Once the coffee was delivered and the friendly conversation, including congratulations and a discussion of Caleb's newborn son was over, Governor Bell got down to business. "Your Rangers have done a fine job so far with the limited resources I've been able to provide, and the pressure on the frontier has lessened somewhat. The Comanches aren't our only problem, though. I want your opinion on a meeting I had with Major Robert Neighbors, who was recently appointed Supervising Federal Agent for Texas Indian affairs, and a letter I received from the new United States Secretary of War, Jefferson Davis."

"I know Neighbors, but not real well," said Caleb. "He was a member of Jack Hays's Ranger Company, too. He was captured in 1842 along with the members of the District Court durin' General Woll's occupation of San Antonio and marched off to prison in Mexico. He's been a Texas Indian agent for a good while. Chief Old Owl adopted him into the Comanche tribe. What did he have to say?"

"Right now Major Neighbors is more concerned with what he refers to as 'the border remnants' of the Indian tribes in west central Texas like the Witchitas, Tonkawas, and the Lipans than he is with the Comanches. Like Sam Houston, he thinks these tribes are caught in 'limbo' between the line of our western settlements and the Comancheria. Our settlers have pushed the game—in numbers the Indians could live on—far beyond their lands, and none of theses tribes would dare venture too far out on the Comanches' range to hunt. Neighbors says they simply wander around on the fringes of the frontier, and they're usually hungry and in some cases actually starvin'. That's why, accordin' to him, they're forced to commit small depredations, like killin' cattle or horses for food. Not much of a choice between stealin' and starvin', is there, Caleb?"

"No sir, there ain't," Caleb replied, "and I agree with everything you've said so far. Even the Penataka Comanches are in bad shape from what I can gather. We've taken over most of their former range, and the only way they've made it through the last few winters is by eatin' their dogs and horses. A horse is a Comanche's most prized possession, Governor. If they've taken to eatin' 'em, the situation is gettin' to be damn desperate. What does Neighbors suggest we do?"

"Major Neighbors and Secretary Davis have come to the same conclusion—these tribes need a reservation. Accordin' to both men, if the tribes were on a reservation, they would have a defined territory. The army would not only be in a position to see that they were fed, but the soldiers would also be able to restrict the Indians to the reservation and take control of them if they strayed off it. Of course, because of our annexation, Texas is in a unique situation. Unlike other states, there are no Federal lands here, and if a reservation is to be established, the Texas legislature would have to set aside the necessary land. The newspapers might be leanin' in that direction, though, with their talk of the pitiable sight the tame Indians make. What do you think about all this, Caleb?"

"Most of it makes good sense, Governor. I agree that the tribes like the Tonkawas and Witchitas would stay on a reservation if they're fed, or taught to feed themselves. They already know some about farmin'. That would take care of both the occasional theft of livestock and the killin' of the Indians by vengeful Texans. I would add a couple things to what Neighbors and Davis suggest, though."

"Like what," asked Bell?

"First," added Caleb warming to the conversation, "the legislature will have to establish two reservations. The Penetakas will never live side-by-side with the Tonkaws and Witchitas, or any other tribe for that matter. They'd look at it as an opportunity to exterminate 'em once and for all. If there were two reservations some miles apart, it would be easier for the army to keep the tribes from fightin'."

Governor Bell smiled. "Neighbors mentioned that, but I rejected the idea on the basis of cost. However, if you both feel so strongly about it, I'll keep it under consideration. Is there anything else?"

Caleb smiled. "As long as the federal government is askin' us for somethin' that'll make their job easier, they can do us a favor in return. The army has got to get some cavalry out here if they're gonna do any good, sir. I realize it's more expensive to maintain cavalry than to man the forts with infantry, but a tribe as mobile as the Comanches can never be subdued, let alone controlled without 'em. We told the army that durin' the war with Mexico, and we told 'em when the war was over, but they refuse to listen. Maybe you can use this reservation request as a little leverage."

Governor Bell nodded his head as he added to the notes he had been taking during the meeting. "That sounds like a very sensible and reasonable request. I'll add it to the letter I'm preparin' for Secretary Davis. If anyone can do anything about the problem it's surely him. By the way, Neighbors mentioned another problem that's been a thorn in his side; white traders stirrin' up trouble by sellin' liquor and firearms to the Indians. There is no federal law against the trade, so the army has no authority to act within the confines of a sovereign state unless state law prohibits it. Unfortunately there is no such law in Texas, or likely to be one for that matter with the amount of campaign contributions that pour into the legislators coffers from the traders. There is one particularly bothersome trader on the upper Brazos some miles above Fort Belknap by the name of George Barnard. When you're up that way, look into it. See if there might be some way to discourage his trade." The Governor raised his eyebrows but said no more, and Caleb asked no questions. "I told you this would be a lengthy meetin'. Do you have any questions about what we've discussed?"

"Not right now, Governor." Caleb rose from his chair. "The company will be headin' for Fort Belknap within two weeks. Send a message if you need me before then."

Caleb stopped in to see Bullock before he went back to the ranch. He found the burly innkeeper behind the bar in the café. There were several customers having lunch at the bar and at the row of tables that stood along the windows facing Pecan Street.

Bullock smiled when he saw Caleb come in. "Howdy, Caleb, how's that new son of yours doin'?"

Caleb laughed. Bullock seldom had to be told anything. "He's three weeks old today, and already the spittin' image of his namesake, my father, Hammond."

"That sure as hell means he looks like you then," Bullock said with a chuckle. "You look more like your pa every day. How's Lucinda?"

"She couldn't be better, Mr. Bullock, and just as happy as can be. By the way, I plan on stoppin' off at Sam's on our next patrol. I'll be sure 'n give him your best." Bullock's brother,

Sam, owned and operated a small trading post north of Austin on the south bank of the Brazos River.

"Much obliged," said Bullock, "I ain't seen the varmint for quite a spell." Bullock slipped a letter from Wanda across the bar. "This came for you the other day. Excuse me; I got a customer in need."

Caleb opened the letter and read it rapidly. Incredibly, Wanda had delivered their baby the same day Lucinda birthed Hammond. He was a healthy boy with curly, reddish-blond hair from his father and mother and big blue eyes from his mother. Wanda named him Joshua after her father. Caleb had to chuckle at the similarities between the two boys—hair from both their father and mother, and eyes from their mothers. There was also a vast difference, and Caleb sobered as he began to ponder the situation. Hammond had a name and an inheritance that Joshua would never have, and he had a father. How could Caleb ever be the father that Josh would need to become a man?

Those thoughts brought him around to Wanda. Had she felt deserted and alone during her pregnancy and the birth of Josh? Who had been there to hold her hand and tell her they loved her the way he had been with Lucinda? The burden was, and still remained, entirely hers, and Caleb had no idea what to do about it. He asked Mr. Bullock if he could use the desk in the hotel's office and sat down to write Wanda a long letter telling her she was in his thoughts and how excited he was about their new son. What more could he do about the situation, and what more could she want of him? Only time would tell.

"Thanks for the wonderful breakfast, Connie," Caleb said as he rose from the table in the great room and kissed Lucinda and the girls. The last few days on the Rocking M had been hectic with the final preparations for the trail drive and the upcoming Ranger patrol underway. Both would pull out at sunup the following morning. "Lucinda, I'm gonna talk with Eph for a minute, and then ride out to the line camp to see how Pedro's doin'."

"Be back early if you can, and make sure to bring Pedro with you," said Lucinda. "Veronica and I are preparing a special supper."

"We'll be here before sundown," Caleb replied as he headed for the door.

Caleb was greeted with smiles and nods as he walked out the hacienda's big gate and headed across the central square, already bustling with activity. As usual, Felix was up well before dawn, working on the irrigation system he was installing along the river on the old Meacham place. Spring planting was also well underway, and women and children were heading for the fields. Caleb waved at Nacho. The big blacksmith was busy checking and replacing the shoes of the horses that would make up the remuda for the trail drive. Cutting through the barn saved a few steps, and Caleb headed for the barracks.

Some of the Rangers were finishing their breakfast at the table in the center of the bunkroom, and Eph, Terrell, and George were sitting at the table in the orderly room having a cup of coffee. Using his shirttail, Caleb picked up the pot from the top of the potbelly stove and poured himself a cup. He sat down at the table, spooned in an ample amount of sugar, and took a sip, smacking his lips in satisfaction. "Are we ready to pull out?" he asked. The entire company would be participating in this patrol.

Eph looked to Jessup and White, and they nodded for him to go ahead. "Nacho checked the shoes on all the horses and replaced the ones that needed it. The supplies are packed and ready to load on the packhorses. All weapons will be inspected this afternoon. Corporal Perez and Corporal Nelson checked the men's boots and clothing last week, and made sure every man has his rain slicker and a blanket."

"Sounds good to me," said Caleb. "After the weapons check, let the men relax and rest today. I'm still wonderin' what the hell we're gonna do about Barnard, other than shoot him, but that's always a possibility. Let me know if y'all come up with anything." Caleb finished his coffee and stood up. "I'm on my way to the line camp to see Pedro. I'll be back before sundown."

Pedro was checking the inventory in the supply wagon against a list Bo gave him, when Caleb rode up and dismounted. Bo would not be going on this drive or any other drive, if Connie had anything to say about it. Pedro hired a cook who Bo recommended, but until the man proved himself reliable, everything he did would be double checked carefully.

"Well, trail boss, you gonna make us a pile of money this trip?" Caleb kidded.

Pedro smiled as he jumped down from the wagon. "I'm only taking fifteen prime horses, but we will be trailing close to four thousand longhorns. That is nearly a hundred thousand dollars on the hoof."

"Just do me a favor, brother, and don't risk your life for one longhorn, or the whole damn herd for that matter. We can always get some more cows, but I need you back here runnin' the ranch so I can Ranger." Caleb smiled. "You're not a bad brother-in-law either. Just remember to keep a good lookout for bandits and stay the hell out of saloons."

"You sound just like Padre," said Pedro.

"Good," Caleb replied with a smile. "Felix has always given me good advice, so it's best you listen to him. If you got everything ready here, let's get on back to the hacienda. The ladies are fixin' a special supper, and I promised Lucinda we'd be home early."

Chapter 18

Late in the afternoon of the third day on the trail, after fording the San Gabriel and Little Rivers, the Rangers rode into Sam Bullock's trading post and general store on the south bank of the Brazos. Sitting on a low bluff overlooking the river, the trading post looked more like a fortified blockhouse than a general store, with its sod-covered roof, loop-holed shutters, and reinforced oaken door that could be barred in case of Indian attack. Down closer to the river, where it could be covered with rifle fire from the windows of the trading post, stood a good sized, low-roofed barn and a big corral, additions that were new since Caleb's last visit nearly two years ago. Bill Thompson, the old man who worked for Sam, was standing at the corral when the Rangers rode up, and he swung the gate open.

"Much obliged, Bill," said Caleb as he led the mounted Rangers into the corral, swung down from the saddle, and began to rub the numbness out of his rear end. "Unsaddle your horses and give 'em a good rubdown, men. We'll water 'em later on, when they've cooled off some." Caleb unsaddled Nasty and hoisted his fancy Mexican saddle onto the top rail of the fence. Using his wool saddle blanket, he rubbed the big stallion down thoroughly then removed the bridle before tossing the blanket and the bridle on the fence beside his saddle. "Jessup, you and George find a good place to set up camp. Me and Lieutenant Daggett are gonna have a talk with Sam. Come on, Eph."

Bill swung the gate closed behind them and secured it before shaking Caleb's hand. "Good to see you again, Ranger. What brings you up this way with all these men?"

"This is my new company," Caleb replied. "We're on our way to Fort Belknap. Bill, this is Lieutenant Ephrain Daggett. Eph, this is Bill Thompson. He works for Sam." The two men shook hands and walked up to the trading post together.

Sam was standing behind the counter talking with a customer when they stepped through the reinforced door. "Two more came up missin' this afternoon. Me and Bill was gatherin' up the stock when we noticed they was gone."

"What did you lose now, Sam?" Caleb interrupted with a big smile.

"Why if it ain't Ranger McAdams," said Sam with a return smile. "How the hell are you? I was just talkin' about our missin' livestock. Not a lot, just an animal or two here and there. Two mules came up missin' this afternoon."

"Where were the critters when they were taken?" Caleb asked.

Sam shook his head. "In the pasture out back, I think, but don't worry about it now. You just got here."

"No trouble, Sam," said Caleb, "it's my job. I'll grab Chako and Juaquin, and take a quick look. By the way, this varmint is my lieutenant and good friend, Eph Daggett. Eph, meet Sam Bullock."

Caleb headed for the door while the men greeted each other. He found the Lipans just outside, leaning on the hitching rail waiting for him. "Come with me. Somebody stole my friend's mules this afternoon. Maybe we can pick up a trail."

They were more than half way around the perimeter of the big pasture that spread out behind the trading post when Juaquin found the tracks they were looking for. "One man, maybe one boy steal mules take west." They followed the tracks for ten minutes until Juaquin stopped and added, "they no ride."

When Caleb and the Lipans retuned to the trading post, the Rangers were sitting around tables eating venison stew with hot biscuits, fresh baked from Sam's big Dutch ovens. Caleb carried a couple bowls of stew and a few biscuits out to Chako and Juaquin, and then after filling his own bowl, joined Sam, Eph, George, and Terrell at a table.

"Did you find anything?" asked Sam around a big spoonful of stew.

"Fresh moccasin tracks," Caleb replied, "looked to be a man and a boy on foot. My curiosity's up now. I plan on followin' the trail in the mornin'. George, I want you to ride with me and the Lipans."

"Don't you want to take a few more men?" asked Eph as he scraped the bottom of his bowl with the big wooden spoon.

Caleb shook his head. "No, I don't think I'll need any more. We're just gonna have a look see, but Jessup, have the men ready just in case."

With the coming of first light, Caleb, George, and the Lipans were mounted and following the moccasin and mule tracks that led away from the pasture to the west. The tracks continued west for a few miles until they struck the North Fork of the Bosque River. From there, they followed the bank of the clear-running, shallow river to the northwest. Chako and Juaquin were riding ahead, and when Caleb saw them retuning, he called for George to rein in and wait for the Lipan scouts.

Chako did not have his usual excited look when he located his quarry. "No warriors," he said "only old men, squaws, and young. They starve, eat mule."

With a report like that Caleb did not know what to think. "How far is their camp?"

"Maybe two miles, small canyon," Chako replied. "Cross river, follow creek."

"I have to see this," Caleb said. "Cross here, Chako, and swing around to the west, so we can come out above the canyon. *Comprende?*" Chako nodded his understanding. "Come on, George." Caleb nudged Nasty into the shallow water and splashed across the creek.

Circling to the west and then back north brought the four riders to some broken high ground and Chako signaled for a halt, leaping down from his Pinto. "We leave horse, climb hill. Caleb and George swung down from their saddles and tied their reins to a gnarly cedar tree. A thin column of smoke spiraled into the sky from the other side of the hill, and the fresh breeze in their faces brought the smell of roasting meat.

"Stay with the horses, Juaquin," said Caleb.

Chako set off up the hill and Caleb and George followed him in single file. Just before reaching the top Chako signaled for them to get down, and they low crawled over the crest and down into some big rocks that formed the west wall of a small canyon. Below, a small group of Indians, Tonkawas Caleb guessed, were gathered around a fire roasting meat. Not too far from the fire, the remainder of a mule carcass hung suspended from the limb of a tree. The other mule stood hobbled on the far side of the canyon.

Chako was right about the makeup of the group, thought Caleb; only old men, women, and children. They looked emaciated, as if this was their first good meal in quite a spell. After a few more minutes, Caleb signaled for a withdrawal. He led the way as they slithered back over the crest of the hill and walked down to the horses. "George, them people are near starvin'. No damn wonder they stole Bullock's mules." Caleb remembered what Governor Bell had said about the central Texas tribes being squeezed between the white frontier and the Comancheria. Texas needs those reservations, he thought, and the sooner the better. "We ain't gonna bother them people none. Let's get on back to the tradin' post. I want to talk with Sam."

Chako and Juaquin looked on Caleb with favor as they all mounted. Red Hair was a good war chief.

Dismounting in front of Sam's trading post, Caleb and George tied their reins to the hitching rail and went inside. Caleb had sent Chako and Juaquin ahead to scout the trail along the Brazos that the Rangers would follow in the morning. Sam and Eph were sitting at a table talking to an old Ranger friend of Caleb's, Shapley Ross. Shapley had ridden with Caleb as a member of Jack Hays' Ranger Company in San Antonio. He now lived a mile from Sam's place in a big double log cabin built on a bluff overlooking the Brazos.

"How you doin', Shapley?" asked Caleb as he and George pulled up chairs and sat down at the table. "It's been a good while since I laid eyes on you." Shapley was a short wiry man with dark curly hair and dark eyes. He always reminded Caleb of Sam Walker. "This is George White, one of my sergeants." The two men shook hands and greeted one another warmly.

"More than ten years," Shapley agreed as he turned to Caleb. "You were still a kid then, but damn good with that Colt as I remember."

Sam's curiosity got the best of him, and he broke into the conversation. "Well, did you find them mules, Caleb?"

"We found your mules alright, but I let the Indians keep 'em." Caleb almost laughed at the look of shock on Sam Bullock's face. "You aint never seen a more pitiful sight, Sam. Nothin' but old folks and women and kids, and they was starvin'. In fact, one of them mules was near roasted when we caught up with 'em. Don't worry. It was my choice to leave the mules, so I'll pay you for 'em."

Sam sighed. "You don't have to do that, Caleb. To be honest, the mules were well past their prime anyways, and I ain't one to see no kids and old folks starve to death. We'll just forget about it."

"The problem is gettin' to be a common one," said Shapley. "For the past few years, I been scoutin' for Major Neighbors, the Indian agent, and most of the tribes, except for the Comanches and Kiowas are in damn poor shape."

"Even the Penetaka are eatin' their dogs and horses in the winter from what I hear," said Caleb. "They all need a little land of their own. The Governor's been dealin' with Neighbors, and he's gonna make a request to the legislature for reservation land. If so, I'll most likely be ridin' up this way again soon to give you and Neighbors a hand."

"We'll be damn glad to have you," Shapley said. "Most of the Indians, except for maybe the Penetakas, will cooperate and come on in when we meet with 'em. It's the damn white Indian haters who'll cause us the problems."

Early in the afternoon of the fifth day out of Sam Bullock's trading post, the Rangers rode into Fort Belknap and reined up at the headquarters building. Fort Belknap was manned by two companies from the Fifth Infantry and two companies from the Second Dragoons. Caleb gave the order for the Rangers to dismount and called for Sergeant White and Sergeant Jessup to join him and Eph. The long ride along the Brazos had been uneventful, and the Rangers' horses remained in good shape.

"Make sure the men walk their horses to cool 'em down before you take 'em to water," Caleb said after the sergeants reported. "Me and Eph are gonna have a talk with the Commandin'

Officer. We'll find out where we can set up camp. Chako, you and Juaquin stick with the sergeants until I get back." The Lipans nodded their understanding and Caleb and Eph headed for the entrance to the headquarters building.

When the guard waved the Rangers through the door and into the orderly room, they removed their sombreros and found themselves standing in front of the post Sergeant Major's desk. The Sergeant Major looked them over carefully from the top of their heads down to the scuffed toes of their boots. They were a rough looking pair, he thought. Both men were tall and clean-shaven, but the tow-headed one was on the lanky side, while the one with the long, copper-red curls was broad across the chest and narrow-hipped. The towhead was dressed in a set of soft buckskins tucked into a pair of mule-eared boots with big Mexican spurs, and the redhead wore a fringed buckskin hunting shirt and faded blue army trousers. They were both armed with new Colt Dragoon revolvers carried low in holsters tied down to their right thighs and huge Bowie knives.

"What can I do for you gentlemen?" the Sergeant Major finally asked.

"I'm Captain Caleb McAdams, Sergeant Major, and this is Lieutenant Eph Daggett. We're Texas Rangers up from Austin, and we'd like to speak with your Commandin' Officer on official business."

"Sergeant Miller, see if the C.O. has a few minutes to talk with some Texas Rangers from Austin," the Sergeant Major said to one of the two clerks who were working at smaller desks behind his. The other clerk was a private.

Sergeant Miller got up and knocked on a door at the rear of the orderly room before entering. He was back in less than a minute. "Captain Stephenson says to go on in."

"You heard the man, gentlemen, go on in," repeated the Sergeant Major. "By the way, would either of you like a cup of coffee?"

"We both would, Sergeant Major," said Caleb as he and Eph headed for Captain Stephenson's office, "and thanks. That's right neighborly."

Captain Stephenson was sitting behind his desk when the Rangers entered his office. He greeted them with a questioning smile. "Sergeant Miller said you'd like a word with me, but I'm curious, gentlemen. What brings volunteers up here all the way from Austin? That's quite a ride."

Caleb handed the Captain his authorization from the governor, and the coffee arrived while he was examining it. When the officer looked up from his reading, Caleb took a sip of his coffee and said, "As you can see, sir, we're not a volunteer outfit. I'm Captain McAdams and this is Lieutenant Daggett. The Texas legislature gave my Company responsibility for protectin' settlers anywhere on the frontier, but Governor Bell also made it plain that he would like for me to coordinate my efforts with the army whenever possible. So far, I haven't had much luck at the other posts."

Captain Stephenson chuckled. "Many of my colleagues do not look favorably on volunteer outfits like the Rangers. Without the discipline of regulars, they tend to get out of control. Professional pride is also involved in not wanting to ask for help. Policing Texas is a big job, though, and I don't mind saying we can use all the help we can get. Did you show these orders to the other officers you've met, Captain?"

Caleb nodded. "Yes sir, but they weren't very impressed."

"Give the army a little time, Captain," said Stephenson. "I'm certainly glad we have some regular Rangers running patrols again. The better the job you do, the sooner the other commanders will accept your outfit. Was there anything else you wanted to discuss?"

"When the Governor and Major Neighbors spoke, they talked about a problem the army is havin' with traders sellin' whiskey and guns to the Indians. One trader was mentioned by name, George Barnard." Stephenson's eyes widened and he sat up straighter. "What can you tell me about him?"

"Barnard is a menace to the peace the army is trying to maintain on the frontier," Captain Stephenson complained. "However, without a Federal law forbidding the sale of liquor and firearms to the Indians, there's not a damn thing we can do about him. Has Texas passed such a law?"

"I'm afraid not," Caleb replied, "but I aim to have a little talk with the man. I just thought it would be best if I paid my respects to the army first."

Stephenson nodded. "I'm glad you did, Captain McAdams. It's good to know if another outfit is operating near here. But what can you possibly hope to accomplish without the necessary legal authority?"

"I'll consider that once I've met Barnard," Caleb replied with a smile. "How far up the river is his tradin' post?"

Captain Stephenson held up his hands. "No more than ten or twelve miles from here, but as far as I'm concerned, this conversation never took place."

It was mid-afternoon of the following day when Caleb, George White, and the Lipans crested a ridge well away from the Brazos and looked down on Barnard's trading post. The rectangular-shaped, log building was situated on the slope of a low hill above the river. The roof was made of thick sod, and the walls were dug down into the ground and back into the side of the hill so that fewer logs were required in construction. The overall effect was a low, squat building that seemed to merge into the grassy prairie. Further on down the slope stood a small barn with a fair sized corral. A large storage building was conveniently situated between the post and the barn, and three buffalo hide lodges stood down near the river. From the markings on the lodges, they appeared to be Penetaka. Two men were working with some horses in the corral, but no one else was in sight.

Caleb decided to have a good look at the trading post without letting Barnard know he was a Ranger, so he had concealed Eph and the remainder of the company in a wooded canyon a few miles back. The four riders moved down the ridge and up the low hill, reining up in front of the post and dismounting. Looping his reins around the hitching rail, Caleb shoved the heavy door open and stepped down into the trading post. George, Chako, and Juaquin followed right behind him. The interior was dimly lit with several smoking oil lamps hanging from the rafters, and it took a few moments for their eyes to adjust. Rows of long tables were stacked high with goods and wide shelves that extended down both sides of the room from floor to ceiling were loaded with merchandise of all descriptions.

"We don't allow Indians in here," growled a man standing behind a counter at the back of the room. "The bastards will steal a man blind." Short and stocky, with a thick neck and bull-like shoulders, the man wore a pair of heavy canvas pants held up by a set of frayed leather braces and an old, red long-handle shirt filled with holes, neither of which had been washed in some time. His unwashed, bushy black hair and unkempt beard added to his slovenly appearance.

Caleb stepped up to the counter. "If you don't allow Indians in here, what do you call them?" He pointed to two young Indian girls sitting on the floor next to the wall.

"Why them two are my girls," the unkempt proprietor said. "You're more 'n welcome to try one of 'em for a dollar, or both for that matter. You can either take 'em in the backroom or to one of the teepees down by the river. You interested? If not, how about a drink?"

Caleb shook his head. "No to both right now, thanks. As for my Indian friends, if you don't want 'em in here you tell 'em to go."

One look into the cruel eyes of the well-armed Lipans told the man behind the counter that to say anything to these Indians would more than likely cost him his life. "Well, keep an eye on 'em then. What can I do for you gents, if you don't want a woman or a drink?"

"Might you be George Barnard?" asked Caleb.

The man nodded with a suspicious look. "That's me alright, and who might you be?" Before Caleb answered, one of the men who had been working in the corral entered the trading post and stood by the door, keeping a close eye on them.

"My name is Caleb, Mister Barnard, and I might be interested in purchasin' two dozen rifles and a couple barrels of whiskey, if the price is right."

That put a smile on Barnard's face. "I keep the rifles and whiskey out in the storeroom. Come with me." The man who entered the trading post followed Barnard out the door.

Caleb took a deep breath of the fresh air on the way to the storeroom, glad to be out of the smelly confines of the trading post. He was sure George and the Lipans felt the same way. Barnard unlocked the chain that held the double doors to the storeroom closed and swung them open. The right side of the storeroom was filled with barrels of whiskey stacked three high. There had to be nearly a hundred barrels of the rot gut, thought Caleb. On the left side of the storeroom kegs of gun powder were stacked up five high alongside several boxes of rifles. Barnard walked over to one of the boxes, and using a small bar that he kept in his pocket, pried off the lid. After removing some loose packing, he drew out a brand new .54 caliber Remington Model 1841 Mississippi Rifle and handed it to Caleb.

Caleb hefted the rifle and brought it to his shoulder. "How much are you askin'?"

Barnard smiled. "They're sweet, ain't they? The rifles are twenty-five dollars each and the whiskey is fifty dollars a barrel. I don't argue over the price; take it or leave it."

"I'm afraid I'll have to leave it for now," said Caleb. "That's a little rich for my blood. Maybe I'll be back after I talk it over with my partners."

"Suit yourself," said Barnard, angry at Caleb for wasting his time, "but the weapons won't be here forever." He snatched the rifle from Caleb's hands and put it back in the crate.

Ignoring Barnard's anger, Caleb turned and headed out the door. "Come on, George, we got to round up a little more cash."

The Rangers were soon mounted and riding out of the trading post. Barnard stared after them with an angry scowl on his face.

Only the lonesome hoot of a prairie owl disturbed the depth of the night as Caleb, George, and Chako slowly crept up on the trading post. Heavy cloud cover blotted out the moon, and they were all probing the darkness with their senses, attempting to locate the guard Caleb was sure Barnard had posted. Reaching the back wall of the storeroom, they moved around to the side nearest the trading post and waited patiently for the man to reveal himself. It was not long before they heard the guard's footsteps approaching the double doors of the storeroom. He rattled the chain holding the doors and then headed back toward the trading post.

Like a phantom, Caleb slipped up on the guard and whacked him hard behind the ear with the long barrel of his Colt. The man dropped like a stone. Caleb and George drug him by the heels off to the side. George used a length of rope he had cut earlier to hogtie the guard, and Caleb took the man's bandana and stuffed it into his mouth. Chako moved off silently toward the trading post to make sure there were no more guards and to intercept anyone who might decide to head to the storeroom.

"Follow me," Caleb whispered to George.

The Rangers moved around to the front of the storeroom and up to the double doors. Caleb pulled a hatchet from his belt and stuck down on the old lock with a sharp blow. In the deathly quiet of the night, the noise sounded as loud as a pistol shot, but the rusty metal gave way easily. They had to move quickly now in case anyone had heard the lock break. As George stood guard at the door, Caleb hurried over to where the powder kegs were stacked up. Using the hatchet, he broke open the top on one of the powder kegs and then another. Caleb tipped over one keg, spilling a good amount of the gunpowder. Picking up the other keg, he quickly poured a powder trail out the door and around to the side of the storeroom. Kneeling down, he struck his flint to the blade of the hatchet and a small shower of sparks fell on the powder trail. With a whoosh and a flash the powder ignited and began to burn back down the trail toward the barn.

"Let's get the hell out of here, George!" Caleb yelped.

The Rangers sprinted up the hill toward the place where Eph and Juaqin waited with the horses. Chako was right behind them. They made it to the top of the hill just as the gunpowder exploded. The thundering blast lit up the trading post like it was daylight, and the Rangers and Lipans quickly mounted and galloped away. The kegs of powder continued to explode one-by-one until they joined in with the whiskey in a huge fiery roar.

"Barnard won't be sellin' rifles and whiskey to the Indians for a good while," Eph commented as they slowed their horses and rode to join the remainder of the company.

Chapter 19

A messenger from the new Governor of Texas, Elisha M. Pease, arrived at the Rocking M shortly after the new year of 1854. Pease wanted to see Captain McAdams in Austin at his earliest convenience on Ranger business. Caleb was only a casual acquaintance of the new Governor, not a good friend as he was with Peter Bell, and he wondered what Pease had in mind for him and his Rangers. He hoped the Governor was not thinking about disbanding the company. As far as Caleb was concerned the Rangers had performed well, and though they were only one small unit, they had had a disproportionate effect on the number and ferocity of Comanche raids on the frontier. Any roving war party now knew they could not simply raid the settlements with impunity or they might end up as the prey, not the hunter.

The long summer and fall leading up to the New Year had also been good seasons for the ranch. Hammond was nearly a year old now, and between Lucinda and the girls, let alone Connie and Veronica, he got more attention lavished on him than any five normal babies. Veronica was also pregnant and due in July, and Pedro was bursting with pride. The cattle drive Pedro led the prior spring had been successful once again, resulting in $55,000.00 being deposited in three Cincinnati banks and $50,000.00 in gold added to the safe in the storeroom. Pedro and Felix were already planning for another drive in early April. This time less than a thousand head would come from Rocking M stock with cattle purchased from nearby ranches for ten dollars a head making up the remainder of a herd that would total nearly four thousand.

Governor Pease was very cordial when he greeted Caleb, immediately allaying any fears that the Rangers might be disbanded. "On the contrary, Captain McAdams, I am currently working with a few key legislators to activate two more companies as soon as this Fall. It seems there may be some question about the original authorization applying to only Governor Bell's authority. Governor Henderson attempted to address the problem, but since his term was only temporary, he couldn't accomplish much." Hansbrough Bell had resigned as governor to fill a vacancy in the United States House of Representatives. James Henderson served the final twenty-eight days of Bell's term. "I had a long conversation with Governor Bell before I took office, and he had only words of praise for the work of you and your Company. I consider it amazing you were able to accomplish so much with so little, and I'm sure your efforts will make it easier to gain approval for the new companies. Governor Bell mentioned that you are acquainted with Major Robert Neighbors, the head Federal Indian agent."

"Yes sir," Caleb replied. "We rode together for a short time with Jack Hays when Texas was still a Republic. Then Neighbors was captured by the Mexicans in San Antonio and thrown into prison."

The governor continued. "After you spoke with Governor Bell about the advisability of establishing two Indian reservations in Texas instead of one, Major Neighbors and Captain Randolph Marcy of the United States Army surveyed two locations totaling nearly seventy thousand acres. The Brazos Reservation, a few miles below Fort Belknap, is slated for use by the Central Texas tribes like the Tonkawas and the Witchitas. The Clear Fork Reservation, about twenty miles to the southwest of Belknap, on the Clear Fork of the Brazos, is designated as the home of the Penataka Comanches."

"I know that area well," said Caleb, "and it's perfect. Both reservations lay in beautiful rolling country with plenty of wood and water."

Governor Pease smiled. "I'm glad you think so, Captain, because the legislature approved both sites the last week of February. That's why I sent for you. I'd like you to tell me what kind of problems you foresee for Major Neighbors when he attempts to establish the reservations."

Caleb thought for a moment. "His first problem is gonna be to convince the tribes to come in. The Central Tribes will be easier, since they're in the worse shape, and they know some about plantin' corn and other kinds of farmin'. The Penetakas aint been doin' too well lately either, but they don't know a lick about farmin' —look on it as woman's work in fact—so they won't care much for bein' penned up. It's gonna depend on how hungry they are. Mostly all the Indians trust Neighbors though, even the Comanches. If anybody can get 'em on a reservation, it's got to be him."

"Do you foresee any other problems?" asked Pease.

"To be honest, Governor," replied Caleb shaking his head in sad resignation, "most settlers on the frontier hate Indians. Nearly to a man, they don't want 'em put on reservations. Given a choice, they want the Indians either driven out of the state or exterminated. The more the Indians like and respect Neighbors as an agent, the more the settlers are gonna hate the man as an Indian lover."

Pease nodded. "Taking into consideration what you've told me, I believe it would be best if you assisted Major Neighbors and the army in their efforts. I realize this assignment may pit your Rangers against the very people you've been trying to protect, but no matter how much the people on the frontier hate Indians, they must not be permitted to take the law into their own hands. I expect you to send back reports as often as you deem necessary, but especially if there are any clashes between your men and the settlers. The legislature may permit us to go only so far, so tread as lightly as you can and still get the job done. Major Neighbors said if I decided to send the Rangers to Fort Belknap, he would like you to arrive no later than the middle of May. Does that cause any problems?"

"I don't think so," replied Caleb. "My partners expect to start our next cattle drive to New Orleans by the end of April. I should be able to head for Belknap by the first week of May."

"That will be fine," said Pease. "Do you have any questions?"

"No sir," said Caleb as he rose to his feet, "the Rangers will get the job done."

It sure as hell won't be easy, though, Caleb thought. I will be forced to make all the decisions on the spot, and the legislature will have plenty of time to second guess whatever I do.

A letter from Jack Hays arrived at the Rocking M in the middle of April. When Caleb opened the letter it began "I have bad news," and it got worse from there. Nathan Frost's body had been fished out of San Francisco Bay. Caleb glanced at the date of the letter; almost three months ago. Frost was shot in the back and then tossed in the bay after he was dead. Jack's investigation revealed that Frost told several people of his involvement in the deaths of Elijah Pate and his brothers, and word of the incident could have reached Ned and Mike. However, there were no witness who could testify to any confrontation between Frost and the Pates, or even if they had ever met, so there was no way to link them to the murder. The authorities may not be able to prove it, Caleb thought, but there was no doubt in his mind. With as much money as the Pates have, they probably hired someone to do their dirty work for them, and Hays said as much in the letter.

Caleb wanted to mount up, ride to California, and finish the bloody feud once and for all, but there was no way he could do that. Jack Hays was no longer the sheriff, and even if he were, there was no way he could let Caleb ride into San Francisco and gun down two of the city's wealthiest citizens without proof that they had committed the murder. No, right now the Pates were out of his reach, but that would not always be the case. One day there would be a time for revenge. Caleb simply had to bide his time until that day came.

Hays went on to say Frost had a will that left everything to Caleb, including some valuable real estate and a bank account of $223,000.00 from the sale of his gold mine. After some serious thought, Caleb wrote to Hays and carefully explained his relationship with Wanda and the birth of Joshua. Hammond of course would inherit Caleb's share of the Rocking M, with some provision for the girls, but Joshua would be in line to inherit nothing. The power of attorney he sent to Hays gave Jack the authority to manage half of the money and all of the real estate in Joshua's name until he came of age, at which time it would all be turned over to Josh. Jack was to bank the remainder of the money in Caleb's name, and invest a portion of it in real estate now and then when he saw a good opportunity.

Caleb had spent much of his time since meeting with the Governor purchasing cattle from smaller spreads all across central Texas. The ranchers had been glad to sell for ten dollars a head cash money, rather than risk everything on a trail drive with only a few cattle. In less than six weeks he and Pedro had assembled a herd of nearly five thousand longhorns, less than a thousand of them Rocking M stock.

"Drivin' all these cattle to New Orleans is gonna be quite a chore little brother," Caleb said, as he and Pedro sat their horses on a ridge overlooking the huge herd grazing its way across a valley on the east end of the Rocking M.

Pedro nodded his agreement. "I hired fifteen extra hands for the drive. With the ten men I'm taking from the ranch, we should be able to handle them okay. Besides, I know the trail like the back of my hand now. That will make things a lot easier."

"Will you need that many extra men?" It seemed to Caleb that ten or fifteen hands would have been plenty.

"I hired ten of the men strictly for their guns," Pedro replied. "They will spend much of the days and nights riding guard. There were some problems on the last trail drive. I discussed them with father, but we decided not to bother you."

That got Caleb's attention. "What kind of problems?"

Pedro sighed. "Caleb, I know it seldom crosses your mind, but my father and I are not Anglos. In Texas, being a *tejano* is enough for some men to hate you or to wish you ill. I made the mistake of hiring two Anglo hands on the last trail drive. They ended up refusing to take my orders. It eventually led to a gunfight, and I was forced to wound one and kill the other. This time I hired only *tejanos*. They need the work and they are good hands. Many along the trail will not like to see only *tejanos* with so many longhorns and a *tejano* trail boss as well. Think about it, Caleb. How many Anglo ranch hands work the Rocking M right now? The answer is not a single man."

Caleb sadly shook his head. "I see what you mean, little brother. Do you still want to trail the cattle?"

Pedro laughed. "Of course I want to lead the drive. These are my cattle now, too. I will never allow anyone to prevent me from doing my job or living like a man. I hired the extra hands to let such men know we will fight for our rights as free men if necessary."

"Unfortunately, strength is the only thing some men respect," Caleb agreed. "You're my brother, Pedro. You always have my support. I don't care if you hire fifty extra men."

Caleb was sitting his horse with Felix, watching as the trail drive headed out three days later, and the movement of so many cattle was a sight to behold. The supply wagon had already pulled out, and Pedro was up front with the remuda. The trail hands and half the guards had the herd surrounded, beating at the bunch quitters with doubled lariats and trying to be everywhere at once, as the contrary beasts did their best to escape from the confines of the herd. Well outside the ring of trail hands rode the remainder of the guards. Caleb and Felix watched until the huge herd slowly moved out of sight into the next valley before reining around and heading for the hacienda.

"I'll be pullin' out with my Rangers in a few days, Felix. The whole company will be ridin' on this patrol, except for the Lipans. We're likely to be gone for at least a month or two, maybe more. I told Chako and Juaquin to keep a sharp lookout for trouble and to report to you regular. By the way, what would you think about addin' on a few more ranch hands?"

"Pedro told me that you two discussed his troubles on the last trail drive. Is that why you feel we need more ranch hands?"

Caleb nodded with a grim set to his features. "I got a bad habit sometimes of closin' my eyes to things I don't want to see, but I ain't totally blind. I know how some ranchers around here treat you and Pedro; in fact, most of the ranchers. It ain't right, but I can't do a damn thing to change their minds. I got a feelin' with all the problems brewin' between the North and the South over slavery things are only gonna get worse. You *tejanos* are likely to get caught in the middle of all the hatred. I can see it comin' plain as day, and the only thing that's gonna keep people like that at bay is strength. This ranch may eventually have to become a fortress before our families are safe. We need folks we can trust, and that means hirin' more family or close friends."

Felix chuckled and noticed the strange look Caleb gave him. "Don't worry. I happen to agree with everything you said, and so does Pedro. We were going to discuss it with you when he returns. It's just that if we don't stop hiring them soon, my whole family will live here on the Rocking M."

Caleb's frown turned to a smile. "With Lucinda and now Hammond, they're all my family, too, and what's more, I trust 'em. Why don't you write and see who you can convince to come north. Send a couple men down to Mexico to recruit if you have to."

Felix nodded. "I will see what I can do."

The cloud lifted from Caleb's day when he walked into the orderly room. Sitting at the table with Eph, Terrell, and George was his long lost partner. "Bigfoot, you son-of-gun," he said with a huge smile as the big man stood to greet him, "what the hell brings you here?"

"I thought it was high time I quit foolin' around with that stage and got back to what I do best. I got my percentage from Mr. Skillman, and all the relay stations are in place, so the job's gettin' a might borin' anyways."

"Well there's plenty for you to do around here," said Caleb. "We leave for Fort Belknap in a couple days. We're gonna be helpin' Major Neighbors round up Indians to fill the two new reservations—one on the Clear Fork of the Brazos for the Penetaka and one just below Belknap on the Brazos for the rest of the tribes."

"We might have more trouble with the white folks up that way than we do with the Indians," Bigfoot said, "and what about the Penetaka? Does Neighbors really think he can get them on a reservation?"

"That's what we're about to find out," said Caleb. "But if anybody can do it Neighbors can. He speaks Comanche, and Old Owl adopted him into the tribe a few years back."

"Maybe so," Bigfoot replied, his voice full of skepticism, "but more 'n likely Neighbors is gonna get nothin' but old folks and little ones to live on a reservation. The warriors will keep on killin' at their pleasure. Either that or they'll use the reservation as a refuge to hide out after they return from a war party."

Caleb shook his head. "Dang, partner, you sound just like the people we're gonna have to keep away from the Indians while Neighbors rounds 'em up. It ain't gonna be too easy, is it?"

"You're damned right it ain't," Bigfoot agreed, "but when did a Ranger's job ever get easy? How do I join this chicken outfit anyways?"

"As far as I'm concerned you're joined," said Caleb. "That other officer's room has had your name on it since the barracks was built."

"Seems to me you already got a damn good second officer," Bigfoot winked at Eph, and Eph smiled in return. "I never hankered to be no officer anyways. What this chicken outfit needs is a damn good First Sergeant. Let's just change the sign above that other door, and I'll move my gear in. Don't be expectin' me to 'sir' you, though, Captain McAdams. You'll always be a snot-nosed youngster to me,"

Everyone at the table had a good laugh at Caleb's expense, but he just shook his head, long ago resigned to Bigfoot's harassment. "Your new sombrero is hangin' on a peg in your room. Welcome to the company, First Sergeant Wallace."

The following morning Caleb made a quick supply run to Cooper's Emporium. When he stopped by the Bullock Hotel there was a letter from Wanda waiting for him. She and Joshua were doing well. Under her new name, the widow Andrews, she had found a job teaching at a fancy girl's school, and she planned to stay in New Orleans for at least another year before returning to Austin. Wanda mentioned a book called "Uncle Tom's Cabin" that was all the rage among the abolitionists up north. The book was already banned in New Orleans. Caleb shook his head in frustration. When would the woman ever learn? She had Josh's safety to consider now, not just her own.

Wanda also wrote about some recent legislation passed by the United States Congress and sponsored by pro-slavery Senator Steven Douglas. The Kansas-Nebraska Act had nullified the Missouri Compromise by stating that citizens of new territories would now be able to vote to decide if their state would be free or slave. Wanda was sure the Act would fan the flames of hatred as both "slavers" and "free-soilers" rushed to the new territories to sway the vote. Caleb suspected she was right. Just another step towards secession and war, he thought. In his return letter, Caleb cautioned her, though he knew it was a waste of time. He also told her about the trust he had set up for Joshua, and that he was very much looking forward to seeing his son.

Chapter 20

By the middle of June, Major Neighbors had gathered a considerable band of Indians from the Central Texas tribes near Fort Graham on the eastern bank of the Brazos at Little Bear Creek. For the past few years the fort had served as the headquarters for Neighbors and other Indian agents in the area. Like most frontier army posts, the fort was without a stockade and consisted of several log and clapboard structures including a commissary, a hospital, officer's quarters, and a crude troop barracks. The post was manned by Company I of the Second Dragoons and Company H of the Eighth Infantry and commanded by Lt. Col. James Bomford.

"Thank you for seein' us, sir," said Major Neighbors. "This is my chief scout Shapley Ross, and this is Captain McAdams, Lieutenant Daggett, and First Sergeant Wallace of the Texas Rangers."

"Please have a seat, gentlemen," said Bomford. "My orders are to assist your efforts in any way I can Major Neighbors. How can I help?"

Not a man to waste time on formalities, Neighbors got right down to business. "Colonel, as you know, I gathered the Indians here before moving them to the Brazos reservation south of Fort Belknap. Unfortunately, it's well over a hundred miles to the fort, and our promised foodstuffs have not yet arrived. The shortage of food is becomin' critical. There's no way I can begin the movement to the reservation without adequate supplies."

"I just received word from a messenger that fourteen supply wagons have been dispatched from the army depot at Nacogdoches," said Colonel Bomford. "They should arrive within the week." The local settlers were becoming restless with the gathering of so many Indians in the area, and Bomford was just as anxious as Neighbors for the savages to depart for the reservation.

Neighbors smiled for the first time. "That is indeed good news, Colonel. I'm plannin' on leavin' today to round up the final band of Tonkawas who'll make up the reservation contingent. I should be back here before the supply wagons arrive. The Tonkawas are presently encamped near the site of former Fort Gates on the north bank of the Leon River just above Coryell Creek. They have suffered constant harassment by the local settlers, and they refuse to move until I can provide them with an adequate escort."

"I'm afraid I can't help you there, Major," said Bomford. "With only two companies assigned to the fort, I don't have enough men to provide an escort. Besides, the army has no jurisdiction over the local settlers. The last thing I want to do is put my men between them and the Indians."

Major Neighbors nodded. "That's quite understandable, Colonel. In any event, the army won't become responsible for the Indians' safety until they are firmly established on the reservation. Keepin' the settlers away from them now is the responsibility of Captain McAdams and his Rangers. So far, his company has done a good job, but now I must ask him to divide his men, so he can protect the Indians I already gathered here and also provide an escort for the Tonkawas who are presently camped on the Leon. I only ask that you support the men he leaves here, should they require it."

Bomford looked to Caleb. "How many men do you have, Captain McAdams, and how many do you propose to leave here?"

"My company is made up of two thirteen-man platoons, sir. I plan to leave Lt. Daggett here with Second Platoon and take First Platoon to escort the Tonkawas. I appreciate Major Neighbors askin' for your help, but I'm sure Lt. Daggett and his men can handle the situation here just fine."

Caleb's assurance brought a smile to Lt. Col. Bomford's face. "Excellent, Captain McAdams, as I said before, coming between the settlers and their hatred for the Indians certainly doesn't make the army any more popular. I'm glad the job is yours and not mine."

First Platoon rode out of Fort Graham with Major Neighbors and the other Indian agents shortly after noon. Less than an hour later, one of the pickets Eph had posted to keep an eye on the settlement rode into the fort with news that forty or fifty settlers were on the way to the Indian camp. According to the Ranger, the settlers appeared to be in an ugly mood. Eph immediately moved out of the fort with Second Platoon, and within minutes the Rangers were waiting on line, blocking the main trail to the Indian camp. The settlers soon reined up in a swirling cloud of dust.

Eph sat his horse in the center of the Ranger line beside Sergeant Jessup, his hands crossed on his saddle horn. "Afternoon, gents," he said in a loud clear voice, "where're y'all headin' in such an all-fired hurry?"

"What right do you have to question us or block our path?" asked a self-appointed spokesman for the settlers. His horse was lathered up and jittery from being ridden hard, and he fought to settle the rambunctious animal and maintain control over the long rifle he carried cradled in his arm.

"My name is Lt. Daggett," replied Eph, keeping his voice calm and even. "My men are Texas Rangers sworn to uphold the law. We ain't blockin' your path unless you're aimin' to head to the Indian encampment."

"You're damn right we're headin' for the Indian camp," replied the settler. "Once we get through with 'em there won't be a need for a reservation."

Now the spokesman got loud support from the others in the crowd and the settlers' mood turned even uglier. "They can't stop us!" a settler yelled. "You're damn right they can't!" someone yelled out in agreement. "Who the hell do these Rangers think they are? Let's just ride over the sons-a-bitches and get on with it!" hollered someone from the back of the group.

Eph finally had enough, and all up and down the line the Rangers tensed for action. "Y'all best turn around and go home before it's too late!"

Ignoring Eph's demand, the settler who started all the commotion brought the barrel of his long rifle to bear. Before he could pull the trigger, the lanky Ranger drew and fired, the big .44 caliber ball from his Colt Dragoon ripping into the settler's shoulder like the kick of a mule and unhorsing him. Every Ranger in the line cleared leather before the wounded settler struck the ground, and a deathly silence settled over the mob as the determined men covered the crowd but held their fire. Thank the lord his Rangers had the discipline and good sense not to open fire, thought Eph. The last thing the Rangers needed was to kill a bunch of civilians.

Eph holstered his Colt. "I'm tellin' y'all now to pick your wounded and go home before somebody gets killed."

Two settlers dismounted, helped the wounded man up on his horse, and then climbed back up on their saddles. To a man, they were eager to take revenge against the Indians for past grievances both real and imagined, but not one man was willing to go up against a determined bunch of Rangers. Grumbling and mumbling their discontent, the settlers reluctantly reined around and rode away.

"Williamson, Sturm," Eph ordered, "make damn sure they clear the area before you return to the fort."

"Hold up, Rory," Williamson said to Rory Sturm as he reined in beside Eph. "Lieutenant, I don't much care for shootin' settlers to protect Indians. It don't sit well with me, or some of the others here either for that matter."

Eph heard some whispered comments between the men, and he rode to the front before reining around to face them. "Thad, when you signed up with this outfit you swore to follow orders," Eph said to Williamson. "That damn well means all the orders you get, not just the ones you like. That goes for all of you! Anybody here thinks I enjoyed what I had to do today don't know Eph Daggett. But my orders are to protect the Indians, and that's damn well what we're all gonna do. If you don't like it, turn your Colt in to Sergeant Jessup now and draw your pay at the ranch. Are there any takers?" Not a man moved or said a word. "Thad, you and Rory get goin' like I said. The rest of you follow me. We're headin' back to the fort." Eph reined around and rode out. Sergeant Jessup and the others fell in behind him.

By noon the following day, the Rangers and Indian agents had covered the forty-five miles to the bend in the Leon River, and Major Neighbors received a warm welcome when he led the small detachment into the Tonkawa encampment. After reining in, they were greeted by a tall warrior dressed in a breechclout and moccasins. His long, raven-black hair was decorated by a cluster of eagle feathers that fluttered in the breeze, and most of his well-muscled body, including his face, was covered by black-lined tattoos.

Stepping forward, the tall Indian raised the palm of his hand to Neighbors in a sign of peace. "Welcome to the camp of the People of the Wolf, my brother." He nodded to Shapely Ross as a friend, but looked at the Rangers with suspicion until he recognized Caleb and Bigfoot.

Neighbors raised his hand in greeting before calling for everyone to dismount. "Thank you for your welcome, Placido." Placido, also known as Ha-shu-ka-na or Can't Kill Him, was the major chief of the Tonkawa people, and a hated enemy of the Comanche. He was the son of a Tonkawa warrior and a captive Comanche woman. Neighbors started to introduce Caleb, but Placido interrupted him.

"Welcome to the camp of the People of the Wolf, Red Hair. Do you remember me from many years ago in the big fight with the Comanche? You were but a youngster then, but now you are a warrior and a hated enemy of my enemy."

"I remember very well," said Caleb as he raised his hand in greeting. "You and your warriors counted many coups on our enemy that day. Thank you for your welcome."

"And you, Bear-of-a-Man," Placido said to Bigfoot. "It is also good to see you once more." Bigfoot nodded his head in greeting. "Come to my lodge. We will all eat and smoke before we talk."

Placido led the way to his lodge, and after they smoked together and enjoyed a good meal he began the talk. "I have not waited for you to come for my people out of fear, my brother," he said to Neighbors. "The whites have threatened us with death if we move toward the reservation, and I know if we fought back, the People of the Wolf would be blamed for the trouble."

Neighbors nodded his agreement. "In this you were very wise, Ha-shu-ka-na. Let Red hair and Bear-of-a-Man and their Rangers deal with the settlers. They have sworn to protect the People of the Wolf on their march to the reservation."

"The word of Red Hair and Bear-of-a-Man is good," said Placido. "The People of the Wolf will follow when you are ready, my brother."

When the bright orange disc of the morning sun peaked over the eastern horizon, Caleb and Bigfoot sat their horses watching as the Tonkawas quickly dismantled their encampment with a precision that would have made an army officer proud of his unit and prepared for the movement to Fort Graham. With a well-practiced ease, the squaws and children took down the teepees and packed up their possessions onto travois. They were ready to move out in little more than an hour.

"Do you expect any trouble?" Bigfoot asked Caleb.

"From what Placido says the settlers have been keepin' a close eye on the camp. That could spell trouble. I'm hopin' they'll back off when they see us ridin' escort."

"Maybe so," Bigfoot replied, "but they just might think we won't interfere with 'em since we ain't the army."

"That would be a serious mistake on their part," said Caleb. "It would cause us some big problems, too. Let's face it, the Governor don't want us dealin' with the settlers like we would a Comanche war party or a gang of bandits. We can't just kill 'em all. It's almost time to move out. Tell George to round up the men so I can have a talk with 'em."

Sergeant White had First Platoon assembled in a few minutes, and Caleb reined up in front of them. "Men, some of you may not like it, but our job is to see that the Tonkawas and the Indians at Fort Graham arrive at the reservation alive and well. If any of you can't see puttin' yourselves between the settlers and the Indians, now's the time to speak up. I'll pay you off and you can be on your way."

"Sir," asked Private Watson, "are we gonna end up shootin' settlers to save the damn Indians? Hell, I joined the Rangers to kill redskins, not settlers."

"I hope it don't come to that, Seth," Caleb replied, "but it damn well could. The settlers have been warned by the army to stand aside. If they don't do what they're told, we're gonna have to deal with 'em. Now," Caleb added as he looked each man in the eyes, "who wants out?" No one opted out, but they did not look any too eager either. "Fine, just remember you're all Rangers and you follow orders, even the ones you don't like. George, take Corporal Nelson and half the platoon and trail the Tonkawas. The rest of the men will ride up front with me and Bigfoot. Keep your eyes open. If there's trouble, shoot to warn or wound first if you can. Let's move out."

Once the Tonkawas were packed and ready, Major Neighbors, Shapley Ross, and Chief Placido joined Caleb and Bigfoot at the front of the procession, and the Chief gave the signal to move out. Thirty or forty Tonkawa warriors rode at the front of the long column, and about the same number joined George and his Rangers at the rear.

The first day of the journey to Fort Graham was peaceful, and the Tonkawas set up camp for the night on the west bank of the Bosque River. Caleb would have preferred to ford the river before establishing the camp, but the amount of graze for the Tonkawa horse herd was much greater on the west bank. Bigfoot told Sergeant White to post guards on both sides of the river and hobble the Rangers' horses. Shortly after dark the silvery moon rose full and round in a star-filled sky, and the occasional yip of a coyote and the echo of its distant answer were the only things that disturbed the tranquility of the night.

Morning twilight brought the camp awake, and the long column was ready to ford the river before the blood-red sun had fully cleared the horizon. Caleb and the Rangers splashed across the shallow river, spreading out to secure the area, and Chief Placido and Major Neighbors began leading the Tonkawas across. Without warning, a well-timed, mounted attack stormed out of the heavily wooded area to the east of the ford, taking the column by surprise and catching half the Tonkawas on one side of the river and half on the other side.

With terrifying whoops and hollers, the settlers drove in among the hapless women and children, killing indiscriminately without mercy and scattering them like a hungry fox in the middle of a flock of chickens. Only a disciplined response from Sergeant White's Rangers prevented the incident from becoming a massacre. White led his men toward the settlers, firing a warning shot above their heads. Suddenly, return fire from the settlers tumbled two of his Rangers out of the saddle.

"That's two Rangers down!" screamed Sergeant White as he leveled his big Colt and blew a settler out of the saddle with a well-aimed shot. Texans or not, White was not about to let his Rangers get slaughtered without fighting back. "Give 'em hell, boys!" The Rangers responded by opening fire in earnest, and a few more casualties quickly took the settlers' attention away from their pursuit of the Tonkawas.

Caleb and Bigfoot circled back across the river with their men, striking the settlers' other flank, and the rout was on. The Rangers, having seen some of their own go down at the hands of the settlers, were boiling mad, and they dished out a full measure of punishment without mercy. A settler aimed his long rifle at Caleb, and Caleb shot the man in the shoulder. The impact of the heavy ball flipped the settler out of the saddle as if he had hit a rope stretched across the trail. Two more settlers were quickly unhorsed, and suddenly, they were all reining in, dropping their weapons and raising their hands.

One of the settlers foolishly decided to change his mind, going for his horse pistol after dropping his rifle. Before the man could get off a shot, Bigfoot rode up and whacked him across the forehead with the long barrel of his Dragoon. The settler tumbled from the saddle, unconscious before he struck the ground. Caleb screamed out for a cease fire before anyone else was hurt, and the call was quickly taken up by the other Rangers. Within moments an eerie silence settled over the scene.

"Round 'em up, Rangers," Caleb yelled! "Pick up their weapons, and make damn sure none of 'em are still armed."

Within minutes the settlers were gathered in a small group. Two of them were draped over their saddles and seven were wounded. One man glared at Caleb, the hatred burning in his eyes. "I'm Dan Ketchum, the leader of these men. Who might you be?"

Caleb maneuvered Smokey closer to the settler. "I'm Captain McAdams of the Texas Rangers, Ketchum."

Ketchum's mouth hung open. "You men are Rangers, and you opposed our attack on these savages! Why? Rangers are supposed to kill Indians, not protect 'em."

"The Governor ordered us to make sure the tribes got to their new reservations safely," Caleb replied as he looked across the field at the Tonkawas gathering their dead and wounded, nearly all of them women and children. "But the way you people make war on squaws and kids, I'd have stopped you anyways."

Ketchum was livid. "You had no right to kill any of my men!"

"Sergeant White, what's the story on our casualties?" Caleb asked, ignoring Ketchum's outburst.

"One dead, Bill Tompkins, and three wounded, Captain," replied White. "Al Chalmers and Stan Redd got wounds that'll lay 'em up for a spell, but Ned Sumter was hit in the chest. He ain't gonna make it."

Caleb turned back to Ketchum. "You and your rabble killed one of my Rangers, and most likely another. That's more 'n the Comanches were able to kill in nearly two years. By rights, I ought to string you and your whole damn bunch up for murder right now." That got Ketchum's attention. "But I ain't gonna do it. You got thirty seconds to get yourself and these men out of my sight. A few of my Rangers will follow along with your weapons. You can have 'em back in four or five miles." Caleb looked to George White, "Sergeant White, see that it gets done. Ketchum, y'all make tracks now before I change my mind. If you show up anywhere near these Tonkawas again, you'll be kickin' at the end of a rope."

When the settlers cleared out, Caleb and Bigfoot rode up to Chief Placido and Major Neighbors. "I'm sorry about all this trouble and your casualties, Placido." said Caleb. "We did our best."

"Only the rocks live forever," said Placido. "Red Hair and Bear-of-a-Man kept their word. You fought well, or many more of my people would have been lost. The People of the Wolf will call you both friends for as long as the grass grows."

Less than a week later, a long column made up of several tribes departed Fort Graham on the 110 mile trek to the new Brazos Reserve reservation just below Fort Belknap. Placido and his Tonkawas led the way, but there were also Caddos, Lipans, Witchitas, and even a few Shawnees and Delawares in the colorful cavalcade. Caleb and the Rangers rode at the front, and a platoon from the Second Dragoons also accompanied the procession. With so many women and children, the column moved at a leisurely pace, and it was more than a week later when the tribes crested a high ridge along the west bank of the Brazos and looked down on the Reserve. A lovely valley spread out in the distance below them, stretching for nearly forty thousand rolling acres with plenty of wood and good water.

"The tribes in this group should do real well on land like this, partner," said Bigfoot. The Rangers had reined off to the side to watch as the long column snaked its way down into the valley. "Even the Tonkawas know how to grow a little corn and live on small game. And tribes like the Wichitas and the Caddos should prosper here if they're left alone. I can't see this kind of life appealin' to Comanches, though. I'm bettin' they ain't gonna be too happy to see us."

"I'm afraid you're right," Caleb agreed. "The Penetakas will have to be sufferin' real bad to give up followin' the buffalo herds and raidin' where it pleases 'em. The Comanche way of life is based on warfare. It ain't gonna be easy for 'em to give it up, even if they do decide to move to the reservation."

Chapter 21

As Caleb and Bigfoot had predicted, the Penetaka Comanches proved much more difficult for Neighbors to deal with than had the Central Texas tribes. Major Neighbors' patrol, consisting of a platoon from the Second Dragoons under the command of Lieutenant Forsythe, and Caleb and Bigfoot, was forced to roam the area west of Fort Belknap for nearly a month before finally locating the Penetaka village on the Salt Fork of the Brazos, some ten miles west of the confluence of the two rivers.

Shapley Ross had been appointed the Indian agent for the Brazos Reserve, and he stayed behind to organize the reservation with the assistance of Eph and the remainder of the Rangers. The Rangers planned to meet up with Caleb and Bigfoot later at the Comanche reservation on the Clear Fork of the Brazos. Neighbors had decided, and Caleb agreed that the sight of so many Texas Rangers early in the negotiations would only serve to stir up the Comanches.

The patrol was met by a well armed party of warriors soon after starting up the Salt Fork, and the welcome was not very warm until the Comanches recognized Neighbors. The Major greeted several warriors personally and spoke to them in Comanche before the column was permitted to continue on to the village. Caleb and Bigfoot also attracted some attention from the warriors who recognized them.

Stretching for more than a mile along the Salt Fork, the Comanche village must have been made up of at least four hundred lodges. That's a hell of a lot of warriors, thought Caleb, probably close to five hundred. He glanced over at Bigfoot as the wild reception committee riding out from the village reached them, but the big man was concentrating his attention on the warriors. War hoops and screamed out greetings deafened their ears and clouds of choking dust filled the air as the column was circled again and again by the galloping warriors, weapons held high but making no aggressive moves. The galloping circle broke apart as the patrol neared the edge of the village and the warriors fell in at a trot on both flanks, escorting the column into the heart of the buffalo hide lodges.

"Quite a reception, uh Bigfoot?" asked Caleb in a voice loud enough to be heard over the surrounding cacophony. "I get the feelin' they'd much rather turn them weapons on us than wave 'em around in the air."

"Did you notice all the rifles?" Bigfoot asked. "They're Remington Model 1841's, just like the ones you were tellin' me about. I counted nearly a hundred of 'em, and there were most likely more. It's a good thing you destroyed the others, or the whole damn tribe would be armed with 'em by now."

A group of chiefs and experienced warriors, including Buffalo Hump, were standing ready to greet Tall Brother, as they called Neighbors, but Caleb locked eyes with the one warrior he was seeking. The Comanche's Spanish metal breastplate, polished by handfuls of river sand, gleamed in the sun as he stood tall, and the lone eagle feather in his long, raven-black hair fluttered in the freshening breeze. So we meet again hated enemy, thought Caleb, as his slate-gray eyes bored into Iron Jacket's pools of deep obsidian.

Determined not to flinch, the Comanche warrior stared back with equal intensity. This time you have come to me Red Hair, Iron Jacket thought, and this time you will not return to your white fort alive. According to the law of the People, Red hair was safe from Iron Jacket as long as he was a guest in the village, but when he left, the Ranger would become fair game for all warriors to hunt and kill. Iron Jacket also saw Bear-of-a-Man standing beside Red Hair. You too will die hated enemy. The thought brought a wicked smile to Iron Jacket's face.

"I see your old friend is glad to see us," Bigfoot said as he nodded a big smiling greeting toward Iron Jacket, surprising the Comanche with his audacity. "My guess is we'll have to fight our way home. I'm sure you knew that before we came on this little ride, though."

"I thought it was possible," Caleb admitted. "As guests of the tribe, we're safe for now, but we'll have to be ready for anything when we pull out of the Clear Fork reservation and head for home. It's high time we killed that son-of-a-bitch anyways. I figured the best way to go about that was to get him to attack us."

"I can't argue with that," agreed Bigfoot as he gave Iron Jacket another a big friendly smile and a wink that infuriated the Comanche.

Caleb and Bigfoot broke their focus on Iron Jacket to observe the meeting between Buffalo Hump and Major Neighbors. It would indeed be a historic event if the Penetaka war chief ever agreed to move onto the reservation. Neighbors dismounted and stepped forward, raising his right hand in peace and friendship to Buffalo Hump. "It is good to see you again, Potsanaquahip. Not since I was in the village of Old Owl several years ago have I seen you."

"Welcome to the gathering of the Penetaka, Tall Brother," said Buffalo Hump. "The People have come together to hear your words as you asked. And though it is not our way to speak of those who have gone before, I too remember my brother well. I only wish the People still had his wisdom to help guide us. Come join me in my lodge and we shall eat." Buffalo Hump turned to Caleb and Bigfoot. "I also invite two of the People's greatest enemies, Red Hair and Bear-of-a-Man to join with us."

The meetings to decide the fate of the Penetakas were conducted in Buffalo Hump's lodge, the largest in the village, and they took place over a period of several days. The last day, however, was the day a decision would be reached. The lodge was packed and tensions ran high. Every warrior present wanted to ensure that his opinion was heard.

The meeting began with the sacred pipe ceremony as explained by Buffalo Hump, "to show respect for Wakan Tanka, to show respect for Mother Earth, to show respect for our fellow man, and to show respect for individual freedom." Buffalo Hump began the ceremony by loading the pipe with kinnic kinnick, an aromatic bark from the red willow tree and sprinkling a small pinch on the ground. "This is for giving back to Mother Earth what we have taken from her." He then faced east, "for the sun and the new day;" south, "for warmth and growth;" west "for where the thunder lives and the rains come;" and north "for winter purity and spring re-growth." He then pointed the pipe down "for Mother Earth" and up "for Father Sky."

After the sacred pipe had made its way around the fire, Buffalo Hump was the first to rise and speak. "I have heard many words in the last week from those who feel it would be best for the Penetaka to move to the Clear Fork, and many words from those who are sure we would not be happy there. All of these words were spoken well and with much thought, and they deserved the careful consideration we have given them. Yet in spite of all these words, there are many here, like me, who have not yet chosen a path. Today Ketumse will first tell us once more why the reservation is a good thing, and then Sanaco will tell us why we should not go there. After they have shared their words others may also speak as is the way of the People. Then we will decide." Buffalo Hump resumed his seat at the fire.

Ketumse rose to his feet. "I have heard many complaints about the size of the reservation on the Clear Fork, but what size would please those who complain. What they demand is our old hunting grounds that stretched all the way to the Shining Water and deep into Mexico. But those days are gone. The Penetaka are now squeezed between the white settlements and the lands of our brothers to the north. Do the Kwahadi to the northwest or the Yamparika to the northeast invite us to hunt buffalo in their lands? No, they guard them with the jealousy of a squaw. The Penetaka are forced to eat deer and antelope which are fine until the starving time comes. Then we are forced to eat our own mules and horses. Compare the size of our herds now to what they were. Soon we will eat them all! Tall brother says we can learn to raise the spotted buffalo of the whites to see us through the winter, and the game on the Clear Fork is plentiful. If the Penetaka are to survive we must accept the reservation. I have spoken."

Ketsume sat down and Sanaco rose to take his place. "My brother Ketsume speaks with his heart, but the reservation is not the way of the People. This land belongs to the People; all of it, not only a tiny bit along the Clear Fork the whites offer us when it is already ours. The People are not meant to sit idle, growing fat and lazy on the spotted buffalo of the whites and learning to scar the land like women. Without the buffalo how will we build our lodges? How will we keep them warm in the winter? How can we hope to maintain our way of life? If we must fight for the right to hunt in the north, then we must fight! If we must fight for the land that stretches to the Shining Water and deep into Mexico, then we must fight! This has always been the way of the people! I have spoken."

Iron Jacket sprang to his feet as soon as Sanaco had regained his seat, his angry words directed more at Caleb and Bigfoot than the others who sat around the council fire. "My brother Sanaco speaks words of wisdom and truth! We must never give in to the white eyes. The way of the People is the way of the war path. How else can our young men prove themselves to be men, if not in war; by raising spotted buffalo, by scarring the earth like squaws? I spit on the ways of the white man! The people have always ridden where they chose, not only where the white eyes allowed. I can ride across the land the whites offer us on the Clear Fork in a single morning. Would the men sitting at this council fire accept being limited to such a small place? We must never give up our land and our way of life for the white road!" Iron Jacket's burned into Caleb's as he added, "The People must fight for what is ours!"

Singing Grass rose slowly to his feet, looking each of the warriors sitting around the fire in the eyes before moving on to the next man. He had not missed the fact that most of Iron Jacket's heated words were directed at Red Hair and Bear-of-a-Man. "Iron Jacket speaks words of war. He says we must kill the white eyes and take back our land; that our young men can only prove themselves in war. He does not speak of the terrible price the People have already paid to fight this unending war against the whites. For every white man we kill, many more take his place. The whites are numbered as the stars in the sky, but not so the People. Once the Penetaka were many and our herds were vast. Now we are few, and we must eat our horses in the starving time. What will we do when they are gone? Iron Jacket's answer is always to fight; to fight for the land that we no longer have, and to fight our brothers in the north for the right to hunt where we are now unwelcome. We will need many warriors to carry on such a fight. From where will they come? Must we fight until every one of us is dead? There comes a time when all men must face the truth. The time of glory for the Penetaka has passed. We can either go to the Clear Fork and begin a new life or move north as we choose and join our brothers who will continue the fight, until one day they have to make the same choice we do today."

A time of quiet and contemplation settled over the council as each warrior searched his own heart for the answer. Eventually Buffalo Hump rose to his feet once again. "As in all things that concern the People each warrior has the right and the duty to seek the path that he feels to be the right one. As for me I will try this life on the Clear Fork as Ketumse and Singing Grass suggest. In my heart I believe it is the only chance for the People to survive. If things turn out to be as my brother Sanaco says they will, or as my brother Iron Jacket warns, then I will leave the reservation and continue the fight with all my strength until the People are no more. Under these conditions, I ask that my brothers in this council join with me."

Even the warriors who strongly opposed the idea of moving to the reservation joined in with Buffalo Hump's reasonable position, and Major Neighbors finally rose to speak. "Today the People have made a wise decision. I promise to do my best to see that none of you regret your choice, and that the army keeps the whites off your land."

That will be easier said than done, thought Caleb. Thankfully, he was wise enough to keep his opinion to himself.

Soon after the council meeting, Iron Jacket met in his lodge with Many Tears and a few more good friends. "We will all go to the reservation as Buffalo Hump wishes. After all, we can raid the settlements from there just as well as we can from any other village or camp. When we return, the blue-coat soldiers will prevent the Rangers from following us onto the reservation." The others smiled for the first time since the meeting, nodding at the truth of Iron Jacket's words, and for the promise that the fight would continue. "But Red Hair and Bear-of-a-Man must die before they reach the white settlements! When they leave the land on the Clear Fork, I will organize a war party to follow them. After the hated Rangers are dead, we will continue on to the settlements and set them aflame."

It took nearly a week for the entire village to traverse the fifty miles to the reservation and slowly file into the lovely valley of the Clear Fork. Caleb could not help but wonder how long it would last. "You heard the talk around the council fire as well as I did, Bigfoot," he said. "What do you think?" Major Neighbors had sat between the Rangers during the councils and acted as an interpreter.

Bigfoot yanked off his sombrero and vigorously scratched at his head, messing up his unruly, matted hair even more than it was. "As far as I'm concerned Sanaco's a tossup. I could see him stayin' and tryin' to make a go of it, if everything works out the way Neighbors is hopin' it will, who knows. But there ain't no way in hell your good friend's gonna stick around. Not unless he launches his raids on the settlements from here, so he can hide behind the army. That Iron Jacket's a sidewinder pure and simple."

Caleb nodded his agreement. "That's pretty much the way I see it. Let's go round up Eph and the rest of the company. The army has things under control here. I think it's high time we said so long to Major Neighbors and hit the trail home."

Chapter 22

A bank of dirty gray clouds hanging low over the Western horizon gave the promise of rain, when the Rangers rode out of the Clear Fork reservation early the following morning. Rangers Al Chalmers and Stan Redd had been left behind at Fort Graham. Once their wounds were sufficiently healed, they would proceed to the Rocking M on their own. Major Neighbors told Caleb he was pleased with the assistance the Rangers had provided and that he would be sure and write the same to Governor Pease.

The company covered nearly forty miles, when the rain failed to materialize, and stopped to cook their evening meal a few miles below the headwaters of Hubbard Creek. Caleb ordered the cook fires smothered in dirt and moved the Rangers to a new location a mile further up the creek when the men had finished eating. After his little talk with Bigfoot, he was sure they were either being followed or soon would be.

"We'll cold camp the first few nights on the trail," Caleb said, after the guards had been posted and the men bedded down.

"I got a bad feelin' Iron Jacket and some of his friends ain't far behind."

Eph glanced at Bigfoot and George. Unlike Sergeant Jessup, the three Rangers had ridden with Caleb long enough to respect his sixth sense for danger.

"Eph," Caleb continued, "tomorrow mornin' you'll take the Company and head for Indian Gap. It's near seventy miles from here, so set up a cold camp when you hole up for the night. Me and Bigfoot are gonna hang back and keep an eye on our back-trail. We'll meet up with you durin' the night. Make damn sure the guards keep a sharp eye. Neither of us hankers to get shot by one of our own men. Bigfoot, what do you think? Am I chasin' around after my own tail?"

Bigfoot shook his head. "To be honest, partner, I ain't sure. Iron Jacket may not want to cause any problems so soon after movin' to the reservation, but I learned a long time ago to follow your hunches. If you want to ride our back-trail for a day or two, I'm all for it."

Early the following morning, after Eph had led the Company out toward Indian Gap, Caleb and Bigfoot splashed their mounts back down Hubbard creek for a mile or so. Being careful to cover their tracks, they left the creek and made a big circle to the east, coming out on some high ground that offered a fine view of their back-trail. After picketing their horses in some good graze in the middle of a small copse of live oak, they took cover and waited. The morning passed slowly, and by early afternoon, the heat of the day made them both drowsy.

Caleb was ready to mount up and ride out when he finally saw what he had been waiting for. Nudging Bigfoot awake with his elbow, he said, "Take a look, partner. That son-of-a-bitch just don't know when to call it quits."

Down in the low ground, near Hubbard Creek, four Comanche scouts slowly circled the previous evening's camp, and then set out to the southeast on the trail left by the Rangers when they headed toward Indian Gap. Within minutes the main body of the war party arrived, stretched out along the creek, with Iron Jacket in the lead on his big silver-gray stallion.

Bigfoot glanced over at Caleb. "I think your friend means business this time. There must be more than a hundred warriors down there."

Caleb paused to make a count. "With the scouts, I make it a hundred and fifty-seven," he said when he was finished. "I had a feelin' there were a bunch of Comanches in that village who wanted to slit our throats. It looks like most of 'em decided to join up with Iron Jacket and give it a try."

"Tryin' is about as far as the varmints are likely to get," said Bigfoot. "I don't give a damn how many Comanches are ridin' against us. It takes a lot of doin to deal with twenty-five well-armed Rangers."

Caleb chuckled. "Let's get mounted. We got some hard ridin' ahead of us, and I got a plan that just might work. We can talk it over on the way."

When Caleb and Bigfoot got back to their horses, they made a wide swing to the east and then picked up the pace to a steady, ground-eating lope that Smokey and Bigfoot's big buckskin, Biscuit could maintain all day long. The Rangers rode through the late afternoon before overtaking the Comanches who had set up for a few hours rest in a cold camp. Soon after midnight the sky partially cleared, and with the aid of a silvery full moon, the Rangers made much better time, meeting up with the company well before dawn.

While Bigfoot got busy waking the men and getting them ready to ride, Caleb briefed Eph and the sergeants on the plan he and Wallace had worked out. "There's a big war party no more 'n a couple hours behind us. The Comanches got scouts out, so we'll ride hard until we find a good spot to defend ourselves. We won't set up there right away, though. Instead we'll ride on for a mile or two then swing wide and double back. Once we're in position, the Comanche scouts should ride right on past us, so we can kick off the fight by stingin' the war party from ambush. That should shake their confidence some."

"How many warriors are you talkin' about?" asked Eph.

"One hundred and fifty seven," Caleb replied as he looked each man in the eye to see their reaction to the number, "so we should all have plenty of targets." They appeared calm and ready, smiling thinly at his poor attempt at humor.

Bigfoot walked up. "The horses are saddled and the men are ready to ride, partner."

"Good! We'll use what's left of this moon and hopefully put some ground between us and that war party." Caleb headed for Smokey. "Let's mount up and get ridin'."

With the knowledge that they would be holing up as soon as they found a likely location to set up the ambush, the Rangers pushed their horses to the limit and gained a little ground on the Comanches. It was mid-morning when the company rode through Indian Gap and Caleb spotted what he was looking for near the headwaters of the Lampasas River. To the west of the spring that served as the source of the Lampasas, the ground rose gradually to a low, tree-covered, rocky hill less than a hundred yards from the river. The Rangers rode on down the shallow river for a couple more miles then made a wide swing to the west before heading back north.

When the company rode into the trees at the top of the hill and dismounted, Caleb could not have been happier with his choice. The flattened area at the summit was a little more than fifty yards long and thirty yards wide, and stretched from the northwest to the southeast roughly along the course of the Lampasas. From the rocky edge of the hill facing the river, there was a clear field of fire over the tops of the trees that covered the slope all the way down to the trail. A bubbling spring cut a deep, L-shaped ravine into the rear of the hill, the water from the small stream eventually winding its way down and back around the base of the hill and on into the Lampasas. The ravine would provide fresh water and a wide enough place to picket the horses where the animals would be out of the line of fire.

Once the horses were picketed, Caleb addressed the Rangers. "Men, this will be a long, tough fight. Conserve your powder and ball and make every shot count. We'll be doin' most of the fightin' with our long rifles unless the Comanches get in close, but make damn sure all four of your cylinders are loaded and ready just in case."

"Sergeant Jessup, you and Sergeant White will place each one of your men personally. For the initial ambush I want every man along the edge of the hill facin' the river. Second Platoon will cover from the center of the hill to the northwest, and First Platoon will cover from the center of the hill to the southeast. Sergeant Jessup will be the last man on the northwest end of the line and Sergeant White will be the last man on the southeast end. Bigfoot and Lieutenant Daggett will remain in the middle with me."

"Jessup, you and White will also locate a position on the rear of the hill for every third man in your platoon. Make damn sure each man knows exactly where they're supposed to go if I give the order. The last thing we need is a bunch of confusion, if the Comanches decide to hit us from the rear. Bigfoot, if that happens, you'll take command back there. Remember, no one fires until I do, or when this is all over, I'll skin you alive! Are there any questions? Good, let's get it done. And make damn sure the men can't be seen from the river!"

The preparations were no sooner completed than the Comanche scouts made their appearance, riding slowly past the spring that served as the source of the Lampasas and heading on down the trail below the hill. Caleb breathed a sigh of relief, but it was short lived. The main war party soon came into sight with Iron Jacket riding at the front. The Comanches were decked out for war, with their colorful, bull-hide shields uncased and their faces painted in bright slashes of vermillion, ocher, white, blue, and black. The horses were also painted, and their tails were tied up and decorated with colorful trade ribbons. As always, Iron Jacket's big silver stallion had lightning bolts brushed down its legs and hailstones daubed across its rump. The war chief's face was decorated in broad horizontal stripes of vermilion and ocher and his metal breastplate gleamed in the sunlight. The lone eagle feather twisted into his long hair danced in the breeze.

Caleb brought the brass butt-plate of the Hawken's stock up into the cup of his shoulder and leveled the long barrel. Taking up a good sight picture, the distinct tip of the front sight blade centered in the blurry V of the rear sight, he found his target and made sure the form of Iron Jacket's torso sat atop the clear tip of the front sight. He set the rear trigger, took a shallow breath, letting half of it out, placed the first pad of his index finger on the front hair trigger, and slowly squeezed.

The throaty roar of the Hawken surprised him, and he lifted his head above the swirling smoke. The .50 caliber ball flew straight and true, but once again the Gods smiled on Caleb's hated enemy. Iron Jacket took that very instant to look up toward the hill and the slight turn of his torso caused the rifle ball to strike a glancing blow off his breast plate instead of plowing into his side. The force of the blow still nearly unhorsed the war chief, and the glancing ball burned a shallow furrow across his left forearm.

All along the rocky face of the hill, the Rangers' long rifles belched smoke and fire, knocking eighteen Comanches off the backs of their ponies with the deadly rain of lead, a few of them hit more than once. Not bad thought Caleb, as he quickly went through the well-practiced routine of loading his long rifle.

Normally he could get off a well-aimed shot every thirty to forty-five seconds. First, he poured a measured amount of gunpowder down the muzzle. Next, he shoved a ball and patch in the barrel with his thumb, and removing the ramrod, seated them snugly. Replacing the ramrod, he brought the rifle to half-cock, pushed a percussion cap on the nipple, and cocked the hammer to full, as he searched the field for another target.

Iron Jacket had already ridden out of range, so Caleb drew down on a warrior adorned with a buffalo horn headdress, set the rear trigger, and slowly squeezed the hair trigger. The warrior's arms flew wide as the heavy rifle ball blasted in between his shoulder-blades and rolled him off his pony. Pandemonium reigned among the Comanches as they scattered in all directions to avoid the death-dealing rifle fire of the Rangers. Some of them took cover in the trees at the base of the hill. They would bear watching, thought Caleb.

Iron Jacket was furious. Most of the warriors had ridden out of range up past the spring by now, but the damage had already been done. Fifteen warriors were killed in the ambush and nearly as many wounded, some of them to the point where they would not recover. How had the scouts missed the ambush? But it was much too late to worry about that now. Words of discontent were already beginning to spread, and he had to take some kind of action to regain the momentum that now belonged to the Rangers.

A frontal attack would be foolish and the casualties would be too high. Looking around, he saw there was also a hill on the east side of the river opposite the hill the Rangers occupied. The hills were less than two hundred yards apart, with the river running nearly equidistant between them. He sent fifty warriors armed with the new rifles around to the rear of the east hill with instructions to climb it and bring the Rangers under fire. With a little luck, their rifle fire would produce a few Ranger casualties and no more casualties of their own.

Fifteen or twenty warriors had taken cover in the trees at the base of the hill when the ambush was sprung. If Iron Jacket could manage to get a few more warriors in the trees, they could help pin down the Rangers in the rocks with rifle fire while he launched an attack on the hill from the rear. However, it was already late in the afternoon. If he waited, he could move the warriors into place during the night for an early morning attack. In the meantime he would send a few more men with rifles to the hill and take the rest with him to offer the Rangers a little surprise Comanche style.

After sending the riflemen to join the warriors already on the hill, Iron jacket took the remaining fifty warriors into the trees to the northwest side of the Ranger hill. Taking their time the Comanches silently worked themselves into bow range. When he was satisfied they were close enough, Iron Jacket told the warriors that on his command they would all fire a volley of arrows high into the air so that they would fall on the ranger position like so many death-dealing raindrops from the sky. The warriors would then quickly fire another volley and then another. By the third volley, the Rangers would find cover, but if the three volleys were quick enough, and the warriors managed to judge the distance correctly, the falling arrows would be deadly surprise for the hated Rangers.

The Comanches were not the best marksmen in the world with their new rifles, but when seventy warriors opened fire on the hill across the river at the same time the Rangers were forced to take heed. Hot led seemed to be flying everywhere, but at first no one was hit.

"Damn," Bigfoot groused as a ball stuck the rocks in front of him and whined away over his head. "It's gettin' to be down right dangerous around here!"

Caleb took careful aim and fired at the smoke from the opposite hillside. "Bigfoot, go down the line and make sure only
our best marksmen are firin' at the smoke. We can't let the Comanches off Scott free, but we can't be wastin' powder and ball
either. I got no idea how long we'll be holed up here."

As Bigfoot came to his feet and started down the line, Caleb
heard a dull thud and a low moan off to his left. Crawling over
to where he heard the moan, he found young Mike Yates lying
on his back, a bloody hole in his chest. Caleb sat up and lifted
Mike's head into his lap. "Tell my Ma," Mike gasped, but never
finished what he had tried to say.

"I'll tell her," Caleb said as he closed the young man's eyes
and sighed in frustration. When would it ever end, he wondered?

Suddenly arrows started to rain out of the sky, two of them
sticking into the ground near Caleb. He heard a distant scream
and then a yelp of pain nearby. "Get under some cover," he
yelled! A second wave of arrows came in and he heard another
scream of pain further down the line. "Get under cover, damn
it!" At least the rifle fire from the hill across the river was beginning to slack off. The return fire from the ranger sharpshooters
must be having some effect, he thought.

Another flight of arrows rained in. When they stopped falling, Caleb came to his feet and ran hunched over to where he
heard the nearby yelp of pain. Billy Allen was sitting up under a
shelf of rocks holding his leg with both hands and grimacing in
pain. An arrow was imbedded deep in his thigh. Caleb saw Niko
Chavez crouching beside a nearby tree and called him over. Expecting another flight of arrows, the young Ranger sprinted for
all he was worth and rolled under the cover of the rocks.

"Get to the packhorse in the ravine, Niko," Caleb ordered.
"I need a bunch of bandages and a couple bottles of whiskey.
Get someone to help if you need it. It looks as if the arrows have
stopped for now, but move from cover to cover for until we're
sure. Niko hesitated for only a moment, and then took off for the
ravine. Thankfully, no more arrows rained in.

Caleb slipped his Bowie from the beaded sheath on his gun belt and cut a long opening in the leg of Billy's wool trousers. Giving the young Ranger a stick to bite down on, he took a firm grip on the shaft of the arrow and shoved it the rest of the way through the thigh, eliciting a sharp groan of pain in spite of the stick. Thankfully, Billy passed out. After he snapped off the feathered end of the shaft, Caleb grasped the bloody end of the arrow just above the arrowhead and slowly pulled it the rest of the way through.

A moment later, Niko arrived with the bandages and whiskey. "Ernie Moyer is bringin' some more. He should be here in a minute."

Caleb nodded as he poured some whiskey into both the entry and the exit wounds. After pressing dressings into place, he wrapped them with a bandage and tied it tightly to slow the bleeding. "That should do it." Caleb stayed under cover for a few more minutes, but no more arrows fell, and the rifle fire from the other side of the river had ceased. It would be dark soon and plans would have to be made for morning. The remaining wounded would also have to be cared for.

Darkness had fallen by the time Iron Jacket gathered his war party once again. He was shocked to learn that two more warriors had been killed while firing from the hill and several more wounded by the accurate return fire of the Rangers. The war chief had no way of knowing whether or not the rifle fire from the Comanches or the arrows launched high in the sky had caused any Ranger casualties, but it made little difference. Already growing weary of the siege, his warriors would give up and return to the reservation if they did not overrun the Ranger position soon.

During the launching of the arrows, Iron Jacket had worked out a plan for an attack in the morning. Well before daylight, he would send thirty warriors into the woods at the rear of the hill to begin firing at the Rangers as soon as there was enough light for them to see their targets. He hoped the Rangers would believe this was the main attack and would move some men to defend against it. In the meantime Iron Jacket would take the remainder of the war party into the woods on the southeast side of the hill near the river. The warriors would use the cover of the trees and darkness to move in as close to the top of the hill as they dared without being discovered. When the sun came up in the Rangers' eyes, the warriors would charge out of the woods and overwhelm the defenders on that side of the hill. Once the Comanches were in among their hated enemies, their numbers would give them the advantage in a close in fight.

Many of the warriors were not in favor of fighting the Rangers while they were dug into the hilltop like so many stubborn prairie dogs. From the beginning, the plan had been to strike their hated enemies on the trail while they were out in the open, but somehow the war party had been discovered. Of course, most of the warriors attributed this fact to the strong medicine of Red Hair and Bear-of-a-Man. If the attack did not go well in the morning, they would surely turn tail and return to the reservation.

Well before sunrise, Caleb rose with thoughts of the previous night's meeting still fresh in his mind. Everyone who spoke up had expected an attack in the morning and various methods had been discussed to meet the threat. Not knowing exactly where the attack would fall, it was decided to adopt Eph's idea of establishing a reaction force. Every third Ranger was taken out of the line, brought to the center of the hilltop, and placed under Eph's command. When the Comanches struck, his men would reinforce the section of the perimeter that was under attack. Caleb and Bigfoot would remain in the middle of the hilltop to direct the entire defense and help out where they were needed.

Caleb heard Bigfoot stir in his bedroll. "You best get up and circle the perimeter, Bigfoot. Make damn sure everyone's awake. It'll be growin' light soon enough."

Bigfoot crawled out of his bedroll and nudged Eph with the toe of his boot. "Get on up from there, Lieutenant, it's time to rise and shine and wake up your men." The big man chuckled as he walked off into the darkness.

Eph stood and stretched, vigorously scratching his head before he pulled on his sombrero. "I'll get right to it, Sergeant," he called out in the darkness to the still chuckling Bigfoot." Eph moved to the men and began shaking them awake. "Get on you feet, Rangers, and start checkin' your weapons."

One by one the Rangers climbed out of their bedrolls, stretching and yawning, and complaining about the lack of a fire and a good cup of hot coffee in the cool dampness of the early morning. By the time Eph had them all on their feet, it was close to sunrise. In the early morning twilight, it was already light enough for Caleb to see the Rangers coming to life all along the perimeter. Suddenly, the sharp crack of a single rifle shot from the woods on the slope behind the hill shattered the tranquility of the peaceful dawn. A Ranger standing guard at the rear of the hill dropped his rifle and slumped to the ground. The single shot was quickly followed by the rolling thunder of a sustained volley, and the shrill Comanche war cries of attacking warriors.

"Let's go, follow me men!" Eph yelled as took off running toward the rear of the hill.

Corporal Nelson and the remainder of the reaction platoon were right on his heels. Quickly joining up with the Rangers on the perimeter, they began returning the Comanches' fire.

"Shouldn't we head over there and give 'em a hand?" Bigfoot asked, returning from his rounds and anxious to join in on the action.

Caleb hesitated, concerned about the dwindling volume of fire from the attackers. If this was a real attack, the rate of fire should be increasing, he thought, not slowing down. He was about to address his concerns to Bigfoot when the first blinding rays of the sun streamed over the eastern horizon and all hell broke loose, as nearly a hundred Comanches came boiling up out of the woods on the eastern slope of the hill, Iron Jacket leading the charge.

The only thing that prevented the screaming warriors from overrunning the hill was the presence on the southeastern perimeter of George White and another young Ranger, Tom Willis. Refusing to yield in spite of the terrible odds, George and Tom came to their feet with both Colts blazing, delivering a devastating, rapid fire volley into the heart of the oncoming Comanche line. Iron Jacket was the first warrior to go down in the hail of .44 caliber lead that spewed from the long barrels of the Rangers' Colt Dragoons. The war chief was quickly joined by more than a dozen others, instantly breaking the momentum of the charge. The Comanches began to mill around uncertain whether to continue the charge or retreat to the cover of the woods. Then Many tears, enraged by what he assumed was the death of his good friend, rallied the confused warriors by drawing an arrow back in his short bow and burying it deep in George White's chest. The Ranger Sergeant dropped his Colts and grabbed at the arrow as he fell to his knees and flopped onto his back. Young Tom was killed soon after by return rifle fire from several warriors as the Comanches resumed the attack.

However, the sacrifices of George and Tom had not been in vain. The brief break in the momentum of the attack lasted long enough to enable Caleb and Bigfoot to reach the downed Rangers and take their place on the perimeter. Once again the Comanche charge was met by a wall of hot lead that tore into their ranks. Caleb shot Many Tears in the face at close range, the .44 caliber ball exiting the back of the unlucky warrior's skull along with most of his brains. Caleb took an arrow in his left arm from a warrior with his face painted half black and half white, but Bigfoot, firing first his right hand Colt and then his left, blew the Comanche off the back of his painted pony.

Eph's reaction force reached the perimeter a moment later, and their added firepower broke the back of the Comanche charge, driving the confused and angry warriors back toward the woods. As Caleb stood holding his bloody arm, he saw Iron Jacket stagger to his feet. The war chief had only been grazed across the top of the head by George's ball and momentarily knocked senseless. Another warrior galloped past. Leaning far off the side of his pony, he swung Iron Jacket up behind him. Caleb fired twice at the war chief with his good arm, but the hurried shots went wide, and Iron Jacket and his rescuer made it to the safety of the woods along with the others.

An eerie quiet settled over the hilltop as the bitter tang of black powder smoke began to clear the air. The area from the woods to the Ranger perimeter where Sergeant White and young Tom Willis had made their final stand was littered with dead and dying warriors. Caleb fought back the tears as he grasped the shaft of the arrow and pulled it from his arm, before kneeling beside George and gently closing his friend's eyes.

Bigfoot and Eph strode through the downed Comanches, finishing off the wounded warriors without mercy. The striking contrast between Caleb's tender mercies and the pure savagery of Bigfoot and Eph's actions went unnoticed among those who were destined to continue the bloody struggle for many years to come.

PART IV

Chapter 23

Cholo poured Caleb a cup of coffee from the big pot that he always kept hot on a small fire near the roundup supply wagon. The old Mexican cook smiled as he added three heaping spoons of sugar and stirred the coffee well before handing it to Caleb. "Be careful, *Jeffe*, it is very hot."

"Gracias, Cholo," Caleb said after carefully tasting the delicious brew and smacking his lips with pleasure. "You make a great cup of coffee." This would be the old Mexican's third cattle drive with Pedro, and he had become a permanent fixture at the Rocking M.

The sunset from the high ridge above the Colorado was spectacular this late spring evening of 1856 and Caleb took a moment to admire the view before joining Felix and Pedro. As the huge orange disk of the sun slowly sank below the far off Texas hill country, its dying rays set fire to a band of fleecy clouds drifting across the deep azure sky, putting on a display of vivid colors that would have been the envy of any artist's palette.

With the birth of Pedro's son, Antonio, last spring, there had not been a cattle drive, but the break gave the Rocking M longhorns an opportunity to breed and mature in abundance. This spring's drive would be much more profitable than the previous year's, when much of the stock had been purchased on consignment. The herd would be made up entirely of Rocking M stock, more than four thousand of the ornery critters.

Financially, the ranch was doing well. There was now nearly $250,000 deposited in Cincinnati banks and more than $100,000 in gold coins in the safe buried in the floor of the storeroom. Caleb and Josh's California investments had also prospered, nearly doubling with the spectacular growth of Oakland, the city Jack Hays had helped to found across the bay from San Francisco. Wanda and Josh were doing well, and she planned to return to Austin in the fall. Caleb was looking forward to seeing Joshua for the first time. Both he and Hammond were three year's old now, and little Ham, reddish-brown curls flying, was the terror of the hacienda.

Being the matron of such a large hacienda, with responsibility for all the wives and children and the operation of a school to teach everyone to speak English, including many of the adults, was a full-time job for Lucinda. If not for the attentions of Ham's watchful sisters, the little bandit would have driven Lucinda crazy. Ilse was already turning into a responsible young lady at twelve, blond, blue-eyed, and beautiful, and Gretchin was every bit as pretty, although at ten still very much of a tomboy, who rode the ranch with her father or Bigfoot at every opportunity. Veronica had bloomed into a beautiful wife and mother, and she provided invaluable assistance to Lucinda when it came to running the bustling household.

Caleb's Rangers had spent most of the last year in the saddle dealing with the Comanches. It seemed as if there were as many raids launched off the reservation on the Clear Fork of the Brazos as there were from out of the Llano Estacado or across the

Red River. Eph and the Second Platoon would be back any day now from their most recent patrol, and Caleb and Bigfoot would be taking out the First Platoon.

After the wounded, including Caleb, had healed up from the big standoff with Iron Jacket, six new Rangers had been recruited, two from San Antonio, and four from Austin and the Bastrop area. Instead of recruiting a new sergeant to take George White's place, Caleb made Bigfoot the sergeant for first Platoon as well as the Company First Sergeant.

The western sky had turned a deep indigo and the first stars were beginning to twinkle overhead by the time Caleb turned away and walked over to fire. Felix and Pedro were finishing up their supper, and Caleb ladled some beans and bacon onto a tin plate and picked up a few tortillas before sitting down to join them. "This is real good eatin'," he mumbled around a big spoonful of beans and a bite of tortilla. "Looks like you're about ready to go, Pedro."

Pedro nodded as he took a sip of his hot coffee, set the cup aside, and scraped his tin plate into the fire. "We should move out in a few days. I planned on driving around four thousand head this year, and we're already there."

"Four thousand longhorns will bring in a heap of gold," Caleb said as he briefly paused in his attack on the plate of beans to take a sip of his coffee. "Felix, are we still plannin' on sendin' some of this money north with Josh?"

"Most of it," Felix replied. "I told Pedro to bring back forty thousand in gold for the safe. With the ten extra hands we hired, the payroll has increased, and I'm also planning to build five new cottages for the married hands; three on the end of the bunkhouse closest to the hacienda and two on the other end."

"I like that idea," said Caleb, nodding his head. "Not only do we need the cottages, but they'll nearly wall in the entire central square. With thirty ranch hands and the five Lipans, we can put up a damn stiff defense, too, if need be."

"Do you think we'll have more problems with the local ranchers now that we hired the extra hands?" asked Pedro.

"No more than we already have," Caleb replied. "But we can't make decisions for the Rockin' M based on what other folks say, 'specially when most of it's pure hatred. By the way, Pedro, if you're still goin' to town for supplies tomorrow, me and Bigfoot are plannin' on stringin' along." Caleb had written Wanda a long letter in the orderly room that he wanted to leave with Richard Bullock before the First Platoon rode out on patrol, and Bigfoot decided to go along to have a beer and say hello to his old friend.

"I'll look forward to the company," Pedro replied. We leave right after breakfast."

It was near noon the following day, when Caleb, Bigfoot, and Pedro rode up Congress Avenue at the head of two Rocking M supply wagons. Manny and Miguel Flores and four other ranch hands trailed the wagons to help load and serve as guards on the way back to the ranch. Being a Saturday, the Avenue was crowded with foot traffic, riders on horseback, and wagons and buggies of all manner and description.

Caleb glanced over at Pedro when they reached Pecan Street. "Me and Bigfoot are headin' on over to Bullock's. We'll meet up with you at the Emporium later on. If you finish early, you can meet up with us."

"*Bueno*," Pedro replied.

Caleb and Bigfoot reined west and headed for the Bullock Hotel. The Rangers dismounted and looped their reins over the hitching rail in front of the hotel. Striding up the steps, they crossed the wide, covered veranda, stepped through the front door, and shoved their way past the swinging, batwing doors into the hotel's café. Two customers were leaning on the far end of the bar, and several of the café' s tables were occupied.

Bullock was swiping a towel down the bar, and a big smile spread across his face when he saw the pair enter. "Bigfoot, you old sidewinder, how the hell you been? You too, Caleb, step on up and have yourselves a beer. Bullock filled two glasses and placed them on the bar. "What brings the two of you to town?"

Bigfoot chuckled. "I can't speak for my redheaded companion, but I missed the stimulatin' conversation you're so famous for, Richard. Course to tell the truth, the beer might have somethin' to do with it, too."

Bullock laughed. "Well, no matter, it's damn good to see you either way. How're Lucinda and the kids doin', Caleb?"

Caleb smiled. "Just fine, Mr. Bullock. Thanks for askin'. Ham's turned into a holy terror now that he's gotten older, but Ilse keeps a tight rein on him. She acts like a grown woman already. Gretchin is still a Tomboy and loves to ride with Bigfoot. My crazy partner is teachin' her to rope and shoot, too. It's about to drive her Ma crazy." Bigfoot beamed. "Would you mind mailin' this for me, Mr. Bullock?" Caleb slid a letter across the bar, and Bullock glanced at Bigfoot. "Don't worry, he knows."

Bullock slipped the letter under the bar. "In that case I guess I can tell you there's a letter for you on my desk."

"Thanks," said Caleb, "I'll be right back." Caleb stepped away from the bar and headed for the office.

Bigfoot shook his head. "The man's playin' with fire, plain and simple."

Caleb ripped the letter open and scanned it quickly to ensure that all was well, then sat back in Bullock's chair to take his time and savor it. "Hello, Caleb," the letter began rather formally, but soon warmed up. "I am growing tired of the hustle and bustle of New Orleans and looking forward to the relative peace and quiet of Austin. I miss my school, too. Every time I look at Joshua I see you. He looks just like his father, except his curly hair is a little lighter and his eyes are blue like mine."

"I was terribly sorry to hear of your friend's death in California, but thank you so much for thinking of Joshua. It comforts me to know that he will have a fine future thanks to his loving father. I am still teaching at the girls' school, but having my own school, no matter how humble it was, brought me a very special kind of freedom and happiness. I was surprised to hear that no one else has opened a school since I've been gone. Remember the book I told you about, *Uncle Tom's Cabin*. It has been officially banned not only in New Orleans, but all across the south, and therefore, I assume in Texas, too. The abolitionists, of which I consider myself one, have refused to let it die. I saved a copy for you as I promised. You must read it when I get home."

Be careful, love, Caleb thought, you have Joshua to think about now, too. Wanda went on to talk about the violence that had erupted in Kansas as a result of the Kansas-Nebraska Act just as she had predicted it would. Supporters of slavery under the leadership of William Quantrill, and those strongly opposed to it under abolitionist John Brown, had flocked to Kansas to ensure their side would carry the vote when the election was finally held. In the meantime violence was rife, and no one could begin to guess what the ultimate outcome would be.

Caleb sat up straight and folded the letter. How would things eventually work out with Wanda, he wondered? He knew how much he loved Hammond, and the thought of Joshua never knowing him as his father hurt deeply. How much could he and Wanda tell the boy, though, before he was really old enough to understand? Then there was the terrible struggle over slavery that was gradually ripping the country apart. Caleb was not ready to stand beside Wanda as an outright abolitionist, but he knew in his heart that she was right. Slavery was inhuman, plain and simple. The terrible truth of the matter was that while most of the people in Texas seemed go along with the idea of slavery, only the eastern planters profited from the peculiar institution. Hardly anyone owned more than a slave or two in west Texas, but it was the issue of states' rights that would doom Texas, not slavery. If the Deep South succeeded from the Union, as many continued to threaten, Texas would follow, and war—a bloody civil war —would almost surely follow that. Would he be drawn into the fight, or could he somehow manage to straddle the fence; a precarious position at best. Only time would tell. He stood, put the letter in the bottom drawer with the others, and retuned to the café.

As he stepped through the batwing doors, Caleb heard the angry snap of a gunshot from the direction of Cooper's Emporium and then another. "Come on, Bigfoot, I think we got trouble!"

The wagons were almost loaded, and Pedro was talking with John Cooper when he heard men yelling from outside the store. "Excuse me, John," Pedro said, heading for the door.

When Pedro emerged into the bright sunlight on the wooden walk, the sight that greeted him nearly sent him into a rage. Two men were holding Manny Flores against the side of one of the supply wagons by pinning his arms, while another man was striking him across the face with a riding quirt. Two other men were holding guns on Miguel and the rest of the Rocking M hands to keep them from coming to Manny's assistance. A large crowd had gathered around to watch the show.

"You filthy greaser!" the man snarled as he raised the quirt high to strike again. "I'll teach you to show respect for a white man."

Snapping the Navy Colt from his right holster, Pedro fired from the hip, the .36 caliber ball neatly severing the quirt just above the startled man's grip. "Let him go and step away," Pedro growled at the two men holding Manny as he holstered the Colt and stepped toward them.

The man who had been using the quit dropped what remained of it and went for his gun. He had barely cleared leather when Pedro drew and fired, dropping the man where he stood with a ball in the center of his chest. This time the smoking Colt remained in his right hand and he filled his left hand from his other holster.

"I thought I told you to let that man go!" Pedro snarled to the men holding Manny. They quickly stepped away and Manny fell to the ground moaning. "Angel, you and Jose pick Manny up and put him in the wagon." Pedro stared at the men with drawn revolvers who were covering the Rocking M hands. "Use those guns or holster them and get out of the way." The men holstered their weapons and stepped back into the crowd, as Angel and Jose began helping Manny into the wagon.

Now voices from the large crowd began to turn uglier, as the two men who had been holding Manny also joined them. "We can't let that damn greaser get away with killin' Tom. You're damn right! We ought to string the bastard up right now! Somebody get a rope!"

Just as Pedro stepped back to face off against the heavy odds, Caleb and Bigfoot galloped up and reined in hard. A billowing cloud of dust swirled up in the street and slowly settled over the ugly scene.

Caleb swung down from the saddle and moved to Pedro's side, eyeing up the dead man lying in the street. "What the hell's goin' on, here brother?"

Before Pedro could answer, Bigfoot stepped up beside Caleb. Angel, Jose, and the other hands joined him. "Appears to me the odds are a little better now, partner."

Pedro pointed to the dead man as he answered Caleb's question. "That man was hitting Manny in the face with a riding quirt while two other men held him against the wagon. When I stopped him, he drew on me, so I shot him."

"That seems like a reasonable thing to do," Caleb said. He looked to the Rocking M hands. "What started all this?"

Reluctant to say anything, the ranch hands looked to one another before young Jose Vaca, Ernesto's son, finally spoke up. "Manny was carrying a box of supplies to the wagon when he accidentally bumped into that *hombre, Jeffe*." Jose pointed to the dead man. "Manny said that he was sorry, but then the *hombre* told him to get off the walk, and that a greaser had no right to use the walk when a white man was using it. This Manny refused to do. That is when the *hombre's* friends grabbed Manny and held him against the side of the wagon. His other friends kept us covered so we could not help while he beat Manny with the quirt."

"Is that the story, Angel?" Caleb asked.

"Si, Jeffe," Angel replied, "Jose is speaking the truth. This is what happened." The other hands were quick to nod their agreement.

Caleb turned to the crowd. "Gents, it appears to me this *hombre* got exactly what was comin' to him."

"Beatin' a greaser with a quirt ain't no crime or no reason to kill a man, McAdams," said one of the men who had been holding Manny, growing bolder now that he had so many men to back him up. "We aim to hang the bastard who did it!"

"Mister," said Caleb maintaining his calm, "I don't care one bit for the word 'greaser'; 'specially when you use it to talk about my brother. The man was beatin' my ranch hand for doing somethin' he had every right to do. Then he was dumb enough to draw down on my brother. I suggest you pick up this man's body and go about your business before any more of you get hurt. One more thing, most of the Rockin' M's hands are my kin, and even the ones who ain't won't bow down to you 'cause you're white. You best leave 'em be, or you'll end up answerin' to me or my brother."

"You can't talk to us like that McAdams," the spokesman for the crowd said, and he was immediately backed up by several others, "even if you are a rich rancher. We got a hell of a lot more men here than you do."

Bigfoot's unexpected laughter unsettled the crowd. "Mister, you must have a serious death wish. There might be more of you, but that just means we got more targets. Most of you are gonna be dead long before you even clear leather." The big man's smile dissolved into a sneer. "In fact, draw or not, I'm gonna kill you and anybody else dumb enough to still be standin' here thirty seconds from now." Bigfoot started to count, but before he reached ten, two men picked up the dead man and the crowd began to quickly disperse. Bigfoot turned to Caleb. "I think it's time we headed on back to the ranch, partner."

Caleb shook his head as he mounted. There was no telling what Bigfoot would do or say next. "You heard the man, Pedro. Somebody see to Manny. Let's go home."

Chapter 24

Second Platoon had just returned from their patrol and Bigfoot, Eph, and Sergeant Jessup were sitting at the table in the orderly room. Caleb poured everybody a cup of coffee from the pot that usually sat on the potbelly stove and joined them. Pedro had departed with the trail drive the previous morning, and Caleb was anxious to move out with First Platoon.

After adding his usual three spoonfuls of sugar, Caleb stirred the coffee well and took a sip. "Well, Lieutenant Daggett, how did it go out there?"

Eph smiled at Caleb's joking formality. "Juaquin spotted a small war party before they reached Indian Gap, and we set up an ambush, but somethin' must've tipped 'em off. Maybe they're startin' to get spooked about usin' the Gap to get at the settlements, but they turned tail just before we were ready to open fire. We still killed one and might've wounded a couple more. Juaquin tracked 'em to the reservation on the Clear Fork.

Then I turned back the way you told me too. I don't have to tell you how happy that made the men."

Caleb nodded. "I know how they feel, but that's what Governor Pease ordered, and that's they way we're gonna play it. Be sure 'n put it in your report so the governor can inform the army command. By the way, I got some great news from Pease this mornin' when I was in town. The Second U. S. Cavalry has arrived in Texas. Major William Hardee established Camp Cooper on the Clear Fork reservation, and the remainder of the regiment, under the command of Colonel Albert Sidney Johnston, set up regimental headquarters at Fort Mason."

"Hoorah," said Bigfoot, "that's the best damn news I heard in a good while. It's about time somebody in Washington got their act together." Everybody at the table shared the big man's sentiments.

"Governor Pease gives all the credit to Jefferson Davis, the current Secretary of War," said Caleb. "Accordin' to Pease, Secretary Davis understands the difference between the Indian problems the United States faced east of the Mississippi, and the problems we're facin' out here in the west. He knows settlers in the west are too spread out to use the old militia system they used back east, and that even if cavalry costs more than infantry, it's gonna be a hell of a lot more effective out here. I wanted to tell Pease that's what the Rangers have been preachin' ever since the war with Mexico, but I thought it best to hold my tongue. Davis plans to establish a few strong garrisons across the western frontier, and then mount expeditions from them to go after the tribes that cause problems."

"The man's talkin' sense," agreed Eph. "If the army operates like that and coordinates their efforts with ours, we can put a squeeze on the Comanches they won't soon forget."

"How long will the army be here, though, once they do get it right?" asked Caleb. "There's a war comin' between the North and the South, just as sure as the sun rises in the mornin', and when it comes it's gonna be terrible to behold. I just wonder if Texas will be a part of it."

"I sure as hell hope so," said Eph. "We all know any Texan can whip ten Yankees without breakin' a sweat."

"You best be careful what you hope for, Eph," Caleb replied. "Takin' into account the number of people who live up North, every Texan may well have to whip at least ten Yankees, to say nothin' of all their factories, railroads, and ships."

The heavy frown that shadowed Eph's features clearly showed his disapproval of Caleb's words, but he kept his further opinions to himself.

On their third night out of the Rocking M, the Rangers of First Platoon stopped to cook their evening meal in a large grove of pecan trees at the junction of the Lampasas and Leon Rivers. When they were finished eating, the patrol would move up the Leon for a few miles and set up a cold camp. The winter had been dry, and the Leon ran shallow and clear as it babbled its way over shelves of limestone rock and course gravel beds before joining up with the Lampasas to form the Little River. Bigfoot made sure the men used only dry driftwood for the cook fire in order to eliminate most of the smoke, and ordered them to smother the fire with dirt when it was time to move out. It was Peso Diaz's turn to do the cooking and soon the heavy aroma of spicy beans and bacon made Caleb's stomach growl.

Since Bigfoot was seeing to the men, Caleb got busy preparing their coffee. A quick trip to the clear running river provided the water to fill his old, fire-blackened coffee pot and he found a place on the edge of the fire to set it near the hot coals. Taking out the soft leather pouch he used to prepare his coffee, he filled it half full with fresh beans and cinched the top tight. Next he laid the pouch on a flat rock and picked up a fist-sized rock, using it to gently pound the beans into a fine powder. By this time the water was boiling, so he used his shirttail to remove the pot from the coals and added the crushed beans, allowing ample time for the grounds to settle. When the coffee was ready he carried it over to where he and Bigfoot had tossed their saddles and poured two big tin cups full. Handing one to Bigfoot, he sugared his as usual and sat down cross-legged near where Bigfoot sat leaning back against the trunk of a fallen tree.

Bigfoot took a sip of his coffee and savored the rich taste. "Tell me more about this war, partner; the one where Eph is so anxious to fight the Yankees. What makes you think it's comin'?"

"Hell, Bigfoot, there's already fightin' and dyin' goin' on right now in Kansas over whether the new state will be slave or free. The southerners are led by a Missourian, William Quantrill, and the free-soilers are led by a radical abolitionist named John Brown. The abolitionists won't be satisfied until all the slaves are free, and the South won't stand for that. The secessionists want out of the Union, and the North won't stand for that. Sooner or later one side or the other is gonna start fightin'."

Bigfoot frowned, his mind slowly running over the possibilities of fighting against the flag he had fought so hard to defend, or the state he loved so much. "You may just be right, partner, but if so, it's gonna leave a lot of men with a bitter choice."

The Rangers arrived at Fort Gates late the following afternoon. The post had been closed for a few years, but the local settlers still used the old stockade for special gatherings or defense in case of a Comanche raid. A crowd of settlers was milling around in the parade ground of the old Fort when Caleb and Bigfoot led the Rangers through the gate and reined in.

A settler stepped forward before the Rangers had a chance to dismount. "Thank the Lord y'all are here! My name's Bill Evans. Comanches hit my place around noon today and made off with my son, Nathan. His ma's near hysterical. Can you help us?"

"How many warriors you talkin' about?" asked Caleb.

"There were ten of the heathen bastards," Evans replied. "At least, that's all I saw. They rode through the settlement, stole a few horses, and headed back up river. Nathan was out in the field near our cabin playin' when they grabbed him. He's only five. He must be plum scared near to death by now."

"They got close to a four hour start on us," Caleb said as he turned to Bigfoot. "There ain't no time to waste."

"You want us to ride with you?" asked Evans.

"No," Caleb replied, "I don't want anyone else to get hurt. Let's ride, boys." Reining Nasty around sharply, he led the Rangers out the gate of the old fort and upriver at a steady lope.

Alternating the pace of the horses between a trot, a walk, and once again back to a steady lope, Caleb pushed the animals as hard as he dared, riding deep into the night before halting for a brief rest in a cold camp. The trail of the war party never wavered from the river, and the Rangers reined up at the head-waters of the Middle Leon late the following day. The upper reaches of the river flowed through a series of rocky hills dotted here and there with small copses of post oak and scrub cedar.

Chako rode up a few minutes later. "Comanches go Clear Fork."

"How far are they ahead of us?" Caleb asked.

The Lipan scout held up two fingers, "Maybe two hour."

Caleb looked to Bigfoot. "It's less than forty miles from here to the reservation. We'll never catch 'em in that short a ride."

Bigfoot shook his head in disgust. "There ain't no way in hell we can just write that boy off, Caleb. We're gonna have to try somethin'."

"Well, we sure as hell can't ride in there and take him back," Caleb replied. "We'd have to fight the army as well as the Co-manches. That's the last damn thing we need. With Comanches, though, there's always the possibility of a trade. Who knows, maybe the army will give us a hand if we ask. We got nothin' to lose?"

The Rangers had no sooner crossed the boundary of the Clear Fork reservation than they were greeted by a squad of horsemen from Company G, Second Cavalry, led by Lieutenant John Bell Hood. Hood's uniform, like those of his cavalrymen, consisted of a dark blue jacket and light blue trousers striped in yellow rather than the orange of the dragoons. They also wore heavy brogans instead of boots, a dark blue, thigh-length cape, and a black Hardee hat with a yellow wool hat cord and the right brim looped up and pinned to the crown. The cavalrymen were mounted on matched gray horses and armed with .58 caliber Model 1855 Springfield rifled muskets, .36 caliber Colt Navy revolvers, and heavy dragoon sabers.

Hood looked Caleb over closely before he spoke. "What business do you gentlemen have on the reservation?"

"We're Texas Rangers, Lieutenant," Caleb replied. "I'm Captain McAdams, and this is my First Sergeant, Bigfoot Wallace. A small bunch of Comanches took a young boy from the settlement near old Fort Gates a few days ago. Our Lipan scout tracked 'em here."

"I'm afraid you have no authority on this reservation, Captain McAdams," said Hood. "This is federal property."

Caleb nodded. "I know the rules, Lieutenant, but I was hopin' to speak with your Commandin' Officer to see if he might help us get the child back. The boy's Ma is near frantic with worry." Caleb saw a glimpse of sympathy in the young man's eyes.

"I can certainly understand her concern," said Hood. "If you'll please follow me, sir, I will escort you and your men to Camp Cooper. I can't promise anything, but I will ask the Major if he will see you. "Hood and his troopers reined around and moved off at a brisk trot. The Rangers fell in behind them.

Camp Cooper was located on a wide stretch of level ground near the north bank of the Clear Fork of the Brazos. A high, steep cliff rose to the rear of the camp that helped protect the cavalrymen from the freezing winter winds, but the cliff also served to cut off any stray breeze that may have reached the sweltering camp in the summer. Mosquitoes and biting flies swarmed thick in the sultry air, and the only nearby source of water came from the brackish Clear Fork. In fact, the area's only attribute were the trees that grew nearby, providing the camp with an abundance of timber.

Camp cooper was laid out in the shape of a huge L. One leg of the L was the parade ground and the other leg was the living quarters for the officers and troopers. Most of the structures that made up the camp were heavy canvas tents, including a headquarters tent, a hospital, a guardhouse, a bakery, and an arsenal. Behind the headquarters tent stood several storehouses, their frames constructed from wood, but sided and roofed with heavy canvas. Close by stood a tented sutler's store. There were no stables. The fine matched cavalry horses of the unit were kept tethered on long picket lines.

Lieutenant Hood halted his squad in front of the headquarters tent, and the Rangers reined in behind them. Everyone dismounted and Hood excused himself and stepped into the tent, emerging a few minutes later to motion Caleb and Bigfoot to enter. The interior of the headquarters tent was spacious, with plenty of headroom. Two clerks and a top sergeant sat at field desks near the front flap, and behind them at a larger desk sat an army major.

Caleb and Bigfoot joined Hood standing in front of the desk and he introduced them. "Major Lee, this is Captain McAdams and Sergeant Wallace of the Texas Rangers. Gentlemen, this is the Commanding Officer of Camp Cooper, Major Lee."

Major Robert E. Lee rose to his feet behind his desk. Lee was of medium height and build with graying hair, a neatly trimmed gray beard, and clear, ice-blue blue eyes that spoke of intelligence. "Captain McAdams, Lieutenant Hood tells me a small boy was kidnapped by a Comanche war party that you tracked to this reservation. Is that right?"

Impressed by Major Lee's look and manner, Caleb removed his gray sombrero and Bigfoot immediately followed suit. "Yes sir, Major. My Lipan scout also circled the reservation to see if the trail led out, but he didn't find a thing. That tells me the boy's still here."

"First of all," said Lee, "I want to thank you for coming to me and not just riding onto the reservation without permission." Caleb nodded. "I'm not sure what you want of me, Captain, but I could have the Comanche village searched? Would that satisfy you?"

"I appreciate your cooperation, sir," Caleb replied, "but I don't think a search would do much good. From what I've run into in the past, the Comanches would just hide the boy and then sell him off later to the Comancheros or some tribe further north of here."

"If not a search of the village, then what method would you suggest, Captain? I simply can't allow you to take the boy back by force."

"I understand that, Major, but the Comanches know me and Sergeant Wallace real well. If you were to go along with us to the village and meet with the chiefs, I think we could arrange a trade for the boy."

Lee frowned as he thought over Caleb's suggestion. "I'm afraid a trade might set a bad precedent, Captain. Every time the Comanches take a prisoner in the future they would expect some kind of exchange."

"I realize that's a possibility, sir," Caleb agreed, "but we may actually have a chance to return this boy to his family. I'd hate to count the times when we've either found stolen children dead or never found 'em at all. I'm willin' to purchase the trade goods from the sutler out of my own pocket, if you'll let me give it a try."

Lee paused for a moment, lost in thought as he examined some paperwork on his desk before finally raising his penetrating blue eyes to meet Caleb's. "Very well, Captain, I'm willin' to give your idea a try. Please purchase the necessary trade goods, while Lieutenant Hood has my horse saddled."

Caleb smiled in relief. "Thank you, sir. Come on, Bigfoot; let's go see what the sutler has to offer."

Major Lee, Lieutenant Hood, and Horace Capron, Robert Neighbors' special agent, led the column into the Comanche village followed by Hood's squad of troopers. Caleb and Bigfoot brought up the rear, each of them with a fine looking bay mare at lead. Both horses had two thick trade blankets and a few miscellaneous trade goods tied to their backs. Packs of lean, snarling camp dogs snapped at the horses' legs as they freely darted in and out of the formation. Finally, fed up with their whining, Nasty launched one of the mangy curs with a solid kick to the ribs, sending the animal yowling in pain as it fled off into the middle of the village.

Close to three hundred buffalo hide lodges were strung out in a haphazard manner along the north bank of the Clear Fork. The village was filthy, with clouds of flies swarming over piles of bones, refuse, and waste—both human and animal. A stench, strong enough to drop a buffalo at fifty paces, hung heavy in the air. Used to moving their villages on a regular basis, the Comanches had not yet learned how to deal with the sanitation problems that came with living in one place for a long period of time. Racks of drying meat and recently skinned hides stood among the tepees, with squaws busy everywhere cooking, scraping hides, making clothes, skinning freshly killed game, and caring for the many naked and noisy children who ran and played among them. Here and there, an idle warrior sat, arrogant in both his look and manner.

Major Lee signaled for a halt when the small column reached the center of the village and ordered the troopers to dismount. The lead chief, Tecumseh, stepped forward to greet Lee. He was accompanied by two lesser chiefs, Sanaco and Ketumse, but neither Buffalo Hump or Iron Jacket were present. With six wives, Tecumseh needed all the space he could get, so he had the roomiest lodge in the village. After everyone was seated around his small council fire, the head chief rose with the ceremonial pipe and conducted the smoking ritual, ending by blowing smoke to Mother Earth and Father Sky.

"Why has the white chief come to visit our village?" Tecumseh asked when he recaptured his seat by the fire. "And why has he brought enemies of the People with him, though Red Hair and Bear-of-a-Man are honored and much respected enemies?" Agent Capron interpreted Tecumseh's words as they were spoken.

Lee looked to Capron, and when the agent nodded he began to speak. "The Rangers are here searching for a boy who was recently taken from a white settlement. The trail of the war party that took the boy led to this village. They wish to return him to his mother and father."

"I have heard of no such white boy in this village," Tecumseh replied immediately. "The hated Lipan dog of the Rangers must have followed the wrong trail."

Caleb did not miss the reference to Chako. The boy must be here, if the Comanches knew of the Lipan scout's presence, he thought.

"It is good that the boy was not taken by a war party from this village," said Lee in response to Tecumseh's denial. "Such an act would be a violation of the agreement between the People and the Great White Father in Washington and would result in punishment for the warriors involved. It is unfortunate, however, that the young boy did not wander onto the reservation by mistake because Red Hair has brought valuable trade goods to exchange for him."

Lee paused for a moment to give the Comanches sitting around the fire an opportunity to digest what he had just suggested. Caleb forced himself not to smile at Major Lee's clever insight. Lee had provided the warriors with a way to profit from the trade of the boy, and at the same time avoid admitting they were out raiding the settlements. This man was no run of the mill army officer; he was something special.

"Sanaco rose to his feet. "My warriors will search the reservation to see if such a boy may be found." The Comanche stepped out of the tent. Major Lee and Tecumseh used the next few minutes to discuss the sanitary conditions on the reservation, and before long Sanaco returned with a veteran warrior in tow, many battle scars covered his bronzed body. Both of them sat down at the fire.

"What news do you bring, Sanaco?" asked Tecumseh.

"Many Coups thinks he may know where the boy is that you have spoken of," said Sanaco, "but before he speaks, he wishes to know what Red Hair will offer in return."

Caleb rose to his feet. "Red Hair does not wish to haggle like a woman over the price of the boy's return. I offer Many Coups the two excellent bay mares that I brought to camp, and an ax and two knives of the finest metal. I also offer his squaw four thick red trade blankets, two cooking pots, many sewing needles, and several lengths of trade ribbon."

Many Coups leaned toward Sanaco and said something in the chief's ear. Sanaco nodded, "Many Coups accepts all that Red hair has offered, but he must also have a fine rifle."

"This I will not do," Caleb replied immediately. "I would never arm my enemy with a weapon to harm me or my Rangers.

Many Coups has my offer, and it is a fair offer. I have said that I will not haggle. He must accept it now, or I will go, but I will not forget."

Sanaco and Many Coups spoke together quietly for a minute before both of them rose to their feet. "Many Coups accepts Red Hair's offer. The boy will be delivered to the army camp before the sun goes to rest this day."

"Caleb nodded. "Red Hair accepts the word of Many Coups. I will wait for him by the river south of camp with the gifts I have promised. Bring the boy there."

Chapter 25

Richard Bullock slid the glass of beer across the hotel bar, with a big smile gracing his craggy features. "What brings you to town on this fine September day, Caleb?"

Caleb lifted the glass of cool beer in a brief salute, took a long swallow to cut the trail dust, and sat the glass back down on the bar. He wiped the beer from his drooping red mustache with the back of his hand. "I got a meetin' with Governor Pease this afternoon, Mr. Bullock, and I'm afraid it ain't gonna be good news."

"What makes you think so?" Bullock asked, eager for the latest tidbit of information in his usual inquisitive manner.

Caleb shook his head in disgust. "From the rumors I been hearin' all summer, it appears the state treasury is broke again. If that's true, the legislators always seem to get around to cuttin' the money for the Rangers first."

"That sounds just like our incompetent legislature alright," agreed Bullock. "Why think about cuttin' their own pay when they can save money by gettin' rid of one of the few things that's actually worth payin' for?" Some customers at a table across the café signaled for Bullock and he excused himself.

Left to his own thoughts, Caleb's mind drifted to the happenings over the summer since his return from the Clear Fork reservation with Nathan Evans. The Fort Gates settlement and Bill and Martha Evans, the boy's parents, were overjoyed with Nathan's return, and Caleb had never mentioned the price he paid for the youngster's release. Whatever the price, the pure joy that the boy's return brought to the Evans family and the sense of pride and accomplishment it gave his Rangers made the money well spent.

Both First and Second Platoon had continued to patrol the frontier throughout the long summer with mixed results. Sometimes preventing a raid and sometimes administering punishment to the raiders after the fact, but more often than not simply maneuvering the war parties back to the reservation before they could do serious harm.

Pedro had also returned from the trail drive with great news. Not only had he delivered more than four thousand longhorns to Josh Tanner in New Orleans, but the price per head of the cattle rose to twenty-eight dollars. That meant Pedro sent close to $100,000 with Josh to Cincinnati, and still returned to the Rocking M with the $40,000 Felix requested. Only Felix, and now to a lesser extent Pedro, understood the complexities of the wealth the partnership had amassed over the last few years, but Caleb knew it was more money than he would ever need. That was to say nothing of his California inheritance and the investments Jack Hays had made in his and Josh's behalf, which were now considerable.

A special kind of excitement stirred Caleb as he sat at the bar and sipped the remainder of his beer. After he finished with the Governor this afternoon, he would cross the Colorado on the ferry and ride to Wanda's cabin. She and Josh had arrived in Austin on the stage nearly two weeks ago. Caleb was eager to see Wanda again and excited about meeting his son for the first time. He wanted to be there to greet them when they got off the stage, but Wanda had expressly forbidden it in her last letter. "The risk was bad enough for their reputations when he had insisted on seeing her off," Wanda said in the letter, "but the rumors would fly if he was also there to greet the 'widowed' school teacher upon her return." Caleb had to admit Wanda was right, but that had not made the waiting any easier.

Bullock returned just as Caleb finished off his beer and sat the glass back down on the bar. "I better get goin', Mr. Bullock, it's near time for my meetin'. It ain't good practice to keep the Governor waitin'."

Bullock retrieved the empty beer glass and swiped at the bar with a rag. "The meetin' with Pease will give you a chance to look over the new governor's mansion. Be sure and give the Governor my regards, and don't forget to say hello to Lucinda and the family for me when you get home."

"I'll be sure and do it, Mr. Bullock," Caleb replied as he turned and headed for the café's swinging doors.

The grounds for the newly constructed Governor's mansion lay to the southwest of the capital and spanned an entire city block between Colorado and Lavaca Streets. Standing in the center of the expansive grounds, the two-story, six thousand square foot mansion was designed in the Greek revival style by Abner Cook a local builder, and was constructed of buff-colored bricks produced in the Colorado River clay pits owned by the designer. Cook also owned a part of the Bastrop sawmill that supplied the lumber for the structure. The mansion's square floor plan allowed for four main rooms on each floor, two on either side of a broad central hallway. There was also a rear wing that held the kitchen and servants' quarters.

As Caleb rode up to the hitching rail near the front steps of the mansion and dismounted, he could not help but admire how well-proportioned the huge structure was. Six, thirty-foot, fluted columns stood equally spaced across the façade of the lovely structure, providing tall ceilings for both the downstairs and up-stairs rooms, and a wide set of steps led up to a deep, covered veranda. On the far side of the veranda stood a centrally placed front door with two floor-length windows set equally spaced to either side. The façade of the second floor was identical to the first, and both the first and second floor verandas were fronted by fancy X-and-Stick balustrades; a trademark of Abner Cook. Bullock was right as usual. The mansion was indeed impressive.

Caleb looped Nasty's reins over the hitching rail and climbed the steps two at a time. Striding across the veranda, he lifted the heavy door knocker and let it fall once. The door was opened almost immediately by a tall, well-dressed black servant. The servant looked Caleb over from head to foot before asking him to identify himself and state his business.

"My name's Captain McAdams," Caleb responded. "I got an appointment with Governor Pease this afternoon. Is he in?"

A smile broke across the servant's face. "He certainly is, Captain, and he's expecting you. Please follow me."

The servant turned, and Caleb followed him into a wide central hall with a highly polished oak floor and a sweeping curved staircase flanked by a double parlor to his left and a dining room to his right. The servant led him past the entrance to the dining room and through a second door on the right that led into the mansion's library. Governor Pease was sitting in a comfortable-looking wingback chair. He rose as Caleb entered, placing the book he had been reading on the table beside him.

"Caleb, thank you for answering my summons so quickly," Pease said as he offered his hand. "Please have a seat. Would you like something to drink?"

Caleb sat down in a matching wingback chair beside Pease. "No thank you, Governor. I'd just as soon get down to business. I spoke with Senator Jenkins the other day, and if what he told me was true, the news you got ain't gonna be to my likin'."

Pease shook his head in disgust; legislative confidences were rarely kept, especially from influential citizens such as Caleb McAdams. "The good Senator was talking 'out of school' shall we say, but if the subject you were discussing was the funding for your Ranger Company, I'm afraid what he told you was true. Once again the State coffers are empty and certain hard choices must be made."

"By now I'm plumb used to Texas bein' dead broke," Caleb replied, the frustration he felt evident in the concerned frown that shrouded his usually pleasant features, "but how come it's always the frontier that suffers first? The western settlers pay a terrible price for tryin' to make a life for themselves out of almost nothin'. They're the ones who're buildin' Texas, Governor, not the eastern slave-holders who refuse to give 'em a hand."

"What you say is absolutely true, Caleb," agreed Pease. "Unfortunately, it's a fact of life that the population in the eastern half of the State and the wealth of the planter class control the balance of power in the Texas legislature, both now and for the foreseeable future. As long as that holds true, the frontier will suffer first and foremost. What will you do now that your funding has been cut off?"

"I've been thinkin' about that ever since I talked to Jenkins," Caleb replied. "I decided to keep on a few men at my own expense. I can keep 'em busy on the ranch between patrols. I know we can't cover as much ground as the entire Company did, but at least the Comanches won't think we forgot about 'em."

Governor Pease smiled. "That's exactly what I hoped you'd say. Even a small presence on the frontier is better than no presence at all. The Comanches would run wild if they knew the Rangers were gone for good. In the meantime, I'll keep pressing the legislature for money, but it seems like all they're worried about theses days are issues dealing with states' rights and secession."

Pease's mention of secession caught Caleb's attention. Though he had already formed his own opinion on the subject, he was eager to hear from someone like the Governor who was in a position to have more of an informed political view. "Do you think Texas will secede from the Union, Governor?"

Governor Pease nodded emphatically. "I certainly do, and though I'm dead set against it, you'll never hear me speak out in public and say so. If you value your hide, you'll follow the same course."

Caleb agreed with Pease completely, but to probe the issue further he asked, "Why do you say that, sir?"

"Because the tide of resentment and hatred against the abolitionists and hence the North is already too relentless to turn back," Pease replied. "Take our mutual friend Sam Houston, for example. In 1848 he voted for the entrance of Oregon as a free territory, standing against a solid bloc of United States Senators from the South. He also refused to sign Senator John C. Calhoun's manifesto on "aggression by the free states." Remember, Caleb, even though Calhoun is dead, his pro slavery position and championing of states' rights are more popular than ever. Then to top it off, Sam debated vehemently against the Kansas-Nebraska Act, which effectively abrogated the old Missouri Compromise and made slavery a possibility above the Mason-Dixon Line."

"What does all that mean for Sam," Caleb asked?

Pease shook his head in resignation. "For the first time since Texas was a state, the Democratic Party held a statewide convention this summer in which almost every county was represented. Calhoun Democrats emerged in complete control of the party.

That means Sam Houston's days as a United States Senator are numbered. There is absolutely no way a Calhoun controlled legislature will reelect him. And if Sam Houston isn't safe to freely speak his mind in Texas, I say no man is, especially a private citizen like you who is subject to having his home burned or even to be lynched. Take my advice and keep your opinions to yourself. It is the only safe course for you and your family."

"I appreciate the information and the advice, Governor," said Caleb. "I promise to take it to heart. Do you have anything else for me?"

"Just one thing," Pease replied. "For the last two years, there's been sporadic trouble between the Mexican carters who haul ox carts full of goods from the port of Indianola overland to San Antonio, and some of the riffraff of Gonzales and Goliad. If the situation gets worse, I may have to organize the militia, but before I do that, I'd like to see if you and your Rangers can handle the problem. I'll let you know if it comes to that."

Caleb rose to his feet. "We'll be ready if you need us."

Unexpected business kept Caleb in town longer than he had planned, and a star-filled blanket of darkness had settled peacefully over the valley of the Lower Colorado by the time he reined up in front of Wanda's cabin and dismounted. Far below the high bluff, the silvery disc of a bright full moon cast a shimmering reflection off the placid, inky-black surface of the river. Caleb looped the reins around the hitching rail and stepped up to the door of the cabin, knocking quietly.

"Who is it?" inquired a soft feminine voice he would have recognized anywhere.

"It's me, Caleb," he replied, and the door flew open.

Standing there silhouetted by the soft glow of candles and firelight was Wanda in a long cotton nightdress with a Colt Navy revolver in her right hand. "Caleb," she nearly shouted as she stepped forward and hugged him close, "it's so good to see you again!"

Caleb smiled as he stood back from Wanda's embrace and took the Navy Colt from her hand. Stepping into the cabin, he placed the revolver on a small stand next to the door. "Where's Josh?"

Wanda chuckled mirthlessly. "So much for my warm greeting, I guess? Josh is still a little boy and he's sleeping, silly. But come with me and you can see him."

Wanda held Caleb's hand and led him across the main room of the cabin to a small bed, where he saw his son for the first time. His eyes moistened as he looked down at the little head full of red-gold curls, but he nearly collapsed when the youngster rolled over in his sleep and he got a good look at his face. As near as Caleb could tell, Josh was Ham's twin in everything except hair color, and according to Wanda, his eyes, which were the color of bluebonnets in the spring like hers.

"Wait until you see Ham, Wanda. There's absolutely no doubt the boys are brothers. My God, the resemblance is remarkable."

Wanda smiled. "That could prove to be a bit of a problem later, but let's not try to deal with it now. Come and sit by the fire and tell me what I've missed." Caleb bent down and gave Josh a kiss, then joined Wanda on the sofa in front of the fire.

Time seemed to stand still for the next hour as Caleb and Wanda talked of all the things they had done and seen since Wanda's departure for New Orleans. The subject eventually got around to politics, though, as it usually did when they had the rare opportunity for a long discussion.

"Did you hear what happened to Senator Sumner late last spring?" asked Wanda.

"You mean the fight he had with that Congressman from South Carolina?" Caleb asked in return.

Wanda laughed. "The newspapers down here are fairly loose with the truth, if that's what you heard. What actually happened was that Senator Sumner gave a speech in the Senate criticizing President Pierce and Senator Butler for sympathizing with the pro-slavery violence occurring in Kansas. Congressman Preston Brooks, Senator Butler's cousin, took offense, walked into the Senate chamber with a gold-headed cane, and proceeded to beat Sumner senseless with it, while his friend, Congressman Keitt, held a gun on the people who tried to put a stop it."

"Sumner is still bedridden from the incident," Wanda continued, "and will remain that way for quite some time. Of course, when it comes to violence the free-soilers are just as bad. Right after the Sumner incident, rabid abolitionist John Brown led a raid on Pottawatome, Kansas and executed five pro-slavery men by chopping off their heads with a broadsword."

Caleb shook his head. "All that violence happened because of the Kansas-Nebraska Act just like you said it would. Governor Pease told me today that Sam Houston would lose his seat in the United States Senate because he voted against the Act and talks down secession."

"I admire Sam," said Wanda. "It's good to know some men in the south aren't afraid to speak up for what they know to be right."

"Pease also said regular folks like us have to be careful what we say," added Caleb. "Times are dangerous, Wanda, and now you got little Josh to think about. Please use your head before you speak out, and for God's sake don't talk to anyone about that book you wrote to me about. A few folks around here have already been tarred and feathered because of it."

Wanda stood up in anger. "I refuse to be intimidated into keeping quiet by a few zealots, Caleb McAdams. Furthermore, I'll teach my students the way I see fit, including *Uncle Tom's Cabin'*. The slavers be damned if they don't like it."

"That's just it, Wanda," Caleb warned. "It ain't just a few zealots causin' the trouble no more; it's most of the folks around here. Now sit back down and let's talk about it."

Wanda flopped back down on the sofa, the fiery anger still present in her eyes. "There's nothing wrong with that book. It tells the truth about slavery."

Caleb shook his head in exasperation. "Wanda I know I ain't got your education, but one thing I learned over the years is that one man's truth is another man's lies. Most folks around here don't own slaves, but they don't want the abolitionists stirrin' 'em up to revolt neither. And they'll never consider blacks as equals. The slaves are here, not up North, and if they were to be set free like the abolitionists want, it's the folks in the South who'll have to deal with 'em."

"I swear, Caleb," replied Wanda in near shock, "please don't tell me you've turned into a proponent of slavery."

"That's not fair, Wanda, and you know it," Caleb retorted, the anger now growing in his voice. "Of course I'm against slavery and secession, too, but this is where I live. That means gettin' along with other folks that live here. It's high time you realized that."

"I suppose you're right," Wanda reluctantly replied, now somewhat contrite. "For you and Josh, I'll try and watch what I say. I refuse to hold totally silent, though, in the face of the injustice and tyranny that goes on here as a matter of course every day."

Ending their brief disagreement brought a sense of calm to the cabin once again, but Caleb knew it would be nearly impossible for Wanda to hold silent. In all honesty, though he usually managed to hold his own tongue in front of others, Caleb often felt as strongly as Wanda did about the peculiar institution of slavery, and he thought the idea of secession was pure lunacy. He would have to keep a close eye on the situation and do all that he could to protect both her and Josh.

Upon his return to the Rocking M from Austin late the following afternoon, Caleb gathered the Rangers together and gave them the bad news about the legislature cutting off the Company's funding. Thanking them for all they'd done, he gave each man a choice to stay on as a Rocking M ranch hand and a part-time Ranger, but only Corporal Nelson and seven others out of the twenty-four men accepted his offer. The men who decided to leave were able to keep their Colts and a good horse plus a month's pay that came out of Caleb's pocket. After the men were dismissed, Caleb met in the orderly room with Bigfoot, Eph, and Sergeant Jessup.

"That was damn good of you to promise everyone a job who wanted to stay on, partner," Bigfoot said when they were sitting around the table sipping a cup of coffee. "I'm surprised more of 'em didn't take you up on the offer."

"I expect most of 'em ain't much for chasin' after ornery longhorns," Caleb replied. "That's why they were ridin' with the Company in the first place. That still leaves you three, though. The offer of a job stands for ya'll, too."

Bigfoot chuckled. "I ain't had a close up look at the rear end of a longhorn for quite a spell, and I don't aim to now. I'm headin' back to my little cabin on the Medina. Maybe I'll take a stage to El Paso now and then for a little excitement. Don't hesitate to give me a call if you need me, though."

"Thanks, Bigfoot, I appreciate that." Caleb looked to Sergeant Jessup and Eph. "What about you two?"

"I'm for movin' on, Captain," said Jessup. "I always had me a hankerin' to see old Mexico, and with winter comin' on now's the time."

Caleb nodded. "I wish you the best, Jessup. There'll always be a place for you on the Rockin' M if you change your mind. What about you, Eph?"

Eph smiled. "I think I'll take you up on that job offer. Like Jessup said, winter's comin' on, and I've grown right fond of my warm room here in the barracks."

"Good," said Caleb, "I'm damn glad you're stayin' on. With you 'n me and the scouts, we'll have ten men to ride patrol. We can even take turns leadin' the patrols, too, if I'm needed here on the ranch."

Caleb headed for the hacienda when he was finished in the barracks, and Lucinda greeted him at the front door with a towel and a bar of lye soap. Caleb attempted to grab her up in a bear hug, but with a tinkling laugh, she gracefully dodged her way out of his grasp.

"There is a bucket of fresh water beside the well, my husband," Lucinda said with a radiant smile and laughing eyes. "Since there is not enough time to take a bath before supper, please use that to clean up before you try and put your arms around me."

Caleb grabbed for her, but she danced away again and fled for the kitchen to render assistance to Connie and Veronica. Laughing to himself, he headed for the well where he stripped off his buckskin hunting shirt and scrubbed his face and upper body thoroughly. After drying off, he slipped on the clean cotton shirt Lucinda had placed beside the bucket, tied off his long copper curls with a leather string, and headed for the supper table in the great room. The family was all seated when Caleb took his place at the head of the table, and Felix, sitting at the other end led the family in prayer.

"Grandpa Felix gave me a new horse today, Papa," said Gretchin in an excited voice before Caleb managed to take a bite of food, "and it's not a pony."

"I wish you hadn't done that Padre," Lucinda scolded. "That horse is much too big for a girl her age."

"She should be working on her lessons more often instead of riding so much anyway," added Ilse, "and learning to cook and sew like other girls, too, instead of how to shoot and rope."

Gretchin stuck out her tongue at her older sister. "Other girls like you, is what you really mean, Ilse!"

"Young lady," Lucinda snapped, "it is not polite to stick your tongue out at your sister! Besides, Ilse is right. You spend far too much time riding."

Ilse gave her younger sister a smug, I told you so look, but Felix came to Gretchin's rescue. "Lucinda, Gretchin does very well at her studies, and she rides as well as most men. It is high time she had a real horse of her own." Gretchin was all smiles as Felix quickly changed the subject before Lucinda could object. "By the way, Caleb, while I am speaking of horses, I also think it is time you put Nasty out to pasture and choose a younger mount. That big, three year old filly I showed you last month would be perfect. Nasty was her sire."

Caleb had to agree with his father-in-law. It was high time Nasty was put out to stud. The big Appaloosa had earned a graceful retirement through years of hard and dependable service. "Let's bring the filly in tomorrow, Felix. I'd like to give her a try. Oh, Pedro, I almost forgot, Eph and eight others decided to stay on as ranch hands. Go ahead and put 'em to work in the mornin'."

"We can use all of them," said Pedro. "We should put Eph in charge over at the old Meacham place and spread the others around."

Caleb nodded. "That sounds real good. We'll see how it works out."

The lively supper conversation continued for the remainder of the meal, with everyone joining in.

Chapter 26

The winter of 1856 was unusually harsh, with long cold spells and abundant rain, and the first breath of spring came as a welcome relief to the valley of the Lower Colorado. After deciding that most of the Rocking M livestock would be left in place for the year to multiply, the majority of the spring trail drive was made up of cattle consigned from nearby ranches and more than fifty prime head of horseflesh. With Veronica near term for her second child, Caleb led the drive, and as usual, most of the profit was sent north with Josh Tanner.

By the time Caleb returned to the ranch from New Orleans, Pedro was the proud father of his second son, Felix. Veronica was also doing fine, and little Felix's grandfather was bursting with pride. Toward the end of June, Caleb led his Rangers on a two week patrol far up the Colorado to the confluence of the Concho River. From the Concho, the patrol swung back south, crossing the San Saba, the Llano, and the Pedernales Rivers, but failed to turn up any trouble.

In late July, a message from Governor Pease arrived at the ranch, requesting that Caleb ride to Goliad with his Rangers to assist the local authorities in dealing with the outlaws known as the "cartcutters." The cartcutters had recently stepped-up their attacks on the Mexican and Tejano carters who transported goods from the port of Indianola to San Antonio. Indianola was the port of entry for many immigrants arriving in Texas. Since most of the new arrivals did not have their own wagons, they hired the Mexican and Tejano carters to haul their belongings. Unfortunately, the carters were forced to pass through or near Goliad on their way inland, and ill will toward Mexicans and Tejanos had been commonplace in the old settlement ever since the massacre of Colonel James Fannin and his men during the Texas Revolution. Many of the carters had been attacked, robbed, and even murdered. When local authorities realized they could no longer cope with the situation, they had requested help from the governor.

The message went on to say that complaints of the atrocities had been received by the Mexican Consulate in Washington, and the situation was beginning to have all the ingredients of an international incident. Governor Pease had requested funds from the Texas legislature to send the state militia south to act as escorts for the Mexican and Tejano teamsters, but the legislative process was slow and something had to be done quickly. The message also contained a letter of introduction from Governor Pease to the mayor of Goliad, explaining Caleb's mission and requesting the mayor's cooperation until such time as the state militia arrived on the scene.

Caleb immediately dispatched Corporal Nelson with a message to Bigfoot, requesting that he meet up with the Rangers south of San Antonio at the confluence of the Medina and San Antonio Rivers. Goliad was located on the southern reaches of the San Antonio River, about twenty miles southwest of Victoria. The Rangers were on the trail the following morning, and on the third day out of the Rocking M, they passed through San Antonio and met up with Bigfoot and Nelson.

Caleb leaned out of the saddle and shook Bigfoot's hand. "I'm damn glad you could ride with us, partner."

Bigfoot smiled. "All you had to do was put out the call. But next time remind the man you send to come up to my cabin real noisy like, so I ain't apt to put a ball twixt his eyes like I nearly done old Nelson here." Corporal Nelson shook his head and smiled. "Hey, Eph, it's good to see you again. How's it goin'?" Eph smiled and nodded his greeting, and Bigfoot returned his attention to Caleb. "Say, partner, that's a new filly you're ridin'. What happened to that mean, red-eyed bastard you used to ride?"

Chuckling at Bigfoot's nonstop banter Caleb replied, "She's new alright." The big Appaloosa filly was brown through the head and shoulders and back to the withers with a white face and white front legs; from the withers through the hind quarters she was white with big brown spots. Caleb had worked with the intelligent filly all winter, and she had performed remarkably well on the spring trail drive. "Her name's Sally Mae, Sally for short. Pretty as a picture, ain't she?"

"That she is, my friend," Bigfoot replied. "And she don't act like she's ready to bite my hand off neither. Quite an improvement I'd say."

"Come on," Caleb said as he nudged Sally with his heels and started her off down a game trail that ran well away from the river, "we're burnin' daylight sittin' here jawin'. I can fill you in on what we're up to while we ride."

Well before noon of their third day since meeting up with Bigfoot, the Rangers rode into the sleepy little town of Goliad and reined in at a long, flat-roofed adobe building. A sign out front said the building housed the county courthouse, the sheriff's office and jail, and the mayor's office. Caleb sent the men across the dusty street to a little cantina and he, Bigfoot, and Eph entered the door marked Office of the Mayor. A skinny, bug-eyed clerk wearing a black vest and a white cotton shirt with the sleeves rolled up sat at a small desk just inside the door.

"May I help you, gentlemen?" the clerk asked in a squeaky voice.

"We're Texas Rangers," Caleb replied. "My name's Captain McAdams, this is Lieutenant Daggett, and this is Sergeant Wallace. We'd like to speak to the mayor."

"And what might your business be with the mayor?" the clerk asked.

Caleb frowned. "I have a letter from the governor explainin' our business."

The clerk looked as if he was growing impatient, but Bigfoot saw that Caleb was getting riled by the little man's self-important attitude. The clerk had best watch his manners, the big man thought.

"Might I see the letter, sir?" the clerk asked.

"I done told you the letter's for the mayor," Caleb snapped. "Now get up out of that chair and fetch him before I drag you out of it!"

Bigfoot and Eph started chuckling and Caleb was about to take action when the door to the mayor's office opened. "What's the commotion out here, Clarence?" asked a man in a dark blue suit jacket and matching waistcoat.

"There ain't no commotion yet, Mr. Mayor," Caleb replied, "if that's who you are, but there was about to be. My name's Captain McAdams of the Texas Rangers. Governor Pease sent me to see you. I have a letter to you from him, but this man insisted on seeing it before he told you we were here. Like I said, the letter's for you, not him."

The mayor scowled at the clerk. "Sometimes Clarence goes too far with his limited authority. Why don't you gentlemen come into my office? I'll take a look at the letter."

The office was big with plenty of chairs for everyone and two men who had been seated rose to their feet. "Gentlemen," said the mayor, "my name is Isaac Van Dohlen, this is Goliad County Judge Ira Mason, and the sheriff of Goliad County, Thomas Anson."

When the introductions were complete, Caleb handed the letter to the mayor and everyone sat down while he read it. The mayor looked up at Caleb when he finished. "Governor Pease appears to have great confidence in you, Captain. It is most fortuitous that you arrived when you did. The Judge, the Sheriff, and I were just discussing the problem of the cartcutters. We got word yesterday that another caravan is on the way from Indianola. How many men did you bring along?"

"Twelve countin' our Lipan scout, sir," replied Caleb.

The mayor was shocked. "You only brought twelve men! The cartcutters operate in several big gangs, Captain. That's why I requested that the governor send the militia. How in the world does he expect you to handle the situation with so few men?"

"Not just twelve men, Mayor," said Caleb, "twelve experienced and very capable Texas Rangers. We'll get the job done alright, but we need the help of your sheriff and the county court to handle the outlaws we bring in."

"You bring them in," said Judge Mason, "and the court will see that justice is meted out in full measure. You can be sure of that."

On the second day riding south along the San Antonio River, the Rangers came across the remains of the caravan that had recently set out from Indianola. The nightmarish scene made many of them turn aside and empty their stomachs, as flocks of buzzards, fat from gorging on human flesh, took wing at their approach. Several coyotes reluctantly abandoned their feast and slunk off into the cover of the nearby trees. Burned out hulks of carts and wagons lined the trail, half-eaten bodies of mostly men and children sprawled among them. Scattered piles of discarded furniture, clothing, dishes, and toys lay strewn across the grizzly scene.

"Looks like the cartcutters carried off most of the women," Caleb observed, fighting to keep from retching.

"We're sure dealin' with some bad *hombres* here, partner," Bigfoot replied. The big Ranger pulled his bandana up over his mouth and nose to cut the stench that hung so thick in the air it was difficult to take a breath. "Hell, I ain't seen much worse from the Comanches."

"There ain't nothin' left to do but bury the poor souls," said Caleb, "so let's get it done. Chako, did you find their trail?"

"Si," Chako replied, "trail easy follow. Much track."

Caleb nodded. "Good, go find their camp. I need to know exactly where they are and how many of 'em we're up against. Then we can decide what we're gonna do with the bastards. We'll set up camp a few miles upriver from here and wait for you."

"As far as I'm concerned," added Eph, when Chako reined around and set out on the cartcutters trail, "there ain't but one thing to do with ornery scum like this; kill or hang every damn one of 'em." To a man, the Rangers within earshot voiced their approval.

Chako rode into the camp just after the sun sank below the horizon, dusting the wide, western sky with the soft pastels of a beautiful summer evening. Sliding off the back of his black and white pinto, the Lipan tethered his single braided rein to a scrub oak and walked over to the small fire where Caleb, Bigfoot, and Eph were enjoying a cup of coffee.

"Camp maybe two hour downriver," Chako reported, "near small stream. This many." The scout showed his fingers three times. "No guards. Much drink."

Caleb reached over and pulled the extra tin cup from his saddlebag, pouring it half full. After adding a heaping spoonful of sugar, he carefully stirred it around, handed it to Chako, and motioned for the Lipan to take a seat on a log beside the fire. Once Chako was comfortable, Caleb bent over, smoothed out a space on the ground with his hand, and handed him a small stick. "Show me."

Chako drew a wavy line in the dirt to represent the San Antonio, and then drew a smaller line heading off to the southeast to represent a stream. A short ways down the stream, on the west bank, he jammed the stick in the ground. "Camp is here."

Taking the stick from Chako, Caleb looked to Bigfoot and Eph. "We'll head out around nine. That should give the cartcutters plenty of time to get good and drunk. Chako will lead us down the river until we're close to the stream, about here." Caleb drew in the dirt with the stick as he talked glancing at Chako from time to time to make sure the Lipan understood what he was saying. "From there, he'll lead us along the stream until we're abreast of the camp. Once we're in position, we move toward the camp at a slow walk until they spot us or I fire a shot. They got us outnumbered pretty good, so we go in blastin'. Remember, if they ain't women or kids, and they ain't tied up, they're bad guys pure and simple. We take 'em out. You got any questions? Good, each of you take a few men and brief 'em. Make damn sure you check their weapons personally and see that all the loose gear on their saddles is tied down tight. We're gonna give those bastards exactly what they deserve."

Darkness was complete, but from the center of the line of Rangers, Caleb could see the shadowy silhouettes of the cartcutters celebrating around their big fires as he walked Sally toward the camp. Bigfoot and Eph rode at either end of the line. Every now and then a woman's anguished scream pierced the raucous singing, boisterous laughter, and loud talk that smothered the usual night sounds around the roaring fires. These people have no idea that the wrath of God is about to descend upon their heads, thought Caleb, as he drew his Colt. Rangers up and down the line followed suit.

The Rangers rode past the bodies of four Mexican carters hanging from stout tree limbs, slowly twisting in the evening breeze at the ends of the ropes that had stretched their necks. Now the Rangers were close enough to see what was going on near the fires, and the sights and sounds turned their stomachs. Naked women, both Mexican and white immigrants, were screaming and begging for mercy, but the brutal, laughing cartcutters offered no mercy. It will be a pleasure to kill these bastards, thought Caleb.

Caleb led the line to the outer edge of the camp before a drunken outlaw finally took note of the Rangers. The cartcutter opened his mouth in surprise, but the tall redhead coldly put a .44 caliber ball in the man's forehead before he could scream out a warning. "Give 'em hell, Rangers!" he yelled as loped the big appaloosa filly into the middle of the camp.

Firing right and left, Caleb knocked an outlaw off his feet with a well-aimed shot to the chest, and then shot man between the shoulder blades as the terrified outlaw made a drunken dash toward the perceived safety of the surrounding darkness. The vengeful Rangers were in among the stunned cartcutters before the outlaws had an opportunity to react. Many of the cartcutters did not even clear leather before they were brutally gunned down in the rapid-firing onslaught. Bigfoot shot a man in the stomach attempting to use a screaming woman as a shield and then finished him off, before catching up with another outlaw as he ran toward the stream at the rear of the camp. From such close range, the ball from his Colt nearly blew the back of the man's head off. A Ranger took a ball in the chest that knocked him out of the saddle, but the outlaw who fired the shot was hit again and again, his bullet-riddled body dancing like a puppet on a string before he flopped to the ground. Outlaws began to drop their weapons and hold their hands in the air, begging for mercy.

A Ranger rode up and gunned down one of the cartcutters who was trying to surrender, and Caleb knew it was time to call a halt to the slaughter. "Cease fire!" he yelled. "Cease fire!" Slowly the echoing of gunfire stopped and Caleb counted only eight outlaws still on their feet, hands held high over their heads. "Drop your gun belts now or you're dead!" he yelled.

The cartcutters hesitated and Bigfoot knocked a man off his feet with a ball that center-punched his chest. "The man said now!" Bigfoot bellowed, smoking Colt in his hand. The remainder of the outlaws quickly complied.

"Bigfoot," Caleb yelled, "you and Eph help me keep these skunks covered. Corporal Nelson, you and Peso check the woods close by and see if you can round anymore of 'em up. Be careful. The rest of you dismount and check for wounded. Make damn sure you disarm all of 'em. As soon as you check for weapons, get these women some blankets or clothes to wear and get 'em in the wagons. We're headin' out of here as soon as Nelson and Diaz get back from searchin' the woods."

Caleb swung down out of the saddle and knelt beside Sancho Pera. The ball from the outlaw's horse pistol had struck the young Ranger in the heart and he was dead. Gently closing Sancho's eyes, Caleb said a silent prayer, wrapped the body in the Ranger's poncho, then carefully picked it up and placed it in one of the wagons on top of some trade goods. He tied the reins to Pera's horse to the rear of the wagon and began to help the others search for wounded.

The dead outlaws' weapons were quickly gathered up and the two wounded men were disarmed. One of them was gut-shot and Caleb was sure he would not last long. There were plenty of trade blankets in one of the wagons, and the women were wrapped up as gently as possible and placed among them. By the time all this was accomplished, Corporal Nelson and Peso Diaz returned from their search of the woods with two more outlaws walking in front of them, their hands held high. One of the cartcutters was wounded, but the wound was not serious. After tying the eleven prisoners securely to ensure that escape was impossible, they were all thrown in an empty wagon bed.

There were six wagons in all, and once the mule teams were hitched and the fires put out, a Ranger tied his horse to the back of each of the wagons, climbed up on the seat, and took up the reins. The wagon with the women was up front with Caleb and Bigfoot, and the wagon with the prisoners took up the rear with Eph and Corporal Nelson riding behind it. Chako had ridden out earlier toward Goliad to make sure the trail was clear. The bodies of eighteen outlaws lay scattered across the camp. They would remain unburied; food for the vultures and other scavengers.

Caleb looked around. Satisfied that all was ready, he raised his hand. "Okay, men, move 'em out."

After a stop in the middle of the night to water and rest the stock, and another brief holdover in a cold camp for a little sleep, the small caravan pulled into Goliad well before noon and reined up in front of the sheriff's office. Sheriff Anson met them out front with Mayor Van Dohlen and Judge Mason in tow.

Caleb dismounted and looped his reins over the hitching rail. "Here's the first sorry bunch, Sheriff. I hope you got room in your jail for all ten of 'em. Two of 'em are wounded, and another was gut-shot and died on the trail. Eighteen more are lying dead in their camp south of here. I'm sorry to say I lost one of my Rangers, Sancho Pera; a damn good man."

"I'm right sorry to here that, Captain," said Mayor Dohlen as the Rangers climbed down from the wagons and began herding the prisoners toward the jail. "But the Governor was right. You did a bang up job."

"We got there too late to help the poor souls they massacred Mayor," said Caleb, "but we managed to save some of the women they was abusin' when we attacked their camp. They're wrapped up in blankets in the first wagon. I'm sure they could use a hand from some of your women folk."

The Mayor was shocked. "My Lord, I should hope so. Clarence," the clerk had just stepped out the door to satisfy his curiosity, "get on down to the house and fetch Emma. Tell her what's happened, and tell her to bring some of the other wives to help. Be damn quick about it." The clerk took off at a run.

"If it's okay, Mayor," said Caleb, "I'll have Ranger Warren take the wagon on down to your house?"

"Certainly," replied Van Dohlen, "I should have thought of that myself. It's the last house down the street, Ranger."

"You heard the man, Jason," said Caleb. "Take the wagon down there now." Ranger Warren whipped up the team and pulled out just as the sheriff and the other Rangers walked out of the jail.

"The prisoners are locked up," said Sheriff Anson, "and I sent my deputy to fetch Doc Sturm for the wounded men."

"They won't be locked up for long," added Judge Mason. "I plan to have the trial this very afternoon."

"Excellent Your Honor," said Mayor Van Dohlen. "Captain McAdams, why don't you, Lieutenant Daggett, and Sergeant Wallace come on in my office and we'll discuss the trial over a cup of coffee? Your men can wait across the street in the cantina. The beer is on me."

"If you don't mind," said Bigfoot, "I'll join the men. I'm sure these fine officers here can do all the talkin' you're gonna need. A nice cool beer sounds a might better to me than a cup of coffee."

The Mayor chuckled, "By all means, Sergeant Wallace, by all means."

The brief trial was conducted outdoors, under the spreading limbs of a huge live oak tree at the north end of the long adobe structure that housed the offices of the judge, the mayor, and the sheriff. By the time Caleb and two of the women had finished testifying, there was not much doubt as to the outcome of the verdict. The jury deliberated only ten minutes before filing in front of the Judge.

"Gentlemen of the jury," asked the Judge, "how do you find the defendants?"

The foreman of the jury stepped forward. "Your Honor, the jury finds the defendants guilty as charged."

The Judge nodded his acceptance of the verdict. "Gentlemen, the Court wishes to thank each of you for doin' your civic duty. You are dismissed." The jury filed off to stand at the rear of the outdoor court. Judge Mason looked to the Sheriff. "Sheriff Anson, please bring the defendants before the court." The prisoners bound hand and foot were led in front of the Judge. "In light of the verdict rendered against you by a jury of your peers, I find each of you guilty as charged for the crimes of robbery, rape, and murder. I hereby sentence you to be hanged by the neck until you are dead, said sentence to be carried out immediately. Sheriff Anson, do your duty."

Ten hanging nooses were quickly fashioned, tossed over the stout limbs of the huge oak tree, and tied off securely to the trunk. Sheriff Anson untied the legs of the first pair of outlaws, and members of the jury helped lift them up onto the saddles of the horses that had been readied for the occasion. The jurors then led the horses over to where the deputy waited. When the outlaws were in place, the deputy leaned out of his saddle and slipped a noose around each man's neck, making sure that the hangman's knot was placed correctly under their ears. When the deputy nodded his head the sheriff smacked the horses on the rump, and both outlaws' protests were cut short as they dropped to their deaths and slowly swung at the end of the ropes. The process was quickly repeated, until all ten cartcutters dangled from the limbs of the huge live oak.

"Leave 'em hang there until mornin' as an example, Sheriff," said Judge Mason. "Perhaps their fate will discourage others of their kind.

Chapter 27

Within the month, Governor Pease received the necessary funding from the legislature to send the state militia to act as escorts for the Mexican carters. Their arrival on the scene diffused the situation, but not before Caleb's Rangers, with the help of the local citizens of Goliad, had removed much of the bad element causing the unrest. However, the same could not be said for the frontier.

During the summer of 1857, Secretary of War Jefferson Davis left the War Office, and the greater part of the Second Cavalry was ordered out of Texas and sent to Utah. Out on the plains, the Comanches remained politically insensitive to many things, but it could never be said they were either blind or stupid. With the threat of the Second Cavalry practically eliminated and the disbandment of the Texas Rangers, attacks all along the frontier increased in both number and ferocity. The line of western settlements was pushed back further to the east with each passing day, as one-by-one, settlers' cabins went up in flames.

As far as Caleb was concerned, the political situation was not much better. At the end of the 1857, state-wide Democratic convention, the Calhoun democrats emerged in complete control of the state, and as former governor Pease had predicted, they refused to reelect Sam Houston to the United States Senate. With no hope of being returned to his Congressional office by the legislature, Houston appealed directly to the people by running for governor against the Democrats' nominee, a wealthy, states' rights planter by the name of Hardin R. Runnels. Caleb threw his full support, both financial and otherwise behind Sam Houston, but the hero of San Jacinto was soundly trounced. The first time the man had ever been repudiated at the polls.

However, defense of the frontier had always lain close to the heart of Texas politics, and when Runnels was sworn in as governor in late December of 1857, he was elected in part because of his promise to solve the Comanche problem. Upon taking office, he addressed this promise, according to the Texas legislature's wishes, by seeking assistance from the federal government. When no assistance was forthcoming, the legislature, finally despairing of federal action, authorized the raising of state troops to get the job done. The Governor immediately appointed Caleb's good friend and long-time Texas Ranger, John Ford, Senior Captain and commander of all Texas forces.

John "Rip" Ford had served with Caleb during the war as the Executive Officer and Regimental Medical Officer for Jack Hays's regiment of Texas Rangers, fighting the guerrillas who attempted to cut General Winfield Scott's supply lines to Mexico City. As the regimental medical officer, Ford had gained the nickname Rip by signing all Ranger death certificates with R.I.P., for rest in peace. Caleb had commanded the regiment's scouts and he and Ford had worked well together. As a result of their friendship and former close working relationship, Ford sent Caleb a message right after his appointment, stating that he had a meeting scheduled with Governor Runnels the following week and requesting that Caleb meet him at the Bullock Hotel around noon on March 10.

Rip was standing at the bar talking to Bullock when Caleb shoved his way through the café's swinging doors. "Caleb," Ford said as he smiled and offered his hand, "good to see you again." The well-groomed Ford was tall and muscular, with a ruddy complexion and deep blue eyes. His handshake was firm and his welcoming smile sincere.

"Howdy, Caleb," Bullock joined in, "would you like to join our new 'Senior Captain' in a cup of my fine coffee?"

Ford shook his head and chuckled at Bullock's dig about the unwanted title Governor Runnels had bestowed on him. "I'd much rather have a beer, but we'll be meetin' with the governor soon enough."

"Coffee's fine," Caleb replied. "I don't know how eager Runnels is gonna be to see me, though, after I threw my support behind Sam Houston in the election."

Ford smiled as Caleb heaped the usual amount of sugar in his cup and stirred it well. "Hell, Caleb, I voted for Houston myself, but Runnels gave me authority to appoint anyone I want, and that sure as hell includes you. I want you to lead my scouts. You got anyone in mind you might want to bring along?"

"Bigfoot and one of my Lipans for sure," Caleb replied. "I'll most likely bring a few of my Rangers, too. Some of 'em are still workin' the Rockin' M."

"Sounds good to me," said Ford. "Finish off that coffee and let's get on over to the Capitol. It doesn't pay to keep the Governor waitin'."

"By the way," added Bullock before they left, "this letter came for you the other day." He slid an envelope across the bar to Caleb.

Caleb picked up the letter and immediately recognized the handwriting. "It's from Jack Hays." He slipped the letter in a pocket of his hunting shirt. "I'll take a look at it later."

"How's Jack been doin' out in California?" asked Ford.

"Damn well," Caleb replied with a smile. "In fact, last time I heard he was filthy rich. I'll tell you about it on the way."

Governor Runnels rose from behind his desk when Ford and Caleb were admitted to his office. The Governor wore a dark suit with a white, high-collared shirt and black tie. His hair and beard were short-cropped, and his thin lips, dark eyes, and stern expression gave him an aristocratic appearance.

Runnels welcomed Ford with a cordial handshake. "Thank you for agreeing to serve Captain Ford."

"It's a pleasure anytime I can be of service to Texas, Governor," Ford replied. "Sir, I'd like you to meet Caleb McAdams. He'll serve as chief of my scouts."

Runnels stern expression showed the barest hint of a smile as he shook Caleb's outstretched hand. "I recognize Mr. McAdams from the campaign. He was an avid supporter of my opponent, if I'm not mistaken."

"I'm afraid that's correct, Governor," said Caleb with a grin as he returned the governor's firm handshake. "My loyalties did lie with Sam."

"With the troubles facing the Texas frontier, the candidate you supported in the election means very little to me, Mr. McAdams," said Runnels. "If Captain Ford thinks he needs you, I'm more than grateful for your help. Please have a seat, gentlemen." Once they were seated, Runnels quickly got down to business. "Captain Ford, you have authority to call up a hundred men and establish a camp somewhere on the northwestern frontier. My wish is that you cooperate as much as you can with the army, the Indian agents, and other federal authorities, but you must brook absolutely no interference with your assigned mission."

"Just exactly what is my mission, Governor?" asked Ford.

"With the most recent ferocious and bloody Comanche raids into Texas, the public is howling for action, Captain. Up to now, the U.S. Army has proved unable to stem the violence, and worse, federal units that were stationed here, including the Second Cavalry, are being transferred out of Texas for reasons that seem to be driven more by politics than military considerations. Although I fully realize federal law and numerous treaties forbid incursion by state forces into protected Indian territories, the situation demands action. You must follow the trail of any and all hostile or suspected hostile Indians you may discover, no matter where they lead, and if possible, overtake and chastise them severely if you find them to be unfriendly."

"Furthermore, you must do so as quickly as possible because your appropriation for the mission is quite limited, and you dare not exceed it. I realize this is a very delicate and difficult assignment, but I feel with certainty that you are the perfect man to accomplish the task. I also know from speaking with former Governor Pease that Mr. McAdams will be of great assistance to you." Runnels smiled. "In fact, if not for his misguided loyalty during the election, this mission may well have been his to command. Do either of you have any questions?" When neither man spoke Runnels continued, "Very well, gentlemen, good luck and good hunting."

Josh ran across the room to Caleb and climbed up on his lap. "Horsy ride, Uncle Caleb, I want a horsy ride!"

Caleb bounced Josh up and down on his knee and Wanda smiled as the little boy squealed in delight. They had just finished a quiet supper, and Caleb was horse-playing with Josh. Having the opportunity to interact with his second son was a cherished opportunity that did not come often enough as far as Caleb was concerned. At home on the ranch, he spent much of his time with his family; riding with Gretchin, reading and talking with Ilse about her plans to continue her education in New Orleans, and romping and playing with little Ham. In truth, his favorite moments on the ranch were when the entire family gathered in the great room in front of a warm fire and spent time enjoying each other's company. He knew it could never be the same with Wanda and Josh, and the realization saddened him.

In spite of his strenuous protests, Wanda picked Josh up off Caleb's lap and stood him up on the floor. "I'll brook no nonsense from you, young man. It's well past your bedtime. Now give Uncle Caleb a kiss and off you go."

"Okay," Josh agreed although from his expression it was apparent that he did not much care at all for the idea of going to bed. Reaching up, he hugged Caleb around the neck. "Goodnight Uncle Caleb. We can play tomorrow."

"Sorry, partner, but I won't be here tomorrow." The look of disappointment on little Josh's face tugged at Caleb's heart. "But I promise I'll be back just as soon as I can, okay?"

"Okay, Uncle Caleb," Josh said as Wanda led him off to bed.

Wanda returned a few minutes later and sat down beside Caleb on the sofa in front of the fire. "Now I guess it's my turn to face disappointment. I thought if I made up a pallet for you in front of the fire, you would stay the night?"

Caleb smiled. "I changed my mind. I'll stay the night and the mornin', too, so I can surprise Josh. I plan on takin' him for a little ride right after breakfast. You're welcome to join us if you've a mind."

Wanda put her head on Caleb's shoulder. "I would love to. I know it's been hard for you to get away once in a while, but both of us miss having you around. What did Jack have to say in his letter?"

"He's doin real fine, and so are the investments he's been makin' for us. He made arrangements for you to have access to the money, if you and Josh need it. You can either write to him or directly to the Bank of San Francisco. He also had the bank send a good amount as a line of credit to John at the emporium." When would the Texas legislature ever get around to letting banks incorporate, Caleb wondered? Making credit and savings arrangements through local merchants like John Cooper was inconvenient at best. Thank goodness for the big safe that was buried in the floor of the storeroom at the Rocking M. "By the way, what does John have to say about all this?"

If you're asking what my brother thinks of our relationship," Wanda replied, "he doesn't approve of it at all. At the same time, he knows I'm an adult capable of making my own decisions. He does his best to ignore the situation by pretending it doesn't exist."

Caleb sat quietly for a moment wondering if he should tell Wanda about the remainder of Jack's letter warning him about the Pates. According to Jack, a friend of his was playing poker with Ned Pate, when Ned mentioned sending someone to Texas to take care of an old family problem. As far as Hays was concerned the "problem" Ned spoke of must have been Caleb. Of course, Caleb would do his best to keep an eye out for trouble, but he decided not to worry Wanda about it.

"By the way," Caleb added after a moment, "I heard your name mentioned in town today. You ain't been takin' my advice about keepin' your opinions to yourself, have you?"

Wanda sat up. "Why do you say that?"

"Caleb shook his head. "Come on, Wanda. How many Anglo kids have been comin' to your school lately? Two or three at most, and I'm bettin' they're German. I'd say you got mostly Tejano kids and a few free Negroes, right?"

"So what if that's all I have?" Wanda asked, immediately going on the defensive. "Tejanos and Negroes need an education, too?"

Caleb sighed. "Of course they do, but that's not the point. Anglo parents refuse to send their kids to your school because of your opinions on slavery and secession."

"Sam Houston is against secession and you supported him," Wanda pointed out.

"He lost the election by a bunch too, didn't he?" asked Caleb. "And he sure as hell didn't come out against slavery like you've been preachin'."

Now, Wanda was angry. "Slavery is wrong Caleb McAdams, and you know it!"

Caleb nodded. "That's right, but I ain't worried about me, Wanda. I can damn well take care of myself. I got a lot of guns at the Rockin' M to discourage people from messin' with my family there, but I can't be here all the time to look after you and little Josh. Please girl, you have to tone it down some or the crazies around here may try 'n harm you. Can't you see how dangerous things are gettin'? I'm not sayin' anybody would intentionally hurt Josh, but he could get caught in the middle. The idea of them comin' after you when I'm not around to help scares me to death."

Wanda was still not convinced. "I can imagine the slavery and states' rights sympathizers trying to put a scare into me, Caleb, but the idea that they would intentionally harm a woman is difficult to believe. It's just not in the code of most Southern gentlemen to do such a thing."

"Wanda, I'm tellin' you the situation is a hell of a lot more dangerous than you think. Most of these states' rights and slavery sympathizers as you describe 'em are rabid zealots that have nothin' but pure hatred for the North and especially for anyone who's an abolitionist. I swear, if you were a man you'd already been tarred and feathered or worse long before now. And even bein' a woman ain't gonna protect you much longer, if you can't learn to keep your opinions to yourself."

Wanda sighed deeply. "I'm sorry Caleb. I'll do my best, but it's so difficult to just sit by and say nothing when these terrible men mouth their hatred so openly."

Caleb realized his words of warning were having little or no effect on Wanda's stubborn need to point out injustice at every turn. Who knows, he thought, maybe I should speak up more often myself and take some of the heat off her. He only hoped with all his heart that his assessment of the situation was wrong, and that Wanda and Josh would remain safe.

Far to the west, in the fancy parlor of a Nob Hill mansion overlooking San Francisco Bay, another conversation was taking place between Ned and Mike Pate, the subject of which was their plans for dealing with Caleb McAdams. Or at least as far as Mike Pate was concerned their lack of any plans at all.

"I'm sick and tired of waitin' to deal with McAdams, Ned," Mike groused from his slouched down position in a comfortable overstuffed chair near the fireplace. "All I hear from you is to be patient. Hell, we took care of the old man long ago. I say it's high time we headed back to Texas and finished the damn feud once and for all."

Ned shook his head at Mike's stupidity, wondering if all the brains in the Pate family had gone to him. "Look Mike," he explained, doing his best to keep from throttling his younger brother, "in the first place we ain't goin' back to Texas, now or ever. Why in the hell would we deal with McAdams on our own when we got all the money in the damn world to hire it done? Are you willin' to face the bastard down?" Ned nearly laughed out loud at the look of fear that widened his brother's eyes. "Don't worry, little brother, I ain't either. I only waited this long to put McAdams off his guard, makin' him think we forgot all about him. We ain't never gonna forget what he done. In fact, I already put a plan in motion."

Mike sat up straight. "What're you talkin' about?"

Ned's lips curled into a sneering smile, giving his cruel features an even more sinister look in the flickering light cast by the fire. "A few months ago I hired an agent and sent him to Texas to find somebody ready and willin' to kill McAdams for the right price. The man's got plenty of money and orders to take his time to find the right killer; somebody who's real close to McAdams, so the bastard won't be suspicious. Time means nothin' now anyways. The only thing that matters is that McAdams will finally get what's comin' to him. That's a promise, little brother, that's a promise.

With his stomach near ready to burst from a delicious picnic lunch, Caleb leaned back against the warmth of the big, sun-heated rock and watched as Lucinda allowed little Ham to wade and splash in the shallow water below the small waterfall. The creek that ran through the east end of the Rocking M and down to the Colorado was one of the family's favorite spots, and the place where Caleb had proposed marriage to Lucinda. Ilse sat beside Caleb quietly reading from one of her favorite books and Gretchin was off riding with Bigfoot.

Caleb heard gunshots off in the distance and Lucinda glanced up at him with worry on her face. "Don't worry, love, Bigfoot said he and Gretchin would be doin' a little target practice."

Lucinda's worried look turned to a frown. "I swear, Caleb, that man is determined to turn Gretchin into a tomboy."

Caleb chuckled. "Gretchin was a tomboy long before she ever met up with Bigfoot. You know darn well she's always liked ridin' a horse more 'n readin' a book. Don't worry; she'll grow out of it one of these days."

"I'm not so sure about that," Lucinda disagreed, "especially with Bigfoot teaching her to rope and shoot, too."

"Give her some time," Caleb replied. "She's only thirteen." Lucinda shook her head in doubt and went back to playing with Ham.

As he watched Lucinda and Ham splash around in the shallow water that rippled over the rocks and sent sparkling flashes of sunlight reflecting into his eyes, Caleb's mind drifted to the upcoming expedition with Rip Ford. After recruiting most of his men, Ford left for the Brazos Reserve in mid-March. He hoped to induce Chief Placido and as many of the reservation Indians as possible to join up with his force. Caleb had not heard from Rip as yet, but he and Bigfoot planned to ride north in the morning with Chako and eight Rangers to join him on the Brazos. From there the expedition would move further north in search of hostile Comanche bands, even if it meant, as Governor Runnels made abundantly clear, moving across the Red River and into Indian Territory for the first time.

Caleb heard the approach of galloping horses and looked up in time to see Gretchin and Bigfoot racing for the stream. The tall roan Gretchin rode had a much lighter load to carry and she slid to a laughing, dust-swirling stop just before Bigfoot reined in on his big buckskin and stepped down out of the saddle. Ilse shook her head disapprovingly at Gretchin's boyish antics and went back to her reading.

Still chuckling, Gretchin jumped down from the saddle to join Bigfoot. "Uncle Bigfoot, you're much too fat to race me."

Bigfoot ruffled Gretchin's hair in a friendly manner as she tried to dodge away from him. "You'll hurt your old Uncle Bigfoot's feelin's with harsh words like that, Little Bit, even if they are true."

After the mismatched pair got down on their knees and took a long drink from the clear running stream, Gretchin pulled off her boots, rolled up her pants, and joined Ham and her mother splashing around in the water. Bigfoot plopped down beside Caleb. Reaching into the nearby picnic basket, the big man pulled out a leftover drumstick and took a huge bite, talking around a mouthful of chicken as he mumbled, "that girl of yours can ride up a storm, Caleb. She'll soon be a dead shot, too, if she keeps on practicin'."

"Not if Lucinda shoots you first for encouagin' the girl into what she thinks of as foolishness," Caleb replied with a chuckle.

Bigfoot nearly choked on the mouthful of chicken as he broke into a hearty laugh, and Caleb had to slap him on the back to help him catch his breath. Once he had regained his composure, the big man glanced over to see that Lucinda was out of earshot then asked, "Did Jack mention the Pates in his last letter?"

Caleb also kept his voice low in response. "He said there were rumors goin' around that Ned sent someone to Texas to take care of an old family problem. Jack seemed to think Ned was talkin' about me."

"Seemed to think," Bigfoot loudly parroted before glancing over at Lucinda and lowering his voice once again. "What the hell else could he be talkin' about, partner? I'm damn glad we brought the girls back to Texas with us, but maybe we should have taken care of them Pates first, after all. I always said they'll be a threat to you and yours until we kill every damn one of 'em, and that's the Gospel truth."

Caleb knew beyond a doubt that he had made the right decision to abandon the chase for Ned and Mike and return with the girls, but right or wrong that still left him and his family in danger. "I have to agree with you, partner. We'll just have to keep an extra sharp eye out for awhile. At least until we can learn a little more."

PART V

Chapter 28

Late in the afternoon of a mid-April day in 1858, Caleb, Big-foot and Eph Daggett led a small band of Rangers into the camp Rip Ford had established on the Middle Fork of the Brazos near the Brazos Reserve. Rip was standing outside his tent alongside Shapley Ross, ready to greet the Rangers when they dismounted.

"Caleb, Bigfoot, good to see you," Ford said with a warm smile as he shook hands. "You too, Eph, it's been a good while since I've laid eyes on you. Welcome to Camp Runnels. Y'all know Shapley, don't you?"

"I've known him for a good while," Caleb replied as he shook Ross's hand. Me 'n Bigfoot rode with him a couple years back, too, when we helped set up the Reserve. Good to see you again, Shapley. How's the family?"

"The wife and kids are just fine, thanks," Shapley replied as he returned Caleb's handshake and followed suit with Bigfoot and Eph. "Sul is off to Alabama goin' to college at Wesleyan University in Florence."

Caleb nodded his approval. "I figured that boy was headed for big things one day. Give him my best next time he's home." Turning back to Ford, Caleb asked, "How many men have signed on, Rip?"

"Countin' you and your ten, we now total a hundred and two men ready to ride. That should do us just fine once we throw in the reservation warriors Shapley's plannin' on recruitin' tonight, with Placido's help."

"There's a big powwow at the reservation this evenin'," added Shapley. "Y'all are more 'n welcome to join in, if you've a mind. As often as the Comanches have been hittin' the reservation lately, though, I don't suppose it's gonna be hard to round up a good many warriors willin' to ride against 'em. In fact, Placido and most of his Tonkawas are so stirred up they're ready to ride out now."

"Let's head on over there," said Rip. "The powwow should be goin' strong by the time we arrive."

"Sounds good to me," Caleb agreed. "We'll be ready to ride just as soon as I make sure Corporal Nelson finds a place for the men to lay out their bedrolls."

"There's a good spot down by the river," said Shapley. "Mount up and I'll take y'all on down there."

"You heard the man," said Caleb as he turned back to his Rangers. "Mount up!"

"Captain," said Corporal Nelson as he swung up in the saddle, "I'd just as soon ride with you and Bigfoot."

"I want you with the men, Nelson," Caleb replied. "Keep 'em together and see they're looked after properly." Nelson did not look happy, but he kept quiet and did as he was ordered.

In the gathering darkness, the Rangers saw the towering blaze long before they dismounted and tethered their horses at the edge of the village. When they walked up to join the gathering at the huge council fire, Placido was standing in front of the reservation warriors, his muscular, tattooed physique silhouetted by the light cast from the leaping flames as he harangued the fighting men of the village about the many atrocities committed by their hated enemies.

"We must not throw away this chance for vengeance, my brothers! The hated Comanches have raided this reservation time and again, stealing our horses, riding off with our women and children, and slaughtering many of our friends and family!" The warriors screamed their approval of Placido's words, urging the war chief on. "Now we have a chance to ride with our white brothers and take revenge by stealing Comanche horses, taking Comanche women and children, and counting coup on many of their warriors! Who will ride with Placido and his Ranger friends on this raid?"

As the leaping flames of the council fire sent towers of shimmering sparks swirling high in the night sky, the frenzied warriors sprang to their feet. Dancing around the huge bonfire, they twisted and turned, stomping their feet to the beat of the drums as they boasted of their prowess and chanted for the Great Spirit to bring them victory. Placido was plainly pleased with his efforts when he walked over to join Ford and the Rangers.

"As you can see, my brother," the war chief said as he stepped up to Shapley, "many of the warriors from this village will journey north with you and Captain Ford." When Shapley voiced his approval, Placido turned to Caleb and Bigfoot. "It also pleases me to see Red Hair and Bear-of-a-Man, and to know they will ride with the People of the Wolf against our hated enemies. This is truly good medicine."

Caleb raised his hand to Placido in a gesture of greeting. "It is good to see you once again, too, Ha-shu-ka-na. Your words are good words; words of strength. I have spoken with Captain Ford, and me and Bear-of-a-Man plan to ride out early tomorrow mornin' on a scout north to the Red River."

"And we plan on ridin' north of the Red if we have to," added Ford, "federal law, be damned. No boundary set by man is gonna keep me from goin' after the Comanches this time. They're gonna pay a severe penalty for all the devilment they've been causin'."

"We'll find 'em, Rip," Caleb said before turning back to Placido. "Ha-shu-ka-na, I plan to leave my Rangers here with Rip. Will you lend me a few of your warriors to ride north on the scout?"

Placido smiled. "It will be a pleasure, my friend. Now come and join the warriors at the fire. We will dance in celebration."

A long column of Rangers, two wagons, a rickety old ambulance, and fifteen pack-mules meandered out of Camp Runnels on April 22, following the winding course of the Clear Fork of the Brazos in a northeasterly direction. On the third day of the march, the column forded the Brazos and headed north for Cottonwood Springs, where, late in the afternoon, they met up with a hundred and thirteen reservation warriors under the command of Placido and Shapley Ross. A camp was established for the night, sentries were posted, and Ford allowed the lighting of several small cook fires with orders to use only dry wood and to put them out well before dark.

The setting sun had fired the scattered clouds that floated across the deep azure of the western horizon in vivid shades of orange and red when Caleb and Bigfoot rode into camp with Chako and the Tonkawa scouts. After tending to their mounts, the Rangers headed for Captain Ford's tent. Ford was sitting out front near the still hot coals of a small cook fire, drinking coffee with Ross, Eph, and his three other lieutenants, William Pitts, John Tankersly, and Waylon Preston.

Ford lifted his cup in greeting. "Pull yourself up a log, boys, and grab a cup of coffee. It ain't much, but it's hot. There's some antelope leftover too, if you've a mind to cook some of it up on the coals before dark."

"As hungry as I am," Bigfoot said to Caleb when he dragged up a log for them to sit on, "I'll do the cookin' while you do the talkin'." Everyone had a good chuckle as the big man went to work spearing some fat chunks of antelope with sharpened green sticks before shoving the other ends of the sticks into the ground so that the meat hung suspended over the hottest coals of the dying fire.

Caleb plopped down, poured himself a cup of coffee, and added his usual heaping measure of sugar, stirring the coffee with his finger before he spoke. "We rode all the way to the Red, and then downstream for twenty miles and didn't see a damn thing, Rip. My guess is the Comanches are scattered out in huntin' camps somewhere along the Washita, or maybe even further north on the Canadian."

"I figured as much," said Ford. "That's why I was glad Runnels gave us the authority to cross the Red if need be. We'll move as far north as we have to. I agree the Comanches are most likely spread out huntin' by now too, and that's gonna make our job a hell of a lot easier once we do find 'em. We'll cross the Red and move upstream. If we don't turn up any Comanche sign in a few days, we'll head straight north for the Washita."

Traveling north from the camp at Cottonwood Springs, the long column of Rangers and reservation warriors forded the Red River on April 29. Fortunately, the usually heavy spring rains had not yet fallen, and while nearly a hundred yards wide where Caleb led the column across, the ford he and the scouts had located was shallow, with a good gravel bottom skirting most of the red mud flats and quicksand that posed a constant hazard along the course of the treacherous river. After fording the Red, the column moved cautiously upstream, making stops every now and then to rest the horses and give the scouts ample opportunity to locate any hostile camps that may have been in the area.

This methodical movement continued until May 7, when Ford, disappointed in finding nothing, after more than a week of diligent searching, finally gave the order to move north along the 98th meridian and head for the Washita. The column reached a winding branch of the Washita on the following day, and Ford ordered the men to set up camp while Caleb and his scouts fanned out to the north and west to discover if there were any Comanche hunting camps nearby. Their search was once again in vain.

Pulling out early the following morning, the column soon reached the Washita where they were forced to cut their way into and out of the river's deeply incised banks before they could manage to drag the wagons and ambulance across the muddy, silt-laden bottom to the north bank. For the next day and a half, movement continued to the northwest following the course of the Washita, with the scouts again well to the front.

Around noon on May 10, Caleb, Bigfoot, and Chako crested a low rise ten miles or so ahead of the column. A good-sized bull buffalo stood near the bottom of the rise. Intending to take advantage of an easy meal for the entire outfit, the riders moved in closer, as Caleb slipped the Hawken long rifle from the fringed scabbard on the left side of his fancy Mexican saddle. The tall redhead was puzzled when the buffalo did not bolt into a run at their approach. Then he saw the animal stagger when it tried to move.

"Bigfoot, either that bull is sick or somethin' has crippled him." Preferring not to risk the noise of a rifle shot unless it was necessary, Caleb shoved his Hawken back into the saddle scabbard. "Chako, ride on down there and finish him with your bow."

Digging his heels into his lively pinto mare, Chako galloped down the rise. The bull attempted to run, but it was plain the animal's heart was not in the effort. Quickly drawing back his powerful bow, Chako sent an arrow deep into the buffalo's lungs, and then drew back and launched another. The bull staggered forward for a few feet until his front legs collapsed, then rolled over and lay still. Caleb and Bigfoot moved down the rise to join Chako and dismounted at the kill.

Bigfoot was the first to notice two other arrows buried deep in the buffalo's ribs. Only the feathers and a short bit of the shafts were visible above the bull's shaggy coat. Kneeling down, he went to work with his Bowie knife and soon held one of the bloody shafts in his hand.

"They're Comanche for sure," the big man said as he handed them up to Caleb before beginning to go to work on the bull. "The column should be catchin' up with us in a few hours. We might as well get this animal skinned and butchered before they get here. Give me a hand, Chako."

"I'm gonna take a little ride around here and look for sign while y'all finish up," said Caleb. "I'll be back shortly."

Bigfoot and Chako skillfully skinned and butchered the buffalo, piling up the good cuts of meat on the bloody hide. By the time they finished wrapping the meat in the fresh hide to keep the flies at bay, it was late afternoon and Caleb returned from his scout.

In the distance Caleb saw the column approaching along the river. "This looks like as good a place as any to set up camp, Bigfoot. We might as well wait for 'em here."

"Did you see any sign?" Bigfoot asked.

"There's been a lot of huntin' northwest of here," Caleb replied. "I'd guess there must be a camp somewhere up that way. I'd bet it's not too far from here either. We'll talk it over with Rip when he gets here and see what he wants to do."

The column arrived within the hour, and Caleb and Bigfoot discussed the situation with Rip. After showing him the arrow they had pulled out of the buffalo. They told him about the results of Caleb's scout.

"I agree with you," Rip said. "The Comanche camp must be off to the northwest. They tend to camp as close as they can to the buffalo herd they're huntin', so the women don't have to carry the meat too far. Tomorrow I'll ride out with you and Bigfoot. We'll take a good look up that way."

Early the following morning, as the shimmering, blood-orange disc of the sun appeared to hover on the distant eastern horizon Ford spoke with Eph and his other lieutenants. "I'm gonna scout to the northwest with Caleb and Bigfoot today. Head the column out that way, and we'll meet up with you by late this afternoon. We're deep into the Comancheria now, men. If we aim to surprise the Comanches, we have to move as quickly and as quietly as possible. So when you move out, leave the wagons and baggage here with a few guards. Make damn sure Shapley keeps a close watch on his Tonkawas, too, or they'll ride off on their own and give us away. Eph, you're in charge until I get back. Keep a point element well out to the front and a few scouts out to the flanks. No command of mine is gonna ride into an ambush, or I'll skin you alive. Caleb, Bigfoot, let's get mounted and ride!"

The three Rangers rode out of camp a few minutes later and headed northwest, with Chako scouting well ahead of them. It was close to noon when the Lipan loped his pinto down from a high ridge and joined them with news the Rangers had been waiting to hear.

"Soldier road at top of ridge," said Chako. "Far down in valley, Comanche hunters chase buffalo."

"The soldier road he's talkin' about has got to be the trail that runs between Fort Smith and Santa Fe," said Ford. "Let's go have us a look."

Within minutes the Rangers dismounted just below the ridgeline and walked up to the Fort Smith trail, making sure not to skyline themselves. Far down in the valley that stretched its way to the north a few Comanche braves were chasing buffalo. Further off, a gaggle of squaws were leading several meat-laden travois away from the scene of the hunt.

"From the direction the squaws are draggin' the travois, the camp definitely lies to the northwest," said Rip, "and not far from here. I think it's high time we started back to the column."

Ford and Bigfoot mounted up, but Caleb hesitated, staring out across the rolling plains as if he could sense the nearness of their elusive quarry. "Rip, you and Bigfoot go ahead and ride on back. I think me and Chako are gonna have us another good look around. We'll be back well before sundown."

Bigfoot frowned. "Don't be takin' too many chances, partner. You'll be a long way from help if you run into somethin' you can't handle."

"Don't worry," Caleb replied, "I ain't lookin' for trouble. We might be able to locate the Comanche hunting camp for certain, though, if we're careful. We sure as hell don't want to stumble across it by accident when we're on the march."

"You're probably right," Rip agreed, "but Bigfoot's advice about bein' careful is right on the money. Be damn sure you heed it. Come on, Bigfoot, let's ride." The pair reined around and headed back down the ridge.

Caleb waited until Bigfoot and Ford had disappeared over the next ridge before mounting up and motioning for Chako to follow him.

Moving slowly to the northwest, Caleb and Chako kept to the low ground to prevent from silhouetting themselves against the skyline on one of the many ridges that swept across the wide grassland of the prairie like the rolling waves on an endless sea. Nearly two hours into the scout they were following the winding course of a shallow stream that flowed north toward the

Canadian River when Caleb's keen sense of smell caught the tangy scent of wood smoke wafting on the wind. He signaled Chako to rein in and carefully let his eyes roam over the length of the next ridge. Less than a mile distant, a faint column of smoke coiled above the ridge like an angry rattler before quickly dissipating in the wind.

"That smoke has to be coming from a Comanche camp, Chako," Caleb observed, "but with only one fire it can't be too big. We'll dismount up ahead in that little copse of cottonwoods and take a closer look on foot." After tying off their animals, the scouts followed the stream towards the suspected campsite until Caleb guessed they were within a hundred yards of the rising smoke. "Let's circle around and come up on the camp from behind this ridge. That should keep us out of sight."

The climb took only a few minutes, and once the scouts were near the top, both men dropped to their bellies and squirmed up the final few feet. Caleb removed his sombrero before joining Chako in taking a peek at the camp over the crest of the ridge. Five tall, buffalo hide lodges stood in a half-moon arc near a bend in the stream. A lone Comanche squaw squatted at a fire in the middle of the arc stirring something in an old iron pot suspended over the flames. Three other squaws and some children were busy gathering firewood near the base of the ridge.

Further downstream a small pony herd grazed peacefully. There were no warriors in sight, and Caleb decided it would be a good idea to clear the area before any of them returned. After nudging Chako with his elbow, he slid back down far enough to stand without being seen from the camp and headed for the horses with the Lipan right behind him. They were soon mounted and heading back for the column.

Reaching the campsite just after sundown, Caleb and Chako were challenged by the sentries guarding the darkened perimeter.

This close to his objective Ford would allow no campfires, bugle calls, shouted orders, and similar nonsense that were common to the army in Indian country. Like many old Rangers, Ford believed he could out-trail, out-sneak, and out-think most Indians, and he was eager to prove it.

Caleb reported to Ford as soon as he had wiped Sally down and fed the sturdy mare a fair measure of grain from a sack on one of the pack mules. "We found a small hunting camp northwest of here, Rip, so the main Comanche camp can't be much further. There were only five lodges, but I don't think we can afford to bypass them without the warriors takin' note and spreadin' the alarm."

Ford nodded, lost in thought for a moment before he replied. "I agree. We'll have to take care of the camp first and hope the noise doesn't alert the village. Well before sunup, I want you to lead Shapley and the Tonkawas to this side of the hunting camp. They will attack just as soon as there's enough light. Before they do, I want you and Bigfoot to take a few warriors and set up on the other side. That'll put you in a good position to cut off anybody who tries to escape and warn the village. I'll be about fifteen minutes behind with the remainder of the column. We'll close up as soon as I hear the Tonkawas open fire. You best grab a couple hours shuteye now while you got the chance. I'll brief the others."

"Sounds like a damn good idea to me, Rip," said Caleb. "My butt still feels like it's bouncin' in the saddle."

Chapter 29

The prairie was still shrouded in a thick blanket of darkness the following morning when Caleb, Bigfoot, and Chako returned from their scout and met up with Shapley and the Tonkawas waiting along the stream that led to the Comanche hunting camp. Placido was doing his best to keep his warriors quiet as Caleb had requested, but the tall redhead was sure the Tonkawa war chief's obedience was more the result of Shapley Ross's presence than anything else. The reservation warriors respected the man, and Caleb was damn glad the Indian Agent had agreed to join the expedition. Shapley, having heard the approach of the scouts, already had Placido and the Tonkawas mounted when Caleb reined in.

"The camp's quiet, Shapley," Caleb said as he settled Sally's jitters with a tight rein. "All you have to do is follow this stream and you'll run right smack into the middle of 'em. Give me ten warriors and about fifteen minutes to get in position on the other side of the camp. It should be growin' light about then anyway.

Move in and hit 'em hard. Placido, be sure 'n hold your warriors up once you ride through the camp. We might shoot some of 'em by accident if they follow on too close to anyone who escapes."

"It will be as you say, Red Hair." The excitement was obvious in the war chief's tone of voice and manner. "We will destroy our hated enemy."

Caleb did not doubt the veracity of Placido's words. He was glad he would have no part in attacking the small camp. Long ago he had vowed not to make war on women and children, but he was sure the Tonkawas would kill without mercy in revenge for similar ruthlessness on the part of the Comanches.

"See you when the fightin's done," Caleb said to Shapley, after Placido had given him the ten warriors he had requested. "Good luck. Come on Bigfoot, let's ride."

Shapley watched in silence as Caleb and the others melted into the surrounding darkness, the muffled sound of their horses' hooves gradually growing fainter until they could no longer be heard. Within minutes the eastern horizon began to glow with a faint aura of light, and the Indian Agent checked the loads in his Colt. "Get 'em ready, Placido. We're goin' in."

The morning sun had not yet broken clear of the horizon when Shapley and Placido led the Tonkawa warriors into the middle of the Comanche camp. In spite of warnings from both leaders, the element of surprise was lost when the Tonkawas began to scream and fire their weapons in the air well before they reached the camp. There were also more Comanche warriors in the camp than expected, and they quickly formed a line of defense, fighting desperately to protect the flight of their women and children. Comanche arrows filled the air. When they began to hit home more than a few reservation warriors took the opportunity to follow the women and children off into the darkness rather than face the hissing death launched by the formidable short bows.

A Comanche brave in the defensive line launched an arrow at Shapley, and the deadly shaft whipped close past his face as he leaned well out of the saddle. Quickly righting himself, Ross put a ball into the luckless warrior's chest and rode on looking for his next target; man, woman, or child. Like Shapley, Placido and his Tonkawas made no distinction when it came to selecting targets. After dispatching a warrior with a well-aimed ball from the Colt revolver Shapley had given him, Placido crushed the skull of a fleeing squaw with a vicious backhanded swipe of his war club. Leaping from his pony, he quickly went to work with his scalping knife to claim his bloody prize.

A few more Comanches went down under the sheer weight of numbers as the deadly struggle turned hand to hand; blood enemies rolling on the ground, chopping and hacking at each other with clubs, hatchets, and knives. The fight did not completely turn in favor of the reservation Indians, however, until Ford and his Rangers thundered into the camp. The added firepower of their roaring Colts made short work of the Comanche warriors still standing or struggling with the Tonkawas, and the remaining women and children fled off into the gathering dawn.

Caleb and Bigfoot had been struggling to maintain control of their Tonkawas ever since the first shot echoed from the Comanche camp, but when the fleeing women and children began to appear several of them were instantly struck down in spite of their efforts. Having long ago sworn off killing women and children, Caleb finally brought an abrupt end to the slaughter when he blew one of the offending Tonkawas off the back of his painted pony with a round to the shoulder and threatened to do the same with a few of the others. The Tonkawas grumbled their displeasure at Caleb's actions, but not one of them was about to incur the wrath of Red Hair. However, in the end, even this drastic measure went for naught when the Tonkawas from the camp appeared on the scene and renewed the execution of the innocents.

In the midst of all the killing, Caleb and Bigfoot managed to round up a few prisoners, herding them into a small group between their horses for safety. Then the true irony of the situation came to the front, when Caleb saw a running squaw armed with a short bow turn from her flight and launch an arrow into the chest of one of the Tonkawas. The warrior's arms flew wide as he released the reins and toppled into the tall prairie grass. Having joined the fight as a warrior, Caleb now considered the squaw fair game, and he dropped her with a single shot from his big Colt.

The shimmering morning sun had climbed well above the horizon by the time the acrid smell of gun smoke cleared the air, and the Rangers and warriors returned to the camp. The Comanche warriors and most of the women and children were dead, and those still alive, including Caleb and Bigfoot's prisoners, were rounded up and placed under guard.

Ford called his lieutenants together for a quick meeting. "There's no time to waste. The sound of gunfire could well have been heard in the main village. Caleb and Bigfoot will lead the way to the northwest along with Shapley and his reservation warriors. The rest of us will follow close behind. Keep a sharp eye, Caleb. The village could be damn close, and the warriors might be lyin' in wait for you."

"Let's go!" shouted Caleb as he kneed Sally into a long lope and led the way out of the camp, with Bigfoot, Shapley, and the Tonkawas right behind.

Thirty minutes later Caleb, Bigfoot, and Shapley crested a long ridge in the middle of the Antelope Hills. As he signaled for a halt, Caleb called for the Tonkawas to come up and join them. Far below stretched a looping bend of the wide-bedded

Canadian River; its flat banks lined here and there with small copses of cottonwoods. The Comanche village was nestled at the top of the bend on the north side of the river, near the mouth of Little Robe Creek. Some three miles distant, the peaks of the buffalo hide lodges glistened white in the new light of the spring morning, looking like the sails of an ancient fleet cast against the greening sea of the vast prairie.

"The river looks shallow enough," said Bigfoot. "It shouldn't be much of a problem to ford."

"It's shallow alright," Caleb agreed, "but from what I hear, the Canadian is one of the most treacherous rivers in the west."

"That's a fact, Bigfoot," added Shapley. "You can hardly find a stretch of the damn thing along here where the mud flats and quicksand will allow you to cross. It looks peaceful alright, but looks can sure as hell be deceivin'."

"Danger or no danger, we're gonna have to find us a ford and be damn quick about it," Bigfoot replied. "Them Comanches sure as hell ain't stupid. It won't take 'em long to find out we're here."

Caleb caught a glimpse of movement in the hills far below the ridge. "It looks like we got company, boys. There's a lone Comanche headed this way."

Shapley carefully swept the area below them with his eyes, frustrated when he saw nothing. "I don't see a damn thing."

Bigfoot chuckled at the Indian Agent's consternation. "I don't see anything either, Shapley, but my compatriot has the eyes of a damn eagle. If he says he saw somethin', it's sure as hell out there."

"He's comin' alright," said Caleb, ignoring Bigfoot's humor. "If we can grab him, he just might show us the ford with a little persuasion."

Things did not work out exactly the way Caleb had planned. As soon as the Comanche crested a far ridge and came into sight of the others, a few of the Tonkawas let out a yelp and took off after him.

Cursing his bad luck, Caleb yelled to Bigfoot and the others to follow him as he kicked Sally Mae into motion. "Come on boys, we might as well join the party!"

Ford and his Rangers galloped up the ridge right behind them, and everyone began a mad rush for the river. Sally Mae was soon stretched out to a full gallop, and it did not take Caleb long to catch up with the foolish Tonkawas. Pressing the big filly for even more speed, he passed them, drew his Colt, and began to close in on the fleeing Comanche until he realized the warrior was intending to cross the river. Why not let him show us the way to the ford, Caleb thought, as he holstered his Colt and reined Sally in, slowing the filly to a steady lope. Ford, Bigfoot, and the rest of the outfit caught up with him as he watched the Comanche splash his pony into the Canadian and quickly make his way to the north bank before heading for the village.

"There's your way across, Rip," Caleb said to Ford as the Rangers and Tonkawas reined in. "How do we handle the attack?"

Ford did not waste time issuing orders. "You and Bigfoot take Shapley and the Indians across the river now and immediately attack the village. Stir the Comanches up real good before they get a chance to set up a defense. I'll get the Rangers across the river and on line as fast as I can and charge straight through the camp behind you. We'll meet up on the other side of the village and regroup for another charge if need be."

"Sounds good," Caleb agreed as he turned in the saddle. "Bigfoot, Shapley, you heard the man. Follow me. Placido, bring your warriors with us."

Caleb, Bigfoot, and Shapley splashed their way across the ford and started for the village at a brisk trot, with Placido and the Tonkawas close behind. The pace soon became a long lope, and then turned into a gallop as the scattered formation barged in among the buffalo hide lodges at the east end of the village. The alarm had been sounded only moments before, but the village was already a beehive of activity, with warriors grabbing up lances and stringing their short bows as they dashed to war ponies tethered nearby. Adding to the near pandemonium, frightened women, children, and old ones screamed their fear as they scattered like coveys of quail toward the ravines and thickets northwest of the village.

Caleb ignored a squaw fleeing with her children as he reined hard around a painted lodge and focused on a Comanche warrior who launched a feathered shaft deep into the chest of one of Placido's Tonkawas. The Tonkawa's arms went wide as he flopped off the back of his pony and bounced across the hard-packed earth, his foot caught up in the loop of rope that circled his pony's belly. The fear-crazed horse dragged the body through the village ahead of the charge. Leveling the long barrel of his Dragoon, Caleb slowly squeezed the trigger. The ball struck the offending Comanche square in the side of the head, nearly decapitating him.

"Keep movin'!" Caleb screamed at Placido and his Tonkawas, as he dropped another Comanche running for his tethered pony. "Drive on through the village!"

Unfortunately, the blood-crazed Tonkawas were too interested in killing Comanches and looting their lodges to obey anyone's orders. Caleb turned in the saddle and saw a small group of Tonkawa warriors run down the squaw and children he had spared earlier, filling them with arrows before leaping to the ground to claim their bloody scalps. In the middle of all the confusion there was absolutely nothing to be done for them. Suddenly Bigfoot's nearby Colt roared. A Comanche who had been riding down on Caleb with his war lance poised for the kill flew off the side of his pony, dead before his body slammed into the ground.

"You best forget about that sort of thing," Bigfoot warned, referring to the massacre of the squaw and her children, "and start watchin' your backside, partner. There ain't a damn thing you can do about it anyways."

Caleb shook his head at the helplessness of the situation and reined away with Bigfoot to join up with Ford, as he led the stampeding Rangers through the village at the gallop, shooting at anything that moved, be it man, woman, or child. Whether Caleb liked it or not, absolutely no mercy would be shown on this day.

Chapter 30

By the time the Rangers had completed their bloody assault through the buffalo hide lodges along Little Robe Creek and began to regroup on a low ridge west of the village, the ground was littered with Comanche dead and dying. Ford, not yet satisfied with the carnage his men had wrought, was busy loping along the ridge, frantically working to get his Rangers and Indians on line for another charge. The remaining Comanche warriors were assembling just outside the village in an area that would place them between Ford's new line and their fleeing families. Resplendent in feathered war bonnets and buffalo horn headdresses, the colorful feathers and scalp locks that adorned their long red war lances and buffalo hide shields fluttering in the wind; the warriors circled their prancing war ponies back and forth across the Ranger front, daring them to launch their attack.

In spite of the Comanches' antics, Ford held his men steady. The Rangers formed a long line of solemn, mostly bearded riders dressed in all manner of clothing from well-worn buckskins to old, shiny-kneed wool pants, their shirts a rainbow of sweat-stained and patched cotton, calmly looking on as the Tonkawas did their best to copy the antics of their hated enemies. It was a scene destined to be repeated on the western plains many times in the coming years. Sitting their horses near the center of the line, Caleb and Bigfoot finished reloading the cylinders of their Colts and checked to ensure that the copper percussion caps were properly seated on the firing nipples.

Caleb looked to Bigfoot. "This fight's gonna be a lot more to my likin' now that the women and children are out of the way, partner."

Bigfoot's attention was focused on the Comanches who had by now formed into their own line. "Look who's headin' this way with a truce flag?"

Glancing back at the long line of warriors, Caleb saw a lone Comanche riding toward the Rangers. The warrior was mounted on a tall, iron-gray stallion, and along with his short bow he carried a war lance topped off with a white flag. Although in the haste of the attack the Comanche did not have time to paint his face and his war pony in the usual manner, Caleb had no trouble recognizing his long-time adversary. Iron Jacket's long black hair and single eagle feather danced in the brisk wind that blew across the prairie and his shining breastplate of Spanish armor glistened in the morning sunlight.

As the war chief closed on the line, several Rangers opened fire, suspecting the white flag was nothing more than an old Comanche ruse. Seemingly unfazed and utterly unharmed by the hot lead that whistled all around him, Iron Jacket paused now and then to launch an arrow in the direction of the Ranger line and yell out his challenge to engage in individual combat. Finally convinced that his challenges would go unanswered, he began to swing his big gray stallion around, intending to return to the Comanche line.

Anticipating the moment, Caleb had earlier slipped his Hawken from the rifle scabbard on the side of his saddle and waited while everyone else was blasting away. Iron Jacket continued to swing his stallion around exposing his side, and Caleb ignored the angry jeers and catcalls of the Rangers as he took careful aim, set the rifle's rear trigger, and slowly squeezed the front hair trigger. The roar of the long rifle echoed up and down the Ranger line and the .50 caliber ball sailed straight and true. Iron Jacket lurched on the back of his big gray as the rifle ball glanced off his armor, nearly unseating him. Caleb swore angrily at his bad luck. Nothing but an errant gust of wind, he thought, as Iron Jacket ripped the white flag from his war lance and defiantly shook it at Caleb before galloping back to his warriors.

Ford sensed the time for action had come. "Now's the time to hit 'em hard, boys," he screamed, "charge!"

The long line of Rangers and reservation Indians exploded into motion, galloping toward the Comanches with Colts blazing, and the air filled with a hail of deadly arrows. Unwilling to face the firepower of the Rangers' Colts out in the open, Iron Jacket led a hasty Comanche retreat, and the long pursuit began.

For the next hour the battle became a shrieking, shooting, galloping series of skirmishes and individual combats fought through the hills and ravines north and west of the village that covered an area six miles in length and more than three in width. Small groups of Rangers and Tonkawas pursued the enemy in every direction. Occasionally the Comanches attempted to make a stand, but time and again they were forced to disperse and run by the overwhelming firepower of the Rangers' Colts. The raucous din of battle, punctuated by the steady report of fire-arms and the shouts of men, rolled back from Little Robe Creek, mingling with the groans of the dying and the terrified cries of the women and children as they continued to scramble for their lives.

Fifteen minutes into the running fight Caleb and Bigfoot, along with Corporal Nelson and a few other Rangers and reservation warriors, chased a small group of Comanches into a wooded ravine along a winding branch of Little Robe Creek. Iron Jacket was not among them. Caleb had lost sight of the war chief once the fighting had begun. The others were about to charge in after the fleeing warriors when Caleb signaled for them to hold up.

Bigfoot was eager to continue the chase. "What the hell we waitin' for, Caleb? We got the bastards on the run. Let's finish 'em off while we got the chance."

"That's exactly what they want us to do," Caleb replied. "Once they get us into the trees at close quarters, we lose the advantage of our Colts. We'll be scattered out and their bows and lances will be a hell of a lot more effective."

"That makes sense alright," Bigfoot conceded after a moment to consider the situation. "How should we handle it?"

"I'll take a few men up the ridge and circle around to the other end of the ravine," Caleb replied. "Give me a couple minutes to get ready then move in fast when you hear us start shootin'. With pressure from both ends, we should be able to rout the bastards back out onto the prairie where we can finish 'em off." Caleb pointed out the Rangers he wanted to follow him. "You four ride with me. Bigfoot, you and Nelson take the rest of the Rangers and the reservation warriors and get 'em ready."

As Caleb led his Rangers up the ridge to circle around to the other end of the ravine, Nelson looked over at Bigfoot. "I think I'll ride along with Captain McAdams."

Bigfoot called Nelson up short as he started to rein away. "Nelson, you'll damn well do as Caleb said. Now get in line with the others and get ready."

Nelson grudgingly complied, and Bigfoot put the incident out of his mind when he heard the sharp report of the Rangers Colts from the other end of the ravine. "Let's get after 'em, boys!" he yelled as he drew his Colt and led the remaining Rangers and Tonkawas into the mouth of the ravine.

Caleb's Rangers took the Comanches by surprise when they charged into the far end of the ravine. Recovering quickly, a warrior lowered his long war lance as he reined his pony around to face off with Caleb, but the big redhead fired his Colt twice. The first shot glanced off the Comanche's leather-tough, bull hide shield, but the second ball slammed into the warrior's side, unhorsing him. Another Ranger finished the downed Comanche with a round to the head as the riders loped past and made their way into the trees, firing at anything that moved. Bigfoot and his Rangers and Tonkawas drove in hard from the other end of the ravine, and as Caleb had predicted, exerting pressure from both ends soon routed the Comanches out onto the prairie. The chase continued for a few more minutes, until Caleb again called a halt when he sensed that Sally Mae and the other horses needed a good blow.

"I don't know about your buckskin," Caleb said to Bigfoot as the Rangers and Tonkawas reluctantly reined in and began milling around, "but Sally's just about used up. She needs a walk to catch her breath and a good long drink. 'Sides, I want to take a look at them hills to the north of us. Every now and then I catch a glimpse of movement in that direction, and it's got the hair on the back of my neck standin' up."

As always, Bigfoot put his trust in Caleb's hunches. "We best take a look if somethin's got you bothered."

Caleb called out to Corporal Nelson, "Take the rest of the men back to the village and rest your horses. Rip should be there by now. Let him know me and Bigfoot are gonna take a look around up north before we head back."

Nelson hesitated. "If it's all right with you, Captain, I'd just as soon ride along with you and Bigfoot."

Caleb sighed. "Nelson, the men are gonna need your help to make sure the Tonkawas do what they're told. Now, head on out to the village right now."

Nelson reined around hard and started after the others, but it was apparent he did not much like it. "I wonder what the hell's got into Nelson lately. He's been actin' strange ever since he got back from that trip to San Antonio to visit his family."

Bigfoot did not bother to comment as he reined north with Caleb and coaxed his big buckskin into a restful lope that matched Sally Mae's. Like the big filly, the gelding could maintain the pace all day, even if he was tired. Turning his head to glance back at Nelson for a moment, Bigfoot too wondered about the man's strange conduct before he forced himself back into the moment. Best to get my mind back on the scout before I get an arrow stuck up my rear for daydreaming, he thought.

The Rangers rode with care, constantly keeping an eye out for danger and sticking to the low ground. A few minutes later, they reined up in a wooded draw. Dismounting, they left their horses in the draw and climbed to the top of a low hill before going to ground to get a good look around without being seen. Off to the northwest, a large band of warriors was moving in the direction of the village at a brisk trot.

Caleb squinted as he peered into the distance. "That's old Peta Nocona leadin' 'em." Peta Nocona was a well known war chief who had taken a captured white woman to wife named Cynthia Ann Parker. His eldest son, Quanah, would one day become the scourge of the West Texas plains. "There're at least two hundred of 'em, Bigfoot. Iron Jacket must have called for help. We best be gettin' back to Rip."

Shapley Ross and his Tonkawas rode into the village about one o'clock in the afternoon, eager to rest their horses, but Ford was already forming the Rangers into a battle line.

Shapley rode up to Ford and reined in. "What's goin' on Rip?"

"Take a look at the hills to the northwest," said Ford. "Peta Nocona has arrived with his warriors."

The hills were swarming with Comanches, but constant movement as the warriors swirled back and forth across the far hillsides on their galloping ponies made it difficult to estimate their true numbers. There must be near three hundred, though, thought Shapley, among them the warriors who remained from the fight with Iron Jacket's village.

"Thank God, Caleb and Bigfoot got back in time to warn me that Peta was on the way," Ford added. "If that bastard had caught us by surprise all scattered out in the open, we would have been in a hell of a mess." When the battle line was formed to Ford's satisfaction, he and Shapley joined Caleb and Bigfoot in the center. "Now we wait and see if Peta rides down out of those hills to attack us. I got Lieutenant Preston and his Rangers out of sight in some low ground on the left ready to hit 'em in the flank if they do."

However, the wily Comanche war chief refused to fall into Ford's trap. Realizing his warriors, with their short bows and lances, could never stand at close quarters in the open against the Rangers and their rapid firing Colts, Peta hoped to lure the Rangers into the wooded hills surrounding Little Robe Creek. With the woods helping to negate the Rangers' superior fire-power, the Comanches' legendary skill on horseback with bows and lances could be brought into play. Three times Peta sent part of his force down off the hills close to the Ranger line before they retreated, even challenging the Rangers to individual com-bat, but Ford and his men refused to be baited.

The Comanches were more successful with their traditional enemies, the Tonkawas. A number of the reservation Indians accepted challenges from the Comanches and engaged in the type of single combat that reminded Caleb and Ford of medieval knights riding in jousting tournaments. The feats of horseman-ship displayed by both sides were breathtaking, and the warriors handled their shields and lances with great skill and precision. Unfortunately, good show or not, Ford began to grow irritated when the Tonkawas proceeded to lose fight after fight to the hated Comanches. The breaking point came when a female Comanche "warrior woman" managed to kill a Tonkawa in single combat.

"That's the final damn straw!" Ford ranted. "Shapley, tell Placido to get control of his warriors. I absolutely forbid any further single combat. Tell him to attack the hills with all his warriors at once. Maybe that will convince Peta to commit his entire force. Then when the Comanches and Tonkawas are engaged, I'll attack with my Rangers. Our superior firepower should win the day. Tell Placido I'll signal with the bugle for him to pull back if I decide not to make the attack."

"If you don't mind, Rip," Shapley replied, "I'm goin' in with 'em."

Ford nodded. "Go on ahead, but be damn careful. And don't wait for the bugle if you think it's time to clear out."

A few minutes later Shapley and Placido led the Tonkawas up the hill in mass, striking the Comanches hard, but once again Peta Nocona reused to take the bait. Even worse, as the fighting progressed the Indian allies began to take another savage beating.

Ford was beside himself when he complained to Caleb and Bigfoot. "We might as well pull the Tonkawas back before the damn Comanches kill 'em all."

Bigfoot's chuckle drew a dirty look from Ford, but undaunted the big man said his piece as usual. "Them Tonkawa never could stand up to the Comanches, but they sure as hell ain't alone. Even the Apaches back down from 'em."

Ford reluctantly nodded his agreement. "Caleb, get hold of the bugler and tell him to sound retreat. Bigfoot, ride down the line and tell Eph and the other officers to get their Rangers ready. Once we get the Tonkawas back on line with us I aim to attack the Comanches with the whole damn outfit. Either we chase 'em off those hills or we die tryin'."

The Tonkawas were glad to be recalled, and once they were in the line alongside the Rangers and their rapid-firing Colts, more than ready to renew the action. Ford stared at the far hills as he spoke to his officers. "I hope Peta will stand and fight, but I ain't countin' on it. Once we hit the Comanches in force, I believe they'll fall back and try and fight a series of holdin' actions to cover the escape of Iron Jacket's women and children and their own people. If they do, we're gonna have another runnin' fight on our hands. Caleb, a few of the prisoners we took have been sayin' Buffalo Hump has a village somewhere downstream on the Canadian with a sizable number of warriors. If Peta does fall back, I want you and Bigfoot to break off take a look down that way. I don't need Buffalo Hump jumpin' in by surprise at the last minute. Keep a close eye, and if you see anything, get back here as fast as you can. The rest of you officers get back with your men"

"We'll take care of it, Rip," Caleb said as he pulled his holstered Colt and checked the loads. "I'll see you at top of the hill."

Ford looked to his left and then to his right. When all was ready he gave the call to move out. The long line of Rangers and Indians started out at a walk and slowly brought the pace up to a brisk trot. As they started up the long slope Comanche arrows began to fall in among them, one taking a reservation Indian in the shoulder and unhorsing him, and another striking a Ranger in the thigh."

"Draw your Colts, men," Ford commanded as he drew his own. Ford gave the command to charge when his men had formed into a rough line, and the Rangers and Tonkawas let out with a whoop as they galloped at the Comanches, Colts at the ready.

Caleb fired at a considerable distance, but the ball from his Colt took a Comanche square in the chest, flipping the warrior off the back of his pony. Bigfoot hoorahed his approval as he and the other Rangers up and down the line opened fire. Peta

Nocona responded exactly as Ford had predicted when the volley of red hot lead began to take its toll on his ranks. The days when the Comanches could ride in among the Rangers and fire five or six arrows while the whites reloaded their single shot weapons were over, and Peta had no intention of allowing his warriors to be caught out in the open facing the Rangers' massed repeating weapons.

Instead he ordered a retreat and once again the battle turned into a chaotic running fight over several miles. However, this time the Comanche withdrawal was far from a rout. At carefully selected locations, where their weapons would be most effective, the warriors stood and fought bravely, delaying the Rangers and Tonkawas to buy time for Iron Jacket's people and their own families further up the Canadian to escape the Rangers' wrath. Peta Nocona's band was even able to pack up their lodges, food supplies, and possessions, and move them out of harm's way. Iron Jacket's people would not be so fortunate.

Though Caleb had concentrated on locating Iron Jacket during the initial fighting, he did not catch sight of the war chief before heading down the Canadian with Bigfoot in search of Buffalo Hump's village. An hour into the Rangers' running fight with the warriors of Peta Nocona, Caleb and Bigfoot, their mounts well lathered from hard riding, caught up with Ford who was sitting on a low hill with Shapley Ross and a few Ranges resting their horses.

"Looks like you pushed your animals hard," said Ford.

"Yours don't look a hell of a lot better, Rip," chided Bigfoot with a toothy grin. "We found what you sent us to look for, though. Ain't that a fact, partner?"

"It's a fact alright," Caleb agreed. "Rip, you were right. Buffalo Hump's got himself a village just a few miles down the Canadian from here, and he's got well over a hundred warriors. They weren't headin' this way when we started back, but they may well be by now."

"I don't like it," Rip replied. "Nocona's been pickin' up warriors here too ever since the fight started. Mostly Kiowas it looks like, but some of 'em might be from another band of Comanches close by. Not only that, but as your big dumb partner just pointed out, our horses are about played out, too." Bigfoot chuckled before Ford added, "Bugler, sound the recall. We're headin' back to the village. Caleb, you and your Rangers ride to the camp site and gather up our supply wagons. Move 'em to the village. We'll load up what supplies we can carry and destroy the rest."

By the time Caleb and Bigfoot arrived at the village with the wagons it was late in the day, and the sun was hanging low on the western horizon. Most of the buffalo hide lodges were ablaze, and the flames of a huge bonfire in the center of the village sent a chimney of glowing sparks towering up into the rapidly darkening sky. Rangers were busy feeding the flames of the hungry blaze with all manner of Comanche possessions from the extra buffalo robes that were meant to keep the people warm during the long winter, to the dried meat and pemmican that would have seen them through the starving months.

Many of the Tonkawa warriors celebrated the victory by decorating their ponies with the hands and feet of their Comanche victims. Caleb noticed that many of the dead warriors were missing other body parts besides their hands and feet, and it sickened his stomach when Bigfoot commented that the bloody leather bags the Tonkawas carried tied to their saddles portended a grizzly victory feast that evening.

However, Rip refused to take action when Caleb confronted him. "I sure as hell don't condone that kind of thing," Rip stated, "but I ain't about to step in and force 'em to change their ways. The Tonkawas and all the rest of the reservation Indians fought a good fight today, and we may damn well need 'em again."

Ford's words did not please Caleb, but he also understood that it was Rip's command, not his. "Okay, Rip it's your show, but I don't have to like it. The boys are nearly finished loadin' the rest of the meat and the buffalo hides in the wagons. If it's all the same to you, me and Bigfoot ain't gonna stick around for the party. We'll take a few volunteers and move the wagons south toward the Washita. You won't have any trouble catchin' up with us tomorrow before we reach the river."

Ford nodded his head in agreement. "No problem, but be sure and post a strong guard tonight. I ain't expectin' any trouble, but it always pays to be careful when you're dealin' with Comanches.

Chapter 31

The column returned to Camp Runnels on May 21. After disbanding the men, Ford, accompanied by Caleb and his Rangers, returned to Austin to render his report to the governor. During the meeting with Runnels, Ford reported that in the engagements with the warriors of Iron Jacket and Peta Nocona, the Rangers and their Indian allies killed seventy-six Comanches and captured eighteen prisoners. The fact that most of the prisoners, as well as the dead, were women and children did not seem to bother Governor Runnels any more than it had Ford. The Rangers also took more than three hundred horses and left an entire village without the necessary foodstuffs, clothing, and housing to see them through the winter. Iron Jacket and his people would be dependent upon the charity of other bands for many months.

Governor Runnels was pleased. "You and your Rangers did a splendid job, Captain Ford. Your assistance also proved invaluable, McAdams. The State of Texas owes both of you a sincere debt of gratitude."

"Thank you, Governor," Ford replied. "We also proved a couple theories me and Caleb have shared for quite some time, sir. We both think they'll serve us well in the future."

"And what might they be, Captain," asked Runnels?

"First, the Comanches have always had an upper hand in close fighting with their short bows and war lances. A good warrior can fire at least five or six well-aimed arrows in the time it takes to load a rifle. We usually had a few Rangers armed with revolvers, but not nearly as many, and not with revolvers as good as we have now. This time we made sure every one of our Rangers was armed with a new Colt, and as a result, we devastated the Comanches in close. I also believe we proved that chasin' after war parties is not the way to fight this war. Relentless pursuit of the Comanche villages is the answer, Governor, especially just before or durin' the winter, right Caleb?"

"Rip's right, Governor," Caleb answered. "Nearly twenty years ago, I rode with Colonel Moore when he proved the way to fight a wanderin' people like the Comanches is to attack their villages in the late fall and winter. Texas has never had the will or the money to follow up on the idea, though. It's gonna take Iron Jacket's people a long time to recover from our attack, and his warriors won't be raidin' the frontier any time soon neither. They're gonna be too busy replacin' the hides and foodstuffs they lost. Now is the time to keep the pressure on. I say we put together an even bigger expedition this fall and do as much damage as we can out on the Comancheria. It'll take the Comanches a good long time to recover from somethin' like that. I already talked the idea over with Rip and he agrees with me."

Ford nodded enthusiastically. "Yes sir, I do"

Governor Runnels' features took on a resigned look. "I appreciate your enthusiasm for the task at hand, gentlemen, but another expedition at this time is simply out of the question. As usual, the treasury is empty, and the legislature refuses to set aside any additional funds." When he saw the look of disappointment on the Rangers' faces, Runnels hastened to add, "However, I recently received a letter from Colonel Twiggs, the Commander of the Department of the Army in Texas. He agrees with your strategy, and he feels that the passive federal policy towards the Comanches must be changed."

"Furthermore, the Colonel wrote to Washington requesting a full regiment of cavalry to pursue the Comanches into the Comancheria in both summer and winter, and to give them so much trouble they'll no longer have time to launch raids into Texas. In the meantime, he has ordered Major Earl Van Dorn of the Second Cavalry to cross the Red River as soon as possible with four companies of cavalry and one company of infantry to attack yet another village."

Ford seemed pleased with the news, but Caleb added, "I'm glad to hear the army's finally beginnin' to come around, Governor, but all this talk about secession causes me worry. I think most people are wrong when they say the North will let us go our own way without a fight. And a war will put a quick end to any help the United States Army may provide."

"Secession is indeed a distinct possibility," counseled Runnels who was above all a devout Calhoun Democrat, "but we'll deal with that issue if and when it becomes necessary."

Ford was still talking to Runnels when Caleb excused himself from the meeting and headed for the café in the Bullock Hotel to meet up with Bigfoot and his Rangers. Bigfoot was standing at the bar with his boot up on the long brass foot railing drinking a beer and laughing with Bullock when Caleb shoved his way through the batwing doors. Corporal Nelson and the other Rangers were having a beer and a bowl of Bullock's famous venison stew at the row of tables along the windows that looked out on Pecan Street. Caleb nodded to the others before stepping up to the bar beside Bigfoot.

"Howdy, partner," Bigfoot said with his usual smile, "I was just tellin' our mutual friend here about the little ride we took up north."

"Good to see you, Mr. Bullock." Caleb shook the proprietor's beefy hand. "How are things goin' in the hotel business?"

"Couldn't be better, my friend," Bullock replied as he returned Caleb's firm handshake. "Don't you think after all these years you might call me Richard, or even worse like your salty friend here often does."

Caleb chuckled along with Bigfoot. "Sorry, Mr. Bullock, but with me old habits are hard to break."

"I know what you mean," Bullock agreed. "Say, I hear Sam Houston's gonna try to run for governor again next year; most likely as an independent against Runnels. 'Course the Calhoun Democrats are still dead set against him which means he's opposed by the whole political structure. What do you think?"

"I backed Sam the last time," Caleb stated, "and I'll sure as hell back him again if he runs. These radical Calhoun Democrats will be the ruin of Texas if they ain't stopped. All I been hearin' lately is secession talk, and I know damn well Sam is against that. I'm tellin' you just like I told Runnels a short while ago; the North won't just walk away. They'll fight like hell to preserve the Union. The best we can hope for is to win after a long hard war that will cost thousands of lives and most likely lead to financial ruin."

"Damn, Caleb," piped in Bigfoot, "sounds to me like you should run for Governor yourself, not back Sam."

Caleb lost the serious frown on his face and then chuckled. "I best get down off my soapbox before somebody does confuse me with a politician."

"I can't say as you're wrong," Bullock added on a serious note, "but talkin' out against secession sure as hell won't make you a popular man in Austin. In fact you'd be tarred and feathered by now if the men around here weren't so scared of that

Colt you wear. Either that or lynched like that free black man was last week. All the poor soul did was put his kids in that school Wanda Andrews runs across the river. The mob said he got what all uppity niggers deserve. They've been makin' ugly threats and sayin' disgustin' things about Mrs. Andrews for a while now, too, and lately it's been gettin' worse. You might warn her if you get a chance."

'Thanks, Mr. Bullock," Caleb replied, "I'll see to it right away. In the meantime I'd like you to do me a favor."

Bullock nodded. "Sure thing, Caleb, I'd be glad to do anything I can?"

Caleb's slate gray eyes took on a narrowed, snake-like appearance that frightened Bullock. "You know most of the people in this town. I want every damn one of 'em to know that if somethin' happens to Wanda or her school, I will personally see that the offenders are suitably punished or buried." Caleb finished the beer that Bullock had set in front of him earlier. "Mr. Bullock, you take care. I'll be seein' you again soon. Bigfoot, are you comin'?"

Bigfoot gulped down the remainder of his beer. "I might as well be ridin'. I can be a good ways towards San Antone before dark. Take care Bullock."

"You too, my friend," Bullock replied.

Bigfoot followed Caleb over to the table where Corporal Nelson was sitting. "Nelson," Caleb said, "make sure the boys get back to the barracks tonight. Tell Felix or Pedro I'll be home around noon tomorrow."

Caleb started to turn away, before Nelson asked, "How come you ain't headin' back with us, Captain?"

Trying to keep the anger out of his voice that had built up during his conversation with Bullock, Caleb answered, "I got some business in town to take care of, and it'll take at least the rest of the day."

"Do you mind if I stick around here for a few days, too," Nelson asked.

Caleb hesitated then relented. "Go ahead. The rest of you head on back to the ranch when you finish eatin'. Be sure 'n tell Felix or Pedro that I'll be home around noon tomorrow. Come on, Bigfoot, let's ride."

A few minutes later Bigfoot looked over at Caleb when they were riding down the hill on Congress Avenue towards the ferry. "That Nelson sure has been actin' strange lately. I wonder what the hell's botherin' him."

With his mind focused on Wanda, Caleb did not give much thought to Bigfoot's comment. "Who knows what's botherin' Nelson. I'm more worried about Josh and Wanda. How in the hell am I gonna convince that woman to keep her opinions to herself?"

Bigfoot chuckled in spite of Caleb's concern. "I ain't much on understandin' women. But if Wanda's anything like the women I've known in my time, you ain't about to convince her of nothin'."

Missing the humor in Bigfoot's reply, Caleb only nodded absentmindedly. "I guess you're right."

The conversation dwindled for the next few minutes during the river crossing on the ferry, as Caleb and Bigfoot kept their thoughts to themselves. After leading the horses down the gangplank to the south bank of the Colorado, they mounted, then reached over and shook hands.

Caleb smiled. "You take care of yourself, Bigfoot. No doubt I'll be seein' you again before summer's out."

Bigfoot nodded. "You do the same partner, and I wish you luck with Wanda."

Reining away, Bigfoot spurred his big buckskin into a long lope. Caleb waited until Bigfoot had ridden out of sight over a near ridge, and then reined Sally Mae towards Wanda's cabin, gently kicking her into motion with the heels of his boots.

The sun hung low in the western sky, its slanting rays sending flashes of gold shimmering across the rippled surface of the river far below the bluff, when Caleb reined in at the dogtrot that ran between Wanda's cabin and her little schoolhouse. Swinging down from the saddle, he looped Sally Mae's reins around the hitching rail just as Wanda stepped out the door with little Josh right behind her.

"Uncle Caleb!" Josh shouted as he ran to his father and jumped into his arms.

Caleb gave Josh a big bear hug then held him straight out. "I swear you're gettin' bigger every day, Sprout."

Josh beamed his pleasure. "I'm glad you're back," he said when Caleb sat him down. "Did you shoot a lot of Indians?"

Wanda frowned, but in spite of her obvious dislike for the question, Caleb answered it. "Only a few bad ones, Sprout; ones that really needed it."

"Come on in and get comfortable," Wanda said. "Are you hungry? Josh and I ate early, but there's a pot of leftover stew on the fire and plenty of biscuits."

"That sounds great," Caleb replied. "Give me a minute to take care of Sally and wash up. I'll be right in."

When Caleb stepped into the cabin a few minutes later, he gave Wanda a brief hug before she began spooning up the stew. Pulling out a chair, he sat down at the small dinner table. Wanda placed the bowl of stew in front of him along with a platter of biscuits and a slab of butter. After pouring him a cup of coffee, she slid the sugar bowl over, then joined him and Josh at the table. Josh had another biscuit while Caleb finished his stew and then they sat on the sofa while Wanda cleaned up. She soon joined them and they spoke of trivial things while Caleb played with Josh. Within the hour Josh fell fast asleep in Caleb's lap, and he helped Wanda tuck the youngster in before rejoining her on the sofa in front of the small fire.

After a few minutes of staring into the flickering flames, Caleb was first to break the peaceful silence. "Tell me about the lynchin', Wanda."

Wanda sat up with a start. "You know about that?"

Caleb sighed deeply. "Know about it? Bullock said the whole town's been talkin' about nothin' else. He also said some people have been sayin' ugly things to you and makin' threats. Is that true?"

Wanda looked away. "They're only threats, Caleb. They want to scare me into either closing my school or banning the free Negroes and Tejano children. I refuse to do that."

Caleb's eyes narrowed, and when Wanda looked back the expression on his face frightened her. "I want the names of the men who've been makin' the threats."

"What are you planning to do?" she asked, already knowing the answer.

"I'll tell you exactly what I plan to do," Caleb coldly stated, the fury he felt apparent in the threatening tone of his voice. "I plan on convincin' every damn one of 'em how unhealthy it is to make threats to you, or even think about harmin' you or Josh. That's what I plan on doin', and the sooner the better."

Now it was Wanda's turn to grow angry. "I can't let you do that, Caleb. You're a man of prominence in Austin and in the state of Texas. You have a position of standing to protect in this community, and a family who depends on you. Why should you put all that in jeopardy for me?"

Caleb laughed, but it was a bitter laugh, not one of joy, and his slate-gray eyes remained ice cold. "Whether we can be together as man and wife or not, I care for you, Wanda. I always have, and I love my son. I will kill every damn man in Austin, if necessary, before I see harm come to either one of you. Can't you see that? But I also know how damn stubborn you are, so I won't ask you again for the names. Besides, I already told Bullock to spread the word. If either of you is harmed, there'll be hell to pay."

Wanda shook her head in exasperation, and when she began talking the anger in her voice was replaced by calm resignation.

"Caleb there's another even more important reason you shouldn't get involved, and I think you know what it is. The people around here aren't blind or stupid. There have already been rumors about us. You're involvement in this affair is only going to confirm those rumors in most people's minds. Do you want Lucinda or Josh to be hurt by what folks will say?"

Caleb shook his head. "No, I don't want Lucinda or Josh hurt, Wanda. One day I'll tell Josh the truth. I'd like him to be a little older, though, so he has a better chance to understand, and not find out from some bigmouth out to hurt him. And, of course, Lucinda would be hurt deeply if she ever found out about us. I could even lose her because of it. If I did, though, she and little Ham would still be alive and safe at the Rockin' M with Felix and Pedro to look after 'em. Wanda, this situation is a hell of a lot more dangerous than you make it out to be. The people around here are beginnin' to work themselves into frenzy over slavery and secession. Anyone, be it man or woman, who opposes their views, is considered a traitor, plain and simple. Who's here to watch over you and little Josh if trouble comes but me? I know you won't close the school, and I know you're too damn stubborn and proud to keep your opinions to yourself, so I don't have much choice."

Wanda sobbed before throwing her arms around Caleb. "You're right, but I must do what my conscience demands no matter what the consequences. Please hold me," she whispered. "Help me gain the courage I'll need."

It was still early when Caleb led Sally Mae down the gangplank of the ferry and onto the north bank of the Colorado. The clear azure of the cloudless sky gave promise of a beautiful day. After paying the toll, he mounted and rode out of town on the River Road, heading east toward the Rocking M. With his thoughts focused on Wanda's abolitionist leanings, he failed to hear the sound of a horse coming up behind him until the rider was fairly close. Tensing for action, Caleb turned in the saddle, but was surprised to see that the rider was Corporal Nelson. Relaxing once again, he slowed the big filly's long lope to a gentle trot. Nelson soon caught up and reined in the gait of his gray gelding to match Sally's.

Caleb glanced over at Nelson with a puzzled look. "I thought you was plannin' on spendin' a couple days in Austin, Nelson. What changed your mind?"

Nelson stared straight ahead for a moment before abruptly bringing his big gray to a halt just before the riders reached a small stream. Caleb was forced to rein Sally around in a tight circle. "What the hell's been gettin' into you lately, Corporal?"

Nelson's shocking reply was to draw his Colt and cock the hammer as he pointed it straight at the center of Caleb's chest. The long barrel of the Dragoon wavered slightly as the heavy weapon shook in Nelson's nervous hand.

Surprisingly Caleb's next emotion was anger, not fear. "Nelson, what in the hell are you doin'? Have you lost your damn mind?"

"I'm real sorry about this, Captain," Nelson replied in a quavering voice, "but I'm gonna have to kill you."

Now, more than anything else, Caleb was puzzled. "Why are you doin' this, Nelson? Haven't I always treated you square?"

"You have, Captain," Nelson agreed, "but this has got nothin' to do with the way I've been treated. My Pa was fixin' to lose his ranch if I didn't come up with a lot of money real soon. I been paid a good deal already, and I'll get a lot more once you're dead."

The Pates again, Caleb thought, as he desperately searched his mind for a way out. His prospects were bleak at best. He might well be lightning fast with his Colt, but Nelson had the drop on him plain and simple, and no quick draw, no matter how fast, would get him out of this situation. Perhaps a bribe would work, or at least distract Nelson long enough for him to have a chance at his Colt. "I'll double whatever they promised to pay you, Nelson."

Chuckling without mirth, Nelson replied, "That sounds real good, Captain, but my Mama didn't raise no fool. I done seen you draw that hog leg of yours before. The second I holster this Colt I'd be a dead man for sure. No, I started this, and now I aim to finish it."

Nelson raised the long barrel of the Colt, aiming it between Caleb's eyes. With death staring him in the face and an attitude that he might as well go down fighting, Caleb was about to go for his Colt when suddenly the side of Nelson's head exploded in a gory red mess. His body was blown clear out of the saddle with the force of the impact. Caleb heard the roar of a familiar long rifle echo down off the hillside from a ridge above the river as Nelson's body flopped to the road and lay still.

A minute or two later, Bigfoot trotted his big buckskin down off the ridge and reined in, his Kentucky long rifle cradled in the crook of his left arm. "I was sure that bastard was up to somethin' when he asked to stay in town, so I decided to stick around and keep an eye on him. Damned if I weren't right, too. You okay, partner?"

Caleb smiled. "I am now, thanks to you. How the hell did you know?"

Bigfoot shrugged his wide shoulders. "I never did know for sure. But it had to be somebody close, and Nelson's been actin' mighty strange lately."

"Well, whatever the reason, I'm damn glad you were here when I needed you." Caleb stared off in the distance. "The Pates ain't never gonna give up, are they, Bigfoot?"

"Hell no, they ain't!" Bigfoot growled. "I've been tellin' you that for a long time now. Either you're gonna have to finish it, or they're gonna finish you, one way or the other."

Caleb nodded, at long last reconciled to the truthfulness of Bigfoot's words. "I'll spend some time thinkin' on it. In the meantime, what're we gonna do with Nelson's body?"

"We should leave the bastard lay for the buzzards, but that would bring up a lot of questions when he was found. 'Sides, the man did do some good rangerin', so I guess he at least deserves to be covered. There's a cutaway on the bank of this stream a little ways up the ridge. We can throw his body under there and cave it in. That should keep the varmints off him."

"Sounds good to me," Caleb agreed. "Let's get it done."

Having been alerted by the Rangers who had returned the previous day, and the outriders who constantly roamed the perimeter of the Rocking M, the entire family was gathered on the front porch of the hacienda when Caleb and Bigfoot rode through the front gate. After dismounting at the hitching rail and tying off his horse, Bigfoot was the first to be greeted when Gretchin ran into his arms screaming how glad she was to see her Uncle Bigfoot. Ham was not far behind as he launched himself off the porch into his father's arms, all stories and tales of what his father had missed during his long absence.

"Hold on Ham," Caleb chuckled, "as he swung the youngster around, "you're talkin' so fast I can hardly understand you. 'Sides, I need to greet your Ma and everybody else too." Caleb sat Ham down as Lucinda stepped off the porch and into his arms. "My but you're a sight for sore eyes," he said, holding his wife at arms length and looking her over the way he loved to do when he had been away from the ranch for a time. Taking Lucinda's hand in his, Caleb stepped up on the porch and greeted first Felix and then Pedro with a firm handshake and a smile. "Looks to me like things are prosperin' around the Rockin' M as usual." Veronica was standing beside Pedro holding little

Antonio's hand with baby Felix in her other arm. Caleb greeted his sister-in-law with a warm peck on the cheek and ruffled Antonio's hair. "It's darn good to see ya'll again."

Bigfoot took his turn greeting everyone before Lucinda said, "Caleb, Bo and Connie are setting the table for supper. Take Bigfoot to the well. You can both wash up before we eat."

A few minutes later the family was gathered around the large oak table in the great room. Connie, Bo, Lucinda, and Veronica had outdone themselves in preparing a huge feast to celebrate Caleb and Bigfoot's homecoming. There was a choice of roast beef, fried chicken, freshly smoked ham, or venison, with bowls of savory gravy, early vegetables fresh from the garden, platters of piping-hot, golden-brown biscuits, and several dried apple pies for desert. Everything looked absolutely delicious, and Lucinda was forced to restrain Hammond from digging in before Felix finished saying grace.

The little imp slammed his spoon down on the table in defiance, and Caleb was not pleased with his son's ill-mannered conduct. "Hammond, you'll not act like that when your mother corrects you, or you and me will take a little trip to the woodshed! I hope you understand me, son?"

Hammond looked contrite, "Yes, Papa. I'm sorry, Mother."

Caleb's smile returned with his son's apology. "Good, that's better, now let's all enjoy this wonderful meal."

Near silence ruled the table while the food was passed around, and everyone helped themselves. When they had all begun to eat, lively conversation was once again the order of the day. Topics ranged from family and ranch life to politics and war.

"Ilse has a beau, Papa," Gretchin soon added with a giggle.

"Mother," screeched Ilse in retaliation, "tell Gretchin to mind her own business. She's just jealous because none of the boys are interested in Tomboys like her." Gretchin stuck her tongue out at her older sister.

"Girls!" snapped Lucinda in her sternest voice. "If you cannot treat each other in a civil manner, I will banish both of you from the table. You can finish eating in your rooms. This meal was prepared to celebrate your father's homecoming. Now behave like young ladies!"

Caleb's curiosity was aroused with the mention of a possible beau, but he would speak to Lucinda about it later to keep from embarrassing Ilse. It was hard for him to believe that the young men were interested in Ilse already, but one look at his lovely daughter told him such a notion on his part was foolish. Nonetheless, it was time to change the subject. "Felix, how are things goin' on the ranch?"

Felix smiled. "They could not be better. Pedro and I decided against buying any cattle for a trail drive this spring. That way we can make a drive next spring with pure Rocking M stock, and it should be our biggest drive ever. The irrigation system along the river on the old Meacham place is finished, and the crops we planted there are flourishing. We have also decided it is time for Pedro to assume the full-time management duties of the ranch, so I may devote my time to improving the hacienda and finish the projects in my workshop that have been begging my attention. What do you think of the idea?"

Caleb raised his glass of wine in a toast to Pedro. "Here's to the new manager of the Rockin' M. As far as I'm concerned, the ranch couldn't be in better hands, brother. I'll help out around the place as usual when I can, but I plan on patrollin' the frontier with my Rangers as often as possible. We stirred up the Comanches real good with our raid into the Comancheria, and the Governor wouldn't let me and Rip finish the job like we wanted. I look for a lot of trouble out that way this summer and fall."

"What about the war," asked Felix? "Are you are still certain it is coming?"

"The more I read about it, the more I'm certain the North will never let the South secede without a fight," Caleb replied.

"And when it comes, the war's gonna be long and bloody, win or lose."

Felix nodded. "Then I think it's high time we hired a northern agent to manage the funds we deposited in Cincinnati. If war does break out as you fear, any southern funds deposited in northern banks may well be confiscated if they're not managed properly."

"That's a darn good idea," Caleb agreed, "but even an agent may not be able to protect our money. I say we have the banks in Cincinnati transfer all but $100,000.00 to Jack Hays in San Francisco, and have him deposit the money in his name. He can leave it to us in his will in case somethin' happens to him. I trusted the man with my life often enough, I won't have any trouble trustin' him with our money."

"Amen to that," added Bigfoot.

"We can have the rest of the cash shipped to the ranch in gold coin," added Caleb. "And we'll have 'em send the gold in four or five separate shipments. That should keep it as safe as possible. What do you and Pedro think?"

"Transactions involving money take time," said Felix. "I think we better put things in motion right away."

"I agree, with Padre" added Pedro, "and the sooner the better."

Chapter 32

As Caleb had predicted, the frontier along the Brazos was aflame for the entire long summer and fall of 1858. Even the United States Army's promised move against the Comancheria led by Major Earl Van Dorn of the Second Cavalry, although successful, had done little to slow down the bloody raids. Marching nearly ninety miles in thirty-seven hours with four companies of cavalry and nearly two hundred reservation Indians under the command of Shapley Ross's son Sul, Van Dorn attacked a sleeping Comanche village, killing fifty-six warriors and scattering the survivors across the hills. Unfortunately, instead of discouraging the Comanches as authorities had hoped, the raid served to incite them to even greater atrocities. Only the onset of winter had ended the ghastly depredations along the Brazos.

Late on a clear May afternoon in 1859, Caleb and Eph led Chako and six Rangers into Camp Runnels and reined up in front of Rip Ford's command tent. Caleb dismounted just as Rip tossed back the flap of the tent and emerged into the sunlight.

Two months prior, Governor Runnels had sent Ford north with a few Rangers to investigate charges of the reservation Indians complicity in the attacks on the white farms along the upper reaches of the Brazos.

"It's damn good to see you again, Caleb," said Ford, "you too Eph." Eph touched the wide brim of his gray sombrero in greeting. "Why don't y'all come on in and join me for a cup of coffee? I'll fill you in on what I've learned since I got here."

"Caleb," said Eph, "if you don't mind, I'll get the men settled in first and join y'all later."

Caleb swung down from the saddle and pulled off his sombrero, slapping it against his thigh to remove the trail dust. "Go on ahead, Eph." Eph reined around and led the Rangers toward the river, as Caleb turned back to Ford and offered his hand.

The old friends gripped hands in friendship, and Ford called for two cups of coffee, one heavily sugared, before leading Caleb into the tent and offering him a seat on an empty crate. Ford inquired about Bigfoot, but Caleb said the big Ranger was replacing the roof of his cabin on the Medina River. They made themselves as comfortable as possible on the crates and shared some additional small talk until the coffee was delivered.

After taking a careful sip of the piping hot brew, Ford got down to business. "In the last two years, the line of Texas settlements has flowed up to and around the Brazos and Clear Fork reservations, and the Indians have been forced to live in close proximity to white farms. That puts 'em between a rock and a hard place. The wild bands of the north despise em for helpin' the whites, and the whites believe they're in cahoots with the northern bands. The Governor sent me here to investigate the situation, but so far, I've found no evidence of reservation Indians takin' part in the attacks. There were a few instances of tracks leadin' to the Clear Fork Reserve after a raid, but the trails were too obvious. I'm sure they were planted by somebody who wants to see the Indians on the reservation blamed."

"Do you have any idea who might have done it?" asked Caleb.

Ford nodded. "I have a hunch a man named John Baylor may be involved. He's a former Indian agent who Major Neighbors dismissed in disgrace from the service. Lately he's been givin' a lot of speeches sayin' the only answer is to drive all the Indians out of Texas; either that or kill every one of 'em."

"I know the type," said Caleb. "What does Major Neighbors have to say?"

"He's plum given up on the idea of reservations in Texas. In fact, he's in Washington City right now askin' that all the Indians in Texas be moved north of the Red River. He's concerned for their safety, and well he should be. Just after Christmas, seven Indians were found shot to death in a reservation camp along the Brazos. Baylor and his men said they'd been trailin' horse thieves and defended themselves in a fair fight, but from what I've been able to find out the Indians were killed in their sleepin' robes. The judge wanted me to arrest Baylor and the others, but I told him I'm here on the Governor's business. He should get the local sheriff to take care of it. Arrestin' the bastards won't do a damn bit of good anyway." Ford shook his head in disgust. "There ain't a jury anywhere around here who'd convict 'em. I expect Neighbors back any day now. Maybe he'll have some answers."

"Maybe so," Caleb agreed. "Is there any way I can help out in the meantime?"

"I'd appreciate it if you and your Rangers kept an eye on the reservations. I look for some more raids by the northern bands soon, and I'll need to know if they get any help from the reservation Indians. Be sure and watch out for Baylor and his bunch. I wouldn't put anything past that bastard."

Caleb rose to his feet and offered his hand. "We'll get on it first thing in the mornin', Rip. Let me know when Neighbors gets back."

Ford shook Caleb's hand. "Take care of yourself."

Caleb and his Rangers had been patrolling along the Clear Fork of the Brazos for nearly a week without incident when they heard the echo of distant gunfire. "That sounds like trouble for sure, Eph," said Caleb. "We best head that way."

A thick column of smoke was already beginning to billow above the tree line to the north as the Rangers reined in that direction and picked up the pace to a steady lope. If there was Comanche trouble, Caleb was anxious to come to the settlers' assistance, but he did not want the horses played out when the Rangers arrived. A few minutes later they reined in on a high bluff overlooking a stretch of bottomland that reached to the river.

Below some two hundred yards distant a dozen or so Comanche warriors were mounting up on their painted ponies and preparing to ride out. The devastation of the small homestead was nearly complete with the cabin already engulfed in flames and the makeshift barn just beginning to burn. What looked to be the bodies of a settler and his wife were sprawled on the hard-packed earth in front of the cabin.

"Come on, Rangers," Caleb yelled, waving his sombrero as he urged Sally Mae over the rim of the bluff.

The big filly went over willingly, squatting into the treacherous slope with stiffened front legs as Caleb leaned far back in the saddle to assist her in the plunging descent. Small rocks and pieces of loose shale cascaded along the slope like a brown avalanche as Sally lightly danced her way down in short leaps and bounds. Clouds of dust boiled into the air when the Rangers recklessly followed their leader down the steep face of the bluff. In spite of the danger, the riders reached the plain that led to the river without incident and were galloping toward the war party before the Comanches spotted them.

Cocking the hammer of his Colt, Caleb leveled the long barrel and fired, blasting a luckless warrior off the back of his pony as the war party started off towards the river. The Comanches were soon in full flight and the Rangers all joined in with Caleb, sending a hail of hot lead in pursuit of the fleeing warriors. Three more Comanches were unhorsed in the fusillade before the war party splashed across the shallow river and disappeared into the tree line on the far side. Not wanting to lead his men into a possible ambush in the trees, Caleb signaled for them to pull up when he reached the river.

The Rangers horses milled in confusion, Caleb settling Sally as he called out to Chako. "Cross downstream a ways," Caleb ordered the Lipan scout. "Make damn sure the Comanches cleared out. The rest of you follow me."

Reining around, Caleb loped Sally Mae back toward the burning homestead, hoping to find someone still alive. The settler was lying facedown between the cabin and the empty corral, the broken shafts of two arrows sticking out of his back. They must have gone in too deep to salvage, thought Caleb. A circular portion of the settler's scalp had been torn off. The man's wife lay on her back in front of the cabin. Caleb grabbed his canteen and leaped from the saddle when he thought he saw the woman move. Running to her side, he knelt in the dust and gently lifted her head. The woman had also been scalped and a shaft protruded from her chest.

"My children," she moaned in anguish, "they're still in the cabin. Please help them."

One look at the roaring flames engulfing the cabin told Caleb the children were far beyond any assistance he might offer. "We'll do what we can, Ma'am" he lied as he heard the woman's dying gasp. After gently lowering her head back to the ground, Caleb rose to his feet. The tall Ranger was swinging back up on the saddle when Chako reined up in a swirl of dust.

"Comanches go," the Lipan reported. "We follow?"

"You're damn right we do," Caleb growled in reply. "Get on their trail pronto. We'll be right behind you. Make sure they don't double back on us." Without a word the Lipan reined around and started his pony off toward the river. "Warren, you and Diaz finish off the Comanches we put down if they ain't dead, then get these poor souls in the ground before you follow on. The rest of you move out with me." Caleb kicked Sally into a long lope and he and the remainder of the Rangers set out after Chako.

Relentless in their pursuit, the Rangers dogged the war party throughout the morning and into the early afternoon, varying the pace to save the horses and halting only when Chako doubled back to tell Caleb that the tracks entered the Clear Fork Reserve. Caleb patted Sally's neck and took a moment to consider the situation.

Anticipating Caleb's concerns, Eph added, "The army ain't gonna like it one bit if they catch us on the reserve. Maybe we should let them take it from here."

Caleb sat looking off in the direction of the tracks for a moment more before replying, "To hell with the army, Eph. For once we got a real trail headin' onto the reservation. I aim to see where the damn thing leads. 'Sides, if we take the time to bring the army in and the war party ain't from here, we'll never catch 'em."

"Do you really think we got a chance to catch up with 'em anyway?" Eph asked, knowing full well how difficult it was to run down a war party on the move.

Caleb nodded. "I do if we ride straight through the night. For the last year or so, the Comanches have been used to headin' home free and clear with nobody givin' 'em a hard chase. Let's see what the bastards do if we don't quit."

"Okay," Eph agreed, "I'm with you. "Let's get after 'em."

The trail of the war party passed directly through the reservation as Caleb had suspected it would, and fortunately the Rangers avoided meeting up with any cavalry patrols during their crossing. The tracks clung to a northerly course making them easy for Chako to follow in the moonlight. Just before dawn, after a long, brutal night in the saddle with only brief halts to walk the horses, Chako rode back to rejoin the pursuers.

Catching sight of the Lipan scout returning to the patrol, Caleb called for a halt. "How far ahead of us are they?" he asked when Chako reined in beside him and wheeled his well-lathered pinto about.

"Comanches close," Chako said, eager and ready as always to engage his hated enemy. "They break camp now. We go fast."

"You boys heard the man," Caleb said as he drew his Colt and carefully examined the percussion caps in the gathering light. "Check your Colts. We're gonna charge into that camp and kill any damn thing that moves. Chako, lead the way!"

Minutes later Chako led the Rangers into the Comanche campsite at the gallop, Colts blazing. Only a few warriors who were already mounted escaped the maelstrom that swept down on them with the suddenness of a wind-blown prairie fire. The rest were left to the mercies of a group of men who were bound and determined to show them no mercy.

Caleb reined Sally Mae up in front of a Comanche who was drawing an arrow back in his short bow. Leaning far off to the side of his saddle to avoid the hissing shaft, the tall Ranger triggered his cocked Colt and put a ball into the warrior's chest from point blank range. The Comanche jerked with the impact of the heavy caliber round as his lifeless body collapsed in a heap. Continuing on into the campsite, Caleb snapped off a shot at another warrior who launched an arrow at Peso Diaz. Diaz was nearly unhorsed when the arrow thudded into his shoulder, but the young Tejano managed to stay mounted long enough to finish off the wounded warrior with a ball to the head.

Chaos reigned across the campsite as panicked Comanches scrambled in all directions, determined to reach their ponies and escape the hellish attack. Eager Rangers bolted after them, just as determined to kill every last Comanche before they were mounted. Bravely running the deadly gauntlet of Ranger fire, a warrior managed to reach his pony, but before he could swing up onto the skittish animal's back, it danced away from him and bolted from the camp. Now forced to fight or die, the Comanche turned, and screaming his war cry, ran at Seth Watson with his war lance lowered for a killing thrust.

From across the clearing, Eph saw that Watson had his back turned to the young warrior, but the deafening cacophony of screaming men and roaring Colts made it impossible to yell a warning. Without the time to take careful aim, he quickly lowered the long barrel of his Colt and squeezed the trigger. The desperate, last second shot struck the running Comanche high in the thigh, knocking him off his feet before he could ram the lance into Seth's back. Eph rode in closer, and two more well-aimed shots from his Colt finished the warrior off for good.

Oblivious to the death that had nearly befallen him, Seth rode down a Comanche who managed to leap onto the back of his pony. Watson fired, and the ball from the young Ranger's Colt slammed into the warrior's side, nearly unhorsing him. The Comanche tried desperately to claw his way back up on his pony, then strength fading, slid slowly to the ground, leaving a bloody trail down the terrified animal's flank. Chako killed the wounded warrior then leaped from his pony to claim the Comanche's scalp. The frightened Indian pony bolted and fled from the camp before Seth could grab its braided rein.

Caleb and young Jason Warren killed the last two Comanches, knocking the warriors off their ponies with well-aimed long shots before they could gallop clear of the campsite. As quick as the fight had started, it was over. The heavy tang of black powder smoke swirled in the air, and the Rangers' ears rang from the echoing blasts of their Colts.

Looking around at the bodies of the dead and dying Comanches, Caleb holstered his smoking Colt. "No use goin' after the few that got away," he said as he dismounted and began tending to Peso's wounded shoulder, "our mounts are near played out. Make damn sure they're all dead and let's get ready to move out."

As the Rangers approached the outskirts of the reservation on their return from the pursuit of the war party, Caleb heard the unmistakable rumble of distant gunfire echo down the valley of the Clear Fork. He had been planning to circle around the reservation to avoid an unwelcome confrontation with the army, but there was always a chance that somebody in trouble needed the Rangers' help. Better safe than sorry, he thought, as he called for the patrol to pick up the pace and headed toward the sound of the gunfire.

When the Rangers arrived on the scene a few minutes later, the army was nowhere in sight. The gunfire was coming from a band of white settlers who had a few reservation Indians pinned down in a small copse of cottonwoods along the river. The settlers were maintaining a steady rate of fire, but did not appear anxious to ride into the trees after the Indians. Without hesitating, Caleb rode into the middle of the mounted men and reined up hard, his Rangers fanning out to either side of the settlers to back him up if necessary.

"Hold your fire, damn it!" Caleb bellowed. "And holster them shootin' irons now!" One look at the grim-faced Rangers convinced the surprised settlers that the big red-headed stranger meant business. Within moments, they had complied with Caleb's demand. "Who the hell are you men, and what gives you the authority to be on reservation land?"

"A settler who looked as if he was in charge reined his big stallion next to Sally Mae and tried to face Caleb down with a glare. "My name's John Baylor, mister, and these men ride with me. We're after some savages who've been raidin' the settlements hereabouts. Who the hell are you?"

Caleb glared back at the stranger, his slate-gray eyes narrowing. "My name's McAdams, Caleb McAdams, and we're Texas Rangers. Them Indians y'all were shootin' at didn't have a damn thing to do with the raids around here."

"Ranger or not, you're dead wrong about that, McAdams," Baylor argued. "My men tracked the savages here, and we aim to kill every damn one of 'em."

Caleb's laugh was more of a humorless scoff. "You're either a fool or a damn liar, mister. We just come from dealin' with the Comanche war party responsible for the raids you're talkin' about, and they were a hell of a long way from here."

Baylor's face flushed beet-red in anger. "I don't give a damn if you are a Ranger! You can't talk to me like that!" The settler went for his Colt, but before he had cleared leather he found himself staring into the cannon-like muzzle of Caleb's Dragoon.

Caleb kept the barrel of the Dragoon centered between the loudmouth's eyes. "I suggest you keep that hog leg in your holster, Mr. Baylor." Raising his voice, Caleb added, "That goes for the rest of you, too." Eph and the other Rangers had drawn their Colts along with Caleb, and Baylor's men had little choice but to sit quiet and comply with the demand.

"The army's here, Caleb," noted Eph who was the first to catch sight of a troop of cavalry approaching from along the river.

As the cavalry troop rode closer, Caleb recognized the young officer in command. He had met him on a previous patrol while trying to ransom the young boy who had been carried off by some Comanches living on the Clear Fork Reservation.

"Afternoon, Lieutenant Hood," Caleb said when the cavalry troop reined in, "good to see you again."

Lieutenant John Bell Hood touched the brim of his well-worn, slouched Hardee hat, the brim no longer pinned to the faded crown and the fancy yellow hat cord long since gone. "It's been a good while, Captain McAdams. We heard some shootin'. What seems to be the trouble here?"

Baylor reined his big stallion between Caleb and Hood. "How long are you gonna allow these Rangers to hold me and my men at gunpoint, Lieutenant?"

Hood looked Baylor over carefully. He knew the man, and when he finally spoke, his words and manner were far from pleasant. "Mr. Baylor, you've been told to stay off this reservation more than once. What are you up to now?"

Baylor was indignant over Hood's lack of sympathy. "We followed a band of savages here from a burnin' homestead a few miles back. We were tryin' to bring 'em to justice when these Rangers came along."

Caleb holstered his Colt and the rest of the Rangers followed suit. "That's not exactly the way it happened, Lieutenant. We were comin' back from a scrape with the war party that attacked the homestead when we heard some shootin'. We didn't mean to step on the army's toes, but I thought somebody might need some help. Them reservation Indians Baylor and his boys were shootin' at didn't have a damn thing to do with the attack on the homestead."

"Are you certain," asked Hood?

Caleb nodded. "You're damn right, I'm certain. My Lipan scout tracked that war party the whole way. He don't make mistakes when it comes to followin' a trail."

Hood glared at Baylor. "I suggest you and your men clear off the reservation right now, Mr. Baylor, before the army is forced to throw you off."

"Your superiors will here about this!" growled Baylor as he reined around. "Come on, men." Putting the spurs to his big stallion, Baylor galloped south with his men close behind.

Hood shook his head in resignation. "Unfortunately, he's probably right. The civilian authorities tend to lean heavily on the army for attempting to protect the Indians. Anyway, I appreciate your help, McAdams."

"We were glad to do it, Lieutenant. You take care now. Come on, Rangers, let's ride."

On June 11, Major Robert Neighbors returned from his trip to Washington with permission to move the reservation Indians north of the Red River into Oklahoma Territory. Meanwhile, Rip Ford had been called back to Austin, and Governor Runnels sent Captain John Henry Brown to take his place and assist the federal troops in keeping order. Caleb had never liked Brown and knew him as a hater of all Indians, good or bad. It did not take long for Major Neighbors to share Caleb's low opinion of the man.

"That's the most unfair and ridiculous thing I've ever heard," snapped Neighbors when Brown told him the reservation Indians would not be allowed to scatter over the area to round up their livestock. "How the hell do you expect 'em to exist once they get to Oklahoma? To say nothin' of what they'll survive on durin' the trip. And what about the corn and the other crops they have in the ground?"

"Governor Runnels wants 'em out of the state now, Neighbors," Brown replied. "There won't be time to harvest any crops, and I don't trust the thievin' bastards roundin' up livestock either. They'll steal everything in sight. Besides, it's the army's job to feed 'em. Get 'em in the wagons right now and no more arguments."

So in spite of Neighbors and Caleb's repeated entreaties, the reservation Indians were marched north, leaving gardens, corn, and cattle behind. Their few pitiful belongings were piled into army wagons, but there was little food or water available for the journey. It was a long, dry, hungry, terrible trek, and even the cavalry troopers who guarded it described the passage in bitter terms. Two weeks later, Neighbors forded the Red with his piti-able crew, and reluctantly turned them over to an Indian agent in a strange land. There is no record of how he said goodbye to the people who had put their trust in him.

After finishing their long patrol, Caleb and his Rangers re-turned to Austin. Word of Major Neighbors fate had preceded them. At Fort Belknap, while Neighbors was talking to a man named Pat Murphy about the deplorable relocation of the reser-vation Indians, Murphy's brother-in-law, Ed Cornett, killed the Indian agent by shooting him in the back.

PART VI

Chapter 33

Two weeks after Caleb's return from the Brazos, in mid-summer of 1859, a political meeting took place in Austin in a smoke-filled room of the Bullock Hotel. The purpose of the meeting was to plan Sam Houston's campaign strategy in his run for the Governor's office. Present at the meeting were hotel proprietor Richard Bullock, former Governor Elisha Pease, editor of the Austin Southern Intelligencer, George Washington Paschal, influential politicians Jessie Webb Throckmorton and B. H. Epperson, and a few other substantial men of property, including Caleb McAdams, who had been selected for their willingness to finance Houston's campaign. The meeting was long and heated, and even the open windows failed to clear all the cigar and pipe smoke from the room.

Former Governor Pease took a sip of his brandy. "Sam, as you well know, the entire political structure of the state is in the hands of the Calhoun Democrats, and they oppose you with a vengeance. They defeated you the last time you ran, and they fully intend to do so once again. They'll obviously back Runnels for re-election, and he's a solid states' righter, but thankfully the great sectional arguments that preoccupy the nation don't carry the same weight in Texas as they do elsewhere. Governor Runnels has none of your personal popularity either, and he has basically neglected the frontier, or so most of the westerners believe."

"Elisha is right, Sam," added Throckmorton, "Texans are worried about the frontier and the trouble beginnin' to stir on the Mexican border with this damn bandit Cortina. Those are the issues you must focus on. And for God's sake, don't mention a word about the Kansas-Nebraska donnybrook. You harped on it continually durin' the last election, and it was damn well instrumental in your defeat."

"You must stand on your stature as a war hero and as a past President and Senator of Texas, Sam," agreed Paschal. "Let the people vote against Runnels on his record, not vote for you on yours. I know how much you hate the idea of secession, as do the men in this room, and even most of the wealthy planters, but please tread lightly. Go against reestablishing the slave trade if you must, but leave slavery alone. And if you have to give some account of your earlier defeat, do it with that famous wit of yours, not by trying to justify yourself."

Sam Houston had listened quietly for most of the meeting, and now he rose to pace back and forth in the little space available to him in the small, crowded room. "All of you are talkin' sense, and I intend to rely on your advice. This election is vitally important, Gentlemen. If we follow the rest of the south on their road to secession the state of Texas will suffer terrible consequences. Given a choice of two evils I would rather see us declare our independence once again than succeed. The north has the necessary population to supply a never ending line of soldiers and the industrial resources to equip them. It only remains to be seen if they have the will to fight a long war, but I'm afraid they do. I plan to carry out a horse and buggy campaign across the entire state. Caleb and his Rangers will ride with me to act as escorts and to provide security at campaign rallies."

As the youngest man in the room, Caleb had been silent during the entire meeting, but he had a question he knew was on everyone's mind. "Sam, can you keep Texas in the Union if you win the election?"

Houston shrugged. "I'm not sure if anyone or anything can do that, but at least I'll be in a position to try. Thank you for being here today, Gentlemen, and thank you for your assistance."

Richard Bullock pulled Caleb aside as the meeting was breaking up. "I hate to bother you with this now, Caleb, but you best have another talk with Wanda. Every time that woman opens her mouth she gets in deeper. I overheard some men in the bar talkin' about her the other day. I warned 'em like you told me, but I ain't sure how much longer that's gonna work. More and more people are linin' up against her everyday, and you can't fight the whole damn town."

"I appreciate your warnin', Mr. Bullock," Caleb replied, no longer smiling. "I'll be sure 'n have a talk with her."

Houston's summer campaign was a whirlwind for Caleb and his Rangers, as they followed Sam's election buggy from town to town and speech to speech all across the wide state of Texas. As planned, Houston stuck to the local issues of importance to Texans like protecting the frontier and dealing with the troubles brewing on the Mexican border. He let Runnels do the preaching on the Democratic platform of states' rights and secession. Humor also played an important role, as in Houston's Nacogdoches speech when a section of the stage collapsed. Sam said, "Did I not tell you platforms were dangerous."

Houston supported slavery as everyone expected he would, but he vigorously opposed the idea of resuming the slave trade.

In between attacking Runnels on his neglect of the problems with the Comanches on the frontier and the Mexican bandits along the Rio Grande, he managed to stand for preservation of the Union. From the reaction of the crowds, Caleb thought Sam's stance on preserving the Union was unpopular at best, but in spite of this, everyone felt the election two weeks hence would be close.

Sam decided to spend the final two weeks of the election campaign in Austin, so Caleb took the opportunity to look in on Wanda. Their last meeting had ended in an argument and harsh words over a discussion of the warning Bullock had given him, and he was anxious to see that she and Josh were doing well. It was a pleasant fall Sunday afternoon when Caleb rode up and dismounted in front of Wanda's cabin and schoolhouse. He was surprised to see a young black face peer out of the corner of the curtain hanging in the schoolhouse window. As he stepped up on the porch that served as a dogtrot between the cabin and the schoolhouse, Wanda opened the front door. Josh was nowhere in sight.

Caleb smiled. "Wanda, it's good to see you again. Where's Josh?"

Wanda nervously smoothed her long blond hair with her hands as she gave him a radiant smile of welcome. "Josh is spending the next few days with his Uncle John. Come on in. I have a fresh pot of coffee on the fire."

Caleb glanced over at the door to the schoolhouse. "Since when did you start teachin' school on Sundays?"

Wanda's smile instantly vanished and her blue eyes took on a suspicious look. "What makes you ask that?"

Now it was Caleb's turn to frown. "I just saw a negro youngster peekin' out the schoolhouse window when I swung down from my horse. If you ain't havin' school, what's he doin' in the schoolhouse?"

Now Wanda looked flustered. "Please come in and I'll explain."

Although uneasy about the strange way Wanda was acting, Caleb pulled off his sombrero and stepped through the door she held open for him. He took a seat at her small kitchen table as Wanda closed the door and went for the coffee pot. She placed a cup in front of him and filled it before sliding the sugar bowl over and offering him a spoon. Taking a seat across from him, Wanda crossed her hands in her lap and waited patiently while he spooned the sugar into his cup and stirred it thoroughly.

Finally Caleb looked up at her with questioning eyes. "Well," he asked, "are you gonna answer my question now?"

Wanda refused to make eye contact with him in her usual manner. "The child and his family are runaways. They just got here an hour or so ago."

Caleb leaped to his feet, jarring the table and sloshing coffee onto the clean, white tablecloth. "Have you lost your damn mind, woman?" Wanda's face darkened, but before she could come up with an angry retort to his outburst, he continued. "With your reputation, don't you think this is one of the first places the slave hunters will come to look for 'em? What about Josh? Do you have any idea how much danger you've put him in, to say nothin' of yourself. My God, woman or not, they will hang you for helpin' runaways, and there's not a damn thing I can do about it. Oh, make no mistake, I'd fight 'em every damn inch of the way to protect you, but they got the law on their side!"

Wanda's anger was swallowed up in her regret and tears dampened her cheeks. "I'm so sorry, Caleb, but what was I to do? They're only hiding out here until some of my Mexican friends come by in the morning to smuggle them towards the border."

Caleb began pacing. "Tomorrow may well be too late. We have to hide 'em right now! Just over the edge of the bluff on the other side of the cabin is a small cave. The trail down to it is concealed from view unless you know right where it is. Me and Josh found it one day when I was out playin' with him. How many are in the family?"

"Four," replied Wanda with renewed hope now that she realized Caleb would help her protect the runaways, "a husband and wife and two young children."

Caleb thought for a moment. "Gather 'em up and, we'll take 'em to the cave. Bring some food and water too, and please hurry. The damn slave hunters could be here any minute."

"Do you really think they'll come here that soon?" Wanda asked.

Caleb shook his head in disgust at Wanda's naiveté. "You can damn well bet on it! The only reason the law ain't breakin' your door down right now is that the slaves probably ain't come up missin' yet. Now hurry!"

Finally driven by Caleb's sense of urgency, Wanda wasted no time in gathering up some food and water, fetching the family, and following Caleb to the edge of the bluff. It looked like a straight drop off to her. She could not imagine where he was leading them until he stopped and held some brush back revealing the entrance to a narrow path that led down the face of the steep bluff.

"Hurry and follow me," Caleb urged as he headed down the path.

Wanda coaxed the slaves to follow Caleb, and a little ways down the path they came to a small cave that was really no more than a hollow fifteen or twenty feet deep into the face of the bluff. Caleb motioned for the slaves to enter, and once they were seated on the ground, Wanda handed them the food and water.

"You must stay quiet," Caleb cautioned. "We'll get you out of here as soon as we can in the mornin'."

The black man finally spoke. "Thank you, suh, and God bless you and this fine lady."

Wanda smiled her encouragement to the runaways before following Caleb back up the path to the edge of the bluff. Caleb felt a twinge of guilt knowing that helping these people was the right thing to do, but also wondering if he would have taken the risk if not for trying to protect Wanda. However, this was no time for self-recrimination; much yet remained to be done.

"I'll put the brush back in place over the path," Caleb said, "then check around the schoolhouse and cabin for any tracks or other sign that the slaves might have left when they got here. You make damn sure there's nothin' left in the schoolhouse." By the time Caleb retuned to the schoolhouse, Wanda had removed all traces of the slaves' presence. "Now we wait in the cabin for the slave hunters, and I'm bettin' it won't be long."

No sooner had Caleb sat down to the coffee that had grown cold than he heard the sound of horses. "Let's go greet your guests," he said with a grim smile as he rose from the table and led the way out the door. "Please don't say a word, Wanda. Let me do the talkin'." They were standing on the porch waiting when the horsemen reined up. Caleb estimated their number at near twenty, and he could tell by the look on the men's faces they were disappointed to see him standing beside Wanda. Hooking his thumbs in his gun belt in a casual manner, he asked, "What can I do for you boys?"

"We're lookin' for some runaways," McAdams," said one of the men who Caleb recognized as a slave chaser by the name of Len Samuels.

Samuels reminded Caleb of a New Orleans dandy, dressed as he was all in black with a fancy vest and flat-brimmed black hat. He wore his oily black hair slicked back, and his hair and pencil thin mustache were neatly trimmed. The wilted, white-ruffled shirt that the slave chaser wore only added to the image of a dandy. Hardly an outfit a man would wear who was forced to work for a living, Caleb thought.

Caleb smiled and enjoyed the way the smile seemed to irritate Samuels. "What makes you think the runaways are hidin' out here, Samuels?"

"We tracked them niggers a good way before we lost the trail, and they were headed this way," Samuels replied."' Sides, your lady friend don't make no secret of which side of the fence she stands on when it comes to slavery."

"They're my slaves," added a man who owned a farm south of Austin on the Colorado. "Are they here?"

"Hidin' runaway slaves is against the law," Caleb replied, "and no matter what you might think of Mrs. Andrew's opinions on slavery, she don't go around breakin' the law."

"In that case," said Samuels with a confident smile, "you won't mind if we take a good look around."

Caleb looked to Wanda. "You'll have to ask Mrs. Andrews about that."

"Feel free to look where you may, gentlemen," said Wanda, "but please be careful with my things."

The men dismounted, and led by Samuels and the farmer who owned the slaves, made a thorough search of not only the schoolhouse and Wanda's cabin, but also of the surrounding area. The search turned up nothing, and when the men returned to their horses empty-handed Samuels was furious.

"I know damn well you're hidin' them niggers somewhere around here, McAdams," the slave chaser groused.

Caleb's slate-gray eyes narrowed snake-like in anger as he stepped down off the porch. Two long strides brought him face to face with Samuels. "I don't care much for the tone of your voice, Samuels, or you either for that matter. Now if you're finished here, I'd be obliged if you mounted up and rode on."

Samuels had been made to look like a fool by insisting that the men would find the slaves at Wanda's place, and he refused to leave well enough alone. "We'll catch you hidin' slaves one day, McAdams, you and that nigger-lovin' whore of yours."

The words were no sooner out of Samuel's mouth than Caleb's big right fist caught him flush on the nose, knocking him off his feet. Nose bleeding and obviously broken, the slave chaser staggered to his feet and made a foolish grab for his gun. He was fast, but Caleb was much faster. The roar of the tall Ranger's

Colt echoed along the high bluff, and the .44 caliber ball sliced a chunk out of Samuels' right arm. The slave chaser dropped his Colt and grabbed his wounded arm.

The horses shied away as Caleb faced up with the remainder of the searchers, the smoking Colt still filling his right hand. "Y'all can help him up and clear out or join him. It's your choice!"

Two of the men quickly dismounted and helped Samuels up on his horse. Without another word, they all reined around and rode out. Caleb and Wanda stood watching the riders until they were out of sight.

Wanda smiled in relief. "Thank God they didn't find the slaves."

"Maybe not this time," Caleb snapped in reply, "but it's a damn good thing they didn't bring any hounds along with 'em! Your slave friends would be danglin' at the end of a rope right now along with us, or dancin' to the snap of a whip. Wanda, you got to promise me this won't happen again. It's just too damn dangerous."

Wanda's smile vanished and she looked contrite as she opened the cabin door. "I understand, Caleb. Come on in and I'll make some fresh coffee."

Caleb shook his head in frustration as he entered the cabin. Wanda may well have been contrite in her manner, but her fancy words had not promised him a thing.

Chapter 34

On a warm, sunny day in late November, Rip Ford was walking down the new wooden sidewalk on Congress Avenue when he ran into Forbes Britton, the state senator from Corpus Christi. Britton looked as if he had been treed by an angry coon dog.

"Captain Ford," Senator Britton nearly yelled in frustration, "the very man I've been lookin' for! That Mexican bandit Juan Cortina has invaded Corpus Christi. The town's been sacked and burned to the ground. Heaven only knows what's become of my family."

Ford was familiar with the situation that had been brewing on the Mexican border. All the newspapers were full of Juan Cortina's exploits since his occupation of Brownsville toward the end of September. The Mexican Bandit had wounded the sheriff in a gunfight before releasing one of his men from the town jail. Of course the term bandit was in the eye of the beholder. Most Mexicans thought of the redheaded Cortina as a patriot. His wealthy family had once owned large tracts of land along the Nueces strip, and Cortina had held a grudge against Texas ever since the war with Mexico ended and the land north of the Rio Grande had been confiscated.

Ford smiled. "Senator, I think you been listenin' to rumors. I know Cortina's been causin' a big fuss along border lately, but it ain't likely he'd ride as far north as Corpus Christi."

Ford continued to reason with Senator Britton for the next several minutes and nearly had the man calmed down when Governor Runnels happened to walk up and join in on the conversation. Ford's efforts in calming the Senator were quickly undone, as Britton nearly went into hysterics explaining the rumored invasion to Runnels. Ford wanted to laugh, but he contained his reaction to the Senator's rant when he noticed how intently the Governor was listening. In fact, Runnels appeared to be taking the senator quite seriously.

Finally the Governor turned to Ford. "Captain Ford, I have already sent a force of Rangers from San Antonio to the border under the command of Captain Tobin, but they've obviously failed in their efforts. Now you must go and settle this situation once and for all!"

Rip Ford rode out of Austin the following morning with only eight men, little food, and not a single dollar of public money. As usual, the state treasury was bare. However, Ford did hold a commission from Governor Runnels appointing him a major in command of all Texas forces on the border, and a pretty good idea where he could find some financial support and a few more good men.

Early the same afternoon, Ford and his Rangers trotted through the gate of the Rocking M hacienda. Having been alerted by one of his Lipan outriders, Caleb was standing on the porch, along with Lucinda and Pedro waiting to greet them.

"Climb down from that saddle and come on in for of cup of coffee, Rip," said Caleb. "Eph's in the barracks out back of the barn with a couple of my Rangers. You can send the rest of your boys out there."

Ford explained to the men where they could find the Ranger barracks and then swung down from the saddle. After looping his reins over the hitching rail, he stepped up on the porch and offered his hand to Caleb with a big smile. "It's damn good to see you again, Caleb, and you too Lucinda."

As Ford shook hands and warmly greeted Pedro, he could not help but notice that although Lucinda had a smile on her face, the warmth of the smile did not reach the depth of her eyes. She knows damn well I am about to borrow her man again, he thought, and she knows that whatever I want him to do will be dangerous. They were soon sitting around the big oak table in the great room. Felix pulled up a chair and joined them while Consuela was pouring the coffee.

Caleb looked up at Ford as he was stirring his heavily sweetened coffee. "Well, Rip, I don't imagine this is a purely social visit."

Ford sighed. "I'm afraid not. Governor Runnels asked me to take command of all the state forces along the Mexican border. That bandit Juan Cortina is causin' big trouble along the Rio Grande."

"Many people on the border think of Juan Cortina as a patriot, not a bandit, Major Ford," said Felix with a sly smile. "His family once owned most of the Nueces Strip. They lost many thousands of acres after the war."

Ford nodded in acceptance of Felix's words. "I realize that, Mr. Vaca, and I can't say as how I'd act any different in his place. However, the law is what it is, and many of the actions Cortina has taken are clearly illegal. As a Texas Ranger I have no choice but to try and bring him to justice."

"My father and I both understand your position, Rip," added Pedro. "And like me, while he sympathizes with Juan Cortina's position, he does not condone his present actions. We also both understand why the government must take action."

"Thanks Pedro," said Ford, "I appreciate that."

Caleb sat silent with a slight smile on his face as Felix and Pedro made their positions clear to Ford. Juan Cortina had been the subject of many of their recent conversations, and it was amusing to see Rip having to justify his position as he had been forced to do. Now Caleb decided it was time to get his good friend off the hook.

"The papers have been harpin' about Cortina for a good while now, Rip," Caleb said. "Has Runnels done anything at all about him up until now?"

Ford was more than glad to get back to the subject at hand. "Six weeks ago he sent some San Antonio Rangers to the border under the command of Captain W. G. Tobin. Unfortunately, it appears most of them were the usual riff-raff who are always the first to join up with any expedition headin' for the Rio Grande. The only thing they've managed to accomplish so far was to storm the Brownsville jail and lynch a sixty-five year old Cortinista who was bein' held for trial. They also got a group of volunteers down there made up of Brownsville men known as the Tigers, but they ain't worth much of a damn either. Pardon me, Ma'am," Ford said to Lucinda. She nodded her acceptance of his apology and he continued. "The United States Army's involved now, too. I'll be meetin' up with them soon as I get down there. I only got eight men and a few supplies, Caleb. I'm gonna need your help to put an outfit together between here and Brownsville, and to act as my scout and second in command. What do you say?"

Caleb saw the disappointment on Lucinda's face, but he knew that like it or not, she would understand. "I'm sorry love. I'll do my best to get back home by Christmas, but Rip needs my help. Pedro, will you need me for anything on the ranch?"

"No problem," Pedro replied. "I can handle things, and if I have any questions, I'll ask my father."

"Well then it's settled," Caleb said as he quickly glanced at Lucinda. "Count me in, Rip. Eph and six of my Rangers will ride with us, too. I'd bring Chako along, but I don't trust the men ridin' with Tobin. There may well be some trigger-happy Indian haters among 'em."

"I can't argue with that," said Ford, his spirits lifted now that he was sure Caleb would ride with him.

"I'll send one of my Rangers to fetch Bigfoot too," Caleb added. "He can round up as many good men as he can find in San Antonio and meet us in Goliad. I got all the packhorses we'll need and enough supplies to get us to Goliad. We can pick up some more when we get there. I don't see any reason why we can't pull out fist thing in the mornin'. Caleb glanced at Lucinda when he added, "the sooner we get there, the sooner we'll be gettin' back."

Early the following morning, Caleb sent Ranger Stan Redd to fetch Bigfoot, and he, Ford, and Eph led the thirteen remaining Rangers east along the Colorado towards the Bastrop ferry. Once across the river they would ride south to Goliad and then on to Brownsville. Ford's orders from Governor Runnels were simple. He was to go to the Rio Grande Valley with all the Rangers he could manage to muster and assume overall command of the Rangers already there. "The service required," Runnels had written, "is to protect the western frontier against Cortina and his band and to arrest them if possible."

Word spread rapidly across southeast Texas that Rip Ford was on his way to the border to deal with Juan Cortina, and many men volunteered to join up along the trail to Goliad. However, Ford and Caleb screened each volunteer carefully, expertly weeding out the troublesome adventurers, and signing up only those men who had the grit to keep going when things got tough and knew how to obey orders. The result was that they arrived in Goliad with nearly forty good men.

Caleb was standing there to greet Bigfoot the next day when his good friend rode into the outskirts of Goliad with Stan Redd and ten more volunteers. "Glad you could make it, partner," said Caleb as he reached up and shook Bigfoot's hand.

Before dismounting, Bigfoot looked over the orderly camp Ford's Rangers had set up, and the hard-looking men who had already joined the outfit. "Looks like a good bunch of fightin' men."

Caleb smiled. "The men you brought along look like they'll fit right in with 'em."

"Sure enough," Bigfoot agreed. "There were a bunch more volunteers, but I weeded out the shirkers right off, too."

"Even so, countin' yours, that still gives us nearly fifty men. Rip's still tryin' to add on a few more here in Goliad if he can find 'em. Me and Rip agreed Eph should act as second in command, so we can ride as scouts for the outfit."

"Just like the old days, partner," Bigfoot replied with a chuckle. "We should have us some good times. By the way, where's Rip got off to? I need to pay my respects."

He's busy pickin' up the supplies the good citizens of Goliad gathered up for us. I bought plenty of extra powder and ball, too, so we should be well set up."

"That's sure a pleasant change of circumstances," said Bigfoot. "I won't know how to act without worryin' about my next meal or bit of powder and ball. When's Rip plannin' on headin' for the border?"

Caleb shoved back the wide brim of his sombrero. "I'm not rightly sure, but I'd guess as early as tomorrow mornin', if he finds the men he's lookin' for."

Rip Ford's Rangers broke camp at sunrise the following day and headed for Brownsville some two hundred miles distant. Including the few men Ford had recruited in Goliad, his company now numbered fifty-three Rangers, all of them trail-hardened fighters who could be relied upon to more than hold their own in any scrape. Caleb loaned out the extra Colts he brought along, and each man in the company was now armed with at least one Walker Colt, a Navy Colt, or a Colt Dragoon.

Riding straight south from Goliad, the Rangers forded the Nueces River just west of the coastal settlement of Corpus Christi on their second day out. After ensuring that the rumors of Cortina's invasion of the settlement were untrue, they continued south at the fastest possible pace without using up the horses, arriving on the outskirts of Brownsville early in the afternoon of their sixth day in the saddle. Ford halted the company when he caught sight of Caleb and Bigfoot returning from their scout.

"What's goin' on?" asked Ford, the eagerness in his voice revealing his desire to engage the Mexican invaders as soon as possible.

"Cortina tried to retake Brownsville," Caleb reported, "but the town folk drove his men back with a little help from Tobin and the army."

"Hear that rifle fire?" Bigfoot asked. "Cortina's mounted men are movin' back across the Rio Grande, and the bandits left without horses moved a little further upstream on this side of the river to cover their withdrawal."

"Well, we sure as hell aint doin' much sittin' around here," said Ford. "Let's ride to the sound of those guns."

Citizen volunteers posted in a church steeple caught sight of Ford's Rangers approaching Brownsville at the gallop and at first mistook them for more of Juan Cortina's men. Thankfully, the oncoming riders were identified as Rangers before anyone fired a shot, and the citizens who had gathered to defend the city cheered lustily as the Rangers galloped through town and headed for the river. In spite of Ford's haste, by the time the Rangers reached the scene of the fighting, the Mexican horseman had escaped across the river, so Caleb and Bigfoot led the charge into the middle of the bandits who were retreating up-river on foot after covering the crossing.

Though they held superior numbers, the panicked Mexicans scattered like a flock of startled chickens when Ford's Rangers struck their exposed flank, pausing every now and then to fire a shot when they found a bit of cover or when they were cornered and forced to fight or die. Caleb dropped low over Sally Mae's neck when a bandit he was chasing suddenly turned and leveled the barrel of his rifle. The muzzle of the Mexican rifle belched fire and smoke, and Caleb heard the hornet-like buzz of the rifle ball as it whizzed past his ear. He snapped off a shot with his Colt in return that took the Mexican high in the chest and blew him off his feet. Caleb reined in sharp when he saw Bigfoot's buckskin go down, but he breathed a sigh of relief when the big man came to his feet spitting mad and dropped the Mexican who had killed his horse before the man could scramble to cover.

The Rangers continued to press the Mexicans hard until one of them was killed and two others were wounded by a heavy concentration of rifle fire coming from a walled hacienda near the river. Realizing his men were in an exposed position, and there was no way to assault the hacienda's walls on horseback, Ford called for an orderly withdrawal to a row of old abandoned warehouses located a hundred yards back down the river. Caleb swung Sally Mae around and hoisted Bigfoot up behind him. With the help of a few others, they laid down a withering cover fire on the walls of the hacienda while the dead and wounded were picked up and their horses recovered. Once this was accomplished, the Rangers fell back.

"Dismount!" Ford yelled when they reached the rear of the warehouses. The buildings were dilapidated and the roofs had long since caved in but their thick adobe walls would provide good cover. "Eph, see to the wounded and take care of the horses. The rest of you find a good spot where you can lay some rifle fire on those damn walls."

Caleb and Bigfoot entered the rear of the first building they came to and moved to a row of windows along the front wall that provided a clear view of the hacienda. Caleb estimated the distance at less than two hundred yards. The volume of fire from the walls had slowed considerably since the Rangers took cover, and only an occasional rifle ball struck the front of the warehouse, sending up a puff of adobe brick.

Along the hacienda wall, Caleb caught an occasional glimpse of a sombrero, as one of the Mexicans rose to fire his rifle. Using the window sill to steady the long barrel of his Hawken, he set the rear trigger and carefully centered the tip of the front sight in the notched rear sight. A sombrero came into view over the tip of the front sight and he gently squeezed the front hair trigger. The long rifle roared, and the Mexican fell back out of sight.

Bigfoot let out a whoop. "Great shot, partner!"

The other Rangers joined in, and their rifle fire was so effective Ford was thinking of moving a flanking force toward the hacienda when the weather decreed otherwise. During the brief skirmish the wind had begun to pick up and the sky had darkened as thick clouds rolled in from the west like long rows of gray soldiers on the march. Soon zigzag flashes of lightning began to rip across the darkening western sky followed by booming claps of thunder that seemed to shake the foundations of the earth. Within minutes blinding rain began to pelt down in nearly horizontal sheets and all fighting quickly ceased.

The roofless buildings helped to keep the howling wind at bay, but they did little to shelter the Rangers from the rain, and as darkness fell the Mexicans were forgotten as everyone sought some kind of cover from the torrential downpour. Like many others, Caleb and Bigfoot threw together a makeshift lean-to, but building a fire was next to impossible, and the rain was such that they were soaked to the bone and chilled by morning.

Thankfully, the sunrise gave way to a clear blue sky, and Bigfoot and Ford sat in front of a warm fire drying their soggy clothes and sipping some hot coffee they'd brewed, while Caleb and Eph went to check on the packhorses. Suddenly the sound of Mexican bugles rang out from the walled hacienda and from further up the river.

"Listen to them bugles," Bigfoot said. "Old Cortina can't be too far off, Rip. It looks as if we might get another shot at the varmint this mornin'."

"You may be right," Ford replied.

"Not from the shape our powder's in," added Caleb as he and Eph returned from checking the packhorses. "The whole supply's so wet it's near ruined."

Anxious to keep the pressure on Cortina after the initial skirmish, Ford was beside himself. "Damn it to hell, we ain't got much choice except to back off now. I want to corral that Mexican bandit more than anybody, but we sure as hell can't throw rocks at the bastard. Help me round up the men, Eph. We'll go see the army about findin' some more powder. I should meet up with the new commander anyhow."

"Me and Bigfoot will check up on the Mexicans while you and Eph get the Rangers ready to pull back," said Caleb. "Come on, Bigfoot. You can use the horse of the Ranger who was killed. We should be able to ride out and pick up your saddle by now."

Bigfoot stood and tossed off the rest of his coffee. "Let's ride!"

Wanda sat alone in front of the fire staring into the flames as they flickered from red to blue to orange and yellow. Ever since the incident when Caleb had helped her conceal the family of escaped slaves in the small cave along the face of the bluff, she had followed his advice about minding her own business. That is until this evening when Thomas had showed up at her door.

Wanda had known Thomas for several years. His owner, Ben Slayton, rented out the slave's services as a handyman, and he had often helped out around the school and the cabin when there was heavy work to be done. On each occasion Wanda had taken the time to teach the slave what she could while he worked, and when he sometimes finished early. Eventually with her help and a lot of secret work on his own part, he had learned his numbers and how to read and write on a basic level. She had even read the forbidden "Uncle Tom's Cabin" to him.

Now he showed up on her doorstep ready for freedom, but he needed her help. Wanda wrestled with Caleb's warning only briefly before deciding to lead Thomas to the cave on the bluff. It was the only thing her conscience would allow her to do. She left him with enough food and water to get by for a day or two until she could contact her Mexican friends and smuggle him south, then covered her tracks as she returned to the cabin.

The sound of horses approaching the high bluff brought Wanda to her feet, but it was the mournful baying of the hounds that filled her with dread. The last time she had faced this situation Caleb said it was fortunate the slave hunters had not brought any hounds along with them. The riders reined up in front of her cabin, and she heard the jingle of harness and the creak of leather as the horses settled.

Suddenly Wanda heard a voice she recognized all too well. "We come for the slave, Thomas! Turn him over now or you'll pay dear when we find him!"

Picking up the Navy Colt revolver that was always on the table by the door, Wanda held it down by her side covered by her flowing dress and pulled the door open. Several of the riders carried burning torches, and the firelight cast eerie shadows of the men and horses across the porch and up onto the walls of the twin cabins. At the head of the mounted men was Len Samuels, the voice she had recognized. He was once again leading the slave chasers.

"Where is he, Mrs. Andrews?" Samuels yelled. "Where's the slave named Thomas? We know damn well he was here 'cause the hounds led us straight to your place. If he's still here turn him over like I said or things are gonna go hard on ya."

Baying like a pack of wolves, the hounds strained at the ropes that held them when Wanda walked out the door and stepped down off the porch, but she refused to be cowed. "Thomas was here earlier, but I sent him away. Now you and the others get off my land, Len Samuels! You have no right to be here!"

"The law says we got all the right we need," Samuels replied. "Ain't that the way it is, sheriff?"

Sheriff Bowles did not care much for the way things were going or for Len Samuels, but the law was on Samuels' side. "I'm afraid he's right, ma'am. A slave owner can track his slaves most anywhere and search where he thinks he might find 'em."

"Loose the hounds!" yelled Samuels, and the dogs charged toward the cabin.

Wanda raised the revolver and squeezed the trigger the way Caleb had taught her, killing the lead hound and scattering the others with yelps of fear before they reached the porch. Before anyone else reacted to this startling development, Samuels drew his revolver and fired. The ball carved a long furrow along the side of Wanda's head, knocking her unconscious. She collapsed on the hard packed earth in front of the cabin and did not move. A small pool of blood spread over the ground below her head.

For a moment no one moved then Sheriff Bowles dismounted and knelt down beside Wanda, making sure to pick up the revolver. "You had no cause to shoot her Samuels. It's a damn good thing she's still alive." Sheriff Bowles untied the bandana that was around his neck and held it against the side of Wanda's head.

Suddenly, one of the remaining hounds picked up the scent of the slave and the pack headed for the bluff, baying for all they were worth. Quickly dismounting, the slave hunters followed the hounds, and within minutes they were dragging a pleading Thomas back up the narrow path.

"Found him just like I said we would, sheriff," crowed Samuels, as they dragged Thomas up to where the sheriff still knelt beside Wanda. Samuels pointed to Wanda. "And she damn well got what was comin' to her for breakin' the law by hidin' the bastard. Now we're gonna hang this nigger as an example to all the other slaves who think they can run off."

"Now wait a damn minute, Samuels," complained Ben Slayton. "I went along with this up to now, but you ain't about to hang Thomas. That nigger's a valuable piece of property, and he belongs to me."

"Do you want your other slaves runnin' away when they see this nigger get off with nothin' more than a lickin'," sneered Samuels." 'Sides, the law will pay you. Ain't that right sheriff?"

Seeing that Wanda would be okay, Bowles tied the bandana around her head and rose to his feet. "Unfortunately, Samuels is right about that, Ben. The law will pay you for any runaway you decide to hang as an example."

Though Slayton was not too happy with the idea of hanging his longtime slave, he sensed the mood of Samuels and the others, and he was not about to go against them. "Go ahead and be done with it then," he reluctantly agreed.

Thomas continued to beg for mercy as one of the men tied a noose at the end of a rope and tossed the other end over the limb of a big live oak that stood near the porch. After tying the slave's hands behind his back, Samuels slipped the noose over his neck. Thomas begged all the harder, but ignoring his pleas, Samuels and another slave chaser heaved on the loose end of the rope, slowly raising Thomas' feet off the ground. They held the slave suspended until he began to kick his feet and twirl at the end of the rope as he slowly strangled to death. When they were sure he was dead they tied the end of the rope off to the trunk of the oak tree and let him swing. The men were silent as they watched Thomas's body slowly turn in the flickering torchlight.

Samuels swung up in the saddle and the rest of the men followed suit, most of them eager to be rid of the sickening scene. Reaching over, Samuels grabbed a torch from one of the men and rode up next to the cabin. "I decided we ain't gonna wait for the good Lord to punish this bitch!" He hurled the flaming torch through the window of the cabin before the sheriff could stop him. "Let's ride, men! She won't be hidin' any more niggers in that cabin." Samuels reined around and galloped off. The other riders followed when they saw Wanda begin to stir, a few of them, including Sheriff Bowles, reluctantly.

Wanda slowly sat up, holding her aching head. She nearly became sick when she saw Thomas hanging from the tree, but both her pain and the slave were quickly forgotten when she noticed the spreading fire. Leaping to her feet, she rushed for the door of the cabin as the kerosene lamp exploded.

"Josh," she screamed in terror!

Chapter 35

Just before noon, Ford led his Rangers up to the gate outside Fort Brown and signaled for them to rein in. "Eph, find a place for the men to rest and water the horses, hopefully somewhere with some decent graze. Once the horses are taken care of, the men can eat and relax. Caleb, you and Bigfoot come with me. We're gonna pay a call on the army and see if we can't get a little powder and a whole lot of cooperation."

The three Rangers dismounted in front of the headquarters building and Ford asked to see the new army commander, Major Heintzelman. From what Ford had learned, the Major arrived in Brownsville on the previous day, December 5, 1859, with 165 men. He immediately joined forces with Tobin's Rangers and attacked Cortina at a place called Ebonal. The Rangers did not give a good account of themselves, but in spite of this, the Mexicans were forced to retreat with the loss of eight men. Ford's Rangers had arrived at the tail end of that fight.

Major Heintzelman was talking to Captain Tobin when Ford, Caleb, and Bigfoot were shown into his office, and he did not appear to be happy. Ford handed the major a copy of his orders written by Governor Runnels, and Heintzelman offered the Rangers a chair while he looked them over.

"Welcome to Brownsville, Major Ford," Heintzelman said after he had finished reading the orders. "I am indeed happy to have you here." In their short acquaintance, the Major had found many problems with Captain Tobin, and he was glad to see a new commander of the Rangers. Besides, Ford's reputation as a fighting man preceded him to Brownsville.

"Did you say Major Ford?" asked Tobin.

"Yes, Captain Tobin," replied Heintzelman with a smile. "It appears the Governor has given Major Ford command of all the Texas Rangers on the border. That obviously includes you and your men." He handed the orders to Tobin.

Tobin looked the orders over closely. He was clearly not pleased when he handed them back to Ford, but he had little choice except to comply. "I am at your orders, Major."

"The Captain and I were just having a little discussion on how to proceed from this point," said Heintzelman. "What would you propose, Major Ford?"

Ford never hesitated. "These two men are my scouts, Caleb McAdams and Bigfoot Wallace. They just returned from upriver, and they say the Mexicans are fallin' back quickly and burnin' every damn ranch and settlement in their path. We must pursue Cortina's forces immediately, Major, and keep the pressure on until they're forced to turn and fight. The sooner we do it the better!"

Heintzelman smiled. "Those are my sentiments exactly, Major Ford." Tobin did not say a word, but it was apparent that he had been arguing against such a strategy. Pointing to a map laid out on his desk, the Major continued, "I propose to move up the Rio Grande with my troops while you and your Rangers attempt to outride Cotina and get on his flank. Send me word once you're in position, Major Ford, and I will launch a frontal assault. That should keep him busy while you roll up his flank."

Ford knew that riding in the brush country away from the river would be much more difficult than following the river, but he also realized, as Tobin must have, that it was a mission made for his rugged Rangers. "I can move out just as soon as we replenish our powder, Major. Most of it was ruined by the blasted rain we had last night."

"Have one of your men see the Quartermaster," said Heintzelman as he offered his hand to Ford. "He will take care of your needs. The army will move at first light."

Caleb and Bigfoot kept a close eye on the Mexicans as they continued their retreat up the lower Rio Grande valley. The trail, littered with pillaged and burning ranches and settlements, was easy to follow. The Neale ranch was among those destroyed, as were the customs house and post office at Edinburg, which was plundered and burned to the ground. A thin haze of smoke hung over the entire lower valley as the Mexicans burned and looted their way west.

Moving through the thorny brush and thick chaparral that grew north of the river was more difficult for the scouts than Caleb had imagined, and he knew the Rangers following only a few miles behind him and Bigfoot must be near exhaustion. Long thorns tore at the scouts and their horses, and if not for the thick chaps they wore, their legs would have been shredded.

"This sure is some nasty damn country down here, partner" complained Bigfoot. "Almost every damn thing in it will jab, poke, or poison you, and if it ain't got horns it's most likely got thorns. Kind of reminds me of the time we rode with old General Somervell on the way to Mier. I sure hope this fandango don't turn out the same damn way."

Caleb kept his thoughts to himself, but he could understand the big man's concern. Wallace had ended up in a Vera Cruz prison after the Mier fiasco.

"By the way," added Bigfoot, "speakin' on the Mier expedition reminds me I been meanin' to ask you about the Pates. Are you plannin' on us headin' out to California soon? You know damn well them bastards ain't gonna give up. We'll have to finish 'em off sooner or later."

"The Pates are never far from my mind, partner," Caleb replied, "but I might've solved the problem, at least for a little while."

Bigfoot looked at Caleb, his eyes wide with astonishment. "Now just how in the hell did you go about that? Hire somebody to kill 'em like they did you?"

Caleb laughed out loud, taking a moment to regain control. "Well, not exactly, but that's pretty damn close." Taking delight in the perplexed look on Bigfoot's face, Caleb continued, "I wrote a note to Ned, and put it in a letter to Jack Hays with instructions to hire a disreputable lookin' character to put the note directly into Ned Pate's hand on a crowded street."

"What the hell good is that gonna do?" Bigfoot wondered.

"Let's see," Caleb replied as he rubbed his chin in thought, "if I remember right, the note said, 'Anyone can hire an assassin. The man who handed you this note would have been just as glad to put a bullet in your brain for a little more money. Leave well enough alone, and I will, too.'"

Bigfoot joined Caleb in laughter. "You beat all, partner, you know that. I'd give twenty dollars to see Ned Pate's face when he reads that note. And who knows, it just may work. At least it should make him think it over before he hires another killer."

The scouts continued to beat their way though the heavy brush north of the river. Though the going was tough, they were rewarded when they finally broke into a large clearing and found ample evidence of a recent Mexican campsite. In fact, after dismounting and examining the fires, Caleb was sure some of Cortina's men had camped there the night before. Continuing the pursuit with little rest, led them to a trail that anyone could have followed. Charred ranch houses, burned fences, and destroyed property of all manner and description littered the path Cortina's men had taken.

Caleb and Bigfoot spent a lonesome Christmas night in a cold camp out in the brush. Caleb was exhausted from a long day in the saddle, but sleep came hard. As he lay in his bedroll taking in the surrounding night sounds and Bigfoot's gentle snoring, his thoughts drifted to Lucinda and the children. He could imagine the happy family celebration he was missing at the hacienda. Sometimes a man paid a heavy price to serve as a Ranger. He also wondered how Wanda and Josh were getting along. She had most likely spent the day at her brother's house, Caleb thought, so she probably had not been alone. Sleep was fitful when it finally came.

Rising well before dawn, the scouts had a quick breakfast of jerky and cold creek water, then mounted and rode close to the outskirts of Rio Grande City before tying off their horses in a dry arroyo and moving in on foot for a closer look. From their perch on a little wooded knoll, it was obvious that most of the local citizens had abandoned the small settlement and fled in the direction of Major Heintzelman's approaching troops. Cortina and his men were thus free to loot and burn at their leisure, and they were taking full advantage of the situation.

"It's high time we reported back," said Caleb disgusted with what he saw. "Ford said they would be camped back near Las Cuevas."

It did not take the scouts long to find the Ranger camp, and after rendering their report, Caleb and Bigfoot accompanied Ford to meet with Major Heintzelman. It was almost sundown when the Rangers arrived at the army camp not far from the Rio Grande, and the setting sun provided a breathtaking panorama of color as it slowly made its way through a bank of scattered clouds before sinking below the western horizon.

"Cortina and his men are in Rio Grande City, Major," said Ford. "Caleb and Bigfoot just got back from there."

Heintzelman nodded. "We must move quickly before he has an opportunity to withdraw his forces again and continue to loot and burn. I will advance my troops tonight and be in a position to launch an attack at daybreak. We'll move directly up the river and make a frontal assault on Rio Grande City at dawn. I want you and your Rangers to slip around the settlement tonight, so we can trap Cortina between us and keep him from escaping further west. Even if we don't round them all up, I want to make sure we drive them back across the river. Do you have any questions?"

Ford shook his head. "The Rangers will be in position before the sun comes up, Major. You can count on it."

A few hours later Caleb and Bigfoot were bulling their way through some thick chaparral a quarter mile ahead of the advancing Ranger column. There was little moonlight and the swirling fog that hung thick in the Rio Grande valley limited visibility. Suddenly, an unsuspected gust of wind blew the heavy mist apart for a moment and Caleb thought he caught a glimpse of a rider in the brush not too far ahead.

"Bigfoot, did you catch sight of anything up ahead just now?" Caleb's question was immediately answered by a muzzle flash and a rifle ball that tore a chunk of bark off a nearby tree limb. Yanking the Colt from his holster, he returned the fire, but the fog had blown back in and he was not sure if he had hit anything. Digging his heels into Sally Mae's ribs, Caleb lit out in pursuit of the rider with Bigfoot close behind, but the man, apparently a scout for Cortina, soon escaped into the fog and thick chaparral.

Caleb called for a halt. "It looks like we lost 'em, partner. We best be gettin' back to the column. Rip's gonna be wonderin' about the gunshots."

"I wouldn't be too worried about losin' him anyways," said Bigfoot as they reined around and headed back toward the column. "It ain't any easier for the Mexicans to cut through this brush than it is for us. And if he does get word back to Cortina tonight, all he can report is seein' a couple scouts."

When the scouts returned to the column and rendered their report, Ford decided he was about as close to Rio Grande City as he was going to get without tipping off the attack. "I'd guess we're mighty close to Ringgold Barracks by now; that abandoned army post on the northwest side of the settlement. We best bed down right here for the rest of the night. Eph, have the men spread their blankets out on the ground beside their horses and keep the reins in their hands." Ford looked to his scouts when Eph rode off. "We got ninety Rangers in this command. You two have been followin' Cortina for quite a spell now. How many men would you estimate he has?"

"At least three hundred," Caleb replied.

"At least that many," Bigfoot quickly agreed, "maybe more."

Ford smiled. "Gentlemen, it looks as if we're in for a right lively fight."

Well before dawn the following morning, December 27, the heavy rumbling of caisson wheels could be heard off in the distance toward the river. Major Heintzelman was moving his artillery down the road toward Rio Grande City in preparation for the attack well before the sun was due to make an appearance. The fog was still as thick as pea soup when the Rangers broke their hasty camp and moved out. Reaching Ringgold Barracks a short while later, the column was met by a smattering of gunfire from an advance party of Cortina's men. Caleb and Bigfoot emptied their Colts into the Mexican ranks, driving them back.

"Caleb," said Ford when he reined up beside the scouts after the firing had ceased, "you 'n Bigfoot follow the Mexicans and try to locate Cortina's main body. The column will follow in short order, so we won't be far behind."

A few minutes later, the scouts rode up out of the swirling fog and reined in at the front of the Ranger column. Caleb reported to Ford. "Cortina pulled his men back, Rip. They're holed up in a thicket of large ebony trees on a rise that overlooks the town."

Ford took a moment to consider the situation. "Eph, we'll approach the rise in two columns. You take one, and I'll take the other. Maybe we can catch Cortina in a cross fire. Bigfoot, I want you to lead Eph's column to the objective and Caleb will lead mine. You two pay close attention. I don't want the columns to drift too far apart in this damn fog or we're likely to lose each other. Eph, take half the men and move off to the left. We'll move out once Bigfoot says you're ready."

Eph and Bigfoot rounded up half the men and moved out. Within a few minutes Bigfoot reappeared out of the fog. "We're all set, Rip. Give me a couple minutes to get back and you can move out." Reining around, Bigfoot once again disappeared into the swirling fog.

When Rip was sure Eph and Bigfoot were ready he nodded to Caleb. "Move out and keep the pace slow and steady."

Caleb nudged Sally Mae with his heels and the big filly moved out at a walk, picking her way carefully through the fog and thorny brush. After fifteen minutes or so Caleb felt the terrain beginning to rise, and he was about to signal Rip that they were getting close when the Mexicans opened fire with two cannons. Grape shot ripped through the trees above the Rangers' heads, shattering limbs and bringing down a shower of leaves.

"Cortina must've posted some men well out in front to let his gunners know when we were in range," said Caleb. "The slope's causin' 'em to fire high."

"Thank God for that," said Ford, flinching in the saddle as another blast of grapeshot ripped into the trees above his head.

"That grape would tear us to pieces." Ford called for a runner. "Tell Lieutenant Daggett to concentrate on the cannon. We'll swing around to the west and try to flank the rise."

The runner spurred his horse towards Eph's column, and Ford moved his men to the right before quickly putting them on line. "Caleb, you stay on this end of the line and I'll move down to the other. When I give a holler we'll charge 'em until we get in close then dismount and hit 'em with rifle fire. I'd push all the way on horseback, but in this fog we might end up shootin' at Eph and his bunch. Have every fourth man hold the horses when we dismount. We'll be in need of 'em if Cortina falls back from that rise towards the river."

Caleb could hear Eph's men engaging the Mexican cannon when Ford gave the command to advance. Hindered by the fog and the rough terrain, the charge was not much more than advancing at the trot, but Caleb soon caught sight of the guns in the swirling mist. "Dismount and find some cover!" he yelled. "Horse holders move back with the horses and hold 'em steady."

Caleb dropped down behind a fallen tree with a few other Rangers and sighted in on one of the Mexican gunners with his Hawken when the fog momentarily swirled clear. The rifle roared as he slowly squeezed the trigger and the Mexican gunner spun to the ground. All along the line the Rangers opened fire with their long rifles, pouring a deadly rain of lead into the swirling fog as the Mexicans attempted to turn the guns.

Cortina's men did their best to protect the gunners with a heavy volume of return fire, and for a few minutes, the battle raged fiercely, the fog so thick that at times that it was difficult for either side to tell who they were shooting at. Suddenly the Mexican buglers sounded the charge and a mounted wave of bandits swept down the slope toward Ford and his men, firing as they came. Cortina had obviously decided that his position could not be held unless the Rangers were driven back. Screaming their hated, the Mexican riders emerged from the fog. Hot lead seemed to be coming at the Rangers from every direction, and it looked as if they were being surrounded.

"Stand firm and use your revolvers!" Caleb shouted over the tumult as he opened fire with both Colts. The Mexicans were met by a thunderous, rapid-fire volley as the other Rangers up and down the line joined in. Horses reared and several Mexicans were unhorsed in the brutal onslaught.

"All right, boys," Caleb heard Ford yell out from the other end of the line when the Mexican charge was broken and the bandits began to retreat, "everybody mount up. Let's give the bastards hell!"

The Rangers ran for the horses, swinging up on their saddles and charging after the fleeing bandits before they had an opportunity to regroup. Eph's Rangers joined in with the men under Ford, and the two Mexican guns were quickly overrun. The battle soon broke up into the kind of galloping melee in which the Texans' marksmanship with their Colts was so effective, and as the fog finally began to clear, the Rangers left a path of destruction in the wake of their pursuit.

A bandit turned in the saddle and fired at Caleb from close range. The pistol ball whizzed past his side, ripping a ragged tear in his buckskin hunting shirt, but Caleb calmly triggered a round that center punched the outlaw in the chest and blew him out of the saddle. Caleb fired again, unhorsing a bandit who was drawing down on Bigfoot. Bigfoot quickly finished the outlaw off as he galloped past and looked around for more, especially Cortina. However, the infamous bandit leader and his body guard had slipped safely across the Rio Grande before the army was able to cut them off.

Ford rode up and joined Caleb and Bigfoot as they sat their horses watching the last of the Mexicans splash up out of the river and ride hard for the cover of the trees and brush that grew thick along the far bank. A few more bandits were knocked out of the saddle with accurate rifle before they reached safety, but soon a welcome silence settled over the battlefield.

"Well, we didn't wipe 'em out completely," said Ford, "but I think we taught Cortina that any more adventures on this side of the river will cost him dearly."

"I sure as hell hope you're right, Rip," Caleb replied, "but one way or the other somethin's tellin' me it's time to head for home. And now that you got things in hand, that's exactly what I plan on doin'. Bigfoot, you ready to ride?"

Bigfoot wondered what the hurry was, but he chuckled anyway. "Like I done told you many a time, partner. I was born ready."

Burning kerosene spread the fire quickly, and raging flames and smoke had filled the main room of the cabin, when Wanda burst through the door screaming Josh's name. The heat from the fire was already so intense she could feel her long blond hair beginning to smolder. In spite of the heat and smoke, Wanda fought her way to the bedroom door with the kind of savage determination and courage only a mother protecting her young child could display. Flames were already licking across the bedroom floor and climbing the walls when she shoved the door open and saw Josh sitting up in his small bed, coughing and crying.

Picking up a heavy stool with strength she never knew she possessed, Wanda heaved it through the window, creating a pathway to safety for her son by shattering the glass and knocking the frame completely out of the sill. She frantically beat at the flames that began to lick up her long dress and burn her legs, but quickly realizing there was not enough time to save them both, Wanda ignored the terrible pain and picked Josh up off the bed. With all the strength that remained in her pain-wracked body, she shoved the young boy roughly through the window to safety. A last piercing, pain-wracked scream filled the night as Wanda fell back into the flames and disappeared. Josh instinctively moved away from the fire as the flames raged on.

A few minutes later, a wagon full of helpful neighbors arrived and found Josh wandering away from the flaming cabin crying for his mother. Suddenly the roof of the cabin collapsed into the raging fire, quickly followed by the roof of the schoolhouse. A swirling shower of sparks towered high into the night sky. With nothing else left to do, the neighbors lifted little Josh into the wagon and headed for John Cooper's house.

Chapter 36

Caleb stood on the high bluff overlooking the Colorado River, tears streaming down his trail-hardened face as he stared in shocked silence at the burned out ruins of Wanda's cabin and little schoolhouse. He had heard part of the story from one of Wanda's neighbors, Mike Sumner. Mike told him Wanda had been caught harboring an escaped slave nearly two weeks ago. It must have been near the time of the Cortina fight, Caleb thought. Neither Mike, nor any of the other neighbors for that matter, knew how the fire had started or the circumstances surrounding Wanda's death. They only knew Josh had somehow survived the disaster and had been taken to his Uncle John's house by one of Wanda's other neighbors. Wanda's remains had been buried with little fanfare in the cemetery located on the east side of Austin.

Realizing he would never be satisfied until he knew all the facts surrounding Wanda's death, Caleb wiped his eyes and face with his bandana, shoved his gray sombrero firmly down over his copper-red curls, and slowly swung his leg up and over his fancy Mexican saddle. If anyone knew what had happened here, it would be Richard Bullock, he thought. Reining Sallie Mae around, Caleb nudged the big filly gently in the ribs with his heels and headed for the ferry that would take him across the Colorado.

Though the noontime sun hung high in the clear azure of the winter sky, it did not put out much heat, and there was a distinct chill in the air when Caleb dismounted and looped his reins around the hitching rail that stood in front of the Bullock Hotel. A strong gust of wind rattled the vacancy sign hanging over the veranda as the tall Texas Ranger slowly climbed the steps and crossed to the front door. Bullock was nowhere in sight near the counter when Caleb entered the hotel, so he moved to the café entrance and shoved his way past the batwing doors.

A cheerful fire that brought him absolutely no warmth danced in the big hearth off to Caleb's left. Across the room, a few customers sat at the tables along the widows that provided a view of Pecan Street, engaging in quiet conversation while they enjoyed their lunch. To his right, Richard Bullock stood behind the long bar, whistling while he washed glasses. Caleb walked across the room in his usual silent manner and stepped up to the bar, resting his boot on the long brass foot-rail.

"Excuse me, Mr. Bullock," Caleb said when he was sure Bullock had not heard him approach.

Bullock jumped back, nearly dropping the glass he'd been washing. "Damn Caleb, you startled me."

"Sorry Mr. Bullock," Caleb replied without his usual smile of greeting, "that wasn't my intent. If you don't mind, I need to talk to you for a few minutes."

Bullock nodded his head, knowing what was on Caleb's mind. "Certainly, anytime, when did you get back from the border?"

Caleb removed his sombrero and ran his fingers through his long curls, sighing deeply. "Not long ago, just this mornin', in fact."

"By that soulful expression on your face," said Bullock, resting his hands on the bar, "I'd guess you've already heard about Miss Wanda." The hotel proprietor shook his head in sorrow. "What a terrible waste."

"I couldn't agree with you more, Mr. Bullock. The thing is, I know what happened to Wanda alright, but I don't know how it happened. That's why I came here. I was hopin' you could fill me in on the details."

Now it was Bullock's turn to sigh heavily as he put down the bar towel. "All I can tell you is what I heard, Caleb, and be advised that all of it may not be true. Truth is, I've heard several versions of what happened that night, and although most of 'em differed somewhat, the one name most people mentioned as bein' responsible was that slave chaser, Len Samuels." Bullock felt uneasy, almost as if he was passing a death sentence on the slaver. "At least I know for sure he's the one who shot her."

"Shot Wanda," Caleb gasped in surprise, "hell I ain't heard nothin' about her bein' shot! I thought she died in the fire."

"She did die in the fire," replied Bullock, "helpin' her son to survive from what it looked like to the neighbors. Len Samuels only wounded her. As far as I know, though, he's the one who started the fire."

Caleb's features took on an even grimmer look. "It sure as hell sounds like Len Samuels is the man I'm after. Do you have any idea where I might find him?"

Now Bullock looked uncertain. "He usually hangs out at old man Manor's saloon, the Dry Gulch, over on Brazos Street. Why don't you go see Sheriff Bowles first, though? He was there that night. He can tell you exactly what happened. I know Samuels is a skunk, but I'd hate to think I got anybody killed who didn't deserve it."

"I'm much obliged for your help, Mr. Bullock," said Caleb as he stepped away from the bar and headed for the door. "And I plan to go see Sheriff Bowles first."

Caleb spent the next thirty minutes at the sheriff's office, and he was not at all happy when Bowles told him exactly what had happened on the night Wanda died. "Why in the hell didn't you arrest that bastard when he shot her?"

"Everythin' weren't quite that cut and dried, Caleb." Bowles replied. "When Wanda fired at that dog, even I wasn't sure what or who she was gunnin' for. And Samuels only wounded her. She was alive when we rode off."

Caleb had to work hard to keep the sneer off his face. "Rode off and left her wounded with the cabin on fire, you mean. What about her son?" Caleb almost said my son. "He was in the cabin when Samuels set fire to it."

"There's a lot of blame goin" round for what happened," said Bowles, his reply almost a plea. "I even got a little comin' myself. But I swear none of us knew the boy was in the cabin. Are you gonna shoot me, too?"

Caleb looked Bowles in the eyes, his own slate gray eyes narrowing in a frightening, snake-like manner. "You damn well could have helped Wanda come around and asked her about the boy before you rode off, Sheriff, or even taken the time to make sure yourself. But to answer your question, if you had started the fire or ridden off knowin' the boy was in the cabin, you'd already be dead, just like Len Samuels will soon be."

Sheriff Bowles came to his feet. "You can't just walk in the saloon and gun Samuels down, Caleb. If he refuses to fight, you'll have to let it go. You may well be the fastest gun in these parts, but I'll charge you with murder, and you'll either hang or be a fugitive for the rest of your life. I hope you understand that."

Caleb shoved his chair back and stood up with a cruel smile. "If it comes down to that, it'll be the next sheriff who tries to hang me, not you, Bowles." Caleb's meaning could not have been clearer, and the sheriff did his best to swallow his fear. "But don't start countin' your days yet. As long as Samuels has a friend or two to back him up, I'm sure he'll fight."

Sheriff Bowles' office was located near the capitol building on Congress Avenue, and Brazos was the next street over to the east from Congress. Caleb swung up in the saddle and trotted Sally Mae over to Brazos before reining down the hill towards the river. The Dry Gulch saloon stood at the bottom of the hill on the corner of Brazos and Water Streets. There were only a few horses standing at the hitching rail in front of the saloon when Caleb reined in and dismounted. After looping the reins over the rail, he drew his Colt and checked the loads. Satisfied, he holstered the big Dragoon and headed for the saloon's swinging doors.

The sharp contrast between the bright winter sunshine that graced the streets of Austin on this chilly winter day and the gloomy interior of the Dry Gulch forced Caleb to pause at the door for a minute to let his eyes adjust. Two men stood at the bar deep in conversation; neither man was Samuels. Old man Manor was busy wiping down the bar. Off to Caleb's left a small fireplace put off little heat, and the saloon remained cold enough that he could see his breath. Further back in the dimly lit establishment, five men sat playing cards, their laughter a sharp contrast to the quiet conversation at the bar. Since the card players were the only other customers in the saloon Caleb headed that way. Well before he reached the table he recognized Samuels' flat-brimmed black hat.

The slave chaser had his back to him, but one of the card players opposite Samuels happened to look up and his eyes went wide, "McAdams!"

Caleb saw Samuels flinch. "Y'all keep your hands on the table where I can see 'em." Everyone around the table complied. "Very good, now if you ain't plannin' on sidin' Samuels in the little fandango the two of us are about to have, I suggest you clear out right now." Three of the card players stood and quickly moved for the door, but the man who had seen him first hesitated. Caleb recognized the man as another slave chaser, Norman Caldwell. "Are you in, Norm?"

Caldwell refused to meet Len Samuels' eyes as he rose to his feet. "I guess I'll be goin', too, sorry Len."

The man would bear watching, Caleb thought. He half turned, keeping his eye on Caldwell until he cleared the swinging doors. "Well, Len, it looks like it's just you and me."

Samuels tossed his cards on the table and finally spoke without turning his head. "That was the first good hand I had all damn day, and you come along and ruined it. How come you're gunnin' for me, McAdams? You're friend was the one breakin' the law. 'Sides, when she shot that dog I had no idea what or who she'd shoot next."

"You might have an argument as far as the shootin' goes, Len, but only because you didn't kill her. The fire is somethin' else altogether. The fire was what killed her and nearly killed her son, too. You're gonna have to pay for that fire with your miserable life."

Still refusing to look around, Samuels shook his head as he raised his gun hand away from his holster. "I ain't gonna draw on you, McAdams. You'd kill me sure as hell."

A cold smile crossed Caleb's face. "If not today, then some other day, but sooner or later I'll get you alone, Len. It's only a matter of patience, unless you're scared enough to run. Otherwise, when we meet you'll either draw on me, or I'll kill you anyway. Just remember I'll be watchin' for my chance." That should do it, Caleb thought, as he turned and started walking to the door, the itchiness in his back telling him to be ready to move.

"You bastard, don't turn your back on me!" Samuels screamed as he spun out of the chair and went for his Colt, knowing it was either kill the big Ranger now or live a life of fear until Caleb finally killed him.

Caleb felt Samuels' ball hum close past his shoulder as he threw himself to the right and snapped the big Colt from his holster. Firing more from instinct than anything else, he put a ball into Samuels' chest that lifted the slave chaser off his feet and slammed him onto the card table, collapsing its legs, cards and chips flying.

Caleb kept rolling to avoid the ball he expected Norman Caldwell to fire at him from the swinging doors and coming up on one knee, fired again. The .44 caliber ball took Caldwell in the right shoulder and spun him around. The slave chaser's Colt clattered to the saloon floor as he dropped to his knees holding the wounded shoulder.

Caleb rose to his feet, slowly walked over to Caldwell, and kicked his Colt across the barroom floor. "You should've stayed out of it, Norm." Holstering his Colt, Caleb turned to old man Manor. "You saw what happened. I'd be obliged if you told Sheriff Bowles, if and when he shows up." Turning away, Caleb shoved his way out the swinging doors.

Not long after the incident at the saloon, Caleb found himself knocking on John Cooper's front door. Before he headed for the ranch he wanted to tell John how sorry he was about Wanda's death, and he wanted to speak with Josh. On the ride over he thought about what he wanted to say to the lad, but nothing he came up with so far sounded right. Perhaps the right words would come when they were together.

John opened the door. "Caleb, It's good to see you, I'm glad you made it back from the border. Please come in out of the cold."

As Caleb stepped into the parlor, he decided not to beat around the bush with small talk. "John, I'm terribly sorry about, Wanda. I know you looked with disfavor on me and her, but I want you to know I cared about her very much. And I tried my best to make her and Josh as much a part of my life as I could."

Cooper stood silent for a moment then sighed. "To be honest Caleb, I never cared for the way you handled the situation between you and Wanda. You should've had the strength to stay away, especially after Josh came along. She was a headstrong woman, there's no doubt of it, but eventually she would've found someone else. All that aside, you weren't responsible for her death. Wanda never learned to keep her opinions to herself even when they were a danger to her and Josh. Hidin' that slave was a foolish thing to do, especially after nearly gettin' caught the first time. She told me you warned her against such a thing, and she obviously ignored your warnin'. However, there's still little Josh to consider. He told me Wanda shoved him out the window before the fire got her."

Caleb nodded, not surprised by Wanda's bravery and self-sacrifice. "I know Josh must be takin' his ma's death real hard. Would it be alright if I spoke with him for a few minutes? We need to begin to work this situation out."

A puzzled look momentarily shadowed John's features. "You haven't been home yet, have you, Caleb?"

"No, I been over at the Dry Gulch takin' care of business with Len Samuels," Caleb replied, wondering what his being home yet had to do with Josh.

John could imagine the business Caleb was referring to with Len Samuels, and the thought of it brought him pleasure. He would have dealt with the slave chaser himself had he possessed Caleb's skill with firearms. "Caleb, Lucinda came here and fetched Josh to the Rockin' M the day after the funeral. She said she had always known about you and Wanda, but in spite of that Josh's place was with his father and his family. I happen to agree with her, but I imagine you're gonna have a lot of explainin' to do when you get home, to both her and Josh. She's a mighty fine woman, Caleb, and I don't envy your task one bit."

Later in the evening Caleb and Lucinda sat in front of the fireplace in the great room of the hacienda, she in her favorite rocking chair and he in one of the overstuffed leather chairs Felix had hand crafted. The well-seasoned mesquite logs in the hearth crackled and snapped as they were slowly devoured by the flames. Unlike his previous homecomings, supper had been a quiet affair, the mood around the table subdued by the presence of Josh and the impending conversation that was bound to take place later on between Caleb and Lucinda. Of course, difficult as it may have been, Lucinda had taken the time to explain the entire situation to the family, including Ham and the girls, before she had fetched Josh home. Pedro and Veronica were shocked, but Felix and the children, led by Ilse, took the news in stride and did their best to make Josh feel at home. Lucinda was extremely proud of them all.

Ham and Josh hit it off right away, going for a long ride with their grandfather soon after Josh's arrival at the Rocking M, for Felix accepted Josh as his grandson without hesitation. The boys had immediately became inseparable, exploring every part of the ranch over the past few days and learning even more ways to get into devilment. Their close companionship did much to help Josh deal with the loss of his mother and the startling news about Caleb being his father.

Although it had long been apparent to him, Caleb marveled at the boys' nearly identical appearance, when he finally saw them side-by-side for the first time at the supper table. Only the color of their hair and eyes, favoring Wanda and Lucinda, made them distinguishable. Their remaining features were clearly stamped from the McAdams mold right down to the tight curls in their long hair. Although Josh still pined for his mother and would for quite some time, surprisingly both he and Ham readily accepted Caleb as Josh's father. Only time would tell how the situation worked itself out.

Caleb glanced over at Lucinda. Ever since he left John Cooper's house, he had been dreading facing her with the truth finally out in the open. "How long have you known?" he finally asked, breaking the long silence.

Staring into the flames, Lucinda let her thoughts dance across Caleb's question for a good while before she answered. "I have told you many times that you cannot hide the truth from me, Caleb. Believe me when I say a wife knows her husband's ways better than any other. If you must know, I have known from the very beginning. You have never treated me less, but I could sense that you still cared about Wanda, too. People also talk, and such a thing cannot be kept a secret forever, especially in a small town like Austin."

Caleb sighed deeply. "I'm sorry I hurt you, Love. Its true Wanda and I have always shared a special friendship, but what happened to bring about Josh happened only once and never again. I swear it. I just couldn't bring myself to abandon them altogether."

Lucinda continued to stare into the fire. "It hurt very much at first, but after I had time to realize you would never leave me, I gradually came to accept it, even though it caused me much pain. I knew the circumstances of our wedding made it difficult for you, and that you still cared for Wanda, but I agreed to marry you anyway. I also know you love me very much, and that is what I would never let myself forget." Lucinda rose from her rocking chair and stood next to Caleb, placing her hand softly on his shoulder.

Caleb pulled Lucinda down onto his lap and kissed her gently. "I promise to never hurt you like that again, Love. And I'll never forget that you made a home here for Josh."

A gentle smile graced Lucinda's lovely face. "Josh is our son now, like Ham is our son, and I love him very much. Along with the girls, we will raise a strong family, you and I." Lucinda laid her head on Caleb's shoulder, and they lost themselves in the warmth of the fire and the love they shared for one another.

Epilogue

Caleb saddled Sally Mae in the dark and rode alone to the top of the high ridge overlooking the hacienda. It was springtime in Texas, and although there was still a chill in the early morning air, he wanted to reach the ridge in time to see the sunrise. As Caleb sat his fancy Mexican saddle looking out over the hacienda and the valley of the Lower Colorado, the deep shadows of the night began to give way to the first signs of dawn. Soon the arc of the blood-orange sun poked above the distant rim of the earth, bringing first light and then spectacular color to the eastern sky as the huge disc began to make its way through a bank of wispy clouds hanging close above the horizon. Caleb held his breath as the new day began in all the glory that only a Texas sunrise could provide.

To even consider that this vast and beautiful land could one day be shattered by a terrible civil war was difficult to contemplate, but Caleb was sure war was coming. In spite of his Unionist sentiments, Sam Houston had been elected governor, but it appeared as if he was fighting a losing battle against the secessionists. All over the South, talk was dominated by men who believed that a state had the right to peacefully succeed from a government it no longer agreed with, but Caleb was sure the whole theory of peaceful secession was simply wishful thinking.

The north would fight to preserve the Union. President Andrew Jackson had proved that during the Nullification crisis back in 1832, when South Carolina claimed the right to nullify a protective tariff passed into law by the United States Congress. Old Hickory threatened to send the army to South Carolina and "burn the damn state to the ground" before the people in favor of states' rights backed down.

Caleb felt he could never fight against the flag that his friends had died for during the war, but neither could he bring himself to fight against his beloved Texas. Remaining neutral was also out of the question, because it was a well known fact that fence sitters were invariably attacked by both sides in any struggle. After much consideration, he decided to see Sam Houston about re-establishing his volunteer Ranger Company under the auspices of the state. War or no war, the frontier still had to be protected from the depredations of the Comanches. They were bound to increase their raids once all the federal troops returned to the North. That way he could fight for Texas without being drawn into the war.

The only thing that was sure in Caleb's mind was that Texas would eventually pay a terrible price for secession. With most of the railroads, heavy industry, and population, the North would invariably defeat the South in spite of the fools who boasted that any good southerner could lick ten Yankees. The South, however, would not be subdued easily, and that meant the war would be both long and bloody. Reining Sally Mae down the ridge, Caleb headed for the hacienda and the delicious breakfast that awaited him on the table in the great room. That and much more importantly, a loving wife and family to welcome him home.

CPSIA information can be obtained at www.ICGtesting.com
Printed in the USA
LVOW130752081112

306371LV00002B/9/P